THE GUMSHOE CHRONICLES
1921

a novel by T. J. Viola

T. J. Viola

outskirtspress
DENVER, COLORADO

This is a work of fiction. The events described herein referring to actual places and/or historical characters are imaginary. All other events and characters described herein are also imaginary and are not intended to refer to specific places or living persons. The opinions expressed in this manuscript are solely the opinions of the author and do not represent the opinions or thoughts of the publisher.

The Gumshoe Chronicles 1921
All Rights Reserved.
Copyright © 2012 TJ Viola
v3.0

This book may not be reproduced, transmitted, or stored in whole or in part by any means, including graphic, electronic, or mechanical without the express written consent of the publisher except in the case of brief quotations embodied in critical articles and reviews.

Outskirts Press, Inc.
http://www.outskirtspress.com

ISBN: 978-1-4327-8795-0

Outskirts Press and the "OP" logo are trademarks belonging to Outskirts Press, Inc.

PRINTED IN THE UNITED STATES OF AMERICA

To Dr. Robert J. Mattauch: my mentor, life-long inspirational guide and friend, who has mastered the art of teaching.

"It is the supreme art of the teacher to awaken joy in creativity and knowledge."
Albert Einstein

Acknowledgements

Special thanks to Teresa R. Funke for her continued encouragement and coaching during our writing journey; Saundie Weiss for copy editing; Kendra Spanjer, graphic designer of The Gumshoe Chronicles unique cover designs; and Don and Bette Sailors for providing a final review.

Also by TJ Viola

The Gumshoe Chronicles – 1920

Chapter 1

The outer office door flew open, hitting the wall so hard the glass panel shattered. "Where's that son-of-a-bitch?" Uncle Luigi yelled. "One week into the new year and Joey's already messin' things up. If he wasn't my nephew, I'd shoot him myself."

I stumbled from behind my desk and stood to the side of the glass partition that separated the two offices to catch Martha's reaction. My secretary was all flapper from her bobbed hair to her short skirt and shapely pins, and she never let anyone push her around.

"Geez, Luigi. Owning the building doesn't give you the right to flip off the tracks and scare the bejesus out of me. Take a seat and I'll see if Joey's available," she said.

"So now I have to wait until my nephew, the great PI, has time for me? What…does he have a broad in there?" he asked, brushing Martha aside.

I rushed back to my chair.

Luigi slapped his brawny hands on the desktop and leaned to within inches of my face. "Don't bother getting up."

"Sounds like you owe me a new door," I said, nudging back my chair.

"That's not important. What matters is that you quit screwin' up my life. You promised to make things right again after the DA demolished my speakeasy."

I pulled a bottle of hooch out of the bottom drawer and poured him a shot.

"You need to calm down or you're gonna pop a blood vessel."

"I didn't come here to get smoked. I—hey, that looks like Canadian Scotch. Where'd you get that?"

"I grabbed a few cases the night the DA raided your joint. I guess I forgot to mention it."

"How convenient."

Jackie walked in and planted a kiss on his cheek. "Martha tells me you're on a rampage. Something about wanting to shoot Joey."

"Serve him right if I did," Luigi grumbled, reaching for his drink.

"I thought you two agreed to forget about last year."

"Who gives a damn about the past? I certainly don't. You didn't see me sit on my ass after the DA busted my joint just because he hates Joey's guts."

"Then what's the problem?" Jackie asked.

"I'll tell ya what the problem is. I had a deal to buy one of Castellano's speakeasies, and now he's backing out."

"What the hell does that have to do with me?"

"You tell me, Joey. Castellano said the deal's dead until I get my nephew under control. That means you."

"I didn't think he'd take his anger out on you."

"Me, you, what the hell's the difference? What did you do to tick him off this time?"

"He ordered us to back off the Kowalski murder."

"And?"

"I said no."

"You still don't get it, do you?"

"What am I supposed to get?"

"He's the boss. He runs this part of New York City. He keeps the neighborhood safe, *and* he's a friend of this family, your family."

"Castellano knows he can trust me."

"What? You think you're still a kid running numbers for him? You threaten his business interests and all relationships are cancelled, permanently. Don't ever forget who you're dealing with! If it comes down to his life or yours, you're dead."

Jackie rested quietly against the wall and watched Luigi pace the room.

"Didn't you learn anything growing up in this hellhole? Gutter rules apply, and that means anything goes. But in the end, we Italians stick together. If the boss says back off, you back the hell off."

Luigi glanced at my desk and picked up a folder I had open. "What's this?"

"O'Reilly slipped us a copy of the homicide report his crew put together on Kowalski's murder."

"You listen to me, and listen good. There are no secrets in this town. If you're gonna spit on a guy, do it to his face. Not behind his back, 'cause in the end he's gonna know, especially Castellano."

I'd had enough of my uncle's tantrum.

"We have a case to solve. I'm not gonna let anyone tell us what we can and can't investigate."

"When that someone is the boss, you should, and so should your partner," Luigi said, pointing to Jackie.

"We have our reasons," Jackie said.

"Then give it to me straight. I wanna know what's goin' on. Do you two think Castellano killed Kowalski? Is that it?"

"He certainly had a motive," I said.

"What motive? Tell me why you're putting my livelihood at risk again."

"Kowalski led the effort to get the dockworkers to join a union. You and I both know if the union is successful, Castellano won't be around long."

"Come with me, both of you."

"Where?"

"You're the PI. Figure it out."

Chapter 2

As we entered La Cucina Restaurant, the proprietress, Maria, rushed over.

"Joey, I overheard Mr. Castellano talking. Maybe you should come back when he's in a better mood. He's still angry over the damage you caused to the restaurant, and now he says you're sticking your nose in his business."

Looking around I was surprised to see that most of the interior still bore scars from the gun battle Martha, Jackie, and I had in December with a crazed killer who had taken Maria hostage.

"Why haven't you replaced the chandelier and the mirrors behind the bar?"

Maria nudged me into a corner so Castellano couldn't see us.

"Feel free to shoot the place up any time. To tell the truth, I'm even sorry I repaired the floor where the dynamite exploded or that I patched up the bullet holes in the walls. Everyone wants to know what happened that night and see the damage. The tables with lead in them are in high demand and reserved only for my best customers. Trust me; this place has turned into a gold mine."

"So why should Castellano complain? Besides, this is your restaurant, not his anymore. Maybe he needs to be reminded of that."

I grabbed Jackie's arm and left Maria standing next to Luigi, with her hand covering her mouth.

Castellano saw us approach and dismissed his bodyguards.

"Grab a seat. I've been expecting you."

"My uncle said you're backing out of a deal 'cause of me."

"I didn't think it would take Luigi long to remind you how things are done in my neighborhood," Castellano said, shoving a forkful of spaghetti into his mouth.

This had always been his neighborhood, but hearing him say it didn't sit right, and I was about to tell him so when Jackie squeezed my thigh. I regained my composure, but not completely.

"Why are you putting pressure on us to get off the Kowalski murder?" I asked.

"Why do you think?"

"You really wanna know? I'll give it to you straight. If the longshoremen unionize, you'll be six feet under lookin' up at a patch of dirt rather than overseeing a neighborhood."

"So you suspect I killed him?"

"Everyone does."

"I didn't ask everyone. I asked you." He turned to Jackie. "What about it? You think I whacked this guy?"

"In Chicago, where I grew up, you'd kill him only as a last resort. Kowalski was well liked; his death would create more problems. No, you would try to bribe him, and if that didn't work, he'd have a fatal accident. Rubbing him out in such dramatic fashion, putting his mutilated body on public display, makes no sense."

Castellano pushed his food aside and looked deeply into Jackie's emerald eyes. "Why don't you leave this guy and work for me? A woman as classy and deadly as you is a rare commodity."

"Don't believe everything you hear. I just know how to take care of myself. The sophistication came later in life, after I met my now deceased husband," Jackie said, giving Castellano her most devilish smile.

Castellano went speechless for a moment, no doubt remembering Jackie's sensational trial for the murder of her husband.

"You're right. In my line of work you don't knock off a guy who has Kowalski's kind of respect. Since he got dusted, I have more dockworkers joining the union than would've signed up in years. Now people will get hurt because I need to keep *my* kind of respect."

"You're talking in riddles," I said.

"Know what your problem is, Joey? You don't listen. I told you once, I own the docks and nothing happens there unless I say so."

"I heard you."

"But obviously you didn't understand. So I'm gonna tell you again, for the last time. No one—look at me—no one snoops around the docks without my say so. You understand now? It's all about respect. Kowalski got his because he was a nice guy. Mine comes from fear. If I lose that, I lose control."

"If you didn't order Kowalski's murder, what's the problem?"

"You know something, Joey? You've got a hell of a lot to learn, and I'm not sure you're gonna have the time you need."

"I don't like being threatened."

"What? You come home from the war with a box full of

medals, take out a few wiseguys, and think that makes you a tough guy. Remember this, all it takes is one bullet to blow someone away," he said, pointing at my head.

Jackie gently pushed his hand back onto the table. "What do you want from us?" she asked.

"See what I mean? This is one smart broad," he said, turning back toward me.

"You tell Sadie you're both working for *me* now on this case. *I* need to find out who killed her father and make an example of him. I do that, everything returns to normal. The unions will slowly fade away and fewer people will get hurt. If not, I have to get rough—because you're right—I can't allow a union to take hold. Not now, not ever."

"That sounds like a confession."

"I'm gonna forget you said that because I think the war has warped your mind."

"What's that supposed to mean?"

"Think about it. You've been home a year, and I don't have enough fingers to count the number of goons you've sent to the morgue."

"It was our lives or theirs," Jackie said.

"Fair enough, then I can assume you don't go around knocking people off when you have a disagreement. What makes you think I do?"

"Leading an effort to unionize is more than a disagreement," I said.

"For your information, Kowalski and I were negotiating a deal."

"What deal?"

"That's none of your damn business. Now I suggest you take my offer and find Kowalski's killer for *me*."

In New York City, the only way to survive is to push

back and not take any guff, but you also need to know when to back off. Jackie and I agreed to Castellano's proposition. We now had free access to the docks and a sizable paycheck due when we delivered Kowalski's killer. The only downside was explaining our deal to Sadie, who was convinced Castellano had ordered her father's murder.

* * * * *

Later that night, after agreeing to work for Castellano, I met O'Reilly at his new watering hole and returned the police file on Kowalski. I dropped the report on the table and pulled up a chair. "Thanks, Mike, but it wasn't much help. Your guys haven't made any significant progress."

"It's a tough case. The only lead we have is from Sadie, who swears her father left their apartment that night to meet Castellano down by the waterfront."

"You think she's telling the truth?"

"No reason to doubt her, but Castellano has a solid alibi. Maria confirmed he was at her restaurant when the murder took place."

"He could've arranged the meeting and had someone else do the dirty work."

"That's usually how it's done. But why would he take such a risk?"

"Maybe someone's setting him up to take the fall."

"That's how I see it," O'Reilly said. He then waved the waitress over and ordered eel to go along with the oysters we were washing down with the piss the joint passed off as beer.

"I'll be glad when my uncle gets his own speakeasy again. The booze in this place is rotting out our insides, and

I'm tired of eating fish every time we meet. You'd think the owners would throw some meat on the menu."

"Yeah, but you gotta admit it has atmosphere, and the food's fresh, caught every day off the piers or brought in from the fish market."

"I never dreamed of being a seaman as a kid, but from the look and smell of this place, I'd say you did."

O'Reilly wiped the back of his hand across his mouth, "Aye, that I did, Joey boy, that I did."

"I gotta go, Mike. I promised Jackie I'd stop by her place tonight."

"So it's true. You two are more than partners."

I could feel my face flush. "You have to admit she's special."

"I'll say. She has everything a guy could want and more, especially in your line of work."

I got up to leave but remembered I had a question about the file.

"About Kowalski, the report has several pictures of the bailing hook the killer used to hang him from the crane. The wooden handle looks rotted and the metal is coated with rust. Doesn't that strike you as odd?"

"We checked the local junk shops and some of the so-called antique stores to see if a similar one was sold in the last few months. Nothing turned up."

"It does tell you one thing," I said.

"What's that?"

"Whoever did Kowalski in came prepared to kill him because you're not gonna find a bailing hook in that condition on a working dock."

I left O'Reilly to ponder that thought and headed home.

* * * * *

My meeting with O'Reilly lasted longer than expected, and by the time I got back to my uncle's brownstone, it was close to ten. His building was typical of those in the neighborhood. The ground floor housed two businesses up front with apartments in back for the owners. Massive concrete stairs separated the shops and led up to the first-floor stoop and a huge, decorative entrance door.

Ma and Pop occupied the entire ground floor, where they ran their shoe store and repair shop. Jackie and I had separate apartments on the third floor, along with our office, and Martha kept an apartment on the fourth. Uncle Luigi had moved out of the building last year when he accepted Castellano's offer to oversee all of his joints. With his own speakeasy shutdown by the DA, he didn't have a choice but to take the job, and he took the opportunity to remodel the second floor into apartments. The vacancy rate was higher than typical for the neighborhood, and I'm sure Luigi blamed me, but so far, he had never complained. A raging gun battle decimated my office a few months after I opened for business, and then a bomb nearly destroyed the ground floor—both couldn't have been good for attracting new tenants. Knowing my uncle, he was waiting until he needed a favor, and then he would hold me liable for the low occupancy rate.

On the way to Jackie's apartment, I noticed my uncle had had someone nail wooden slats over the broken glass panel on my door. The lights were out and the door locked, so I continued down the hall. Before I could knock, Jackie opened the door and slipped into my arms.

"I was thinking of taking Castellano up on his offer to

work for him if you kept me waiting much longer," she said, leading me inside.

"It doesn't sound like it would take much for you to dissolve our partnership."

"Well then that's something we should work on tonight," she said, sliding shut the bolt to the door. "I don't mind being tied down under the right circumstances."

Chapter 3

The next morning I had just entered my apartment when Luigi pounded on the door. As soon as I pulled back the latch, he burst in and caught me in one of his crushing bear hugs, burrowing his head into my chest and wrapping his powerful arms around my waist. Over the years, I'd learned how to limit any unintentional damage caused by his gregarious shows of affection.

"The deal with Castellano is set, thanks to you. Twenty-five grand, and I have my own joint again. Any problem if I heist the dough from the stash I'm holding for you in my safe?"

That was almost half the money I had taken from Sal Santangelo when he'd conveniently died with his safe open. Sal should've taken Jackie's offer to forget about the past, but instead, he'd become unhinged when he discovered she was still alive. I guess he'd felt secure with two of his hatchet men standing guard over me, but none of them survived. The army had done its job and turned me into a real button man when threatened.

"Twenty-five grand? Can't you give him half now and the rest after you get some dough flowing in?"

"I tried. It's all or nothin'. The boss drives a hard bargain."

"I need to think on it. If I hand over that much dough, I might not have enough to run my business if money gets tight. One thing's for sure, if you and I cut a deal, I don't want you to mention anything that happened last year ever again."

"What's there to mention? We all made it through your first year as a PI. Hopefully you've learned from your mistakes. Sorry... it just slipped out," he said, with a submissive gesture.

I tried to look upset but couldn't hold back a grin. "So, where's this joint you're buying? It better be something special for that kind of cabbage."

"It's the one next to La Cucina Restaurant. It's always packed, and the price includes all the furnishings, the existing hooch, and a two-month supply of booze on its way down from Canada."

I had to get something more out of the deal or my uncle would think I was a pushover. "Tell you what, if I can get all of the apartments rent free—the office, Jackie's, Martha's, and mine—the scratch is yours."

"I can't believe you have the moxie to even suggest that. Do you know how many vacant flats I have because of you?"

Luigi stood with his arms folded across his chest, waiting for a response. I sat in a chair and pretended to read an old paper, but finally relented.

"Okay, take the dough, but I want something in return for the loan."

"Loan? Nephew, even with that much money, you're still in my debt."

"Now you're sounding like one of Castellano's shylocks, jacking up the juice so a debt can never be paid off. I'm sure someday I'll take a bullet for you, and then we'll be even on that score. But right now we're talking about money, and I don't owe you anything."

"Don't get so touchy. I'm just giving you a hard time.

Tell ya what. Give me the dough and I'll cut the rent in half," he said.

We left the apartment and headed toward my office. "One more thing. I want a table in your new joint reserved for O'Reilly. We gotta quit meeting at that hash house he's been using since your old place shut down."

"Done."

I rapped on the wooden slats covering the hole in my office door, "What about my glass panel?" I asked.

"It'll be fixed in a few days, with gold lettering. Nothing but the best for my favorite nephew. Besides, I can't have my building looking run down. Not good for business."

The one thing I could say about Luigi is that he could always make me laugh, no matter the situation. His favorite nephew. I'm his only nephew.

* * * * *

The rest of the week, Jackie and I hung around the docks asking questions of anyone who would talk about Kowalski's brutal murder. There was considerable anger toward Castellano. No one came right out and accused him of personally killing Kowalski, but most thought he had given the order. Sadie, Kowalski's daughter, had certainly stirred up a hornet's nest. The growing anger among the dockworkers ran deeper than their fear of Castellano or of losing their jobs. They wanted justice, and to them that meant joining the union Kowalski had fought for and, in their minds, died to establish.

Castellano had it right. He had to find Kowalski's killer before he lost control of the waterfront.

On the outside platform that ran the length of the covered

pier where Kowalski was killed, I asked one of the longshoremen to show me how to work the hoist used to hang his body over the water. Even though the crime scene was months old, I still held out hope some clue might turn up to get the investigation moving. It took both of us to crank the wooden crane back toward the platform, but it was worth the effort. I was able to pinpoint several possible loading positions for the crane and the likely vicinity where the killer confronted Kowalski.

Unfortunately, any indications of a struggle, such as bloodstains, were washed away long ago by the high-power hoses used each evening to rinse down the platform. I didn't see anything else helpful and decided my only option was to ask O'Reilly for the crime scene pictures again, in case I had missed something.

Back on the main road running along the waterfront, I found Jackie jawing with Gino, one of the local bums. He'd gotten me out of a jam with the DA last year, and I'd been looking for him to return the favor. Pop had reluctantly agreed to give Gino a job in his shoe repair shop; all I had to do now was convince him to accept the offer.

"Gino, you're a hard guy to find."

"It's best to move around, otherwise some skid rogue will think you got a good deal goin' and knock ya off to get your spot. Life is considered cheap when you're a bum, even among ya own kind."

"I didn't think about looking for you around the waterfront. This has got to be one of the worst places to hang out in winter."

"A few of the dockworkers fixed up a space for me to stay so I'd be out of the cold at night. Just a few empty crates stacked together inside this pier warehouse. The good thing is the other bums can't take it over because the night watchman looks out for me."

"I'm surprised they would do that for you. They usually try to keep the street people off the piers."

"I go way back with some of them," Gino said.

While we were jawing, Jackie walked over to his makeshift cubbyhole and slipped a few bills into his bedroll.

"I hear you're looking to find who knocked off Kowalski," he said.

"Guess the word's out. You wouldn't know anything, would ya?"

"I was tellin' Jackie I talked to Kowalski the night he got whacked. He was standing by that second overhead light above the platform, just before a storm rolled in around midnight. He said he was waiting to meet someone."

"Did he say who?"

"If I knew that, I would've told you as soon as I heard you were snooping around."

"Did he look nervous or scared?"

"He seemed in a good mood. Said things were gonna get better. Who knows, maybe they have for him because he's dead."

"That's an odd thing to say."

"It all depends on what you're carrying around inside. But even without considering that burden, it's damn tough out here for the likes of me. As you said, the winters are brutal, even with these crates. Too much moisture in the air, and when the wind whips up, it feels like your insides are frozen stiff."

"I want to talk to you about that. Pop needs some help in his shop. Not a bad deal, you get three squares and a warm place to bunk down."

Gino pulled out a bottle of hooch and took a few swigs. "I know what you're trying to do, but I'm handcuffed to this stuff. You don't want me around. No one does. I died a long time ago. All I'm doing is waiting for this body to realize the game's over."

"Think about Pop's offer, and let me know if you hear anything about Kowalski." Gino nodded and shuffled off to his crates.

* * * * *

That night during dinner, I told Pop it would take time to convince Gino to get off the streets.

"I can't wait for him to decide. I need help now."

Ma put her fork down with some force. "You have a short memory."

"What are you talkin' about? I remember things going back to the old country—from when I was a boy," Pop said, lifting his hands in frustration.

"But you can't remember who your first customer was?"

"It was Dr. Par—."

"That's right, Dr. Parisi—Gino—and he told all his patients and friends what a great shoemaker you were. He sent a lot of customers our way."

"That was a long time ago," Pop said, hunched over his food.

Ma was about to pounce on Pop's last remark, when Martha jumped into the conversation.

"Are you saying Gino was a croaker?"

"One of the best doctors around," Ma said. "And he did a lot for free. He was more concerned with helping others than making money."

"What happened?" Jackie asked.

Pop didn't respond, so Luigi cleared a place in front of himself, making sure his wine glass wouldn't get knocked over as he told the story, but Ma cut him off.

"I think Vito should explain why Dr. Parisi turned into a street bum. Go ahead, dear. Maybe thinking back twenty years will help improve your memory."

"That woman can drive a man to drink," Pop said, pointing to Ma with his knife.

"They all have that talent. That's why the speakeasy business is so profitable," Luigi said with a vigorous laugh. He abruptly stopped when the women turned and stared at him.

"Gino was Dr. Richard Parisi," Pop said. "One day a couple of lowlifes broke into his home and demanded money. He gave them what he had, but that didn't satisfy them. Thinking he was holding out, they killed his wife and young daughter and left him for dead. Dr. Parisi simply disappeared once he recovered from his injuries. Three years later, he showed up wandering our streets with scraggly hair down to his shoulders and a beard to match."

Martha sat back in her chair with tear-filled eyes. Jackie showed no emotion at first, then became angry.

"Nobody did anything to help? They just let him suffer and become a bum? What's the matter with people in this town?"

Pop pushed his chair back and planted his hands on the table to stand. His neck turned a deep red, and the color rapidly crept up the side of his face.

"Vito!" Ma cautioned.

"It's easy to judge when you don't know the facts. Richard just disappeared. How the hell were we supposed to know he took it upon himself to find the scum that killed his family?

He figured the best way to search the city was to pretend to be a bum because bums are invisible. No one pays them any mind. As time passed, his money ran out and he turned to booze to keep himself warm. Eventually he no longer had to *pretend* to be a boozehound. When it was too late to do anything to help him, he came back to the neighborhood."

"He wouldn't listen to anyone, just kept drinking his gin. That's how he got the name Gino," Ma said. "Kids can be cruel."

"If you ask me, it's time to do something," Jackie said. "I know what it's like to live on the streets feeling hopeless. Gino may say he doesn't want help, but he does."

"You'd be wasting your breath. Most everyone tried at one time or another," Pop said.

Jackie got up from the table to go find Gino. "You just need to know what Gino wants more than anything else and it seems pretty obvious what that is," she said.

"Wait for me," Martha shouted.

"Pop, I think you'll have help in the shop soon. Once those two broads get an idea in their heads, there's no stopping them. Gino doesn't stand a chance."

"Well, I wish them luck. But I gotta tell you, I can't have a drunk around my customers."

"We'll do what we can," Ma said. "Dr. Parisi gave us a start and now it's our turn. The first thing we're gonna do is quit calling him Gino. His name is Richard."

Pop and I looked at each other. Richard just didn't seem to fit. To me, he would always be Gino.

* * * * *

Usually Jackie and Martha helped clean up after dinner,

but since they'd left to corral Gino, I chipped in. Ma didn't say much as we worked.

"Out with it, Ma. What's the problem?"

"Am I that obvious?"

"I can tell when you're having difficulty putting into words what's on your mind."

"What are you talking about? I never have trouble telling people what I think."

"So, out with it."

She turned off the water and faced me. "You know I love to cook, so that's no problem. And don't get me wrong, I like Jackie and Martha, but food is getting expensive. Your uncle doesn't help because he gives us a break on the rent, which doesn't even cover half the wine he downs each night."

"Are you telling me he sells you the booze we drink around here? That's hard to believe. How can anyone be so cheap?"

Ma laughed. "You don't know your uncle as well as you think. Do yourself a favor and don't ever lend him dough or get sucked into negotiating anything with him. I hate to say it, but he's a scoundrel when it comes to money."

I was ready to go tell Luigi off when I realized I was a worse offender. I felt like a heel. "Sorry Ma. I've been so focused on work I didn't realize things were getting tight for you and Pop. I had told Jackie and Martha that food was part of their salary, but I failed to let you both know."

"It would be fine, but we're also supporting Rosalie, and it's costing us a bundle to send her to nursing school. You know she's like a daughter. No doubt she'll pay us back when she gets a job, but that's a ways off."

"Tell you what, I'll take care of Rosalie's expenses and throw in some extra to cover the food bill."

"That would really help, but you can't tell Pop. He feels good about helping you and Rosalie."

"That's a lot of dough. He's gonna find out."

Ma handed me a dish to dry. "Don't worry. Pop thinks he's in control, but I handle the purse strings. He hates to deal with money."

She might have been satisfied, but I was determined to find a way to shame Luigi into providing us with free booze.

Chapter 4

Luigi kept his word. Our office door sported a new, frosted-glass panel with large golden lettering, *Private Investigators - Joey Batista and Jackie Forsythe.*

The place was empty. I suspected Jackie and Martha were again at the pier working Gino over to join the ranks of the employed.

The first thing I noticed when I walked into my office was a file with a note attached from Martha on my desk. *O'Reilly thought you might be interested in the coroner's report, along with the Kowalski crime scene pictures you requested.* The file covered the cigar burn Castellano had ground into the mahogany surface back in December when he first warned me off the case. The scar reminded me to proceed with caution when it came to Castellano.

The coroner's report clearly showed whoever killed Kowalski didn't have a conscience. It concluded that Kowalski died an agonizing death, drowning in his own blood. The killer pierced the front of his neck with a bailing hook, then attached a rope to the handle, and used a block and tackle to hoist him off his feet. I had assumed Kowalski had been dead before the killer put his body on display for everyone to see when the morning shift arrived. The coroner's description of how blood filled his throat, as he struggled to pull himself off the hook, made me sick and even more determined to find the bastard who had done this.

And when I did, I vowed he'd wish he could trade places with Kowalski.

Finished with the written report, I looked at the crime scene shots again. Most of the pictures were taken during the day when the body was discovered, but some were taken that night to capture the conditions under which the murder took place. At first they didn't reveal anything interesting, until I put the pictures showing the neck wounds side-by-side. The entrance and exit holes in his neck didn't line up. The hook entered his throat about one to one and a half inches lower than it had exited the back of his neck. My first thought was that the murderer was taller than Kowalski, which didn't rule out Castellano. He had at least five inches on him, but then again, so did most of the dockworkers. After further reflection, I realized the wounds would look the same if Kowalski had been pushed to the ground and the killer had stood over him and yanked the bailing hook through the front of his neck as Kowalski struggled to push himself up off the wooden planks.

I was about to call O'Reilly when the girls returned.

Jackie shook snow from her coat and hung it on the wooden rack by the door. "Any new leads?" she asked.

"Castellano is still the only logical suspect," I said. "But I can't believe he would order Kowalski killed so brutally. Like you said, it makes no sense. Frankly, if you ask me, Castellano liked Kowalski. When Castellano's son, Carmine, had a crush on Sadie years back, I often saw Castellano and Kowalski talking over drinks or playing chess outside the local pizza shop."

"When are you going to realize he's a Mafia boss? Relationships don't mean much to him. His loyalty is to the syndicate," Jackie stated.

Martha walked into our inner office rubbing her hands together. "Damn, it's cold in here. Next time I see your uncle I'm gonna tell him to raise the heat in the building or I'm gonna get the tenants to hold back next month's rent."

"If you do, I suggest you don't sit next to him during dinner. You might end up with a plate of spaghetti on your lap," I said.

"I'll keep that in mind. Did you see the stuff O'Reilly sent over?"

"Yep. I found somethin' of interest but nothing that really helps. Why don't you two take a look? You might pick up a clue I missed."

Martha cleared off the surface of my desk and laid out the pictures in three rows of five.

"I saw this technique down at the DA's office. Whenever anyone has pictures to inspect, they tack them on a wallboard in sequence. It's easier to go from one to another and back again."

The three of us stared at Kowalski's murder scene in silence until Jackie and I reached for the same picture, a shot taken from the front of the pier looking down along the outside platform.

"Didn't Gino say he saw Kowalski waiting under this second light?" she asked.

"That's right, and the crane's cable is positioned about thirty feet farther down the platform. Why would Kowalski move toward the end of the platform after Castellano left?" I thought aloud.

"I would expect him to wait for Castellano's car to drive off and then head home. He would have no reason to move in the opposite direction," Martha said.

"Unless he heard a noise or saw someone he didn't expect.

Maybe he ran. Here's a close-up picture of the platform under a light, but I can't tell if it's the second light," Jackie said, after she arranged all the pictures with lights together.

I tapped one of them. "This is where Kowalski and Castellano met. When I walked around the other day, I remember seeing this large gash in the cargo bay frame under the second light."

Martha left the room and returned with a magnifying glass. "What's that black spot on the platform at the edge of the light's reflection?"

"Looks like a stogie," I said. "Compared to the width of one of the wooden planks, I'd say it hadn't been smoked or was dropped soon after being lit."

"Did Kowalski smoke?" Jackie asked.

"Not that I know of, but Castellano smokes them," I said.

"So does every other immigrant from the old country. And if you ask me, it's a disgusting habit. Don't they realize how bad those cigars smell?" Martha asked.

"You get used to them," I said.

I took a more careful look with the magnifying glass and noticed something else of interest. After I confirmed my finding with several of the other pictures, I mentioned it to the girls.

"There are crab cages over the side of the pier. Look at the pilings that hold up the platform and you'll see a thin, taut rope that enters the water from several of them, but only in the nighttime shots." I handed the magnifier to Jackie.

"Why is that important?" Martha asked.

"We might have a witness. You can't fish during the day. The piers are too busy. Whoever owns those cages sets them at night and takes them in before sunrise."

Jackie agreed to track down the fisherman, and Martha

took on the task of asking Sadie if her father smoked stogies. They were headed back to their desks when Jackie hesitated. "Who would benefit from discrediting Castellano?"

My first reaction was to say the union leaders, but there were other possibilities. "Any number of people: a disgruntled member of his organization, someone holding a grudge, and let's not forget the outside union instigators."

"Why are we so focused on Castellano? What about Kowalski? This could have nothing to do with Castellano. Isn't it possible that someone just wanted Kowalski out of the way?" Martha asked. "Wasn't Kowalski promoted to foreman a few months before he got knocked off? Maybe we should talk to the fella who ended up with his job."

Jackie didn't say much after that. She didn't have to. She knew she and Martha had just given us some new directions to pursue.

While I still had their attention, I asked about Gino. "Did you two ever get a chance to track down Gino?"

"We did, but we had to wait until he returned to the pier where he beds down at night," Jackie said. "But I'm afraid he's pretty far gone. He blames himself for the death of his wife and daughter and doesn't want to live or associate with other people."

"I'm surprised he gave up searching for their killers."

"That's not fair. He didn't give up. The booze took control of his life, and given what had happened, I can't blame him," Martha said.

We stood there looking at each other deep in our own thoughts, then went back to our desks and pretended to work, not knowing what to say or how to help Gino. Gino was an example of how quickly life can change. A lesson I learned before and during the war.

Chapter 5

The next evening I went to meet Castellano at my uncle's newly acquired speakeasy. Everything was top-notch, from the highly polished redwood bar to the jazz band that accompanied a talented canary. She could really belt out a song.

This joint was certainly several notches above his old dive, which had catered to locals only interested in a safe place to drink.

At first I didn't notice Luigi making his way through the crowd. I never expected to see him in a formal suit with a bow tie. He looked uncomfortable, so I figured the tie would last at most a few days.

"Hey, Joey. Whatdoya think? Pretty nice, huh?"

"You're movin' up in the world, Uncle. You sure Castellano isn't dragging you into his web?"

"What? You think I don't take my own advice?"

"Just wondering how you're keeping the DA off your back?"

Luigi moved in closer. "I learned a trick or two while overseeing Castellano's speakeasies. Ten percent off the top and the DA looks the other way, even for me."

I couldn't resist a little dig. "What was that advice you gave me? Give Castellano a finger and he'll take your soul."

Luigi poked me in the chest. "I didn't know you were

such a wise ass. I'm no longer on Castellano's payroll. What about *you*? This is the second job you're doing for him. Make sure *you* don't become a regular."

"Don't worry, finding work as a PI hasn't been a problem. I'll catch you later. Castellano's waving me over."

Luigi yanked me back. "Make him wait. I'm tellin' ya, Joey, it's a slow process how the Mafia reels you in. If you're not careful, one day you'll wake up in bed with them and there'll be no way out."

I wasn't worried, but he did have a point. I acknowledged Castellano and hung back with Luigi for a few more minutes. "You're right. I'll let him stew a bit."

"Now you've got the idea. Don't ever give him control of your life."

"Good advice. I'll be sure to follow it."

After a bit Luigi gave me a nudge on the arm and said, "Don't overdo it."

I headed toward Castellano but then turned back. "Before I forget, Ma mentioned her booze supply is runnin' low. Why don't you fix up a case and I'll pick it up on my way out. We all appreciate your generosity."

That was the first time I'd ever seen my uncle stumble for words, and I had to laugh. At that point he knew I was giving him a hard time about charging my folks for the booze.

"Did your ma put you up to this or was it your idea?"

"I don't know what you're talkin' about," I said, leaving him to wonder.

* * * * *

Every time I spotted Castellano he had at least two of his bodyguards around. Tonight one of them was Butch, the man who had saved my life last year. When I approached his table, Castellano ordered them to scram. Butch maneuvered awkwardly out of the booth, spilling their drinks. He was a massive brute who often had trouble controlling his own strength. As he continued to struggle, I flashed back to the image of him standing in my office holding onto the door he had accidently ripped off its hinges.

"Butch, I never got the chance to thank you for taking out Tommy Stefano. That was one hell of a shot."

Butch looked confused and turned to Castellano for an explanation.

"He saw you leave the street before the cops arrived," Castellano said.

"I owe you one, Butch, but do me a favor. If you ever need to enter my office again, try turning the knob before pushing your way in and make sure you duck your head," I said with a smile.

"They don't make doors like they used to," he growled.

Butch and the other goon went to the bar and sat where they could keep an eye on their boss.

Castellano got right down to business. "Why the meeting, Joey? You got something?"

"Not much, but I can understand why you're concerned about the union. More dockworkers are signing up every day."

"Tell me something I don't know."

"Right now everyone believes you had the most to gain from Kowalski's death. I think it's time we gave them someone else to suspect."

"Who?"

"The union organizers."

"Why would anyone believe they would kill one of their strongest supporters?"

"You said it yourself. Look what's happened since the murder. Soon the union will be telling *you* how to run the docks."

"Don't worry. I'll never let things get that far out of control. What are ya gonna do to put suspicion on the union?"

"Stir up some dust, ask questions, and hopefully plant seeds of doubt among the dockworkers."

"If I were you, I'd be careful. They know you're working for me, and I'm about to make life a little more difficult for everyone."

"You gonna tell me what you're planning?"

"In the morning, head down to Pier 17, you'll get the idea. In fact, if you want to confront the union leader, he's renting two storefronts across from the pier. You can't miss them. They both have huge signs hanging outside."

"You got a name?" I asked.

"Sure, Jack Donnelly. He's as tall as Butch with twice the brains and half the brawn. Tell him I sent ya. I'm sure he'll welcome you with open arms," Castellano said with a hearty laugh. He then called a waitress over to order drinks.

We jabbered for a few more minutes until I saw Uncle Luigi corner O'Reilly at the entrance of the speakeasy and take him to his private booth. I got up to join O'Reilly. Castellano grabbed my arm and said he wasn't finished.

"You remember I told you Tommy Stefano had a brother in the hoosegow. Well, Bobby Stefano gets out next week, and I hear he's set on avenging his brother's death. He'll be heading straight for you."

With all that had happened last year, I'd forgotten Castellano's warning about Tommy's brother. "What's he like?"

"All you need to know is that he's smart and ruthless. You can bet he won't come alone."

"You'd mentioned he's connected with the Jersey mob. How connected?"

"Enough for you to worry. I know you can handle yourself, but Bobby Stefano isn't just out to get you. He's gonna bury everyone you care about first."

Castellano went back to eating. He had ended our conversation.

O'Reilly had already ordered drinks and nursed a beer while he waited for me to join him. "Thanks for the set-up. My own private booth, what can be better than this?"

"Where's the usual shot of whiskey?" I asked.

"I'm trying to cut back. I feel different now that my brother's murderer finally got his. I know the Lord said, 'Vengeance is Mine,' but I can tell ya, it feels a hell of a lot better when you do it yourself."

Eight years ago I was there when O'Reilly's younger brother, Shawn, took a blade in the gut. The rest of the gang scattered, but I stayed to comfort him as he died. That's how O'Reilly and I became friends. He was the neighborhood flattie back then and had come running around the corner waving his nightstick, expecting to break up a rumble. I'll never forget the look on his face when he saw the life pouring out of his brother.

"Hey, what ya thinking about?" O'Reilly asked.

"Nothing, just that it's interesting you should mention vengeance. Castellano told me Bobby Stefano is getting out of the big house and heading my way."

O'Reilly put his glass down and ordered a whiskey. "He's trouble."

"Can you track his movements once he's back on the streets? I need to know where he'll be hanging out."

"That's easy. What ya gonna do once you catch up with him?"

"Take the advice my uncle gave me from his hospital bed after Tommy Stefano shot up my office. Get to him before he gets to me."

Chapter 6

Jack Donnelly stood outside his union headquarters staring at the barbwire-laced, chain-link fence that blocked the entrance to Pier 17. The fence had been erected during the night and others were springing up all along the waterfront. Dock security protected the construction crews and prevented union members from entering the piers for work.

I walked over to Donnelly. "What's going on?"

He glanced up and down the waterfront, "That bastard Castellano intends to shut out my union members."

Donnelly bumped my shoulder when he turned in disgust to enter his office. "You're not a dockworker."

"Joey Batista, private investigator."

"I heard about you. You're that private dick Castellano hired to find Kowalski's killer. You got the guts to finger your boss?" he asked, ignoring my hand.

"If it comes down to that, but he has a solid alibi."

"What? Are you naïve or just lousy at your job? He had one of his blokes do it."

"That's likely, *if* he was involved. But most murder cases encompass many different characters who have hidden motives to whack someone. Take yourself, for instance, you've benefited from Kowalski's murder."

"Oh yeah? How did ya come to that conclusion?"

"Union membership has increased since Kowalski's death."

"And that proves what?"

"Just one of two interesting facts."

"What's the other?" Donnelly asked, heading into the building.

"Whoever killed Kowalski was tall, like you. Where were you the night of the murder?"

"I don't need to answer your questions, Batista, but to save us both time, I will. I was sound asleep at home, the same as most people."

"Can you prove that?"

He sat behind his desk and lit a cigar. "No, I can't. Can you prove where you were?"

"You're not from around here, so what do you get outta all this?" I asked, glancing around the sparsely furnished room cluttered with union signs.

Donnelly shot up from his chair. "Maybe I believe in workers' rights. Why don't you get the hell out of here and do your gumshoeing someplace else rather than wasting my time?"

I calmly took a step closer. "Did I just witness one of your more subtle negotiating techniques?"

He cracked a smile, "At times it can be effective."

"If I were you, I'd think of a different strategy. You're dealing with the Mafia, not to mention a growing crowd of angry dockworkers milling outside your office."

Donnelly pointed toward the crowd, "I'll let the pressure build then call a strike. No one will work the docks. You watch, sooner or later Castellano will cave."

"I've know Castellano all my life and I can tell you one thing. He's thought through the consequences of his actions and how to deal with them."

"Thanks for the advice, but I can handle a small-time hood."

Donnelly sat back down and picked up some papers, ignoring my presence. I got the message but couldn't resist one last comment in case he was the one who was clueless.

"You're not looking at the big picture. If you succeed in unionizing the dockworkers, then the truckers will follow and maybe the garbage men will join. After that, who knows, possibly the construction workers? Don't kid yourself, Donnelly; you're dealing with more than Castellano. You're dealing with the entire syndicate." For the first time during our confrontation he looked worried.

Back on the street, I muscled my way through the confused crowd of longshoremen until I heard my name called. "Hey, Batista, whataya doin' with Donnelly? You switchin' sides?"

"I don't take sides. Just lookin' for the truth."

Someone else shouted back, "You want the truth? Spend more time checkin' on your pal Castellano."

When I broke through the throng, I turned to face them. "How many of you joined the union since Kowalski got whacked?" I asked. Two-thirds raised their arms.

"Look around and you'll understand why I wanted to know where Donnelly was the night Kowalski got chilled."

Donnelly barreled through the crowd, waving a wicked-looking stick. "Get the hell outta here, Batista, before I smash ya one," he howled.

From the expressions on the longshoremen's faces, I didn't have to respond to his challenge. The rumors would start that Castellano wasn't the only one with a motive to get rid of Kowalski.

On the way back to the office, I made a mental note to have Martha check Donnelly's background. Someone with his temper had probably had a few run-ins with the law.

* * * * *

The next day, truckloads of longshoremen arrived from Brooklyn, Queens, and the Bronx, along with increased "security" armed with bats and crowbars. I suspected Castellano was getting more help than he wanted.

Each morning that the union workers tried to stop the trucks, dock security smashed a few heads. Bats collided and eventually the mass of humanity came to a standstill as everyone maneuvered for room to swing a fist. Soon after, the chivs would come out.

The police stood and watched the same scene unfold day after day, unable to hold back the surging walls of flesh. Mangled bodies soon overwhelmed the local hospitals, and the morgues filled to capacity. The local papers called for city officials to take action, but the police chief refused to order his men into the fray, knowing the Mafia had a hand in the violence. He was satisfied with containing the mayhem to the waterfront.

The strike lasted a little more than a week and ended the morning after Carmine, Castellano's son, stormed into my uncle's joint looking for his dad.

"When are you gonna put an end to this union mess?" Carmine asked, interrupting my discussion with Castellano. "I've come home from vacation and there's complete chaos."

"You need to learn patience and a little respect," Castellano said to his son. "Your lack of respect for me we can talk about later, but Joey is a good friend of yours, and this is how you treat him? You don't even acknowledge his presence?"

"Pop, why are you talkin' about respect at a time like

this? My customers have ships lined up in the harbor with merchandise that needs to be unloaded. They don't understand this strike shit and neither do I. All you have to do is take this Donnelly guy out."

"Things will get worse if I do that."

"They can't get any worse. You need to end this or someone else will, and if that happens, it's not just *your* life at risk. Once the syndicate decides you're no longer of value to them, they won't leave any family members behind to take revenge," Carmine said.

Carmine turned to me and we shook hands. "Do me a favor, Joey, and talk some sense into my father before it's too late," he said and then left.

Castellano ended our discussion, so I headed home.

Later that night, Donnelly's offices were gutted by firebombs.

* * * * *

Early the following morning, Castellano stopped by my office and asked me to walk with him to the waterfront. When we got there, he stopped each truckload of scabs then headed toward the remains of the union headquarters. The crowd parted to reveal Donnelly standing in the middle of the street, gripping his shillelagh.

"It's time for you to decide if this union business is worth your life," Castellano said to Donnelly.

"You got a piece?" Donnelly asked.

"Don't need one."

Donnelly struck his palm with the club. "Are you sure?"

"I'm sure. Batista's all the protection I need against your puny stick."

I was more shocked by Castellano's words than Donnelly's next action. He raised his club in a blinding fury with deadly intent. Castellano didn't flinch. I instinctively stepped in front of Castellano, absorbed the blow with wrists crossed above my head, pivoted, disarmed Donnelly in one motion, and then slammed the club behind his knees. He crumbled to the ground with a screech.

The dockworkers surged forward, but abruptly halted when Castellano faced the crowd.

"Tell me something. Had anyone ever died on these docks before this so-called union organizer showed up? Who has benefited from this strike? *You've* been out of work, and *I* have cargo piled up on the docks and ships waiting in the harbor. Who are you fighting? You're not fighting me. The men in those trucks aren't mine. Our neighborhood has attracted attention from forces larger than all of us. If we don't find a way to end this, and end it now, more good men will die, and your lives, along with the life of this neighborhood, will change forever."

Sadie pushed her way through the crowd. "You killed my father," she shouted.

Castellano told me and his bodyguards to stay back, no matter what happened. He then pointed to some of the union members. "Jorgensen, Germino, Rossi, do you think I would kill you or have one of my men harm any of you because of some grievances?" No one responded. He walked up to Sadie, who stood alone, gripping a knife by her side. "Sadie, I didn't kill your father," he said and extended his hand.

"I don't believe you." She whipped her knife up to his throat. "And when I know for sure, you're gonna pay." She withdrew her chiv and melted back into the masses.

Castellano ordered his men to open the gates to the piers and the trucks, loaded with scabs, to go back where they'd come from. He offered the dockworkers back pay for time lost, and when they had dispersed and headed to their cargo bays, he told Donnelly to follow us to a local restaurant. Once we entered, the place emptied out. The conversation was brief.

"Donnelly," Castellano said. "You have one of three choices, and I want a decision now. Leave town, die for a lost cause, or come work for *me*. I need a representative for the dockworkers."

Butch, who had never let Castellano out of his sight, stood by the front door. When he slid the massive metal bolt to lock the only exit, the sound of metal striking metal reverberated throughout the room.

Donnelly was smart enough to know when to cave, "How much does the job pay?"

Castellano smiled, "Enough."

Donnelly ended up with an office, a high-paying job, and a broad grin.

Castellano and I walked back along Front Street toward Market Street after the crowds had dispersed along the waterfront. On the way, I asked, "Why the hell did you hire Donnelly?"

"It keeps him in town. Like you said, he had a strong motive to kill Kowalski."

"Destroying the union offices and hiring Donnelly won't keep the union out. Whoever sent Donnelly will try again," I said.

"By the time they send someone new, I'll have my own union up and running. I don't know why I didn't think of this before. I'll have everyone paying me for the privilege to work. I see a lot of potential for that. Maybe unions aren't so bad after all."

I stopped walking, and when Castellano realized I was no longer by his side, he came back.

"I want to get something straight," I said. "I'm not one of your goons."

"I didn't bring you along for that reason. The dockworkers know about your war medals and they respect you. Like I said, respect means something in this town. Besides, I knew if I needed protection, I could count on you. But just in case, Butch would have torn him apart or blown his brains out if necessary.

We continued toward Market Street in silence until he grabbed my arm and pulled me toward him.

"You better solve Kowalski's case soon. I'd hate to see something bad happen to Sadie."

We walked the rest of the way in silence. He had made his point. Sadie had publicly challenged Castellano. Someday soon, he would have to respond to that insult if she didn't publicly apologize.

Chapter 7

Some scars of war run deeper than physical wounds. They never fully heal, and fester below the surface ready to ooze their poisonous memories in the dead of night. That night I knew my nightmares would come and they did. During the endless hours of darkness, my apartment walls seemed to move closer, encasing me in a familiar rodent-infested cell. They were first filled with memories of my torture during the war in the dungeon of a decaying castle and then with outlandish dreams of Castellano dragging Kowalski's struggling body by a rusty bailing hook to a block and tackle—only to have the scene repeated with Sadie suffering the same fate.

As with most anguish-filled nights, I found myself on the verge of oblivion just before feeling an urgent need to take a leak. Given that darkness still enshrouded the room, I was surprised by the time. An overcast sky had blocked out the morning sun, and two feet of snow had delayed the inevitable onslaught of commerce along Market Street that normally woke me from a restless sleep.

Faced with the reality of what I had to do that morning, I rolled over and buried my face in the pillow. Convincing Sadie she needed protection wouldn't be easy. I'd barely made it out of her apartment alive the day I told her I was investigating her father's murder, not for her but for Castellano. Sadie and I had been friends all our lives, but that day she'd made it clear that friendship had its limits. Luckily she possessed a bad aim and had run out of flower pots, as I was able to dive out her kitchen window onto the fire escape and clamber down to safety.

An hour after first waking, I successfully dragged myself out of bed and into the embrace of a hot shower, only to have it interrupted by a vigorous knock. I scurried to open the apartment door while wearing just a towel wrapped around my waist. To my surprise, there stood Jackie and Martha, staring at my towel and looking down at the puddle that had formed at my feet.

"You didn't show up for work, so we came to you," Jackie said upon entering.

She took a seat at the kitchen table, but Martha turned back and closed the door.

"You wouldn't have a towel handy?" she asked, reaching out and giving my towel a strong yank.

I held on tight, turned away, and then released my grip. She stumbled back holding her prize. I walked to the bedroom buck naked, accompanied by a chorus of laughter.

Dressed and feeling more in control, I poured a cup of joe from the pot the girls had brewed while they waited.

"I take it you both have information that couldn't wait until I came to the office."

"Just thought we'd add some excitement to your otherwise boring life," Martha said with a hint of sarcasm.

"We heard you and Castellano faced down an angry mob yesterday. Seems to us you're becoming a bit chummy with a Mafia boss, even if he's a friend of your family," Jackie said.

It was bad enough that I had my uncle warning me away from Castellano; I didn't need the girls doing the same. I felt an irrational anger well up inside and knew I would say something nasty if I responded to Jackie's accusation. To buy time, I went to the window with my coffee and watched the neighborhood struggle with the ongoing snow.

"Is that what this invasion is about, or do you have some real work to discuss?" I asked, facing them again.

They didn't react.

"Martha, did you ever discover if Kowalski smoked stogies? And Jackie, what about those crab lines?"

Jackie stiffened, brushed aside a strand of red hair, and joined me at the window.

"I'm a partner in this business, and what we do affects each other. I have a right to be concerned if we're getting entangled with the Mafia, and so does Martha."

I felt like a real jingle-brain. "Look, I'm sorry. I have things under control with Castellano. He just happens to be in the middle of everything that has to do with the Kowalski murder. If it wasn't for this case, we would have very little to do with Castellano."

I turned to Martha, "Are you finished with that towel? It's one of my favorites." She threw it at me, breaking the tension that had developed.

We sat around the table, and Jackie gave a rundown on what she had discovered about the crab lines.

"Unfortunately, the cages could belong to any of over thirty fishermen who work the piers. They seem to randomly decide which pier to fish on any given night, so it's impossible to know who might have been hanging around when Kowalski got bumped off. I have another ten to fifteen to track down, but I'm afraid I'll get the same answer. Nobody knows anything, or they're afraid."

It occurred to me that by snooping around we may

have inadvertently alerted the killer there was a potential witness.

"Most everyone on the docks knows we work together, so I suspect they figured out that a fisherman has something to do with the Kowalski case. We need to find this guy and we need to do it fast before the killer does," I said.

Jackie turned pale, "I don't see how it's possible. It will take at least another week to locate who owned those cages."

"When I was a kid, Pop and Luigi fished the docks for eel and threw out one or two crab cages just in case they got lucky. You're right, like the other fishermen, they moved around, but they had two, maybe three favorite piers. If I were you, I'd stay focused on Pier 17 and see who shows up."

Martha had met with Sadie and confirmed that her father didn't smoke. Though I had forgotten to ask her to dig into Donnelly's past, she had taken the initiative on her own.

"It seemed to me nothing good has happened since this Donnelly fella came to town, so I did some checking," she said. "He arrived from Detroit eight months ago. He tried to organize the autoworkers there, but they practically tarred and feathered him. Ford pays well above the average wage in the area, so the employees viewed Donnelly as a troublemaker."

"Did he use any underhanded tactics to gain support?" I asked.

"He didn't have a chance to get established, but over the years, he's been arrested several times for inciting riots and once for murder. He beat the murder rap."

"How?"

Martha handed me her notes. "Thanks to a contact I've

been cultivating in the DA's office," she said with a smile, "I called the prosecuting attorney in Cleveland, and according to him, a fight broke out between Donnelly and three others during a card game. They accused him of cheating. Donnelly allegedly pulled a knife and fatally stabbed one of the guys and seriously injured another. The prosecutor was confident he was going to get a conviction, but then, several last-minute witnesses testified that Donnelly was the only one in the fight who didn't have his own weapon. According to them, he disarmed one of his attackers and defended himself."

I thought back to the encounter I'd had with Donnelly when he attacked Castellano. Donnelly wasn't much of a street fighter. In my opinion, it was unlikely he would've survived the fight Martha described without his own chiv.

"I suspected Donnelly had some heavyweights behind his efforts to form unions and now I'm sure," I said.

"What makes you say that?" Jackie asked.

"Witnesses can be bought or intimidated."

"I'll keep digging into his background. Anything else you need me to do?" Martha asked.

I was about to answer her when Ma knocked and entered. "O'Reilly's waiting in your office. He said it's important."

Chapter 8

O'Reilly sat back with his shoes on the desk, sipping a shot of my whiskey.

"I could get used to this life," he said when we entered the office. "Why am I wasting time working homicide when I could have two beautiful dames at my side and not be hampered by all the bureaucratic corruption that dominates City Hall?"

"Join us. There's plenty of work," I said.

"Nah, when it comes right down to it, I like the badge. Besides, you're now talking to *Lieutenant* O'Reilly."

We gathered around and congratulated him by knocking off what was left of the scotch whiskey. It turned out Lieutenant Sullivan of the Staten Island Homicide Division recommended O'Reilly for the promotion due to his involvement in the apprehension of a serial killer—the one I filled with daylight in La Cucina Restaurant at the end of last year. It never bothered me that I didn't try real hard to take him in alive; my first love, Anita, was one of his early victims.

"I didn't come over just to brag, but to let you know Bobby Stefano moved into a Brooklyn dive near the Bridge."

"I thought he operated out of Jersey. What's he doing in Brooklyn?" I asked.

"He and his brother grew up there. My guess is he's looking to take care of some unfinished business—you. From what I hear, the mob turned down his request for a hit due to your family's connections in Chicago. He's probably going it alone, recruiting outside help from his old neighborhood."

Jackie stepped toward O'Reilly. "What's the address? We need to settle this before he gets organized."

"Not so fast. First, I want something in return. What about Kowalski? Did you guys pick up any leads we might've missed?"

We gave O'Reilly what we had, and he agreed to track down who owned the crab lines so Jackie could join me in dealing with Stefano. O'Reilly didn't question Jackie's involvement, since she was there when Tommy Stefano shot up my office and killed one of Luigi's bodyguards. That was the first day Jackie and I met, and the first time she saved my life.

* * * * *

We were eager to head to Brooklyn and confront Bobby Stefano, but our first priority was to warn Sadie about the dangers she faced. We ventured into the snowstorm and headed to her apartment, located a few buildings down the street over the local drug store. We didn't have far to go, but the walk wasn't easy. We had to push against the freezing wind and blinding snow with our heads down, holding on to each other for support. With each step, our lungs burned from inhaling the frigid air. Once inside the building, we rushed to join two store customers huddled over the hall radiator and stomped our feet in unison to theirs in an effort to get warm. We may have looked ridiculous, but no one paid attention to our antics since it was a winter ritual practiced by all, often accompanied with the slapping and rubbing of hands over the heater.

I rapped several times on Sadie's door, calling her name. We knew she was home because we heard a small commotion inside. I was about to pound again when Chris, a member of my old gang, stepped out into the hall, closing Sadie's door behind him.

"Hey, Joey, Jackie. I'm afraid Sadie never wants to speak to you again," he said to me.

Seeing Chris caught me off guard. "What're you doin' with Sadie? I thought you and Rosalie had a thing goin'."

"We broke up a few weeks ago. She didn't have time for anything other than school. I'm surprised you didn't know. She has dinner every night with you and your family. I guess she's not exactly heartbroken."

"By the looks of things, neither are you," Jackie said.

"Unlike Joey, I don't get out of the neighborhood much. Pickin's are slim, so those of us who are still single tend to bounce around, if you know what I mean. Who knows? Rosalie and I might still end up together in the end."

"Right now I need a favor," I said. "Try to convince Sadie to see us. We'd like to speak with her in private."

"Why the hell not? I was about to leave anyway. You better wait here. She bought several new flower pots since your last visit," he said with a smile.

A few minutes later Chris came back into the hall and wished us luck. When we entered the apartment, a strong aroma of coffee greeted us. Sadie didn't acknowledge our presence. She sat at her table clutching a mug and watching the steam rise.

"Mind if we help ourselves?" I asked. She didn't answer, so Jackie poured two cups.

I sat opposite Sadie and reached for her hand. She jerked it back and folded her arms tightly against her chest.

"My father liked you, and so did I. I thought we were friends," she said, still looking down at her coffee.

"You can't grow up together in this neighborhood and not be friends. Nothing can change that, nothing. We've been through too much—shed too much blood protecting each other," I said.

She jumped out of her chair. "Then why the hell are you working for my father's killer?"

I stood but kept my distance. "I told you last time, if Castellano had anything to do with your father's death, I won't back down. That's a promise."

"You two looked pretty chummy the other day at the waterfront when you protected him from that union guy. You sure you're not turning into one of Castellano's palookas?"

Jackie put her cup on the kitchen table and stood by my side.

"Joey and I have done nothing but work on this case for the past several weeks and we've uncovered some interesting leads the police overlooked."

Sadie got into Jackie's face. "Why should I believe you any more than him? You two work together, and from what I hear, you guys spend more time in the sack than at the office. Tell me, what the hell was Joey doing with Castellano at the docks?"

Jackie didn't flinch. "Trying to find who benefited from your father's death. And if you would take a minute to think, you'd realize that killing your father in such a dramatic fashion would be the dumbest thing Castellano could've done. The waterfront has been practically shutdown. He needs to find your father's killer because the docks could explode again into chaos at any time."

Sadie leaned against the table and broke down. I heard she hadn't shed a tear for her father, and now everything poured out. I'd never seen Sadie cry, not even when she took a blade in the shoulder during a street fight. She always stood with the guys no matter how dangerous. I knew she'd be there for me if I needed her, but right now it was my turn.

I watched as she left the room to regain her composure. Her blonde hair framed a lean, sculptured face with light blue eyes and features that matched her petite stature. She was now a confident woman determined to have justice, no longer the young girl who wore baggy pants and shirts to hide her femininity. When she returned and sat at the table, she was ready to talk.

"What do you want from me?"

"We think your life's in danger, especially after you threatened Castellano in front of half the city."

"Wait a minute! You can't have it both ways. She just told me Castellano would've been crazy to kill my father. Wouldn't the same apply to me?"

This time Sadie didn't pull away when I reached for her hand. "Castellano has no choice but to respond to the threat you made unless you publicly apologize. If he doesn't do something, his days as a mob boss are numbered. It basically comes down to your life or his. My guess is you will simply disappear. But, in my opinion, Castellano is the least of your problems."

"You're both making my head spin. Just tell me why my father was murdered, and if not by Castellano, then by whom?"

"Jackie and I have asked that very question. We think it's possible that someone is trying to bring down Castellano and take over the waterfront without an outright confrontation. Then there are the union organizers. You can't deny the union has benefited from your father's murder."

Sadie leaned back and thought about what I had said. Then, without saying a word, poured the last of the coffee and got up to brew a new pot. On her way back to the table, she seemed to notice frost forming on the window and cranked up the heat in the apartment. Given her state of mind, I didn't think it a good idea to mention that it wouldn't help given how cold it was outside.

"I'm trying to follow what you're saying, but I've been consumed with hatred for Castellano. I can't accept any other explanation," Sadie said.

"We understand," Jackie said. "But if we're right, and Castellano had nothing to do with your father's death, you will be the killer's next victim."

"Why?"

I was about to answer when Jackie put her hand on my shoulder.

"Think about what Joey just said. If you are killed, the whole waterfront will become unionized, and if that happens, Castellano will be replaced. If I were the killer and wanted to bring down Castellano, I'd hang your mutilated body from the same crane I used to display your father's."

Visibly shaken, Sadie walked over to the window and rubbed her hand in a circle to wipe away the frost so she could see the neighborhood.

"What do you want me to do, run away? This is my home. I have no place to go, no place to hide."

"Stay at Jackie's for awhile. She and I need to leave for a day or two. My uncle can post someone outside the door at night. During the day, you can help Martha at the office."

"How soon do I have to leave?"

"Now. Pack what you need and don't forget your stiletto," I said.

Sadie turned away from the window and placed both arms by her side gripping the edge of the sill.

"No! I'll not run and cower, but I will stay inside. I work downstairs at the drugstore and have plenty of food. Just find out what happened to my father and do it soon. I'll not stay cooped up for long."

Knowing Sadie, I could see her mind was made up. It seemed like a reasonable compromise. As promised, before Jackie and I left for Brooklyn I arranged with my uncle to have someone stand guard outside Sadie's apartment.

Chapter 9

Jackie and I spent a couple of nights observing Stefano's movements to see if he developed a routine. Like most mobsters, he frequented a favorite speakeasy. On the third night, we slipped into the joint with a large group that had piled out of several hacks.

Even though the place was packed, Stefano was easy to pick out of the crowd based on the description O'Reilly had given us before we left for Brooklyn. He was bald, a head taller than everyone else, drunk, loud, and angry at someone at his table. Before long the two men got into a fight and Stefano tossed the guy across the room into a barstool. I went over, helped the fella up, and offered to buy him a drink. Jackie slipped into the space next to him.

"Looks like you could use some tiger milk," I said.

"Thanks. That guy's off his rocker. Been out of the can a few days and already wants to rub out half the city."

"Sounds like he spent too much time in the bing. Solitary confinement can do that to a guy."

"Nah, he's always had a few screws loose. Thinks he can come back after all these years and get his old gang to do whatever he wants. He must think everyone sat around waitin' for him to get out."

"If he's crazy like you said, who knows what's going through his head?" I said, finishing off my drink.

"Geez, I can't believe he still shaves his head. What a

fool. If it was me and I'd just did a five-spot, I'd be holed up with some broad and not hangin' with a bunch of drunks plannin' on whackin' someone." He downed his hooch. I ordered a couple more.

"Who's he after?" I asked.

"While he was up the river some guy iced his brother, and he wants us to take out the guy and his family. If you ask me, his brother Tommy probably deserved what he got. He was another nut case."

Stefano strode over, grabbed the guy by his coat collar, hurled him back toward the table, and then planted both his paws on the bar.

"Who the hell are you?" he demanded.

"None of your damn business," I said, lowering my fedora and turning back toward the bar. I didn't want to take a chance someone had given him my description.

Stefano grabbed my shoulder. "Hey Bozo, I'm talking to you."

Before he could spin me around, Jackie plunged a hunting knife deep into the surface of the bar through the back of his left palm with the blade pointing in the direction of his fingers. He let out a howl and loosened his grip. I yanked his hand off my shoulder and snapped it back hard against his wrist. With one hand pinned to the bar by Jackie's chiv and his other in a wrist lock, Stefano was completely immobilized. I snatched the roscoe out of his shoulder holster and jammed the barrel up under his chin.

"The name's Joey Batista. Maybe you heard of me? If I were you, I wouldn't move your other hand or they'll be calling you Bobby Split Fingers."

"You're a dead man, Batista."

"Funny, that's what your brother said."

He tried to free his left hand but stopped as the blade moved between his knuckles. One of his old gang members stood and pulled a rod, but before he could get off a shot, Jackie had a chiv launched that caught him under the shoulder blade. In less than a second, she drew another blade from the knife harness she wore under her coat, a handy contraption my pop had built for her last year when we realized she was an expert knife thrower.

"Take a good look at this face, Stefano. It's the last thing you're gonna see if you make a move to put a hit on me or my family. And trust me, I'll know."

"If I were you, Batista, I'd pull that trigger because you're not gonna get another chance."

"I'll pick the time and place, and when I do, there won't be any witnesses," I said.

Jackie kept everyone at bay by brandishing two knives at the crowd, and then walked toward the door creating a pathway of startled onlookers. When she was in position, I shoved Stefano forward, letting loose of his wrist as I backed away. Stefano desperately tried to maintain his balance, slamming his freed hand into a surprised bystander. He then let out a hellish yell, pulled the hunting knife out of the wooden bar, and loped toward me, splattering onlookers with blood from his hand.

I had only seconds to react. I knew Jackie would bring him down with one of her knives if he got too close. The last thing we needed was a dead body the DA could hang around our necks. I had no alternative but to shoot. The bullet ripped through Stefano's shoe, stopping his stride. He lunged and crashed to the floor. On the way down, the knife in his outstretched hand grazed my coat. I moved in, stomped on his arm, and retrieved the blade.

"Thanks for returning the chiv, Bobby, but remember, if we meet again, I won't be so cordial."

I turned to the crowd. "You know, all we wanted was a beer. You really should be more hospitable. You're gonna give Brooklyn a bad reputation."

* * * * *

When I cranked up the Ford and pulled into traffic, Jackie let me have it.

"You should've taken my advice and finished the guy in an alleyway when we had the element of surprise. He's a real Bruno and we just pushed him over the edge. I wouldn't be surprised if he comes after us with a chopper squad. Oh, and don't forget, you owe me a knife for the one I left buried in that goon's shoulder, the one about to fill you with lead."

It wasn't my intent to confront Stefano in the speakeasy, but that's how things had turned out. I'd killed too many in the war based solely on orders, never knowing why. I needed to make sure Stefano was obsessed with avenging his brother. To kill him without knowing would have moved me back to the killer the army had created and further from the person I wished to become again.

Now I knew. The next time we confronted each other, only one of us would survive.

Chapter 10

O'Reilly slapped us with some bad news, soon after Jackie and I returned from Brooklyn.

"We lost track of Stefano."

Jackie had been right. I should've killed the bastard when I had the chance.

"How the hell did that happen?" I said, angrier with myself than with O'Reilly.

"Take it easy, we'll pick him up again. He got into a brawl, and after getting patched up, slipped out the back of the hospital."

"How badly was he hurt?"

"He'll be limping around for a few weeks and having someone wiping his ass for a couple of days. Some dame drove a knife through his hand while her Bird nearly broke his wrist and shot a hole in his foot," he said, with a knowing look and a grin. "If he's in the City, we'll find him. I have every beat cop in the five boroughs checkin' around."

"What about Jersey?" I asked. "Castellano said he'd hung out in Newark before he went to the big house."

"That's a problem. But don't worry, I know a couple of guys who know a couple of guys who work the Newark area."

"That's doesn't give me a sense of confidence."

O'Reilly knocked off his beer and ordered another. "It shouldn't. If you're right, and he surfaces in Jersey, it'll be next to impossible to pick up his whereabouts."

That wasn't all O'Reilly had to say.

"I'm not done with the bad news. Gino was found sprawled inside a makeshift shelter down by the waterfront. He went and got his head bashed in during one of the union brawls. The old croaker patched it up himself, but he didn't have what he needed to do a proper job. Some of the dockworkers dragged him to the hospital when they saw his condition."

I had assumed Gino moved out of the area as soon as the fences went up and hadn't given him a second thought. "Is he gonna make it?" I asked.

"He'll be fine; he's already asking for his gin."

"I'll check with my folks to see if he can stay with us when he gets out."

"You don't have to worry. He's being cared for at the local orphanage. Apparently one of the Sisters making her daily rounds at the hospital recognized Gino from years ago. He used to volunteer at the orphanage when he had his medical practice."

"How do you know all this?"

O'Reilly smiled. "I'm a detective."

* * * * *

A week later Gino joined us for breakfast with his head wrapped in several layers of bandages. He sat between the girls and had come clean-shaven, wearing a white shirt that matched his turban, a striped tie, and a Cheshire grin. If it wasn't for the bandages, I don't think I would've recognized him.

Rosalie, who normally had an early morning class, was also at the table sitting next to Luigi.

"Gino, I'm glad to see you reconsidered my offer," I said.

Ma corrected me, "*Richard* and your father have agreed to a month's trial."

"He'll be living behind the repair shop, and there will be no booze," Pop said.

Both Martha and Jackie flashed me a look of concern. I knew what they were thinking. Gino would *need* an occasional drink, if not more.

"Then *I* think Richard should have a nice breakfast, dump the clean shirt and tie, go back on the street, and find a new place to bed down."

"What? You didn't hear me? He can use the room in the back of the shop," Pop said with a mouthful of food.

"Pop, you can't expect Richard to stop drinking just because you say so. It's gonna take time."

Rosalie spoke up.

"Mr. Batista, Joey's right. Once alcohol has a hold of you, it's difficult to get free. I saw my father try for years, but he never could. I'm sure you remember how often I ran down those stairs at night clutching my pillow when he went into one of his rages."

"Rosalie, how many times I gotta tell you to call me Vito or Pop. No more mister crap."

Knowing Pop, he didn't appreciate everyone piling on and had taken his frustration out on Rosalie.

"Vito, I'm afraid this young lady is correct," Gino said. "I won't drink on the job, but what I do in my room should be my business."

"Not in my house," Pop said.

"All I can do is give it my best try. And I will," Gino said.

Everyone stopped eating, expecting Pop to continue his rant, but instead he went into the kitchen, poured himself another cup of joe, came back, and put a gentle hand on Rosalie's shoulder as he looked over at Gino. That simple gesture was his way of apologizing to her for what he had said in anger. "*Richard*," Pop said, "Ma reminded me of your kindness when we first arrived in this country. If you fall down, we will be there to pick you up, as long as you keep tryin'."

Luigi went over and gave his brother a rare hug.

Before anyone could say anything else, Gino spoke up.

"I know you're all trying to be nice, but please don't call me Richard. That part of my life is over. Gino suits me fine."

Ma was about to object, so the rest of us quickly agreed with Gino.

* * * * *

My uncle brought up another controversial topic. "I hear Tommy Stefano's brother is out of the slammer and looking for revenge. What are you planning?" Luigi asked me.

Ma stopped clearing the plates, looked first at Luigi, then in my direction.

"No one told me Stefano had a brother. When was I supposed to find this out, when I have a bullet in my head?"

"Don't worry, Ma. Jackie and I took care of Bobby Stefano a few nights ago."

"Good, then he's dead," she stated.

"Not quite."

"What does that mean? Either he's dead or he's not."

"He's hurt."

That got Pop's attention. "I thought you were an assassin during the war. I never heard of an assassin who goes around only hurting people who threaten him."

"Easy, Vito," Luigi said. "Joey, do you know where Bobby is hanging out?"

All eyes turned towards me.

"We did. O'Reilly had some of his buddies tracking him, but Stefano slipped out the back of a hospital."

"How badly was he hurt?" Pop asked.

"Not bad enough," Jackie said.

Ma turned down the flame under a teapot, and the rest of us listened to the whistle trail off. Pop pushed back from the table. Rosalie slumped in her chair, probably recalling that the last time a Mafia boss wanted me dead, she had ended up plunging a fire ax into the back of a thug about to blow my head off. No one else moved or said a word until Gino broke the silence.

"Maybe Joey's right. I might be better off back on the street."

"Nobody worry," Luigi said. "I've got everything under control. Carmella, you still got that thigh holster I gave you?"

Ma placed the teapot on the table, put her leg on a chair, and pulled up her skirt.

"What? You think I'm crazy after what happened last year? Living with this family is like surviving in a war zone."

Luigi complimented her on being prepared and then continued to give orders.

"Rosalie, sorry, but you need to drop out of school until this is settled." He turned to me, ignoring Rosalie's protest. "Joey, get this bastard, and this time do it right. I'll take care of the home front. I know exactly what type of redecorating this place needs to give us some protection."

A moment ago Gino was kidding about going back on the street. But seeing his eyes bug out as he stared at the gun Ma pulled from her holster, I knew he was truly scared.

* * * * *

Over the next few days, Jackie and I followed up on several leads from O'Reilly about where Stefano might be hanging out in Newark. This time we focused on surveillance, not wanting to tip off Stefano that we were again in the hunt. If Stefano was around, he had gone deep underground, probably nursing his wounds. We had no doubt that sooner or later he would round up a crew and make a move, but in his own time. It became apparent that all we could do was return home and prepare for the inevitable showdown.

Chapter 11

After spending a futile week in Newark on the prowl for Stefano, we walked into the office and found Frank Galvano, the lawyer who had the flat next to ours, attempting to rehire Martha as his secretary.

"I made a mistake. I'm sorry, but I really didn't *fire* you the last time," he said.

"Oh right. You didn't have enough work for me. What a lame excuse. You just don't like others, especially women, telling you what they think."

"Now Martha, that's not fair. You needed more experience. My clients don't want to hear that they wouldn't require a lawyer if they got their shit together."

We all broke out laughing, including Martha. "I guess that was a little extreme," she said.

I stepped into the conversation to make sure Frank didn't have a chance to snatch Martha from us. "Sorry, Frank, as far as we're concerned, Martha's not available. She's a crucial part of our ability to investigate and solve crimes. Besides, she just got a hefty raise."

"I did?"

"Sure, it was gonna be a surprise, but he blew it for us."

"Frank, come back in six months and make me another offer," Martha said. "I'll split my next raise with you fifty-fifty."

Martha walked Frank into the inner office. "You guys coming? Frank has a case for us."

"Only if it doesn't involve another good-looking dame who ends up dead," I said.

Frank heard my comment and stuck his head through the doorway.

"Not a chance. This dame's already on ice and she was eighty-two."

We pulled the chairs together, and Frank explained what he needed.

"I have a client who wants to protest his aunt's will and find out who ran her down in broad daylight."

"You're joking," I said.

"Don't worry. There's only one will, not three like last time."

"What's the problem? Why would he think someone purposely ran her over?"

"He's her sole relative, and she recently disowned him and left the bulk of the estate to her domestic staff and a few others."

"I don't see a case. I imagine things like that happen all the time."

"According to my client, his aunt had intended to change back to her original will on the very day she died, leaving the new beneficiaries with nothing."

"I'll admit it's quite a coincidence. What do you want from us?" I asked.

Frank took a folder from his valise. "Poke around. Check into the background of the beneficiaries. If you don't find anything suspicious, case closed. I have all the information you'll need right here."

"You do realize you just mentioned that three wills are involved," I said, reaching for the folder. That's when I noticed the girls' reactions. Martha clutched her steno pad tighter, and Jackie leaned back in her chair and crossed her legs in the opposite direction.

I shook my head and pulled my hand back. "Sorry Frank, we have too much goin' on. Tommy Stefano's brother, Bobby, is out of the slammer and dead set on revenge. We're still baffled by the Kowalski murder, and Jackie has a minor case hanging over from last year."

"And we have to find the creeps who killed Gino's family," Martha added.

"I wondered how you guys convinced Gino to take Pop's job," I said. "Maybe next time you might consult me before taking on a new case, especially one that's two decades old."

"Oh, we will," Jackie said crossing her fingers.

Frank dropped the folder on my desk with a loud thump.

"I understand your hesitation, especially with Stefano's brother on the loose, but there's no hurry. An injunction has been issued against executing the will, and the next hearing isn't scheduled for a few months. You have plenty of time."

Frank headed for the door but then turned to face me. "How do you figure three wills? I only mentioned two."

"The original, the new one that removed her nephew, and the one she intended to change back to the original."

"That's only two," Frank said.

"Only if you assume the nephew told the truth about her changing the second back to the original," I said.

Frank thought for a second. "I guess that's why I'm not a detective. Look, do this for me. Ruth, the woman who died, did more for the underprivileged in this town than all the city agencies combined. I know firsthand."

I got the sense Frank didn't want to elaborate, so I didn't

probe. With Frank gone, we discussed the current cases and how to deal with Stefano.

"Jackie, what's happening with Mr. Cafiero? You haven't mentioned him since December," I said.

"I didn't find any reason for him to be concerned about his safety. You may recall, he sees Mafia hit men around every corner. I've spent considerable time hanging out in his neighborhood and haven't spotted any suspicious characters. In my opinion, he's a lonely old man in need of company."

"Did he ever explain why he thought the Mafia wanted him dead?" I asked.

"No, just that he had his reasons."

"Can we close out the case?"

"Soon. I did notice some street thugs hanging around the neighborhood, which isn't unusual. I guess there's a chance they're watching him, although it's hard to tell from the way they blend into the background. Someone did ransack his place a few times, but they didn't take anything."

"What do you recommend?"

"I'm trying to convince him to move in with one of his kids, but I'm doing that on my own time. I like the guy and don't think he should be living alone."

I understood why Jackie wanted to help the old man. She'd never had a family life, and from an early age, she had to survive by her wits on the streets of Chicago.

"Okay, we'll consider the case closed unless you say differently."

"Fine with me."

Martha picked up the file Frank left behind and flipped through the pages. "Why don't I check the background of the beneficiaries? You guys are working the Kowalski murder, and I really don't have much to keep me busy other than sitting around worrying that Bobby Stefano might show up."

Past experience told me not to argue with Martha. She becomes a real bitch when she gets bored. We agreed and shifted our focus to Stefano.

"Until we get more information from O'Reilly, there isn't much we can do other than wait for Stefano to make a move. We should travel in pairs and be prepared for the worst," I said, chambering a round in each of my Colt .45 pistols. The girls did the same with their revolvers.

"That reminds me," Martha said. "Luigi brought over an armful of weapons this morning. We each have a shotgun by our desks and an extra revolver in the top drawer."

Jackie picked up her shotgun, racked a shell, and placed it back against the wall behind her desk. "We should track down O'Reilly and see if he's made any progress locating who owns those crab cages and get the latest on Stefano," she said.

Martha thumbed through her note pad. "I was so distracted by Frank that I forgot to mention O'Reilly called. He said he wanted to meet you guys at the Slippery Eel around six tonight."

"Did he say why?" I asked.

"No, just that he had some information. I tried to get more details, but he was in a hurry and said you'd find out when you showed up."

"Where's the Slippery Eel?" Jackie asked.

"It's a dive along the waterfront. He hung out there after Luigi's old speakeasy shut down. I suggest we get something to eat before we go. The food's not the greatest."

* * * * *

To get to the back of the joint where O'Reilly usually sat, we had to barrel our way through a throng of burly men, jostling to get a front row seat to the finals of a spittoon-spitting competition.

"You should have told us there was a contest tonight. I would've practiced my technique," I said to O'Reilly.

"You wouldn't stand a chance. These guys can blind someone at ten paces. Keep that in mind if you ever tangle with an old timer," O'Reilly said with a slight slur.

The waitress brought over two more beers for O'Reilly, removed four empties, and took our order. When she left, we waited for O'Reilly to say why he wanted to meet. I could tell from the way he was downing his drinks that he had something unpleasant on his mind.

"Let's have it, Mike."

O'Reilly lurched forward, grabbed my tie, and yanked me across the table until our faces almost touched.

"You have no one to blame but yourself for Stefano going underground. Even our more reliable stool-pigeons have clammed up, which should make you damn nervous."

"I needed to make sure."

He let loose of the tie and slumped back in his chair. "Are you kidding me? You know how things work around this town. Stefano thinks you killed his brother. You should've drilled him when you had the chance."

"Look, Mike, I left a string of bodies stretched across Europe, and when I came home from the war, the killing didn't stop. It was easier when I was following orders. I didn't have to think about why, just how to get the job done and survive."

"Damn it, Joey," he said, slamming his fist onto the table and sending the beer mugs skittering across the surface. "The only difference now is that your orders are coming from your gut. I know damn well there was no doubt in your mind that Bobby Stefano would want to avenge his brother. You would if you were him."

O'Reilly had essentially repeated what Jackie said the night we confronted Stefano. Even my family had expected the same. I had promised everyone last year that I wouldn't put them in danger again, and I had failed. Ma got it right when she said we live in a war zone. If I wanted to stay in the PI business and live in this city, I needed to let go of the Joey Batista who loved a sweet girl and tried to negotiate between street gangs as a kid. I needed to be the Joey Batista who survived behind enemy lines in France and Germany.

I knocked off my beer and looked O'Reilly squarely in the eyes. "You're right. It won't happen again. Now, tell us about the fishing gear. Any leads?"

"I'm not done with Stefano. We did pick up some talk about a couple of Detroit droppers coming to Newark. At most, you have a few days before they make their move."

"Where in Newark?"

"Don't know, just rumors at this point."

"Do you know who they are? How they operate?" Jackie asked.

"I don't have details, just that they're coming."

Jackie grabbed hold of both our hands and pulled them to her.

"Let's not forget we're in this together. If I know Joey, he won't make the same mistake twice. As for me, I've been living by my instincts all my life. We'll deal with these hit men when the time comes. For right now we have to focus on who killed Kowalski. The killer knows there's a witness, and it's our fault. Did you find our fisherman?" Jackie asked O'Reilly.

Before he could answer, the waitress brought over our drinks, and O'Reilly shifted his attention to her. "Betty, would you tell Dominic I'd like him to join us when he gets a chance?"

"Sure, Mike, but he hasn't been around lately. He might have the week off. I'll check with the guys in the kitchen."

"Who's Dominic?" Jackie asked.

"He's one of the cooks. He fishes after hours to make extra dough by selling his catch to the local restaurants. A buddy of mine, who works this beat, told me Dominic and two other guys fish off Pier 17 every chance they get."

"Have you talked to the others?" I asked.

"I have, and they were both confident Dominic had his lines out the night Kowalski got bumped."

"How can they be so sure? It's been months," Jackie said.

"I'll admit it's not unusual for bodies to wash up around the waterfront, but not many are found dangling from a crane. I think you'd remember if you were fishing there the night it happened."

The waitress came back and handed O'Reilly a note with Dominic's address.

"The boss said Dominic hasn't shown up the last few days. He thinks he's on one of his binges. If Dominic wasn't such a good cook, the boss would've fired him a long time ago."

O'Reilly finished his drink and was halfway through the crowd before we knew what happened. "Let's go," he shouted back at us.

* * * * *

Dominic lived two blocks from the restaurant in a roach-infested, timber-framed row house that leaned to the left. O'Reilly took the stairs in two leaps and banged on the door. When I got to the landing, we hit the door in unison, sending it crashing to the floor.

"Flip the light switch," O'Reilly shouted.

"There isn't one. Wait a minute, there's an oil lamp on this hutch."

The light cast an eerie glow over a blood-soaked body sprawled in a corner not far from an over-turned table. O'Reilly lit another lamp and crouched beside the stiff.

Jackie stepped on some broken glass as she entered. O'Reilly looked up and ordered us to wait outside. Within a few minutes, he joined us.

"Looks like Dominic saw the grim reaper when he opened the door. He didn't stand a chance. The murderer shoved him back across the room into a small table. Dominic had knocked off two bottles of booze and was well into his third when he answered the door. I'm surprised he had the strength to hurl the bottle at his intruder. After that, all it took was a carving knife to the gut. I'd say the killer took less than two minutes."

O'Reilly let us back into the apartment, and I checked out the kitchen.

"Where'd he get the knife? Most murderers don't walk around with a butcher knife in their hands. It doesn't look like they fought in here," I said from the doorway. O'Reilly joined me in the kitchen.

Jackie squatted next to the body.

"This is *my* knife," she said in a soft whisper.

"What?" O'Reilly said.

"From the other night in Brooklyn. I used this chiv to stop Stefano's friend from shooting Joey."

It didn't take O'Reilly long to assess the situation and take action. He returned to the kitchen, overturned a few chairs, and swept his arm across the counter, crashing soiled dishes and glasses onto the floor. He knocked a set of carving knives over, put on a glove, and took one of the knives with him into the main room. Without saying a word, he removed Jackie's knife from Dominic's gut and plunged the one he held into the wound. I grabbed a dishcloth and wrapped the bloody knife.

"Let's get the hell out of here," O'Reilly said.

We walked across the street to one of the piers and shared a smoke.

"What the hell's goin' on?" I asked.

O'Reilly took a long drag while staring at the ground and then pulverized the cigarette butt into the pavement with the heel of his boot.

"I just put my job on the line for you guys because our killer is trying to get you out of the way. Everyone knows Jackie wanted to find who owned those crab lines. It wouldn't take the DA long to have both of you sweating it out in one of his interrogation cells. A few witnesses from the other night testifying how Jackie handles a knife and her prints on that chiv would be sufficient to bury you both."

"This doesn't make any sense," Jackie said. "How did this murderous lunatic get a hold of my knife?"

"My guess is Kowalski's killer has hooked up with Stefano to get us off his back. That can only mean our boy has mob connections or knows someone who does," I said.

The three of us fell silent as we absorbed the implications

of what I'd said. As impossible as it sounded, they couldn't come up with a more logical explanation.

"You two better scram," O'Reilly said. "I need to get my team over here. Make sure you ditch that knife."

"Maybe you'll get lucky and find the killer's fingerprints," Jackie said.

"Our guy isn't that stupid. This is a dead end murder, and I knew it the minute I saw the body. That reminds me, I need to wipe Joey's prints off the oil lamp."

I grabbed Jackie's arm and turned to O'Reilly. "You better check on the other two fishermen. I got a feeling they're on his list." O'Reilly nodded.

I hurried Jackie along. My gut told me to get to Sadie's. Once the killer eliminated everyone who might be able to finger him as the guy who killed Kowalski, he'd get back to his original target—Castellano. He didn't want him dead; he wanted to destroy him. He'd killed Kowalski to incite riots and to strengthen the union. Sadie's death would be the final blow that would ignite the longshoremen into an uncontrollable frenzy, eliminating Castellano's grip on the waterfront and his usefulness to the Mafia.

When we got to Sadie's place, she wasn't home. The bodyguard Luigi had assigned was also gone. I picked the lock and nudged the door open with my .45. Everything looked normal. We waited.

The sun came up with its usual promise of a bright day, only to be masked by the ever present blanket of clouds that blew in from the Atlantic. As the clouds rolled in, so did Sadie.

Chapter 12

Once again, Sadie flat out refused to abandon her apartment.

"Do me a favor and take your crazy theories someplace else. I have a life to live."

"I'm telling ya, Sadie, you'll be a lot safer with us," I said.

"Sure, have you looked around lately? The neighborhood's crawling with Castellano's men trying to protect you and your family. They're even on some of the rooftops, and you want me to move in with you because my life's in danger?"

Jackie strode past Sadie, went into her bedroom, pulled a suitcase from under the bed, and ransacked her bureau and closet. Jackie's actions were so unexpected that Sadie froze at first, but then she reacted. I grabbed her around the waist, dragged her to the couch, and held her down.

"Joey, you don't understand. I'm barely able to pay my bills now that Dad's gone, and I don't have the skills to get a decent job. If I don't show up for work at the drugstore, I'll get fired. I can't leave."

"You're not gonna need a job if you're dead."

Jackie came over carrying the suitcase and offered her hand to Sadie. "I'm guessing that while you've been arguing, O'Reilly has found two more bodies. We came here to help, and if we're right, you're running out of time."

Sadie grudgingly agreed to leave.

* * * * *

I left to inform Ma and Pop to expect another guest, while Sadie and Jackie gathered additional belongings and notified her boss that she needed time off.

Under Luigi's direction, a construction crew had already descended upon my folks' apartment and was in the process of turning it into an impenetrable fortress. They had torn the back wall of Pop's old shoe store, which separated the shop from their apartment, down to the wooden slats and were lining it with steel plates. At the same time, the crew was ripping apart the wall in the hallway that led to the apartment entrance. The workbench in Pop's shoe repair shop, on the other side of the hall, had also been laid bare and reinforced with steel. In the midst of all this commotion, Luigi barked orders as Ma stood among the rubble with her arms folded, shaking her head.

"Joey, do you know what you're doing to Pop's business? When our customers hear about what's goin' on, they won't come anywhere near this place."

"Don't worry," Luigi yelled. "We're ahead of schedule. In two days, no one will remember what went on here."

"Sorry Ma, but we can't take any chances. I'll cover any lost business."

"Where are you gettin' all this money? Luigi told me you're paying the girls' rent and gave him the dough to buy Castellano's speakeasy. Are you working for Castellano? What are you doin' for him?"

"Nothing illegal."

Before I could say more, Jackie and Sadie entered the

apartment building. I turned back to Ma and gave her a kiss on the cheek. "Sadie's gonna stay with us until we find who killed her father. I'm sure you won't mind if she joins us for meals."

I grabbed Sadie's suitcase and rushed her and Jackie past the confusion, up to our office on the third floor. Ma had her hackles up, and I didn't want to take the risk she might say something that would cause Sadie to change her mind.

Martha immediately noticed the suitcase. "Welcome to Fort Batista," she said with a smile, leading the way into the inner office.

Jackie and I explained all that had happened. When asked, Martha didn't hesitate to share her apartment with Sadie and agreed to keep her busy around the office. Once she got Sadie settled, Martha dumped some bad news on us.

"Gino tipped a few too many last night and got completely smoked. I think all the guns and preparation for what might happen have brought back vivid memories of his family's slaughter."

"Is anyone with him?" I asked.

"Rosalie, but I gotta tell ya, she's not happy either with what's goin' on."

I made my way past the construction crew to Gino's room, located behind Pop's shoe repair shop. Rosalie came out and quietly closed the door.

"He's resting. You and I haven't had the chance to talk for a long time, and to tell the truth, I don't appreciate that my life, and everyone else's around here, has to change because of your need to learn on the job how to be a private investigator," she said, poking me in the chest.

Shocked by her aggression, I hesitated before responding.

"I know it's tough to lose time from school, but Luigi's right. Everyone around me is a potential target for Bobby Stefano. We need to take extra precautions."

"How long do you expect us to live like this?"

Rosalie and I were like brother and sister, so I knew she expected a straight answer about Stefano.

"Until one of us is dead."

Her eyes filled with tears and her anger melted away. She put her arms around my waist and rested her head against my shoulder. "I'm sorry, Joey. I'm not thinking straight."

"I'm the one who's sorry. I put us all in danger. I promise this is the last time."

She pulled back. "In your line of work, I don't think you can keep that promise."

We both knew she was right. To change the subject, I asked if Gino was sober enough to talk.

"He's lucid."

* * * * *

Gino sat hunched over on the edge of the bed with his elbows on his knees, cradling his head in both hands. I pulled up a chair. "I don't think you've been honest with us."

Gino looked up with bloodshot eyes and reached toward the nightstand for a bottle of gin. I got to it first.

"You've had enough of that rot gut. It's time to level with me."

"I don't know what you're talking about."

"That's bull and you know it. Tell me now what you really saw the night Kowalski got bumped."

"I already told you everything. Kowalski waited on the platform for Castellano," he said, fixated on the bottle I held.

"Do you expect me to believe you didn't see anyone setting crab traps that night? You didn't hear the cages hit the water?"

"Jackie already asked. I didn't see anything, I swear," he said, again reaching for the gin.

"Do you know a chef over at the Slippery Eel named Dominic?"

"Sure, he's always good for a handout."

"Not anymore. He's dead, took a knife in the gut."

It took a moment for what I'd said to register. "Why would anyone kill Dominic?"

"I just told you, someone had their crab cages out the night Kowalski was murdered, and Dominic usually fished Pier 17."

"He's not the only one that crabs there," Gino said.

"That's right, and I suspect two others have already met the same fate. It's too bad you didn't see anything that night because we probably could've saved their lives."

Gino rubbed his face and suddenly looked completely sober.

"I'm tellin' ya, Gino, it's time to come clean, if for no other reason than to save your own hide. You want to know why? Because I suspect you're on the killer's list. You're one of the few bums who routinely hung around that pier at night."

I let Gino grab the bottle and take a long gulp.

"I was scared. I heard Castellano yelling at Kowalski and saw him shove Kowalski against the wall."

"What was Castellano upset about?"

"I don't know, a storm was rolling in, but in between the thunder I did hear him say he'd kill Kowalski if he went to the papers."

"Did you see anyone else?"

"Just one of Castellano's drivers. He waited in the car."

"Which driver?"

"I didn't get a good look."

Castellano had a solid alibi, and until that moment, I really didn't think he was involved in Kowalski's death.

"Did Castellano kill Kowalski?" I asked with my back to Gino.

"I don't know. I ran away, afraid Castellano would see me and think I heard what they were saying. I didn't know Kowalski was dead until I saw him the next morning hanging like a side of beef."

I couldn't blame him for being afraid, given what had happened to his family. To Gino, Castellano, as the local Mafia boss, represented everything evil in this world.

"Did you see who set the crab cages?"

"Dominic, he was at the end of the pier when Castellano's car drove up, and he hid in the shadows."

"Did Dominic ever say what he saw that night?"

"I never asked him. I didn't want to get involved," Gino said with a sob.

I placed a hand on his shoulder. "It's not your fault that Dominic's dead. I inadvertently alerted the killer that there was a witness when we asked around for who was crabbing that night."

There wasn't much more I could say, so I left Gino with his bottle.

* * * * *

Given Gino's new revelation, Jackie and I were discussing

how best to confront Castellano when Martha burst into the office.

"I just got off the horn with O'Reilly. They found the other fishermen with their throats slit."

"Is O'Reilly still on the line?" I asked.

"He said all hell broke loose when he reported the murders, and then he hung up."

Sadie overheard the end of the conversation. "What's goin' on?"

"Two more bodies were found. Count yourself lucky you came with us last night," Jackie said.

Sadie turned pale and lowered herself onto one of the leather chairs. I nodded to Martha, and she went back to her desk.

"Sadie, I know this isn't the best time, but things are moving fast. We need to know exactly what your father said before goin' to the pier the night he was killed."

"I already told you. He had a meeting with Castellano."

"That's it? He didn't say why or if he was going with someone else?"

Sadie took a deep breath. "He went alone. He said he knew how to get Castellano to cave in on some of the union's demands."

"Wasn't your father fighting to form the union? Why wouldn't he insist Castellano meet *all* the demands?"

"My father realized the other Mafia bosses would never allow the dockworkers to unionize. He just wanted a few changes, just a few. He understood Castellano couldn't afford to look weak. He actually liked him and knew it would be bad for the neighborhood if Castellano got replaced."

"What information did he have?" Jackie asked.

"He wouldn't say, but obviously Castellano didn't want

to have the discussion in the open. Why else would they meet on a deserted pier at night?"

I'd had the same thought. Kowalski must have known something that could damage Castellano's business interests, and he planned to use it to his advantage.

When Sadie left to join Martha, Jackie slowly closed the door behind her and then turned, leaning back against the door.

"What are you gonna do?" she asked, looking as sexy as I've ever seen her.

I sighed. "Well, I know what I'd like to do," I said, reaching for her waist.

"That will have to wait. What I really meant was what are you gonna' do about Castellano?"

"Confront him."

She backed me up against a chair and wrapped her arms around my neck. "Be careful. Sometimes I think you don't see Castellano for who he really is, and that can be dangerous."

"Don't worry. I know how to handle him. Why don't we have dinner tonight at La Cucina's? It'll give me something to look forward to while I'm deflecting death threats from Castellano."

"Not tonight, I already have a date…with Cafiero. I promised the old guy I'd check in with him once in a while. But how about a few drinks at my place, say around nine?"

"Sounds like a much better offer, but you need to be careful. I don't like the idea of you out alone with Stefano on the loose. Why don't you take Martha along?"

On the way out of the office, Martha suggested I wipe the lipstick off my face.

Chapter 13

A few days a week Castellano and his bodyguards hung out at a small pizza shop where he had an office in the back for conducting neighborhood business. I knew I'd find him there.

Butch blocked the door to the office and wouldn't budge. "You wanna see the boss, you need an appointment," he said.

When I reached for the doorknob, he planted his huge hand on my chest and shoved. Instinctively I reached for my piece, but stopped. Castellano had opened the door to let an elderly woman pass.

"Don't worry, Mrs. Marino. Your grandson will get the medical care he needs."

She grabbed Castellano's hand and kissed it. "God bless you. You're a good man."

Castellano walked her to the front of the store and then came over to me. "You wanna talk or are you here for the pizza?"

"We need to talk, now." I said.

Castellano stared at me for a long moment and turned to Butch. "Make sure we're not disturbed."

"Sure, Boss, but he's got a rod."

"Butch, if I can't trust Joey, then I can't trust nobody. Besides, if Joey wanted to kill me, he'd come at night, and not even you would be able to stop him. Ain't that right, Joey?"

Castellano closed the door, spun around, and shoved a gun in my gut. "I thought I told you once to show me respect when I'm around my men. One more slipup like that and I'm gonna forget you're the son of a dear friend. Don't order me around again, ever!"

This wasn't the Castellano I knew. The words came slow and deliberate, and as he spoke, his stare turned to ice, void of emotion other than hatred. I had crossed a line he wouldn't tolerate, but I really didn't give a damn.

"I know you argued with Kowalski on the pier the night he was knocked off."

"So, that's it? Once again you think I killed him. For a PI you have trouble making up your mind and controlling your emotions. How the hell a spy and assassin with your temperament made it through the war is beyond me!"

"You lied!" I said, pushing aside the gun he still held on me.

"You're damn right. I lie all the time, and in my position, you'd do the same."

"If you want me to find Kowalski's killer, I need the truth."

Castellano holstered his gun and sat behind his desk. "Since you won't take my word that I didn't kill him, I'm gonna give it to you straight, even though it won't help find his killer." He paused to light a stogie. "I'm only telling you because I intend to use you in the future."

At that point I should've gotten up and left, but curiosity held me there.

"Everyone knows what I do and who I am," Castellano said. "I run this little sliver of New York. In return for that privilege, I'm expected to pay the organization a percentage of my take and act in their interest—no matter what, including standing against family and friends. You might want to remember that. If I don't deliver, then someone else will move in after I'm dead, before I'm even buried. That's how quickly things will change around here."

"You don't have to tell me any of this. All I need to know is what time you met with Kowalski, and if he was alone, when you left him. That's it."

Castellano went on as if he hadn't heard me.

"Did you ever ask yourself how I make money? I'll tell you, the saloons, now the speakeasies, bootlegging, and the docks. That's it. Ask your pop. Did I ever shake him or any other merchant down for protection money? Do you see my guys pushing drugs? Are there can houses lining the streets? The answer is no! Don't think I don't get pressure to do those things. That's how most of the bosses make dough for the syndicate."

"Booze I understand, but how much can you make running the docks?" I found myself sitting on the edge of my seat.

"Illegal contraband, especially drugs and human cargo, go for a high price. There's more: weapons, machinery, just about anything someone doesn't want to go through customs. I deliver the goods and I get a cut. That's what Kowalski wanted to talk about. He knew how everything goes down and threatened to snitch to the *Daily News*. City Hall or the police, I don't really give a damn about. They already know. But if the newspapers get a hold of what's goin' on, they can cause trouble. We had an intense argument, and if I'd had my rod with me, I probably would've nailed him. But I didn't, and in the end, we agreed on a compromise."

"What compromise?"

"That's none of your business."

"What time did you leave?"

"An hour or so past midnight. I looked back when my car pulled away and saw Kowalski light a cigarette. So I know he was alive."

"He didn't smoke!"

Castellano gazed past me. "I'm sure I saw a match flicker."

"Does anyone in your organization smoke stogies, besides you?"

"Are you kidding? These young punks wouldn't go near a stogie. It's a poor man's smoke. A habit us immigrants, like your pop, picked up in the old country."

He interrupted me before I could get off the next question.

"Wait a minute. I did see Donnelly, that damn union organizer, smoking one. He's still a pain in my ass. You better hurry up and solve this case so I can fire the bum."

"I never saw an Irishman smoke a stogie."

"What does that prove? I drink Irish whiskey."

I had to fight to suppress a laugh.

"Let's get back to Kowalski. How did you get Maria to lie for you? She said you were in the restaurant until past two in the morning."

"She didn't lie. She didn't see me leave. There's a secret passageway in the basement that leads to the adjacent building. Actually, it connects to the basement of your uncle's speakeasy. After my meeting with Kowalski, I returned to her restaurant the same way I'd left."

"How do you get the cargo off the docks?"

"I'm telling you, Joey, you don't need to know. And if I were you, I wouldn't try to find out."

"It's too late for that. I'm not working in the dark any longer. I need to know what went down with Kowalski."

Castellano stood and looked out a window with his hands clutched behind him. He moved over to a portable bar and spoke with his back to me.

"Your parents, your two uncles, and I go back a long way. I promised I wouldn't drag you into my world."

I didn't respond.

"Okay, have it your way," he said facing me. "Crates, containing legit merchandise, not on a ship's cargo lists, arrive piecemeal over a period of weeks to avoid detection. The crates are unloaded at night and stored in a hidden holding area. When the illegal payloads arrive, we unload the contraband and replace the crates with the ones in storage. The hard part is to make sure all the merchandise that leaves the dock matches the ship's manifest. It's a coordination nightmare, and a lot of hands get greased, not just here, but also from the points of origin. Human cargo is much easier. They get loaded onto trucks the same day they arrive."

"How do you get the contraband past dock security?"

"We break it down and move it out at night in small skiffs."

Castellano was right. This was an interesting insight into how the Mafia weaves its tentacles throughout the city, but it was of no real use to my investigation, other than the fact that Kowalski, a shift foreman, had been corrupted and had coordinated the movement of contraband.

"You said you and Kowalski reached a compromise. I think you can now tell me the details."

"I agreed to do what I could to improve working conditions, and in return, he would quit supporting the union. He didn't really give a damn about moving contraband as long as it stayed out of the neighborhood."

I wanted to believe him, but as Jackie said, Castellano is a Mafia boss.

"With Kowalski dead, why hire a so-called worker representative?"

Castellano walked me to the door. "Kowalski and I made a deal, and he would've kept his end. Besides, like I said, it's a good way to keep Donnelly in town. He definitely benefited from Kowalski's death."

I reentered the pizza parlor but then pushed into the door to Castellano's office before it closed, and stepped back inside.

"One last question. If you were taken down, who would take over your organization?"

Castellano laughed. "You have a hell of a lot to learn. Everything stays in the family. My son, Carmine, is in line for my position, but if I don't deliver, he'd be taken out with me. Trust me, if that happened, there would be a blood bath among the other bosses to gain control."

"Sounds like longevity isn't one of the Mafia's selling points."

"That depends on the circumstances and where you stand in the pecking order. At my level, all I have to watch out for is when others get greedy."

Castellano held open the door. "In my opinion, Joey, unless you learn to work within the system, your days are numbered. It seems that every case you're involved with draws you in direct conflict with the Mafia. If that continues, you won't last long."

On the way out I ordered a pizza and bumped gums with a few of Castellano's men. I was hoping to find out who drove him to the pier the night Kowalski got zotzed and who took over Kowalski's foreman position. These were questions Castellano could've answered, but my gut told me the less he knew about my investigation, the better.

* * * * *

Later I looked for O'Reilly at my uncle's joint, but he never showed. I was about to leave when Luigi tapped me on the shoulder and led me into his office.

"I called Torrio in Chicago to get a line on those two button men Stefano hired out of Detroit. The news ain't good."

Luigi paused to look for a cigar in his desk drawers. There was one sticking out from under some papers, but I didn't tell him. The short, wrinkly, black stogies look like something a constipated Chihuahua would leave behind and smelled twice as bad. Unfortunately, he found one.

"You gonna tell me what Torrio said before I die of suspense?" I asked.

He leaned hard against his desk, shifting it a few inches. "You better be as good as I think you are or we're all in deep shit. They're known as The Twins. One's a sniper and the other works in close. They should arrive in town next week; they're on another job. That's all I know."

We both knew my best chance for survival was to flush out The Twins before they moved in for the kill, but without more details about how they conducted their business, we weren't able to come up with a reasonable plan. Anticipating an evening with Jackie, I turned down my uncle's offer to continue our discussion over drinks. But I took a moment to ask about Carmine.

"Castellano told me Carmine would take over if something happened to him. That doesn't make sense. Carmine has never been involved in his dad's business."

"You're wrong about that. Carmine makes everything work," Luigi said.

"How's that possible? He manages the largest shipping company in New York and has nothing to do with the Maf—." I stopped in mid-sentence when I recalled Castellano's comment about the amount of coordination required to make everything work.

I should have known Carmine was the brains behind the scene. When we were kids, he always had a new scheme for making some scratch.

* * * * *

It was past ten by the time I got back to the apartment building. I walked past the office and checked to see if the lights were out and the door locked, just in case Jackie was catching up on some work while she waited. I continued down the hall to her apartment. She wasn't there either. I didn't like it, so I ran upstairs to Martha's. Anthony Brown, the assistant DA and Martha's latest beau, answered the door.

That's when I realized Jackie hadn't asked Martha to go along to have dinner with Cafiero. She must have known Martha had a prior engagement.

Chapter 14

I found Cafiero's phone number in Jackie's case file, but he didn't answer. Martha had tracked down Luigi, who was on his way over, and she had left a message for O'Reilly to join us at my parents' apartment. Before I left for Cafiero's in search of Jackie, I had to make certain that everyone understood something had happened to her and that they all needed to be vigilant.

In the middle of answering questions, someone banged on the apartment door with what sounded like a heavy object. I waited for Pop to rack his shotgun before opening the door.

Stooped before me was a broad-shouldered, elderly man leaning on a hand-carved walking stick. He had a mane of white hair and a worried look.

"Young man, would you run upstairs and tell Joey Batista I need to see him? It's urgent. I don't think I can make those stairs."

Martha's friend, assistant DA Brown, and I helped him over to the sofa.

"I'm Joey. What can I do for you?"

He handed me a note.

"They think Jackie's my daughter."

"Are you Cafiero?"

"Read the note. They want money."

"Who gave you this?"

"It was tacked to my door. I thought the Mafia was following me, but Jackie said they were just a bunch of street thugs."

As Cafiero talked, Luigi arrived, grabbed the note from my hand, and read it aloud, *We'll exchange the dame for money outside your place tomorrow at noon. You better hand over your stash and it better be plenty if you ever want to see your daughter again.* Luigi paused, shaking his head. "What the hell kinda ransom note is this? The jerks don't even say how much they want."

"That tells me Jackie was right. We're dealing with a bunch of local street thugs and not Stefano or Kowalski's killer," I said.

"What are we gonna do?" Martha asked.

"Pay them. Luigi, get me two grand. Martha, find Vic and Chris from my old gang and ask them to round up the neighborhood street kids. I want every rooftop and alleyway covered for three blocks around Cafiero's place. Pay each kid a sawbuck up front, and promise another if anyone tells me where these guys are holding Jackie."

Martha was gone before I finished, but Luigi didn't budge.

"Why give them two grand? They probably think the most the old man has is a couple of hundred, if that."

"I don't want to take the chance they'll ask for more and not turn Jackie over. I'm gonna deliver the money. Once she's safe, I'll get the dough back."

"I shouldn't tell you this," the assistant DA said, "but the DA had some men following Jackie."

"Why the hell would he do that?" I shouted.

"I have no idea. But I can tell you, the men I saw in his office weren't local detectives. I'm not sayin' the DA has Jackie, but he might know who does."

I wanted to smash his head against the wall for not telling

us sooner, but the last thing I needed was for Martha to go bonkers.

I asked Luigi to follow me to my room. I had to get ready to take Cafiero home and needed his help. Once in my apartment, I headed straight for my closet and took my army duffle bag down from the top shelf.

"I need you to stick with the family. This could be a ploy by Stefano and his men to separate us, so stay close to Ma and Pop," I said.

"Don't worry. Nothing will happen to them."

I removed my jacket and put on a chainmail vest overlaid with leather that held several different types of combat knives and two automatic pistols. Next, I grabbed a black metal case that contained a disassembled sniper rifle.

Luigi stroked the chainmail, "I gotta get one of these."

"I'll see what I can do, but right now, I need you to put on my coat and hat and slip out the back into my car. I don't want anyone to see you, so crouch down low in the backseat."

"I thought you wanted me to stay here to protect the family?"

"I think everything's goin' down tomorrow, but just in case, I'll ask the assistant DA to stay until you return. He carries a piece; I just hope he knows how to use it. In any case, Pop will be here to protect Ma and Rosalie."

"What do you want me to do after I'm in the car?"

"If anyone's watching our building, I'll make sure they see me enter the car. It'll look like I'm driving Cafiero home alone. When we get close to his place, I'll pull the car over and get out. You drive the rest of the way to Cafiero's. Drop him off and leave. If his place is staked out, they'll think you're me and that I returned home for the night."

"What are you gonna' do?"

"I'll run the rest of the way along the back alley and sneak into Cafiero's apartment building. He'll get there before I do, so he can let me into his place."

"It feels like we're being manipulated," Luigi said.

"We are. I just don't know who's pulling the strings."

Chapter 15

A blast of frigid air hit me when Cafiero opened the door to his apartment. I looked at the windows to see if one was ajar, then to the radiators that clanged incessantly. The radiators were glazed over with frost and water dripped from an icicle clinging to the kitchen faucet.

"Have you called the super? You can't live like this," I said.

"I try not to call attention to myself. The heat will eventually turn back on."

"I don't think so. Air is trapped in the pipes, preventing hot water from circulating. You should know how to fix the problem."

Cafiero didn't say anything.

I flipped open the pressure relief valve on the side of each radiator until moisture spurted out, releasing the air pockets in the inner coils. Then I fired up a pot of coffee and lit the remaining burners for immediate warmth. Within a half hour, the radiators were hot to the touch and the room livable.

Cafiero was grateful for the mug of joe I placed in front of him until I interrogated him about what happened to Jackie. I had suspected something wasn't right about his case all along. I never mentioned my concerns to Jackie because she liked the old guy. I also didn't want her to think I lacked confidence in her judgment.

The fact that Cafiero didn't know how to get his radiators working told me my suspicions were correct. He'd never lived in a low-rent district before. The old coot was on the lam, laying low.

"What time did Jackie drop you off after dinner?"

"Sometime between eight and eight-thirty. She said she had an important date."

"We were gonna meet at nine."

"I had no idea this would happen."

"Well, it has, and I don't think you've been up front with us. The average bloke doesn't go around thinking the Mafia is watching him. What's really goin' on? Are you running some type of flimflam and taking us for a pair of chumps or is there a contract on your head?"

Cafiero's right eye twitched as he shifted in his chair. "I used to work for the Mafia, and when I wanted out, I took along some protection."

"What were you, a bookkeeper? You got financial records about their illegal businesses?"

Cafiero snickered. He reached down and picked up my rifle case.

I grabbed for the case. "Be careful with that," I said.

He pulled the case out of my reach, flipped open the latches, and in seconds, assembled the rifle, and adjusted the scope.

"When's the last time you used this baby?" he asked.

"About two years ago. Why?"

He limped over to the closet, brought out a cleaning kit, and preceded to field strip the rifle. "It needs oiling."

I could've wrung his neck. He was a damn button man for the mob, and he had knowingly placed Jackie in a dangerous situation when he didn't tell us the truth.

"Who'd you work for?"

"For anyone who could afford my services. I traveled from Jersey to where the work took me."

If the Jersey mob was watching Cafiero, then there was the possibility that Stefano might be involved. The chance that Kowalski's killer was also somehow tied into the picture was slim, but not impossible, since we believed they were now working together. Throw in the fact that the DA had men stalking her, and the best outcome would indeed be if a local gang of young thugs kidnapped Jackie for ransom. For the first time, I realized that Jackie might be in greater danger than I had anticipated.

"With your experience, why the hell did you need to hire us?"

"Since I took one in the hip, I can't move around like I used to. I thought it best to let someone else nose around."

"Do you know a guy named Bobby Stefano?" I asked.

"Sure, I did some work for him. The last I heard he's doin' time. Why do you ask?"

"He's out of the slammer and after me for killing his brother. He also has it in for Jackie."

He took a sip of his coffee. "If Stefano took Jackie, she's already dead," he said.

He showed no emotion, just made a statement of fact, and we both knew he was right. There was nothing more to discuss, no point in hashing over the past or getting angry at Cafiero for putting Jackie into this predicament. I needed to rest while I could. Death was about to descend upon Cafiero's neighborhood, and if Jackie had any chance of surviving, I'd be the one doing the killing. I stretched out on the couch and suggested he get some sleep.

* * * * *

An ice storm had swept through the city during the night, creating a virtual ghost town encased in a frozen shroud of moisture. As the sun rose above the skyline, eerie streams of vapor billowed from roof vents, escaped through broken windows, and spewed from the mouths of a few hardy residents who inched along the streets like lost zombies.

Cafiero and I took turns with his binoculars, looking to see if Vic and Chris were able to round up enough street urchins to blanket the area. Around nine, I saw a flurry of activity on the rooftops opposite Cafiero's building. Down on the street, I spotted Vic running to catch up with a couple of bums who had emerged from a small church. They were a few of the lucky ones who had found shelter during the night.

With everyone in position, all we could do was watch and wait until the specified time to make the ransom exchange for Jackie. When Cafiero relieved me of the binoculars, I hit the sack again. The army had taught me to rest under any conditions because a lack of sleep dulls the senses and slows a person's reaction time. An hour into his watch Cafiero spotted trouble.

"We have two snipers and one's a pro," he said, handing me the binoculars.

"I only see one—third floor apartment directly across the street."

"Three buildings over to the right, fourth floor," Cafiero said.

At first I didn't see anything unusual, but then noticed a circular hole in a window, a little left of center. The guy across the street was the amateur. His window was open about an inch. He intended to rest his rifle on the windowsill.

The other shooter most likely had some type of collapsible stand to support his rifle. It wouldn't be visible from outside the building when he took his shot.

"It looks like you and Jackie have made some serious enemies," Cafiero said.

"What makes you think at least one of these guys isn't after you?"

"I operated in the shadows. No one knew my real name or saw my face. I was simply known as Mr. Reliable. When I retired, I made it clear to my clients that if I died of natural causes, records of my kills would be destroyed. If my death was suspicious in any way, the newspapers would have enough front-page copy for a month, including who paid for my services. They wouldn't take me out until they secured those records."

"Are you telling the truth?"

"Perception is truth."

"You didn't answer my question."

"I always did what I said; one of the reasons why I was valuable to my clients."

"I don't see you trusting someone with your life. The person holding those documents could make a bundle."

As he turned away from the window, it felt like the temperature suddenly dropped. "I *don't* trust anyone," he said.

"Then it's not true. The evidence you have against your former employers would die with you."

"The advantage of being consistent all your life is that you get to be inconsistent once—an opportunity I used wisely."

"So, if no one in the Mafia knows what you look like, and they believe you can bring them all down with information you have hidden away, why were you concerned?"

"Someone had ransacked my apartment twice, and during that same time, I had the feeling I was being followed. I needed help to find out if my cover was blown. I've learned over the years that nothing is certain. But it turned out, Jackie was right. It's just a bunch of local punks who think I have some dough stashed away."

I knew what he was thinking. Given the amateurish ransom note, a local gang had stalked Cafiero with the intent of robbing him. Failing to locate his source of income, they resorted to kidnapping someone they thought he cared about. In that case, the snipers didn't fit; they had to be after me. But what I couldn't figure out was how they knew about Jackie's abduction and that I'd be here? Who were they?

"It's my turn to ask questions," Cafiero said. "Who besides Stefano wants you dead?"

"The Chicago mob isn't too happy with me, but we have a truce. That leaves Stefano, who contracted with a couple of button men to take me out. The DA isn't fond of me either, and for some strange reason, hired some men to stalk Jackie. I should also mention that Jackie and I have been on the trail of a killer."

"Great, of all the PIs in New York City, I end up with a private dick that has a bull's-eye tattooed on his forehead. Do you know who Stefano hired?"

"They're brothers, twins out of Chicago, but I don't expect them for a few more days. They're on another job."

Cafiero picked up the binoculars and scanned the buildings again. When he turned to face me, I noticed perspiration staining his shirt.

"My guess is they finished early, and the pro behind the window down the street is Benny—he doesn't miss. His twin brother, Denny, fancies himself some type of ninja warrior, preferring hand-to-hand combat. He's sadistic, likes his victims to die slowly. These guys are two of the best in the business."

"Wait a minute. Did you say their names were Benny and Denny?"

"What can I say? I guess their mother had a sense of humor. I can tell you this; no one they ever went after is around to joke about their names."

"If you're right, then Denny's the one I'm most concerned about. We don't know where he is," I said.

"Don't forget the bloke across the street. He might not be a professional, but I'm sure he's deadly. What's more unnerving is that we don't know *who* he is."

Over the next two hours we worked out a plan and waited for the ransom exchange. All I could think about was getting Jackie back. Cafiero, in a trance-like state, stripped and cleaned his rifle, Betsy, with the loving care you'd give a newborn, and then he did it again. I put my rifle back in its case and briefly wondered why I had never given it a name. Cafiero interrupted my thoughts.

"The guy across the street would have taken one of us out before we knew he was there, so he's not after us, at least not yet. The twin, he has a bad angle. My guess he's waiting for you to step outside."

"None of this makes sense," I said. "How do the twins know I'm here? They couldn't have been in town for more than a day."

"They were probably setting up surveillance to track your routine when all hell broke out last night after I arrived at your place. My guess is they followed you and saw you get out a few buildings down the way. That's why they're watching the wrong building."

"When they see me making the exchange for Jackie, they'll move in for the kill," I said, more to myself than Cafiero.

"I'll do my best to keep Benny pinned down, but you'll have to handle Denny by yourself, if you even see him comin'," Cafiero said, chambering his rifle.

* * * * *

We had agreed that I would position myself under the front stoop of the building on the left side so the sniper, Benny, further down the street, couldn't get a clean shot. Cafiero would take out the guy in the opposite building when the barrel of his rifle protruded from the open window.

It was time to head to the basement level for the exchange and deal with whatever situation might develop. In the middle of strapping on the gear I needed, someone rapped on Cafiero's door. Startled, I backed off to the side and drew my gun. Cafiero had his rifle aimed at the door.

"Joey, open up. It's me, Vic."

I released the latch and remained off to the side just in case the missing twin had forced Vic to set us up. Vic rushed in and went straight for the table. He collapsed in a chair, breathing hard from running up three flights of stairs.

Unable to sit still, Vic jumped up and moved frantically around the room. "Geez, Joey, you won't believe the shit that's goin' down. We tried to get Jackie, but she was gone. Bodies were scattered everywhere."

"Vic, you're not makin' sense. Calm down and give it to me again."

"I found a bum who saw some local thugs grab Jackie last night. He told us where they hang out. I went in with some of our old gang expectin' to rumble, but there was blood everywhere. I'm tellin' ya, those young punks didn't have a chance."

I wanted to choke the dumb bastard, but Cafiero got between us.

"Let him talk," Cafiero said and poured Vic a cup of coffee.

"Why the hell didn't you get me before you went in?" I shouted.

"We figured this place was being watched."

"Jackie—what about Jackie?"

"Whoever wiped out the street gang took her. There was one guy alive—half out of his mind— going from body to body, trying to wake his buddies. God, it was worse than anything I saw in the war."

I grabbed Vic's coat and pulled him to me. "Do you have him? Does he know where Jackie is?"

"Hey, Joey, I'm on your side."

"Sorry Vic, I—."

"Forget it. I know how you feel about her."

"Where is this guy?"

"He'll be here soon to give you a message from the blokes who snatched her from him. He wants money to get out of town. We tried to get information, but he won't talk to anyone but you."

Cafiero stood by the window with the binoculars.

"I think I see him. He's across the street. Shit, you should see this guy, he's covered in blood."

"No matter what happens, he's a dead man. They can't let him live," I said.

"Now we know who the sniper across the street is going to take out," Cafiero said.

I finished strapping on my gear and ran out the door.

Chapter 16

A tall, lanky kid, who looked like he'd just clawed his way out of hell, shuffled toward the brownstone, his blood-streaked arms dangling by his side. Startled when I called out from below street level, he slipped on the ice-covered sidewalk and crashed to the ground at the foot of the stairs. Ignoring his pathetic whimpering, I reached through the wrought-iron fence that separated us and yanked his face against the metal bars, shocking life back into his eyes.

I let up on the pressure so he could move his lips. "Is she hurt?" I shouted.

"No, no. They just took her. We didn't touch her, I swear. My guys wanted to, but I stopped them. Look, give me some dough to get the hell out of town and I'll tell you everything."

"Did she put up a fight?"

"We took her by surprise, but she's a tough bitch. Broke the nose of one of my guys."

"Did she cut anyone?"

"What?"

I counted out five hundred and told him to hop the fence and come down to my level to get it.

"No way, just hand it over."

"They're not gonna let you live. You saw who they were."

"Give it to me and I'm outta here."

I held on as he tried to grab the bills. "What's the message?"

"They said you got something the DA wants. You have two days to deliver it to him if you ever want to see the bitch again."

"That's it? They didn't say what it was?"

"No. The DA didn't tell them. He said you'd know. Now give me the damn money."

At first I didn't get it, but then the message became clear. The DA wanted Jackie's dead husband's record of the city officials he had bribed, a list I had used to get Jackie's murder charge dismissed last year. I knew the DA was crooked, but he wasn't nuts. The guys he'd hired to nab Jackie must've overreacted when the street gang grabbed her first. In the last twenty-four hours, the DA's life had gotten more complicated. Now he not only had to deal with me, but he had to explain away a blood bath in his precinct.

Shots rang out as I let go of the bills. I ducked and took off. I didn't have to look back to know the kid's fate.

* * * * *

I ran along the pathway beneath the stoops until I was several units beyond where the second sniper, the twin Benny, had taken up position. The guy who'd just killed the kid was either shot by Cafiero or long gone. One way or the other, his job was done. I heard more shots. Cafiero was giving me cover. I ran across the street and entered the building with the sniper, avoiding shards of glass that came raining down as the fourth-floor window was obliterated by Cafiero's bullets.

With my gun drawn, I took two steps at a time, focusing on the landings above me. When I rounded the second corner, bullets slammed into the wall inches above my head. I flattened onto the tiled floor and fired back. Benny ran up the stairs holding a handgun rather than a rifle. On the fourth-floor landing I noticed blood on the floor, which explained Benny's rush to beat it out of the building and leave his gear behind. Cafiero was one hell of a shot to get a direct hit at that distance without a clear view of his target.

Benny made his way to the rooftop and fired again before exiting the stairwell. I rammed the steel door low, flinging it open. My bullets struck an instant late, hitting the brick wall that lined the edge of the roof. Benny had slid over the side of the building onto the fire escape.

Rather than follow, I clambered back down the stairs, thinking he'd be slowed by the ice-covered metal steps and platforms. I kicked in the door of a second-floor apartment and waited, ready to fire through the window. Benny came into view and slid across the landing. The first bullet ripped into his side, throwing him against the metal railing. My second bullet caught him dead center in the chest when he turned to get off a shot. Our eyes locked before he flipped backwards over the railing. He never made a sound other than his body hitting the sidewalk.

I bolted back up to the roof, ignoring the shouts of terrified tenants, and went down the opposite fire escape attached to the back of the building. Skirting behind the apartment houses, I made my way several blocks up from the commotion as police responded to the bloody scene that littered the neighborhood. When I felt safe, I crossed the street, ran down an alleyway between two brownstones, and vaulted over backyard fences to get to the back of Cafiero's building.

Sunlight streamed through the open door, illuminating streaks of blood on the wall opposite Cafiero's apartment. I dropped into a crouch and inched along, until a gargled moan and the familiar stench of imminent death assaulted my senses. Vic lay sprawled on the floor, his stomach slashed open with his guts viciously yanked from their cavity. I fell to my knees and swore I would show Denny no more mercy than he had shown Vic. The guy had to be sick to do what he did to Vic.

"I'm here, Vic. I'm here. I won't leave you."

Vic opened his eyes and tried to speak. I cradled his head and lowered my ear to his mouth.

"Do me, Joey, do me. It hurts. It hurts bad."

Tears blurred my vision, as all the good times we had shared growing up flashed through my mind. I maintained eye contact with Vic, shoved the barrel of my gun into a pillow I held over his chest to muffle the sound, and pulled the trigger.

I didn't have much time. Cops were now crawling all over the neighborhood and would soon be going door to door. Cafiero was gone and so were his suitcase and weapons stash. A small pool of blood by the window and drops of blood splattered over the floor told me he had taken a hit.

* * * * *

The next thing I knew, I was standing in front of Jackie's apartment. I tossed aside my gear, kicked in the door, and searched for her knife harness. It wasn't in the apartment. I thanked God that she'd had sense enough to wear it when she had gone alone to meet Cafiero for dinner. At least she was armed with an array of knives. My pop had designed the harness to feel like a girdle, so as long as her captors hadn't molested her, they would never suspect her deadly potential. It must have taken great self-control not to defend herself. Street wise, she had sense enough to know it would've been useless given the circumstances.

I needed to exhibit the same restraint. Chances were the DA had her stashed under guard in some isolated location, unknown to the judicial system. I had time. The DA knew if he harmed Jackie, he wouldn't get what he wanted, but more importantly, he'd be a dead man. What he didn't know was that no matter what happened from this point forward, he was a goner.

When I came out of Jackie's bedroom, I was surprised to see Martha standing in the doorway of the apartment.

"Where's Jackie? You said you'd bring her back," she screamed, hammering my chest with her fists. I pulled her close.

"It's not your fault, Martha. Jackie should've never left alone. I know I promised to bring her home, and I will, but I can't do it alone."

She looked up, "Tell me what to do."

The old Martha was back, serious and efficient.

"Get everyone together at my parents' place as soon as possible, including O'Reilly and Castellano."

She headed for the door. "One more thing," I said. "Whatever you hear, you can't tell your friend the assistant DA."

"Why? Maybe he can help."

"Trust me. I'll explain later. Right now find Sadie and bring her to my office. Vic's dead, and I don't want Sadie to hear it from O'Reilly. I need to tell her myself. At one time we were all close."

Martha froze. "What's goin' on?"

"I'm not sure I fully understand myself. But Jackie is in more danger than I realized. You'll get the full story, along with everyone else. Right now I need you to find Sadie."

* * * * *

O'Reilly, along with every other homicide detective in the city, had been working the crime scenes in Cafiero's neighborhood and didn't join the rest of us until after midnight.

When I announced that Vic was killed by one of the hit men sent to eliminate me, an unnatural silence swept the room. But it didn't last long.

"Give the DA what he wants. It's your only chance to get Jackie back in one piece," Ma said.

Luigi stood and pounded the table. "No! That book of payoffs is the only thing keeping her alive. She's witnessed a wholesale slaughter by some palookas the DA hired."

"Luigi's right I'm afraid," O'Reilly said. "We need to stall until we find where she's being held."

Since O'Reilly had arrived late, we didn't have a chance to talk in private. I was curious to know how the DA planned to manage the chaos that would erupt over the number of dead bodies.

"It might help if we knew how the DA's office intends to handle the press," I said to him.

"He knows how to twist things to his advantage. They're calling it street violence, two rival gangs fighting over territory. Not a shock to anyone. A few days of headlines, speeches by the mayor, the DA asking for more state funds to fight crime, and then some other atrocity will grab everyone's attention."

"That won't explain away the dead gunman in the building opposite Cafiero's or the twin I shot who landed in the street. The press will discover they're from out of town," I said, frustrated that the DA might get away with so much crap.

"The DA had their bodies removed before he let the reporters on the scene," O'Reilly said. "Vic was easy to explain, since he was from another part of town. Just another street punk."

The room fell quiet again. Vic's death was a blow, and unless I acted quickly, more of us would die. Looking around the room, I realized they were all having the same thoughts and expected me to get things under control.

"Martha and Sadie, you're both moving into my apartment tonight. Ma, Pop, Luigi, I want you to become inseparable. O'Reilly, do what you can to find where the DA is holding Jackie. Castellano, I'd appreciate it if you would double the men guarding the neighborhood." I then ushered Martha and Sadie out of their chairs and over to the door to head upstairs.

"What about you?" O'Reilly asked.

"I'm gonna try to buy time from the DA and then rescue Jackie, but first, I have to figure out where the hell he has her stashed. Once she's safe, I'm goin' after the other twin before he gets to us. Then, if I'm still alive, I'm gonna put tremendous pressure on the Jersey mob to hand over Bobby Stefano so I can kill the bastard."

Chapter 17

The next morning, I found the DA standing in front of City Hall dancing around reporters' questions concerning the wholesale massacre of a local street gang and the ever-escalating crime rate in the ethnic sections of the city. To avoid getting caught up in the hullabaloo, I moved past the throng of journalists and climbed the massive stairs to the building's side entrance. Glancing back, I saw the DA look in my direction. Once inside City Hall's cavernous antechamber, I stepped aside and took a deep breath before heading to the DA's office. I wanted to rip his heart out, but that wouldn't help Jackie. Her only hope was for me to use my military training. This was no different than a mission behind enemy lines, where I had to keep my emotions in check and choose the right moment to act. It didn't take me long, once deployed, to realize that an officer would never turn traitor even when faced with death. The DA would behave the same way. Violence seldom led to success; the key to obtaining information was through the women in their lives. Wives knew less than their mistresses, and the secretaries knew all. I did whatever it took to complete my missions, and I would do the same to save Jackie. As long as I had what the DA wanted, she was safe. I had time, but God help anyone who got in my way.

A short while later the DA came sprinting down the hallway toward his office. His secretary scurried from behind her desk to catch up with him, reading from her steno pad.

"The mayor wants you to call and the police chief will be here in thirty minutes to get an update on the investigation. Oh, this young man mentioned you urgently wanted to see him."

"Get the mayor on the line, and when I'm finished, send in Mr. Batista. I've been expecting him."

The DA slammed his office door shut. His secretary kept her composure, flicked aside a few strands of dark hair, and walked toward her desk. Her high cheekbones drew my attention away from her sculptured body to her black pearl eyes.

"He's extremely busy. It seems the city is always in crisis," she said, still fidgeting with her hair.

From time to time she looked up from her paperwork, and when our eyes met, the coloring in her face brightened ever so slightly. She was interested, and so was I, but for different reasons. She might not know it, but she had information about Jackie's whereabouts.

I walked over and offered her a cigarette. "How long have you worked for this guy?" I asked.

"No thanks. About three years."

"He seems like all business and no play."

"That's the way I like it. Life is complicated enough without mixing pleasure with work. But don't let him fool ya, he's tried."

"I don't blame him. So, what does a fella have to do to get a dinner date?"

"Depends on the guy. Some just have to ask," she said with an inviting smile.

"I hope I fall into that category."

"It's easy to find out."

"What time do you get off?"

"Five." A light blinked on her switchboard. "You can go in now."

"I'll be waiting downstairs," I said, and then entered the DA's office.

* * * * *

"Most people knock," the DA said, without looking up from the report he was reading. "You got the book?"

I planted my stiletto into a stack of papers on his desk and yanked him out of his chair. Before he could say anything, I held my knife to his throat.

"If anyone touches her, you'll be eating your own body parts before I'm through with you."

He was more shocked than afraid and maintained his self- control. "She's safer with me than you. From what I hear you won't last the week with the talent Bobby Stefano hired. The twins have an enviable reputation if you're in that line of work."

"Don't count on it," I said. "There were two and now there's one. By the way, thanks for having your guys scrape him off the street yesterday. I appreciate you cleaning up after me."

He gritted his teeth and a snarl gurgled up in his throat. I pulled his face closer.

"Now, where's Jackie?"

"Hand over the book."

"You expect me to trust you?"

"Anyone in City Hall who ever took a bribe knows his name's in that book and they want it destroyed. You want Jackie, give me the book."

I shoved him back into his chair, convinced he wouldn't call for help.

"You'll get the book when I have Jackie. I'll call to set up the exchange—after I get to my safety deposit box, Monday morning."

"Batista, when this is over, if Stefano doesn't kill you first, I'll find a way to take you down," he said, rubbing his neck.

"The only thing you should be thinking about is how long it will take you to die if anything happens to Jackie."

"I'm just the middle man. Killing me won't solve your problems. You should have been smart enough to have turned that book over to the judge last year when you had the chance. What happens to Jackie is on your head, not mine."

"Just make sure your goons keep their mitts off her—because if they don't, nothing will stop me from getting to you."

Closing the door, I walked over to his secretary's desk.

"Sounds like things got a little rough in there," she said.

"You might say we have a mutual hatred for each other. Why didn't you call in the cavalry?"

"That's the way most of his meetings go."

"You got a name?"

"Gloria."

"Well, Gloria, do we have a date?"

"See ya at five," she said with a warm smile.

* * * * *

It turned out that Martha knew Gloria, due to her frequent visits to the assistant DA's office, and O'Reilly was on friendly terms with her since he interacted with the DA on homicide cases. I asked them to join me for dinner in the hope that Gloria might feel more comfortable talking to them once she knew what I really wanted. Gloria would know something was up the minute she saw Martha and O'Reilly waiting for us, but I didn't have any other option. We were running out of time to save Jackie, and bringing Gloria into our confidence seemed like a good strategy.

Gloria and I got to La Cucina Restaurant later than I'd planned. She had insisted on going to her apartment to change into something more suitable for dinner. When she was ready, she mixed a few drinks and brought them over to her couch.

"You seem in a hurry. Is this how you treat your dates?" she asked.

It occurred to me that the DA might have asked her to pump me for information, since he had expected me to show up at his office.

"I've made reservations for dinner and I don't know how long the restaurant will hold them. Besides, I don't like coming across too aggressive on a first date."

"Normally I would agree, but I feel like I already know you. The DA has mentioned you numerous times, and last year you were front page news more often than President Harding," she said.

"I thought it was too easy to get a date with such a beautiful woman. So why the interest? I'm sure his comments weren't favorable."

"Let just say I like men who are physically attractive and who live dangerously."

"We could always find another restaurant if they don't hold our table," I said.

She smiled and grazed the scar on my cheek with the back of her hand. Her kiss was warm and inviting, making me wonder if I really needed Martha or O'Reilly's help to get the information I needed.

* * * * *

Martha and O'Reilly were sitting nursing their drinks when Gloria and I finally arrived at the restaurant. Gloria demanded an explanation when she realized we were heading for their table.

"What's this? Why are *they* here?"

I pulled out a chair. "If you'll take a seat, I'll explain. You're among friends."

"I'm not so sure," she said with a penetrating stare. "Friends don't use each other."

I sat between her and O'Reilly. "If you've heard about me from the DA, you must also be familiar with Jacqueline Forsythe. Since her murder trial, we've become partners in my PI business," I said.

"What's this have to do with her?"

"The DA had some men kidnap Jackie in order to get his hands on an incriminating document I have. It's a document that would turn City Hall upside down."

"I don't believe it. I know the DA is aggressive and skirts the edge of the law to get convictions, but you're talking about a major crime."

"It gets worse," O'Reilly said. "The young men that were killed the other day got in the way. The DA didn't personally ice any of them, and I'm sure he didn't intend for anyone to get killed, but he paid the hoods to kidnap Jackie; therefore, he's guilty of murder."

"This whole conversation is absurd. How can you be certain the DA's involved?" she demanded.

"Someone who works in your office informed us that he was having Jackie watched. That's why I confronted him today. He admitted he had Jackie and would exchange her for the document," I said.

Gloria drained her drink and ordered another. She knew O'Reilly to be a good cop and quickly surmised that the assistant DA was my source in her office since he dated Martha. She asked several more questions. When she was satisfied, she and Martha left the table for the ladies' room, which gave me a chance to talk with O'Reilly.

"Sorry Joey, none of my stool-pigeons know a thing about Jackie, and my buddies on the force haven't heard anything either."

"Then Gloria is our only chance to locate Jackie. I hope we can get her to cooperate. I'll do whatever it takes," I said.

O'Reilly picked up his mug, "Sounds like a tough assignment. Let me know if you're not up to the task."

The girls came back as the food arrived. Gloria shoved her plate aside and asked how she could help.

"We need to find where he's holding Jackie before Monday. That's when the DA expects Joey to hand over the document. Did you hear any talk around the office?" O'Reilly asked.

"This is the first I've heard of a kidnapping."

"If the DA had to hide someone, where would it be? Does he have a second home? Where does he go on vacation?" I asked.

"I don't know much about his personal life. To tell the truth, I don't think he has one."

I pushed back from the table. "Gloria, you know where she is. You just need to think."

"Look, don't put this on me. Why not give him what he wants?" she said, reaching for O'Reilly's beer.

I grabbed her arm. "Gloria, you must understand something. Jackie witnessed the slaughter of all those young men. Once I hand over the document, she's dead. He has no other choice."

Gloria glanced over at O'Reilly, who gently nodded. "Joey's right; we only have a few days."

"Mike, if I didn't know you to be a damn good cop, I'd tell you guys to leave me out of this mess. The DA's a tough man, but you're accusing him of murder."

"I've known Joey since he was a kid, and I'd stand with him over the DA any day," O'Reilly said.

"I need time to think," Gloria said and walked out of the restaurant. We didn't follow.

Puffing furiously on a cigarette, she walked back and forth in front of the restaurant window. Suddenly she stopped, flung open the door and came back to our table.

"The DA has several 'safe' houses around the city he uses to keep high profile witnesses before they testify at trial. The other day he told me the one on Staten Island was no longer available. I thought it strange at the time because we didn't have anyone who needed protection."

"Where?" O'Reilly and I both blurted out.

"Tottenville, Staten Island, on about ten acres of land." She wrote down the address.

"What about security?" O'Reilly asked.

"The houses aren't staffed when vacant so the amount of security depends on the risk to the witness."

"Any dogs?"

"Not practical, since the places are used so infrequently."

"Have you been to this particular house?"

"I was with him when he selected the location. The only concern he had was a ditch running along the back of the property. A guard is always posted somewhere along the ditch when the house is in use."

Outside the restaurant, Martha gave Gloria a hug. "Thanks for helping. I know this has been a shock."

"I'm gonna resign in the morning. I don't want to go back to work knowing he's responsible for the deaths of so many."

I didn't like that idea, but I said nothing.

Martha, Mike, and I agreed to meet in the morning with Pop and my uncle to put together a plan for rescuing Jackie. O'Reilly was working the night shift and said he would try to get information about the Staten Island safe house without raising suspicion.

He gave Martha a ride home, and I drove Gloria back to her apartment.

* * * * *

Gloria fumbled with the key and then turned toward me as the latch clicked back. I thanked her for the risk she had taken for Jackie. Walking away, I felt her watching me. Halfway down the hall I heard the door close with a slow click. I stopped and went back. I needed to make sure she wouldn't change her mind in the morning and tell the DA about our conversation. If she did, I would be leading O'Reilly and my family into a death trap. I knew only one way to make sure she was sincere. I gently knocked.

She opened the door and stood aside so I could enter.

"I have another favor to ask."

She shut the door and reached up, stretching, to secure a bolt. She knew I was watching and smiled as she ran her hands along the side of her skirt to smooth out the wrinkles that had formed. "Have a seat and I'll be with you shortly," she said.

Gloria removed the glasses we'd used earlier in the evening and brought over fresh drinks. Once again she placed her arm along the top of the sofa. It was as if we had never left the apartment for dinner.

"What can I do for you?" she asked, putting down her drink.

At first I couldn't think of what to say, then remembered one of the reasons I had returned. "I need you to stick it out at your job until we rescue Jackie."

"Why?"

"I want the DA to come to the safe house. Do you think you can get him there this weekend?"

"He's preparing for a Monday morning trial that will give him the headlines he craves. He asked me to work both Saturday and Sunday to help prepare."

"I'll call the office when we have Jackie. Tell him someone from the safe house asked him to come over."

"Why would he make such a long trip?"

"He'll assume I was lying about having the book he wants in my safety deposit box. He's clever enough to know that I was trying to buy time. He'll think Jackie is ready to tell him where the book is really stashed."

"Are you going to kill him?"

"I don't know."

She moved closer. "Is Jackie more than a partner?"

"We're good friends," I said.

I put my drink down next to hers and pulled her close. "Very good friends."

"Are you still using me?"

I didn't answer and she didn't resist my advance.

Chapter 18

I left Gloria's apartment early in the morning, confident she wouldn't betray us. We had spent part of the night discussing what she would do next after quitting her job at the DA's office. She seemed excited to get back to Texas now that she had acquired work experience that would provide for a decent living. She was convinced she would never feel comfortable in New York, because she would always be considered an outsider.

Driving home, my focus shifted back to Jackie's rescue. I had no doubt, even though it had been over a year since my last military mission, that the skills the army had honed in me would kick in when needed. I already felt the effects of an adrenalin surge and, in some perverse way, looked forward to the action.

The instant I turned onto Market Street, my body quivered. The street vendors were nowhere in sight. A closed sign hung in Castellano's pizza joint. Nearer home, I noticed that Castellano's men were gone.

I drove past our stoop, turned the corner, and parked in the alleyway behind the row of brownstones. I ran past the back of the buildings, nearly colliding with several store owners putting out their trash for the morning pick up. When I entered the back of my parents' apartment, I heard familiar banter echoing down the narrow hall from the dining area. Martha noticed me first, shot up from the table, and shoved me back into the hallway.

"Where were you last night? I waited past midnight to talk about Gloria, but you didn't return to your apartment."

Taken aback, I waved her aside. "Don't worry about Gloria. She's not going to betray us. I took care of that."

"I bet you did."

"I don't have time for this right now. We're all in danger."

I had everyone's attention.

"Where's Castellano?" I asked. "He should be here by now."

"How should we know?" Pop said. "Maybe Castellano's waiting for O'Reilly to finish his shift before he joins us. We can't make much of a plan to rescue Jackie without O'Reilly, since he'll want his say."

"What's goin' on? Why so panicked?" Luigi asked.

"Castellano's men are gone, and the street's nearly deserted. I think we're gonna get hit. There's no time for questions. Everybody out the back, *now!*" I shouted. "Uncle Luigi, lead them over to Tony the Butcher's."

The whole group rose simultaneously, grabbed the various weapons my uncle had stashed around the apartment, and gathered by the back door.

"Uncle, if you see a guy with blond hair about six feet tall, shoot the bastard. He's the one who killed Vic."

"How do you know what he looks like? I thought you found Vic dying."

"Didn't I tell you I had killed his twin brother?"

"Forget I asked. What are you gonna be doin? I'm not leavin' you here alone," Luigi said.

"Castellano would never pull his men without telling us. He's either dead or needs my help."

Luigi gripped the back of my neck, gave me a gentle

shake, and joined the others. He went into the alleyway first. Martha hadn't moved from where I had left her in the hall. I grabbed her shoulder and pushed her forward. She stumbled and then came back at me.

"You're a real bastard," she said. "I saw the way you were ogling Gloria last night. For all we know Jackie could be dead and you're playing the field."

"Gloria could've been working for the DA. I had to make sure she intended to help us."

"You didn't have to sleep with her to find that out. If you're gonna sleep around on Jackie, why not with me, and not some bimbo you just met? I thought there was something between us."

"Look, Martha, you couldn't pick a worse time to have this conversation. I'm not sleeping around on Jackie, besides she and I are not hitched. We've made no promises to each other. She knows we had a relationship and that I still have feelings for you, but you're with the assistant DA now. Don't forget it was *you* who told me that our intimacy would end when you found someone else."

"Him? He's just filler. He's too prissy for me, you should know that. I've been using him to get information to help track down Stefano and Kowalski's killer."

"Can we talk about this later? I need to get you over to Tony's with the others and then find Castellano. When Jackie's safe, we can untangle our relationships."

Satisfied, her face softened, and she ran to catch up with the others.

With Martha out of the way, I went to get additional hardware from my room. I didn't know for sure what to expect, but I had a pretty good guess that Bobby Stefano was making his move while he still had one of the twins.

* * * * *

Running down the alleyway, opposite the pizza shop, I saw Castellano's car screech to a halt. Butch jumped out and rushed to the back of the pizzeria. I bolted across the street and got to Butch in time to grab his arm before he knocked on the side door.

"What the hell's happening Butch? Where's everyone?"

"Shit, Joey. Two guys came into the pizza shop early this mornin' and one of them slaughtered three of our guys without firing a shot. The other held a gun to my head."

"Where's Castellano?"

"Inside. They said if I didn't pull our men off the street and down to the docks, they'd slit his throat. They gave me thirty minutes. I'm to knock three times to get back inside once the streets are cleared."

"Open that door and you're gonna get plugged."

Butch lowered his arm and stepped away.

"Go ahead and knock. I'll take care of whoever comes out," I said.

He pulled his rod, rapped on the door, and then moved to the side. Blondie, the twin, came out. Someone slammed the door behind him, and we heard the sound of a heavy bolt being locked from the inside. "You pull that trigger and your boss is history," he said.

Butch smiled and aimed at his head. "If you think I'm gonna trade my life for his, you're mistaken."

From what Cafiero said about this guy, Butch didn't stand a chance. He'd be dead before he knew what happened. "I understand you enjoy hand-to-hand combat." I said. "So do I."

Blondie turned. "You're the one who killed my brother."

"That's hard to say. My guess is he actually died when he flipped over the fire escape railing and splattered head first onto the pavement."

I expected to get a reaction, which would give me a chance to make a move, but he only grinned. "Damn, I wish I could've seen that," he said.

"Stay out of the way, Joey, so I can plug the bastard before he kills us both. I ain't never seen anyone move as fast as him."

I ignored Butch's warning and flipped open my chiv. "This is now between him and me. You can have him next if he's still alive." I moved Butch back a few steps. "Just so we get it straight on the tombstones, are you Benny or Denny?"

"Denny," he said with a smile. Then he reached both hands behind his back and brought out two of the weirdest looking weapons I had ever seen. They were crescent-shaped blades with a handle connecting each end of the crescent. Weapons designed for slicing rather than thrusting.

He moved with the precision of a cat on the prowl, crisscrossing the blades in front of him. Images of Vic lying in Cafiero's apartment with his stomach splayed open flashed before me as the glistening steel came closer and closer. I'd never defended against such a lethal set of blades. It was obvious that my chiv was useless. My only chance was to take a blow and hope the chain link vest I wore under my shirt would limit the damage. Focusing on the timing of his arm movements, I closed in and took a slice to my right side. I then grabbed the wrist of his other arm as it made its descent.

I twisted under his arm and yanked his wrist downward, flipping him to the ground. Stepping on his shoulder, I continued twisting and pulled the handle from his grip. I thought

I had him, but he performed a one-handed push-up, curled around, releasing the strain on his arm, and at the same time kicked the legs out from under me. I landed on my back, gripping one of his crescent blades. He pulled out a pearl-handled knife with eight inches of glistening steel and dove toward me. I resisted the urge to roll to my left, grabbed the handle of the crescent blade I held with both hands, and fully extended my arms. When the sharp metal struck his breastbone, I shifted to my left, slicing open his chest muscles and the tendons in his right shoulder.

Incredibly, he wasn't finished. He pulled his legs to his chest, hurled them forward, while twisting his good shoulder frontward, and landed upright. I blocked his left arm as it came down to strike a lethal blow, and then I leaned forward with one knee bent and struck his pelvic area with a powerful palm thrust. He staggered, unable to support his weight. I twirled him around and buried the curved blade deep into the small of his back. He crumbled into a heap without making a sound.

In hand-to-hand combat, every muscle responds to intense training, every offensive and defensive move instinctive. Letting emotion take control of your reactions is often deadly. A lesson Denny had ignored. He should have retreated when he had a chance.

Butch, with his gun still extended, stood mesmerized.

"Why didn't you shoot the bastard when I distracted him?" I said holding my side.

Butch looked confused. "You said it was between you two."

"Damn Butch, since when did you get honorable?" He didn't know what to say. "I'm goin' around front to get Stefano," I said. "Give me five minutes and then bang on the door. I need a distraction when I break into Castellano's office. Is anyone alive in the pizza shop?"

Butch shook his head, his mouth hanging open as he stared at the slice across my shirt. I lifted up the chainmail undergarment to inspect the wound. There was plenty of blood, but the cut to my side along the hip didn't look life threatening. The metal links had absorbed most of the blow.

Butch smiled and said, "I gotta get me one of those vests."

"You're gonna have to wait. My uncle's first in line." I turned to leave.

Butch tossed over a set of keys: one for the pizza shop and another for Castellano's office door. "You'll need these," he said. "If you don't mind, I'll take your vest if you don't make it out of there alive."

I caught the keys and left to deal with Stefano. For some reason it gave me great pleasure knowing that my vest would never fit Butch.

Chapter 19

Gun drawn, I crossed the threshold of the gruesome pizza shop. The bloody carnage Denny had heaped on those inside triggered a flashback to one of my wartime nightmares. I'll never know how long I stood frozen in the doorway facing a kaleidoscope of past images that overwhelmed my consciousness.

I was to meet Bernadette, a member of the French underground, in the parlor of a small family-owned hotel. A gray-haired man sat on a stool behind an oak reception area with his head resting on one arm flung along the counter. The floor creaked under my weight. I reached in and shook his shoulder. His upper torso slid sideways, and then his lifeless body flipped back against the wooden structure that held the room keys and messages. The blood-stained stool swayed slightly then stood stoically in place as his body slid off and collapsed onto the floor.

I parted a set of colorful curtains that partitioned the reception area from the parlor. There sat Bernadette at the back of the room with the yellow ribbon in her hair that identified her. My eyes locked on hers. I didn't want to see what lay before me. I stepped into the room and stumbled over the lifeless body of a young boy who still clutched a loaf of bread. Slowly, I made my way to Bernadette. She didn't move or say anything—just stared, watching my every move.

With each step, blood squished from under my boots and

with each step, we came closer. I lifted her outstretched hand and removed the cigarette case she had hidden under her palm resting on the table. Before she had died, Bernadette had reached into her purse and pulled out the case that held my instructions. Then the bullet had struck her chest. I hadn't realized her real sacrifice until I looked around the entire room and noticed that Bernadette was the only person near the back exit. Everyone else close to the door made it out alive, but she chose to stay and complete her mission. I returned to her side, took the ribbon from her hair to keep so I would never forget her, and then gently closed her eyelids to shut out the slaughter she had witnessed.

That night, with the information she'd hidden in her cigarette case, I made sure she didn't die in vain.

Gunshots pierced the silence, bringing me back to the present. Butch had created the diversion I needed. I turned the key and barreled through the office door, landing behind the small portable bar. Mirror fragments showered down and whiskey bottles exploded, drenching the floor in liquor. Stefano sounded like a madman, spewing obscenities with each shot. I peered around the end of the bar. *It wasn't Stefano.* One of his hired goons had Castellano in a one-arm choke hold and was holding a gun in his other hand. I fired two shots that struck the wall above the creep's head. He didn't fire back but slouched behind Castellano and shoved the gun against Castellano's temple.

"Throw out your gun, Batista, or I'll scatter his brains all over the place."

I stood with my piece gripped in both hands, ready to shoot. I had him. If he moved his arm, I'd fire, and all he'd have left would be a bloody stump. If he shot Castellano, I'd nail him.

"You're making a big assumption," I said, using a line from Butch.

"Yeah, what's that?"

"That I give a shit about him."

"I know all about you, Batista. Castellano's close to your family, like an uncle."

"If I were you, I wouldn't move. Just drop the gun. At this distance I could pluck out your eyeballs."

Castellano's eyes opened wide. He stopped struggling and took a deep breath. He knew about my marksmanship and had gotten the message that I was going to take a shot. He nodded, and I fired. The bullet struck Castellano a few centimeters below his shoulder blade sending him and the thug against the wall. The bullet went through Castellano and obliterated his attacker's clavicle. The man's gun jerked forward and discharged, missing Castellano, who had thrown himself to the floor. The guy stood exposed, with his arm dangling by his side still holding his rod. He reached for the gun with his other hand, but the sudden movement intensified the pain and the gun dropped to the floor. Castellano yelled for me to finish him off.

Castellano's attacker rushed toward me with a long chiv in his good hand. It had appeared out of nowhere, as did mine. I had brought along Denny's pearl-handled knife. This was how it was going to end. I holstered my gun and watched him come closer.

My head jerked to the side in reaction to gunshots fired close to my ear. The big brute staggered back, then collapsed. Castellano had picked up his gun from the floor.

Castellano spit on the carcass, then turned to me. "Are you crazy? Why didn't you shoot the bastard?"

"He didn't have a gun."

Castellano took hold of my tie and yanked me down. He winced from the pain in his wounded shoulder.

"You get this through your noggin. Someone tries to kill you; you take him out with whatever you got. Shoot him, stab him, hit him over the head with a lead pipe, set him on fire, drown him, use whatever you got; just kill the bastard."

I got Castellano to a chair and tried to stop the bleeding. He yanked the towel I held against his shoulder from my hand and said to get the hell out. "There was another bastard who left to order his crew to take out your family. He has two car loads of guys waiting for his signal. Your folks don't stand a chance."

"Don't worry about that butcher. He's outside and not goin' anywhere," I said.

Butch pounded on the door. I was going to let him in when Castellano stopped me.

"This palooka shot me and I shot him. Capisch? Now, let Butch in and get outta here. My chopper is behind the desk, and take my overcoat. If you walk down the street waving that heat around, half the cops in the city will be on you."

* * * * *

I didn't have a second to waste. The crew that was waiting for Denny's signal to shoot up our apartment building might get antsy and attack.

Luigi saw me walking past our building and joined me in the street.

"What's happening?" he asked.

"The twin's dead, Castellano's shot, but he'll live, and now, I'm gonna deal with Stefano's men."

"You got a plan?"

"You got your chopper?"

"He pulled open his coat and held up his Tommy gun. "Yep."

"That's plan enough. You take the right side, I'll take the left."

"What are we looking for?" he asked.

"One or more cars parked around the corner with a bunch of hoods hanging around, but don't act on your own," I said. "I'll be watching you, and you do the same for me."

When I hit the corner, I turned left and crossed the street, but didn't see anything suspicious. Satisfied, I headed in Luigi's direction. He was on the opposite side hunched behind a parked car. When he saw me, he pointed to two new flivvers on my side of the street. Four men leaned against the cars smoking, and two others paced the sidewalk. Cigarette butts littered the ground.

I took a chance. If Cafiero had gone to great lengths to protect his identity, I assumed the twins did the same. I walked up to the hoods and got their attention by showing my Tommy gun. They hadn't seen the twins, so it wasn't hard to convince them I was Denny. In all likelihood Stefano had hired the bozos and instructed them to wait until they were given the all clear to move in and wipe out my family.

"You ready?" I said.

"Geez, it's about time," said the leader. "Hop in."

"I wouldn't do that if I were you," I said. "It's not safe."

"What the hell are you talkin' about?"

Luigi opened fire and riddled the back car.

They all cowered behind the first car, but when the firing stopped, they reached inside for their heavier hardware. I fired a blast in the air, and they flopped to the ground again.

"For a bunch of torpedoes, you guys have short memories.

I just told you it wasn't safe to get in the cars. I suggest you toss your pistols in the backseat and hoof it back to Newark. Don't forget to tell Stefano that Batista sends his regards."

Sirens were blaring. Luigi rushed to ransack the cars and took out four choppers and two handguns. The hoods had split in different directions, and we disappeared into an alleyway, seconds before the police converged onto the scene.

"These will make a nice addition to my arsenal, but it's too bad I had to leave a bunch behind," Luigi said, with a grin that quickly faded. Ma greeted us at the back door of our apartment building, none too happy.

* * * * *

O'Reilly, Pop, Luigi, and I had roughed out a plan for rescuing Jackie and were about to leave for the Island when Martha burst into my office with an entourage.

"Always playing the hero," she said accusingly. "Why didn't you tell us you were injured? There are droplets of blood all over the stairs."

Ma brushed her aside and barked out orders with the authority of a drill sergeant. O'Reilly and Luigi grabbed me under the shoulders and planted me on the couch. Next thing I knew, Rosalie and Gino were removing my shirt and protective gear. They then lowered my trousers. To my embarrassment, everyone looked on, including Sadie.

The slice in my side was deeper than I thought, exposing the top of my hipbone. Gino told Ma to call a doctor. O'Reilly and I both knew that would create unwanted complications.

"I have medical supplies in my car," O'Reilly said.

Ma insisted we get a doctor and headed for the door. I gave Pop a look, and he stopped her with one command.

"No doctor!"

"I have a field medical kit in a duffle bag stashed in my closet," I said to Martha. "It contains everything needed to cauterize and stitch the wound."

Martha returned in no time and handed the box to Gino.

"I can't do this," he said, with the box shaking in his hand.

Rosalie grabbed the kit and said she'd assist. She walked Gino into the bathroom where they scrubbed down. Upon returning, Rosalie opened the box and laid out the supplies. Pop got the bottle of whiskey from my desk. Gino took a heavy swig and went to work.

"It looks a lot worse than it is; there are no major arteries involved," he said.

The shot of morphine Gino jabbed me with did its job. The next thing I remember, I was waking up in bed surrounded by Rosalie, Martha, and Sadie.

"What time is it?" I asked.

"Early Sunday morning," Martha said.

"Oh God, we've got to get going."

I threw the covers off, only to quickly pull them back. "Where are my clothes?"

Martha walked out, but Rosalie and Sadie stayed put, laughing at my predicament, each insisting they should be the one to help me dress. I threw my pillows and ordered them out. I was sore but could maneuver without much pain. I showered and once again strapped on my military gear. Only this time I wore the entire outfit, including boots, and an impressive array of small arms weapons. I carried my sniper gear and several different types of explosives in a specially designed rucksack that also contained gear for camouflage maneuvers in snow. With my rucksack slung over my shoulder, I headed downstairs. To my relief, O'Reilly and the others had waited and were ready to leave for the Island. During the night they had modified our original plan.

"The best way to get Jackie the hell out of that place is to make sure she knows we've come for her. The only way we could think of doing that is to have Martha drive up to the house pretending she needs directions," O'Reilly said.

"That's insane," I said. "Why would they even let her near the place? We could end up with two women in danger."

"I'm surprised that you care. You don't seem to have any trouble getting women. I'm going," Martha said. "You're wasting valuable time."

"Don't you remember what Gloria said?" O'Reilly asked. "The DA tries to make his safe houses look like ordinary vacation homes. I'm sure they'll have surveillance, but anyone should be able to drive up to the house, especially a woman."

Out voted, I got hold of Gloria on the phone and told her to give the message we had discussed to the DA at two in the afternoon. Hopefully we'd have the house secured and Jackie safe by the time he arrived.

Chapter 20

Covered in snow from the recent storm, the Staten Island summer vacation neighborhood looked deserted—with one exception. We followed in the icy ruts made by previous cars headed for the safe house, which sat at the end of the tree-lined road. Parked a short distance from our destination, Pop and Martha stayed with the car while the rest of us went in on foot.

O'Reilly and Luigi hung back in the foliage, watching as I reconnoitered the layout. The left side of the driveway had a natural knoll sprinkled with overgrown shrubs and dense, snow-laden pine trees that blocked the view from the house. I skirted behind the knoll and positioned myself between two bushes that gave me sufficient cover and a clear side view of the house and surrounding area.

A horseshoe driveway curved to the steps of a covered porch that spanned the length of the two-story house. The whole structure looked in disrepair, including a wooden bench, the lone object on the porch. The backyard lay bare except for an old oak tree, rooted close to a ditch, and an outhouse to the left of the back of the house. The ditch and the tree trunk would provide adequate protection from gunfire coming from the house. I didn't see movement near the windows, which were closed and covered with sheer drapes to let in the sunlight. I removed binoculars from my backpack and inspected the acreage close to the house and along the driveway, and then focused on the entrance from the road. When I first made my way onto the property, I had noticed trampled snow off to the right, leading to a tree partially hidden by a mound of snow. I suspected a guard was posted there. I backtracked toward the main road until I had a different angle to get a better look. I was right. A sentry rested against the tree, guzzling from a bottle of booze and taking an occasional bite of a sandwich. He obviously didn't expect company.

I returned to my original vantage point and concentrated on the drainage ditch behind the house, remembering Gloria had said the DA believed it was a point of vulnerability. There was no sign of a sentry, but the snow around the outhouse was trampled down, so the possibility existed that he was taking a crap. I waited. I was about to change locations to get a better view along the ditch, when I saw someone climbing down from a hollowed-out notch high up in the main trunk of the oak tree. He wore a white hood and overcoat and had a shotgun slung over his shoulder. Once on the ground, he headed for the latrine. Satisfied that I knew where the guards were posted, I inched down the knoll, careful not to brush the snow from low-hanging tree limbs, and headed back to the others. I froze when I heard a door slam shut. Peering over the knoll, I saw a different brute on the front porch attempting to light a cigarette. He didn't have a coat and soon went back inside. Unfortunately, he had a chopper slung over his shoulder.

I met the others back at the car to make final plans.

"There's at least four watching Jackie. One's behind the house, another near the entrance to the drive on the right side. The two others are inside. One came out for a smoke, so there must be at least one more who's keeping an eye on Jackie," I said.

"We should assume there's five, maybe six," O'Reilly said.

"Jackie doesn't stand a chance. When those goons realize what's goin' on, they'll kill her," Martha said. "Let's give the DA what he wants."

"We've already had that discussion. If we do, she'll be done for," Luigi said. "At least this way she has a chance. Just pray she hears you and understands what we need her to do."

"We don't have to worry about Jackie getting the message. She's smart and knows we're looking for her," I said.

"All this has to end," Pop stated. "If anyone, including the DA, makes it out of this alive, we'll be in constant danger."

We all agreed, but I had some hesitation. Gloria knew what was taking place at the safe house, and if the DA turned up dead, she just might testify against us. I decided to see how things played out. What was important at the moment was to get Jackie the hell out of that house.

* * * * *

Martha gave us twenty minutes to get ready before driving up to the house. When her car entered the driveway, O'Reilly took advantage of the distraction and dispatched the guard at the entrance to the grounds. I watched him retrieve his knife, wipe the blade on the trousers of his victim, and then maneuver into position to cover the front and right side of the house. Until then I had never pictured O'Reilly as a street kid, where handling a chiv was a rite of passage, but he'd clearly had practice.

Luigi had taken my sniper rifle and positioned himself

in the same spot I had previously used, giving him a clear view of the front and left side of the house, including the outhouse. Pop and I maneuvered around back from opposite sides. My job was to eliminate the guard watching the ditch area without firing a shot, and Pop's was to provide cover if someone spotted me from inside.

Martha drove along the curved driveway and stopped in front of the porch steps. She kept the flivver running and honked twice. When no one responded, she stepped out of the car and climbed up the porch stairs, stomping her feet to rid them of snow before knocking. She was making as much noise as possible and banged harder and harder until someone answered the door. When it flung open, she stumbled back.

"Whaddaya want lady?"

"I've been driving for two miles and haven't come across another soul. What is this, a ghost town?"

"Then how'd ya know we were here?"

"I followed your tire tracks."

"I said whaddaya want?"

"Directions, I'm obviously lost. How do I get to Amboy Road?"

"Go back the way you came and you'll run into Amboy. You missed the turn."

"You got a john I can use?"

"Sorry lady, you best be leavin'. All we got is an outhouse and it's in use. There are some places on Amboy you can stop."

"I can wait."

"Be on your way, lady."

"Thanks for nothin'," Martha said and drove away.

All we could do was hope Jackie had recognized Martha's

voice and understood the message. Ten minutes later, Jackie stepped onto the porch, accompanied by a burly-looking fella who led her to the outhouse, untied her hands and stood guard. The guy in the tree above the ditch climbed down and headed for his buddy; that's when I made my move.

I approached him from behind, covered his mouth with one hand, and drove my knife home. In the struggle, I lost my footing and dragged us both to the ground. The guy guarding Jackie heard the commotion, pulled his gun, and would've nailed me if Luigi hadn't taken him out with a shot to the head.

Jackie darted out of the outhouse and dove into the ditch. A blast from a Tommy gun riddled the structure as Pop opened fire. I dashed along the ditch and scrambled over to Jackie. Luigi blasted the side of the house, shattering windows to draw attention away from us. Luigi, from his vantage point, also had the front of the house covered, so O'Reilly went around the opposite end and shot out several windows.

Once Jackie and I had sufficient cover, we embraced. Her eyes were filled with tears.

"I knew you'd come for me, but it took you forever."

"It's a long story," I said.

She noticed blood on her hand. "You're shot."

My stitches had split open. "Not shot. Like I said, it's a long story. Now get up the hill to Luigi and stay there. I'll be fine."

"We should leave before one of us gets killed."

"We don't have that option; this needs to end here. These guys can't afford to let us live." She was about to argue, but I grabbed her by the arm and handed her a gun.

"You might need this."

"Be careful, there are three left in the house and they're heavily armed."

When she reached Luigi, I signaled to Pop that I was going to make a move for the back door. He pointed to an upstairs window. I waited, then saw a curtain move slightly to the side. Pop waved for O'Reilly to make his way around back, and when he was in position, Pop exposed himself by running toward the massive oak tree. The gunman upstairs let loose with a chopper. I fired two shots, and a body fell through the window, landing head first into a snow drift. It looked like Pop had taken a hit. O'Reilly scrambled to his side. Heavy fire came from two rooms on the bottom floor.

I couldn't worry about Pop, realizing I might not get this opportunity again. Two gunmen were inside, and I knew exactly where they were located. I scrambled along the ditch toward the outhouse, entered the foliage and made a dash for the back door of the house. Jackie ran to the front of the house at the same time. I didn't know what she had in mind, but I had to stay focused to take the pressure off O'Reilly and Pop.

O'Reilly saw what I intended, and in returning fire, purposely blasted the door-locking mechanism so I could enter through the back. I went in low within seconds of Jackie entering the front door. We were on either ends of a long hallway that ran the lenght of the house. Jackie signaled she would take the far room and that the door in the hallway where I stood led to a room with one of the gunmen. He was still firing a chopper out a window. If I tried to enter, it would be easy for him to turn and spray the entire hallway within seconds. I got into position, kicked the door, and bolted down the hall to the main room, outpacing a barrage of bullets. Jackie had indicated that there was a second door to the bedroom off the front room of the house. By the time the gunman realized I was standing in the main doorway to his room, it was too late.

The gunfire suddenly ceased and a sense of calmness settled over the house. I entered the second bedroom and found Jackie retrieving one of her knives. It had found its mark, as did two bullets from her gun.

O'Reilly had put a tourniquet around Pop's leg and helped him into the house. I retrieved my rucksack from Luigi and bandaged the wound. A bullet had gone through Pop's leg, about six inches above the knee.

Luigi stayed in position, waiting for the DA to arrive. We had deliberately attacked the house from the sides and rear to avoid visible damage to the front so the DA wouldn't suspect anything was wrong when he drove up the driveway. O'Reilly and I carried the bodies inside with just minutes to spare before his car entered the drive.

* * * * *

The DA got out of his car first, followed by two of his henchmen, both holding Tommy guns.

"Joey, I've come to bargain," he yelled out.

O'Reilly looked over at me, and all I could do was shrug. I had no clue how he knew I was there.

"You have nothing to bargain with," I said from an open window. "Make a wrong move and my uncle will drop all three of you. He doesn't miss."

The DA reached into the backseat and pulled Gloria out of the car. Her hands were tied behind her.

"Oh, I wouldn't say we have nothing to bargain with. It seems to me you would hate to see my dedicated secretary get her brains blown out. I know how close you two have become."

Jackie punched me in the side. "Is that why it took you so damn long to come for me?"

The rest of my stitches split open from the blow. When she realized what she had done, she backed away. I signaled everyone to get down low and take cover. I put my gun in my waistband around back, opened the front door, and stood leaning against the frame.

Both Pop and O'Reilly shattered a window pane on either side of the door with the butts of their pistols and took aim at the DA.

"Bring Gloria to me and I'll give you what you want," I said, patting my back pocket.

The DA came onto the porch. "Looks like you've been shot. I hope it's not serious," he said grinning. "She stays put until I see the book. Now hand it over."

I reached behind my back, and when he saw the gun, the DA turned to run. I threw my body forward, hitting him in the back with my shoulder, sending him flying down the steps. Before I fell onto the porch landing, I managed to get off two shots at the car. The gunmen that had come with the DA panicked when their boss tumbled down the stairs and wildly blasted the house. Before they could control their aim, Luigi had dispatched them both. Gloria had wisely fallen back into the car at the first sign of trouble.

O'Reilly pulled the DA to his feet.

The DA stood among the carnage and ranted, "O'Reilly, I'll not only have your badge, but you'll fry along with Joey and everyone else."

O'Reilly picked up the DA's fedora, dusted it off, and calmly handed it to him. "You have all the explaining to do.

Why would you hire a bunch of palookas from out of town to watch one of your safe houses? What were they doing here? Who were they hiding and why? Then, there's the fact that ballistics will tie them to the murders of the street gang that took place two days ago."

"I'll find a way to explain everything and you'll all roast," he said.

I stuck one of the mobsters' guns in his gut. "In that case, you leave us no choice."

Jackie pushed me aside and decked the DA. "I don't think killing a district attorney is a good idea; there would be a huge investigation."

"Looks like you have a problem, Joey," the DA said, rubbing his jaw.

Once freed, Gloria took me aside and said she could prove the DA hired all the goons in the house, including the sniper who had shot the leader of the street gang that had been slaughtered. She had paid them from an illegal checking account the DA kept. At the time she didn't know why he had hired them. She also had their names listed in her ledger.

Gloria and I turned to the DA. "It appears you left a paper trail linking you to these guys. I don't think you'll be pressing charges against us anytime soon. I suggest *you* find a way to get yourself out of this mess."

He sat down on the wooden bench on the porch and cursed the bunch of us. We were about to leave when he stood, looking like his arrogant self.

"O'Reilly, I need you to stay with me," he said. "I wouldn't come here with only two men. This is what we're gonna say. You got a tip that the guys who shot up the street gang were hiding out on the Island, and I insisted we check before asking for local support. They opened fire and a battle ensued. We'll put the body of one of my guys in the backyard and the other in the house. I don't know how you all managed to get the upper hand on these guys, but that's the story we'll tell. It'll sound genuine, especially when you give the details of the actual gun battle."

"How you gonna explain away the fact that all this took place in one of your safe houses?" O'Reilly asked.

"None of the houses are traceable back to my office. That's why they're *safe* houses."

"Don't do it, O'Reilly. Come with us. You can't trust this bastard. He'll shoot you when he gets the chance and take all the glory," I said and Luigi agreed.

Sirens blared off in the distance.

"You better get the hell out of here," O'Reilly said. "Don't worry about me. I won't let him near a gun. This place is about to be swarmed with cops. You gotta give him credit, he's gonna end up looking like a hero. He might even become the next mayor."

"I like the sound of that… mayor. Just think, I'll owe it all to you, Joey."

We could still hear the DA laughing from halfway down the deserted street.

* * * * *

The morning headlines reported a horrific gun battle on Staten Island involving one of the New York City's district attorneys, members of his precinct's homicide and police divisions, and the suspected killers of a youth gang.

The DA had cleverly solved his dilemma, and we were in the clear—at least until the DA figured out a way to get revenge. Gloria understood this better than any of us and didn't waste any time getting out of town.

Back home again, Ma prepared a feast while Gino and Rosalie patched Pop's leg and re-stitched my hip. Halfway through desert, Ma informed us that tomorrow was our last chance to view Vic's body before his burial.

Chapter 21

I hate funerals, always have, but this one was particularly painful. Not because the entire neighborhood knew Vic died doing me a favor trying to rescue Jackie. And not because I had shot him through the heart to stop his suffering. He would've done the same for me. It was because I'd lost another childhood friend. First there was Shawn, O'Reilly's brother, then Anita, whom I loved deeply, friends lost during the war, then Bobby Balcone, poor guy could never catch a break, and now Vic. It felt like it wasn't part of our destiny to grow old.

Vic's mother, Millie Ligotti, had asked Ma to sit with her alongside the casket and help her stand to greet those who came to pay their respects. Otherwise, she would have been alone. Vic's father had died when he was a kid, and his only other relative was his uncle Ronnie, who had left the neighborhood years ago to make his fortune in Detroit. He faithfully sent Vic money on his birthday, but that was all anyone ever heard from him.

During the two days of mourning, the whole neighborhood embraced Millie and said their final goodbyes to Vic. As custom dictated, many folks lingered, sitting in row upon row of wooden folding chairs that faced the casket. It was a sad time, but also a chance to reconnect with old friends and bury differences that tended to creep into relationships.

The funeral parlor was abuzz with local gossip that

stopped abruptly when Jackie and I entered. All heads turned to the front of the room to see what Mrs. Ligotti would do.

Jackie spoke first. "I'm so sorry for your loss, Mrs. Ligotti. Vic gave his life to save mine. I will never forget his sacrifice."

Mrs. Ligotti struggled to stand with Ma's help and then gave Jackie a hug. She moved back holding onto Jackie's hands. "Child, we are all put here for a reason, and Vic fulfilled his. There is no blame."

I was leaning forward to give Mrs. Ligotti an embrace when a strong hand gripped my shoulder and pulled me upright.

"Millie, why don't you take this young lady up to the casket to pay her respects while I talk with Joey?"

I recognized Vic's Uncle Ronnie immediately by the scar that ran from his right temple down to his jaw. In that instant of recognition, my mind flashed back more than fifteen years to an alleyway where Vic and I had hidden behind some crates. By the age of ten, we'd both seen plenty of bloody fights, but you never forget the first time you witness a brutal death.

Vic and I had seen a stranger hiding behind a trash bin with his gun drawn and knew something bad was about to happen. Scared, we backed up and ran behind the building and down the next alley. Looking back over our shoulders to see if we were being followed, we collided into Ronnie as we shot out between the two buildings onto the sidewalk. When we told Ronnie what we saw, he ran to where the stranger was waiting to ambush someone. We followed and hid where we could watch. Ronnie snuck up on the guy, buried his chiv into his back, and grabbed the man's gun. In the ensuing struggle the guy pulled out a glistening steel blade and sliced open the side of Ronnie's face. Ronnie backed away, fired twice, and then stomped the guy's face with the heel of his boot. Soon after, Ronnie left town.

Unknown to Vic and me at the time, Ronnie, armed with only his stiletto, had gone up against a hit man hired to kill Uncle Luigi and Castellano. Even to this day, every kid raised in our neighborhood has heard of Ronnie.

"You remember me?" he asked, pulling me back to the present. I nodded.

"Good. Let's step outside and have a smoke. We need to talk."

Mrs. Ligotti and Jackie had already approached the casket, so I decided not to tell Jackie I was leaving the room. On the way out I did overhear part of their conversation.

"Doesn't he look good?" Mrs. Ligotti asked.

"It's as if he's sleeping," Jackie responded.

"He is, child, and some day he will wake with the rest of us."

I turned back and saw Ma supporting Mrs. Ligotti with her arm around her waist, and Mrs. Ligotti placing hers around Jackie. I never appreciated my parents' devotion to church, but in those few words and simple gestures, I understood the meaning of faith.

Ronnie and I went out back and walked to the edge of the parking area to get away from the other men who were taking a break from the depressing atmosphere of the funeral home. Ronnie obviously didn't want anyone to listen to our conversation. I waited for him to say what he had on his mind.

"I'm told Vic tried to kill you when you arrived home from overseas."

"We got things straightened out. Just a misunderstanding," I said.

"So I hear. You've made quite an impression around the neighborhood. I'm not sure it's all good. You seem to attract trouble."

He reached inside his jacket for his pack of smokes, and that's when I noticed he had a small, intricately engraved, pearl-handled, 9mm semiautomatic pistol in a shoulder holster. He followed my gaze and brushed open my jacket to reveal my own guns.

"The word on the street is you're pretty damn good with those and that your broad has special talents of her own," he said, tapping one of my rods.

"My *broad's* name is Jackie, and she's my partner. Now if you don't mind, I should be inside. In a way, it's my fault Vic died."

"Hold on," he said, grabbing my arm. "That's what I want to talk about. Tell me why Vic died and who killed him."

"For reasons I'm not going to go into now, the DA had Jackie kidnapped. Vic and members of our old gang were helping find out what went down."

"So the DA's responsible?"

"In a way," I said. "If Jackie wasn't kidnapped, Vic wouldn't have been involved in my business. He was actually killed by one of two hired guns out of Chicago who were on a contract to take me out. Vic got in the way."

"These guys from Chicago, you know who they are?"

"Benny and Denny. They're twins. They're both dead."

Ronnie let out a slow whistle. "The twins I know by reputation; they were two of the best. But I don't think they killed Vic. I think you did."

I took a step back.

"This neighborhood," he said, glancing around at some of the old buildings, "has a long memory. I've been gone for some time, yet I still know most of the people inside. The coroner, who worked on Vic, and I were in the same gang. He tells me Vic died from a gunshot through his heart and that cloth fibers were found in the wound. He also said if he wasn't shot, Vic would've lingered for days in agony. Any attempt by doctors to save him would have been futile because a horrible infection would have developed and eventually kill him."

It felt good to tell someone. "I saw gut wounds in the war and his was horrific. We both knew he didn't have a chance. He asked me to stop his suffering and I did. Coppers were crawling all over the place so I used a pillow to muffle the sound. Then I got the hell out of the area."

Ronnie threw down his cigarette and ground it into the pavement with the toe of his shoe. "I think it's time to go back inside and pay your respects," he said.

* * * * *

Pop pulled me aside. "What did Ronnie want with you?"

"He's digging into what happened to Vic."

"I'm surprised he showed his face."

"Why? Wasn't Vic his godchild?"

"He's on the lam. Castellano has him holed up in Little Italy."

Luigi and Castellano joined us.

"Vito, you mind if we talk business with Joey?" Luigi asked.

Once Pop left, Castellano put his arm around my shoulder, and the three of us walked across the hall to an empty room.

"Ronnie has asked for my help," Castellano said.

"What's goin' on?"

"There's a warrant out for his arrest," Luigi said.

"What's the charge?"

"Murder."

"Listen, Joey," my uncle said, leading me deeper into the room. "After you deal with Bobby Stefano, we'd like you to go to Detroit and take care of things for Ronnie."

I backed away and walked over to the window where I saw a hearse parked in front of the funeral hall. I needed time to think and that's when I realized my uncle had much deeper ties to Castellano than I suspected.

"Why get involved when Ronnie hasn't been back to the neighborhood for years, and why me?"

A commotion from across the hall interrupted our conversation. Everyone had begun leaving the building followed by Vic's mother, Ronnie, and my parents, all walking beside the casket.

"We'll continue this discussion after the burial," Castellano said. He caught up with the procession and stood by Mrs. Ligotti's side.

When I got to my car, Jackie was already in the passenger seat.

"That was difficult," she said. "I didn't expect you'd leave me alone in there. It felt like everyone blamed me for Vic's death."

"Vic's mother absolved you of any responsibility once she gave you an embrace and walked you to the casket."

"It would've helped if I had known that."

"Sorry, I got tied up with Vic's uncle, then Luigi and Castellano."

"You gonna tell me what's goin' on?"

"Did you meet Vic's uncle, Ronnie Ligotti?"

"He introduced himself after he came back into the parlor."

"He's asked Castellano for help, and both he and my uncle are obligated to him."

"What for?"

"I'm guessin' it's because he saved their lives years ago."

"What kind of help?"

"All I know is Ronnie's wanted in Detroit for murder. They've asked me to get involved."

"How can they expect you do anything with Stefano and a crazed killer still on the loose? I'm surprised Luigi would put you in such a position."

I had the same thought but didn't say anything. We picked Martha up at La Cucina's where she'd been helping Maria prepare food for the large gathering about to descend upon the establishment after Vic's burial. Martha wasn't happy either and a lot more blunt about her feelings when we filled her in on what had transpired at the wake.

"I think all men are nuts when it comes to honor and loyalty. They don't owe this guy anything. You said yourself it's been almost two decades since he showed his face around here."

I tended to agree with her until I thought about the oath my family made with their close friends. When they'd departed from the ship that took them to America in search of their dreams, they'd pledged to support each other under any and all circumstances. My family had grown up in a different time and place, so some of my values are different from theirs, but I was obliged to honor that difference.

* * * * *

Vic's burial took place in the local church cemetery after a long, drawn-out Mass service. I'm convinced the priest had set a personal goal that everyone who attended would shed at least one tear. He succeeded.

Each mourner passed by the lowered casket and tossed a handful of dirt and a rose into the grave to say their last goodbyes. The motorcade then proceeded to the restaurant where a remembrance of the life of Victor Ligotti erupted into a frenzy of storytelling. Castellano opened with a toast to Vic's memory, followed by Mrs. Ligotti, who told of some of the antics her son had pulled on his dad as a small child, the funniest being when Vic put a small garden snake in his father's plate of pasta. When the snake's head popped through the layer of tomato sauce, his dad tumbled back, hitting the table with his knee, sending the plate in the air and onto his lap. According to Millie, Vic paid a steep price and wasn't able to sit for a week. I wondered if Vic pulled that stunt more than once because he was always asking the gang if we knew where he could find some garden snakes.

Those of us who were left from the old gang got up next, one at a time—some laughing, some crying—as we shared our memorable moments.

I told of the time a group of neighborhood girls surprised us at the end of a pier while we were skinny dipping on a hot, humid August day. When we spotted them running toward us, we jumped over the edge into the water and yelled for them to leave. They finally did, but they left with our clothes. There we stood, after climbing the ladder attached to the pier, stark naked and about a half mile from home. No one knew what to do, except for Vic. He headed down the pier holding a garbage can lid in front, but nothing behind. A while later he came back with a pair of pants for each of us. From that day forward, Vic was the undisputed leader of our gang.

When Castellano's son, Carmine, got up to speak, his wife, Angela, came over with my godchild, Antonio, and sat next to Jackie. Antonio climbed onto my lap and gave me a big hug.

"Mom told me you have medals from the war. Can I see them?" he asked.

"Sure. Next time your mother comes over to visit with my ma, you tell her I said you could have one of my medals to keep."

"You mean it? I can have any one I want?"

"Yep, but you have to treat it with respect. Is it a deal?"

Antonio and I horsed around while Jackie and his mother got to know each other. I couldn't help but overhear their conversation.

"We haven't met, but I've heard so much about you from Joey's mother. I'm Angela, Carmine's wife."

"Nice to meet you. Your son is adorable. How old is he?"

"He's six, and quite a handful," Angela said and then hesitated before speaking again. "Joey's mom told me what you went through when you were kidnapped. I just wanted to make sure you knew that no one blames you for what happened to Vic."

"That's nice of you. I don't think I would have survived if Joey's friends hadn't searched for me. I do feel devastated that Vic died the way he did."

"He chose to help and knew the risk. His memory will

live on for generations in the neighborhood. Knowing Vic, I think he would've liked that," Angela said.

Jackie brushed aside a tear. Angela took hold of her hand, and they sat listening to Carmine speak. When he was done, Jackie asked Angela if she also grew up in the neighborhood.

"I've known Joey all my life. I'm sure you noticed that all his friends are about the same age. My father often joked that the boat ride to America was very long and there wasn't much to do."

When Carmine finished speaking, he spent a few minutes at Mrs. Ligotti's table. Seeing him get up to leave, Angela lifted Antonio off my lap and gave me a kiss on the cheek. She returned to her table to be with her husband and Castellano.

When the stories ended, the food appeared and the booze flowed. Everyone in attendance brought along a body flask filled with their favorite hooch and made the rounds visiting with old friends. Near the end of the evening, Luigi waved me over to where he and Castellano were sitting with Pop. I got up and grabbed Jackie's arm.

"You sure you want me along?" she asked.

"We're partners."

Castellano shuffled uncomfortably in his seat, but before he spoke, I addressed the issue of Jackie's involvement.

"I don't know what this is all about, but what you're asking will impact our business, and therefore, Jackie." I pulled out a chair for her and sat alongside.

"It's not clear how you expect me to get Ronnie out of a murder rap, but before we go any further, I want to know why you're both mixed up in his affairs?"

Luigi leaned forward and, at the same time, Castellano moved his chair back.

"You may not remember, since you were maybe nine or ten at the time," Luigi said. "But just before Ronnie left the neighborhood, a stranger staggered out from the alleyway by the pizza joint and keeled over in the street from a knife wound and some gut shots. He later died."

"I know about that fight. Even the kids on the street today tell the story."

Vic and I had never told anyone about the fight we'd witnessed. We were too scared at the time and decided it best to keep our traps shut. I stuck to that decision as my uncle continued.

"Then you know he was one of Ben Napoli's button men waiting to ambush Castellano and myself. If it wasn't for Ronnie, we'd be dead."

"Did Ronnie even know who the guy was and that you two were his intended victims?"

"Ronnie was working for us and knew that we were goin' up against a strong Mafia boss," my uncle said.

Castellano turned to me. "I never wanted the job of being the boss of this neighborhood, but Napoli was moving in to take control of the docks. Luigi and I knew what that would mean for our families and neighbors. Somebody had to pull everyone together and stand up to Napoli. Your uncle and I drew straws. I lost."

"We don't like what Ronnie has become, but when we needed him, he stepped up and risked his life more times than I can remember," Luigi said.

Castellano put a hand on Luigi's arm, as if to say that's enough, and waved Ronnie over to join us.

"Explain to Joey what you need," Castellano said.

Ronnie looked at Jackie. "You can trust everyone at this table," I said.

"I was framed! A competitor of mine shelled out considerable cash to set me up for the gruesome murders of two prominent city officials. The only way I can get back to Detroit and deal with him is to get the charges dropped."

"Not being familiar with Detroit, we wouldn't know where to begin to find the real killer," Jackie said.

"You don't have to. All you need to do is get scratch into the right hands—money I can't get to," Ronnie said.

Jackie persisted. She clearly didn't like the idea of getting involved in Ronnie's affairs. "Why not use one of your own men?" she asked.

"They couldn't get near the mayor or chief of police to bribe them. There's also the matter of trust. If I gave any of them access to my stash, they'd blow town."

Castellano gave Jackie a look that said to keep her mouth shut.

"Ronnie knows about Stefano and the other issues we face with the killings taking place on my docks. He understands you both have higher priorities," Castellano said.

"I'm gonna continue to lay low to let the heat die down in Detroit. When you have things taken care of here, I'd appreciate your help," Ronnie said to Jackie and me.

A hullabaloo erupted at the front of the restaurant. The DA and some of his men entered. Ronnie slipped down to the basement and out the secret passageway that Castellano had previously mentioned. It connected La Cucina Restaurant to my uncle's speakeasy next door. If Ronnie had any smarts, he was halfway to Little Italy by the time Castellano confronted the DA.

"This is a private event. I would think even you would have the decency to show respect, if not for the dead, for the family," Castellano said.

"Just doing my job. There happens to be a warrant out for the arrest of Ronnie Ligotti. Knowing how much family means to you Italians I thought he might be stupid enough to show up," he said to Castellano, as his men walked the room. Leaving Castellano, he went over to Mrs. Ligotti's table and expressed his sincere regrets for the loss of her son. Satisfied that Ronnie wasn't around, he pulled his men back to the entrance and went back to Castellano.

"My boys tell me you're getting soft and losing your grip on the waterfront. Never a good sign for a Mafia boss; the vultures are always circling for easy pickings."

Heading out the door, he turned to Castellano again.

"From what I hear you may want to watch out for your old friend, Ben Napoli. He has a huge appetite and would like nothing better than taking over all the docks in the city. You stopped him once, I'm not sure you can do it again, especially if you don't have the support of the other bosses."

"If it comes to that, just be ready to clean up the mess and don't take sides. You'll regret it if you do," Castellano shouted.

The room fell silent until the DA left, and Castellano returned to his table and lifted his glass.

* * * * *

With Ronnie gone, the discussion ended and the deal was sealed. Jackie had had sense enough not to ask more questions about Ronnie once she was satisfied that I wouldn't leave until Stefano was eliminated. She understood from her experience in Chicago that you don't turn down the boss when he asks for a favor. Sometime in the future I would be heading to Detroit to bribe some officials to clear Ronnie's name. I had no idea how I was expected to accomplish this feat without ending up in the hoosegow or in the morgue.

Pop hadn't said much, but he made it clear that our family owed Ronnie a debt. He knew the ways of the streets and accepted them. His immediate concern after the meeting was to get home and off his injured leg. I agreed, noticing blood staining his pant leg. The same was happening to my shirt, as blood seeped from my hip wound. It had been a long day and an even longer weekend, and we both had ignored Gino's advice to stay off our feet for a few days.

* * * * *

Pop and I got the royal treatment when we got home. Even Sadie spent time mothering me to speed my recovery, although I soon discovered she had an ulterior motive.

"I can't stay here forever. Are you gonna get back to finding my father's murderer?" she asked, when it looked like the stitches were finally holding.

"We haven't forgotten the danger you face from your father's killer."

"Then do me a favor, quit saving Castellano's life. I still think he's responsible."

"Get that idea out of your head. It'll just lead to more trouble. If I find he's guilty, then we'll deal with it."

The hatred she harbored toward her father's killer had changed her appearance, especially her eyes. They had lost their sparkle.

"Sadie, I know you don't want to hear this, but you need to let go and get on with your life. You're changing into someone I no longer recognize."

"I can't, I just can't. My father suffered a terrible death.

Sometimes at night it's as if I feel his pain. I can't get the image of him dangling from that horrible hook out of my mind."

* * * * *

After only two days back on the job, Martha brought a well-dressed gentleman into our office.

"This is Mr. Genovisi, a lawyer. He says he has a client who needs our services," Martha said. She remained in the room.

"What can we do for you, Mr. Genovisi?" Jackie asked.

"My client, who represents others with similar interests, has secured my services to obtain a document you have in your possession—one that would prove embarrassing to many in City Hall if exposed."

Martha walked right up to him and backed him into one of the chairs. "If you work for the DA, tell him to go to hell," she said.

Jackie got between the two of them and nudged Martha back. "Let's hear what he has to say before we kill the messenger."

I poured Mr. Genovisi a shot of whiskey and assured him he was perfectly safe, explaining that we nearly lost our lives because of the document he referred to.

"My client anticipated your reluctance, especially after what has transpired. He wanted me to assure you he never expected the DA to take such draconian action resulting in Mrs. Forsythe's kidnapping and so many unfortunate deaths," he said, after placing his empty shot glass on the desk.

"Who is this mystery man who hired you?" I asked.

"He suggests you contact him to confirm my authenticity.

He said you would know whom to call, since you used this document so skillfully last year in his courtroom."

I called Judge Andrew Harrington, who had presided over Jackie's murder trial. I asked Genovisi to wait outside with Martha. The judge apologized profusely to Jackie and assured us we would be given special consideration if either of us had to face the judicial system in the future; this was in addition to the cash he had authorized Genovisi to pay out. Jackie and I both grinned when he mentioned a cash offer. We, in turn, assured him no other record of the Forsythe payoffs existed.

"What do you think?" I asked Jackie before calling Genovisi back into our office.

"My deceased husband's little book of names has caused us nothing but trouble, and it's only gonna get worse. As word gets around, everyone who took a bribe from my husband will be after us. I don't know about you, but I'm not willing to risk our lives for a book that will destroy others and make little difference in the end."

"What do you mean?" I asked.

"The only real value it has to us is to keep us out of jail in the future. If the judge is a man of his word, he has just assured us of a fair trial if we ever get tied up in the legal system again."

"We could expose all the crooked politicians," I said.

"Do you really think that will change anything?"

I knew what she meant. It's not just the officials who are corrupt, but the whole system. "You're right. Most people today get fair trials and the hoodlums will always find a way around the law even if all the judges were replaced."

"Then let's get out of this mess in one piece."

Genovisi came back and immediately reached for the book on my desk.

"Not so fast," I said. "There's the little issue of compensation."

A grin spread across Genovisi's face. "Of course. I forgot to mention that detail." He reached into his valise and handed over a stack of hundred-dollar bills.

Martha took the valise from his lap and spilled the contents onto my desk. Five more bundles scattered across the surface. Genovisi took the book and was ushered out of the office by Martha.

Jackie closed the door and turned with an impish smile. "Now that you're feeling better and this whole affair is behind us, how about telling me why it took you so long to come to my rescue? And where did Gloria fit into the picture?"

I felt my face flush. I started to tell Jackie about that night and how I had to be sure Gloria wouldn't betray us. Fortunately, Luigi barged in just as I got to the part about Gloria's role in her rescue.

"Hey, how about you guys help me unload my stuff from the truck outside? I've decided to move back into my old apartment. I was gone for only a few months, and in that time you almost got the whole family wiped out. Besides, I'm missing too many of your ma's meals."

Luigi had moved out last year when he went to work for Castellano, overseeing all his speakeasies. I was out the door and downstairs before he finished his last sentence, hoping Jackie would forget to ask again about Gloria.

Chapter 22

It didn't take the DA long to tighten the screws after we rescued Jackie and demolished his safe house. He busted O'Reilly back to sergeant under the pretense that Mike hadn't solved the Waterfront Homicides, most notably Kowalski's and the three fishermen. Anthony Brown, the assistant DA, chose to dump Martha rather than lose his job. And I had acquired a new friend. At first I thought he might be one of Stefano's henchmen tracking my schedule. It wasn't until I pulled him into an alley and put a gun to his head that I found out he worked for the DA on special assignment.

To make matters worse, the public did hail the district attorney a hero for personally tracking down and killing a gang of murderers in a dramatic gun battle. Our only solace was that Judge Harrington had indicated that the higher-ups in City Hall saw the DA for what he was, a bungling idiot.

O'Reilly didn't care much for titles, and since his new pay level hadn't kicked in yet, he didn't dwell on his demotion. My shadow and I struck a deal that suited both our needs. His name was Pete Fitzpatrick, a seasoned sergeant six months from retirement. Each morning Martha gave him typed details of my planned activities, along with an updated version of the previous day if it was necessary. Needless to say, Pete Fitzpatrick's reports showed I spent considerable time in my office, which certainly wasn't true. In return for my cooperation, Fitzpatrick made himself scarce, showing up occasionally at my uncle's speakeasy to sample the goods. Martha was a different story. She needed a man around and felt I was available again, since I had spent the night with Gloria. Not one to hide her emotions or to betray a friend, she took a direct approach at the worst possible time.

Jackie hadn't dropped her questions about Gloria and one morning insisted on knowing everything. I was in the middle of trying to explain to her why I felt it was necessary to spend the night with Gloria when Martha entered the office and pulled up a chair.

"Sorry, Martha, Joey and I are having a private discussion," Jackie said.

"I overheard part of your conversation, and I think it also involves me."

"What makes you say that?" Jackie asked.

"We both know Joey slept with Gloria, and from what I've observed, you really don't care. Joey and I had a relationship before you came along, and when it looked like he chose you over me, I backed off."

"Martha, that's not fair, you found someone else," I said.

"A lot of good that did me."

"Joey, if I were you, I'd stay out of this," Jackie said and turned back to Martha. "If you're asking if you can see Joey outside of work, that's fine with me. Joey and I are business partners and friends, nothing more."

"Really? Then that's how things will be," Martha said, and she left the office.

Jackie stared at the door. "You were a big help. Why didn't you say something?"

At that moment, I longed for the simplicity of the battlefield where everything was black and white, good guy versus bad guy. Life was dangerous, but you focused on one thing—survival.

Sensing my hesitation, Jackie answered for both of us. "It hasn't been that long since my husband died. I know that sounds strange, given that he was a crook and tried to kill me, but I'm still dealing with his betrayal. I'm not sure I can trust a man ever again. Besides, I don't know what I want to do with my life, and I don't think you do either."

I thought I would feel relieved by her answer, but instead, I felt empty. "Are you saying you don't have a problem if Martha and I see each other again?"

"It's not ideal, but it's worked before. Like I said, it doesn't seem like either of us is ready to settle down. Besides, I like my job. I have no desire to sit at home changing diapers."

I pulled her closer, and as we kissed, I felt the knife harness she wore under her dress jacket. She definitely wasn't ready for motherhood.

* * * * *

Over the next few days I took full advantage of my perceived freedom, which was naïve. Inevitably, tensions developed around the office again, but this time I confronted the issue before things got out of control, or so I thought.

Martha came into the main office to discuss a couple of potential cases, and I found myself sitting between her and Jackie rather than in our usual circle. I moved my chair back and let them have it.

"This has gone far enough. I thought we made a deal that what goes on outside the office stays outside. We'll never solve a case if you two can't work together."

Neither of the girls said a word, refusing to acknowledge

the other. I took hold of their hands and tried again. "Look, I care for you both and would put my life on the line for either of you without hesitation, but I'm not ready to make a commitment. From what I understand, neither are you."

"Let me explain something to you," Jackie said. "Normally, if I were dating someone who had other girlfriends, it wouldn't bother me. But we all work in the same office and live in the same building. We know what's goin' on."

"I still don't understand. Martha has made it clear that she wants to settle down with someone with a more stable future and is waiting for the right guy to come along, and you and I have agreed that we're not ready for a deeper relationship. So what's the problem?" I left the office and closed the door.

Sadie sat behind Martha's desk and shook her head. "I couldn't help but overhear what you said, and believe me when I say you would have been better off letting them work things out on their own."

"Why would you say that?"

"Because—" Before she could finish, both office doors flew open. O'Reilly entered through one and Martha stormed out of the other.

Martha pushed O'Reilly aside and poked me in the chest. "You can get yourself another office manager," she said, slamming the door on the way out.

"While you're at it, find a new partner," Jackie said. She also left.

"Damn, you lead an exciting life, but you better get them back. All hell is breaking lose down at the waterfront, and we're gonna need their help," O'Reilly said, glancing over at Sadie.

I found the girls being corralled by Ma from the downstairs hallway into her apartment. "What's goin' on? I've never seen the two of you so angry," she said.

"Joey!" They both answered.

I stayed hidden, curious to hear what Ma would say.

"I know what the problem is, and there's only one solution," Ma said. "You both have to leave and find other jobs."

I was about to enter the room, when Ma nodded for me to stay away.

"I don't want another job," Martha said.

"Neither do I," Jackie said.

"Then I guess you'll just have to find a way to make things work," Ma said. She then waved me over. "Joey, the girls are in here if you're looking for them."

When I told them what O'Reilly had said, they followed me back to the office, more out of curiosity than anything else.

Upon entering, O'Reilly broke the news to us. "Donnelly was found this morning hanging from the same crane as Sadie's dad."

"Where's Castellano?" I asked.

"He's trying to calm the situation. The dockworkers are milling around aimlessly and remnants of the union are accusing him of all the recent murders."

"Why, when Donnelly worked for Castellano? And what possible motive would Castellano have for killing the fishermen?"

"He and Donnelly got into a shouting match yesterday in front of the longshoremen, and the rumor has resurfaced that the fishermen who were murdered had witnessed Castellano killing Kowalski."

"I *told* you he killed my father," Sadie shouted.

Martha and Jackie led Sadie to the couch in the inner office.

"You're not thinking straight. Castellano is not stupid enough to confront Donnelly in public and then have him killed," Jackie said.

I sat beside Sadie. "Do you want your life to get back to normal?"

She nodded.

"Then you need to go with us to the waterfront and show support for Castellano." Her eyes bulged, and tears trickled down her flushed cheeks.

"Someone is trying to destroy Castellano, and if that man is not successful this time, I'm certain you're his next victim," I said. "No one will believe Castellano didn't kill you for threatening him in public."

"Listen to Joey," O'Reilly said. "You need to convince everyone you no longer believe Castellano killed your father."

"How can any of you be so sure he had nothing to do with it?"

"You're letting your emotions get the better of you," I said. "Castellano has been the boss of this neighborhood our entire lives. How many mob killings have there been? I'm not saying he's a saint—he's not—but do you really believe he killed your father last year and then four more people in the last few weeks?"

"You're asking me to save Castellano's life."

"We're also asking you to save your own," Martha said.

* * * * *

Castellano stood alone atop a massive crate surrounded by a sea of angry men. Shots rang out from the rooftops, silencing the crowd. Castellano looked up and ordered his henchman to put away their weapons.

"I will not shed your blood to save mine," he shouted to the crowd.

The angry mob cautiously crept closer with clenched fists raised in defiance. Castellano calmly faced certain death, proclaiming his innocence, only to have his words washed out to sea on a tide of hatred.

We made our way back behind the commotion and helped Sadie climb on top of Castellano's crate. She stood next to him, then stepped forward, and raised her hands to the crowd. Suddenly, the squeal of seagulls filled the air as the mob fell silent.

"You knew my father and you know me," she shouted. "He fought for your rights. If my father was here, he would tell you to stop and think about what you're doing and why. O'Reilly and Batista tell me Castellano didn't kill my father or any of the other men, and I believe them. Someone in this crowd, possibly one of you or someone in Castellano's organization, or someone sitting in one of these building laughing at our stupidity, killed them."

Sadie turned toward Castellano, gave him a hug, and whispered, "If you killed my father, I will spit on your mangy carcass after I slit your throat."

The edges of the mob moved away. Castellano helped Sadie off the crate and into our outstretched arms. I held her close, kissed her gently on the cheek, and whispered, "I will not stop until your father has peace."

Chapter 23

A few days after the dock incident, Sadie felt safe enough to return to her own apartment. The girls and I had gathered around to say goodbye when Frank Galvano popped in to check if we'd made progress investigating the death of his client's aunt. The injunction imposed against dispersing her estate was scheduled to expire near the end of June.

Martha took the opportunity to ask Frank if he still needed a secretary. Jackie and I were surprised, since the three of us had been trying to work through our relationship issues. It was clear from our discussions that Martha and Jackie liked each other and that I had inadvertently upset Martha when I stopped asking her out once she dated others. And, they both had a problem with how eagerly I had seduced Gloria.

"Sure," Frank said. "I'll throw in an extra ten percent over whatever Joey's paying you." Frank looked over at me. "Nothing personal, Joey, but I hear you guys are on the outs. I'm trying to help."

Jackie grabbed Martha's arm and dragged her toward our office. She then turned to me.

"Don't just stand there with your mouth open. Get in here."

I asked Frank and Sadie to wait as I closed the door behind me. Jackie pushed Martha onto the couch, and when she tried to get up, she shoved her back down.

"I thought we had agreed to work together and not let the relationships between the three of us get in the way. We're a damn good team, and I'm not going to let us fall apart because we're not mature enough to deal with the feelings we have for each other. If necessary, we both need to quit dating Joey."

Martha tried to respond. "That's not necessary. I'm not—"

"Let me finish," Jackie said. "This is the first time in my life I'm doing something I like with people I care about and who care for me. You saved my life last year when I took one in the side and you held that crazed killer down so he couldn't get off another round. That took guts, because you're a lousy shot. What about the risk you just took to get me out of that house full of murderers so I wouldn't get caught in the crossfire when the shooting erupted? How the hell can we put our lives on the line for each other and then let jealousy destroy what we have together?"

Jackie turned her fury on me. "I'm telling you right now, if she leaves, I'm gone. You can run this so-called detective agency by yourself, and it would serve you right. Damn it, say something."

"Over the last few days, I've said all I can. I explained why I used Gloria the way I did, and you both know how I feel toward you. We're a great team, and I want us to stay together."

Martha wiped away a tear. "I'm not planning on leaving," she said. She called Frank and Sadie into the inner office.

"Thanks for the offer, Frank," Martha said. "But I was asking for Sadie. She's the one who needs to find work; she can type, take shorthand, and knows when to keep her mouth shut."

Frank turned to Sadie. "I didn't know you worked as a secretary."

"I never have, but I've learned from Martha these past weeks and I would like a chance."

"If I say no, these guys will never talk to me again. How about we give it a try for two months and then go from there?"

Sadie dropped her suitcase and gave Frank a crushing hug.

"Good," Martha said. "She can take notes as we update you on our progress."

I looked over at Jackie. She shrugged. Neither one of us had had the time to do anything on Frank's case.

* * * * *

I felt it was in Frank's best interest if he gave the case to another detective agency. "Stefano could rear up at any moment, so we need to stay on the offensive. I suggest you hire another detective," I said to Frank.

"Are you sure? The pay's great."

"How great?"

"Ten percent of the estate, split fifty-fifty."

"What if your client loses?" Jackie asked.

"Then there's no estate, but I'll still split everything fifty-fifty," Frank said with a smile.

"How much are we talking about?" I asked.

"She and her husband were loaded. My guess is twenty-five grand each, at least, if we win."

My gut still said to walk away until we got back to a normal routine.

"Would you and Sadie mind waiting outside again? We need to talk this over."

"Not a problem. Just come up with the right answer," Frank said.

I ushered them out and then asked the girls what they thought.

"I say stick with the case," Jackie said. "We really have only one active investigation."

"Explain."

"We already concluded Kowalski's killer is likely the same one who killed Donnelly and the fishermen. We know from the knife we found that somehow he hooked up with Stefano and that his primary motivation is to destroy Castellano."

"What about Gino's case?"

"He's waited over twenty years. I think he can wait a few more months."

Martha hadn't said anything, so I turned to her. She opened a folder she held on her lap.

"Sadie and I have been looking into Ruth's death, and based on the information Frank dropped off, we think there is a chance her nephew could win and have Ruth's will nullified."

Martha's initiative was impressive, but Stefano was still my biggest concern. I didn't see how I could focus on anything else until he was wearing a wooden kimono, and I said as much.

Jackie went over to the couch and sat next to Martha, "Don't forget," Jackie said. "I'm an equal partner in this agency, and so far you've been working Stefano by yourself. And from the sound of it, you'll have to deal with Ronnie's situation in Detroit on your own. Unless you want me twiddling my thumbs, I suggest Martha and I work Frank's case while you flush out Stefano."

I let out a deep sigh. Jackie took advantage of my hesitation and opened the door. She took charge of the conversation when Frank and Sadie entered.

"Martha and I will continue to investigate your case while Joey takes care of Stefano. Don't worry about a thing. We gotcha covered."

Martha opened her folder and went through the backgrounds of all the beneficiaries. When she was done, Frank insisted on weekly updates and the right to pull the case if he felt we weren't making progress. The girls agreed.

* * * * *

Martha and Jackie were huddled together in the outer office preparing to meet Frank to give him his first weekly update when Luigi strode past them with my sniper case. The girls dropped everything and followed him into my office.

"Hey, kid, I thought you might want this back. Your rifle's ready for action, cleaned and oiled by an expert."

"Speaking of experts, I've been meaning to thank you for saving my life back at the safe house. That was one hell of a shot."

"Which one?"

"When you dropped the creep by the outhouse. I didn't think you had the angle to get a clean shot."

"I didn't."

"You didn't have the angle or you didn't take the shot?"

"Both. I assumed you had someone backing us up who wanted to remain nameless, so I never said anything."

"What are you talking about? Who else could have been there?" Jackie asked, looking at me.

I only knew of one other person who could've made that

shot, Cafiero. He liked Jackie and might have followed me, knowing I'd find a way to rescue her.

"Cafiero's not who he said he was. He was a hired gun for anyone who would pay his price. He retired a few years ago and came to us because he suspected his cover was blown. He thought if he had us tail him, we would determine if he was being watched."

Jackie folded her hands in her lap and bit down on her lip as I spoke.

"That's crazy, he's an old guy. How could he be a button man?" Luigi asked in disbelief.

"That's what I thought. When I found Vic in his room, Cafiero was gone and so were his weapons, but he left behind several wigs and a make-up kit. He's probably a master of disguise, as well as a sharpshooter."

Jackie went over to Martha and tugged on her arm. "Let's go. We have to meet with Frank."

"That's all you have to say?" I asked.

"What do you want me to say? I spent months with this guy, feeling sorry for him, and you're telling me it was all an act and I fell for it."

"We all did. He's a professional."

"What about the limp?" she asked.

"It's real, which is why he retired."

"I don't believe it. Why didn't he save Vic if he was so good?"

"I wish I knew," I said, as Jackie walked out the door.

Moments later she barreled back, walked right up to me, and poked my chest. "I guess this means if I ever forget to tell you something important, you'll understand, because I sure as hell don't." She left to join Martha in Frank's office.

I knew Jackie had two sides to her personality, but normally she dealt with stress in a more refined manner.

Luigi had no sympathy for my predicament. He would pay any price to work with two gorgeous broads.

"You know, Joey, all good things in life come with a price tag," he said with a grin. "Sorry if I caused a problem."

"It's not your fault," I said, thinking that the shroud of sophistication Jackie wore when I first met her was quickly disappearing. Our cases pulled her back to an environment similar to the days of her childhood, homeless and fighting for survival. I had a feeling the longer she worked as a PI, the harsher she'd become.

"You got a minute? I could use some advice," I asked my uncle.

"About women? Forget it. I gave up trying to work that puzzle a long time ago."

"It's about Stefano. O'Reilly's not having luck tracking him down."

"Why are you relying on O'Reilly?"

"What else can I do?"

"Do you hear yourself? You're the guy that faced down the Chicago mob. Castellano owes you his life, not once, but twice. Your uncle Torrio is the biggest mobster in the country, and you're a trained assassin. Get off your ass and flush this guy out. Quit worrying about us. We can take care of ourselves. Go on the offensive. Isn't that what kept you alive in the war?"

Luigi's verbal beating made me realize my concern for everyone around me had actually increased the danger we faced. It was time to act.

Chapter 24

I had made arrangements with Maria, the owner of La Cucina Restaurant, for a private booth and a gourmet meal especially prepared for Martha, Jackie, and me. It was the first time I had invited both women out together, and their curiosity ran wild.

"Now that you filled us with delicious food and enough illegal booze to lower our resistance to your manly charms, we were wondering what you had in mind for the rest of the evening?" Jackie asked.

I felt a sudden surge of blood rush to my face, as they both reached for my hand. I couldn't help but marvel at how two women could look so different yet both possess the essence of natural beauty.

"You make it sound like I have some evil intent."

"Now that we've called a truce, we have been comparing notes, and it seems every time one of us has had dinner with you, we end up in bed," Martha said, squeezing my hand.

They both laughed as I fidgeted, looking over my shoulder to see if anyone could hear our conversation. "I'm beginning to think the two of you are too fast for me because that idea never crossed my mind, but it might eliminate some of the fits of jealousy that erupt from time to time."

"Not likely," Jackie said. "Let's stop fooling around and tell us what's goin' on."

"Stefano."

"What about him?"

"I can't wait around any longer. This is no way to live."

"What else can we do?" Martha asked.

"I want you and Jackie to stay close together, no matter what. I'm heading to Newark to see if I can track him down."

"Alone?" Jackie asked.

"Gino will be with me and—"

Martha moved closer. "Are you nuts? He's still a boozehound."

"He can get information I can't. No one notices a bum."

Jackie's eyes glazed as she pushed her chair back. I caught her hand and pulled her back down into her seat.

"Jackie, I need you and Luigi here to protect my parents and Rosalie. Frank is also counting on the both of you to solve his case, and we don't have much time."

"Your uncle is more than capable, and Martha is doing a great job on Frank's case. What's the real reason you don't want me along?"

"Stefano will recognize you from a block away, and he knows what you're capable of doing, so the element of surprise will be gone."

"Do you honestly believe Stefano won't remember what you look like when you shoved your face into his and told him it would be the last thing he'd see if he came after us?" Jackie said.

"I can disguise my features better than you can. Besides every guy looks at a beautiful dame," I said. "Don't forget, it was you who suggested we split our focus, and that I take on Stefano."

Jackie pulled her hand away and reached for a drink. "We shoulda killed the bastard when we had the chance."

I wanted to review Frank's case, and this was a good time to change the subject. "We need to get back to the PI business. We've spent most of this year trying to stay alive."

"I don't see anything wrong with that priority," Jackie said.

"That may be, but it doesn't pay the bills," I said, then turned toward Martha. "I missed the last meeting with Frank. How about giving me a rundown on what the two of you have learned?"

Martha had faded into the background while Jackie and I had our little spat, but she re-engaged with enthusiasm. She was in her element. She had the facts.

"At first it sounded like the beginning of a bad joke. Ruth Capelli, the old lady who got run over, left everything to her priest, her rabbi, her lawyer, her companion, and her chauffeur. She cut the nephew out completely."

"Why a priest and a rabbi?" I asked.

"Covering her bases, I guess. One or the other has to be right," Jackie said with a hint of a smile.

"Could be," Martha said. "Her husband was Catholic and she was Jewish. When he died, she still attended both the synagogue and the Catholic church."

"Why did she leave the butler, the maid, and the cook out of her will?" I asked, unable to hold back a chuckle.

"Actually, she didn't. The companion did all those jobs and more. They became good friends, and Ruth treated her like a daughter rather than a servant."

Jackie took on a more serious demeanor. "There were a few unusual occurrences prior to her death. For one, she had a blowup with her nephew."

"When did this happen?"

"Two to three weeks before her death," Jackie said. "She told him not to expect much when she passed away."

"Why?"

"We don't have the details yet. It seems he's been too busy to meet with us," Jackie said.

"What else?" I asked.

"Wait until you hear this," Martha said. "When her new will was completed, she held a dinner party for the beneficiaries and announced she was leaving her estate to them. The very next day, she was run over and died."

"Sounds like the old girl was a bit eccentric," I said.

"That's not all," Jackie said. "On the morning of her death, she called a new lawyer and made an appointment to change her will again."

"Let me make sure I have this straight," I said. "The first thing she did on the morning after she announced her new will was to hire a different lawyer to change her will again. Is that right?"

"Yes," they both said.

"How did you find all this out, and do you know the name of the new mouthpiece?"

"Remember Frank mentioned the wills, but he didn't know about the new lawyer," Jackie said.

"We searched her apartment, and I noticed a slip of paper behind the phone with a scribbled number and an appointment date. The appointment was for the same day she died. I called the number, and it was the new attorney," Martha said.

"What did he have to say?" I asked.

"I arranged a meeting to get more details, but he said he never met Ruth. She died on the way to his office."

Impressed, I asked what they planned next.

Martha picked up her drink and finished it off, while Jackie moved her glass in a circular pattern on the table.

"Before I answer that question," Jackie said, "I want to make sure Martha and I understand what's goin' on. You're gonna go off with Gino to somehow deal with Stefano. Then you're headed for Detroit to do God knows what to clear Ronnie of murder charges, all because Castellano owes him a favor. Do I have this right?"

"That's right," I said.

"Good, I'm glad we understand. My real question is, do *you* understand?"

"I don't get what you're sayin."

"When we leave this restaurant, Frank's case is mine. Not yours, not ours, mine. Unless I ask you for help or decide to give you an update, after tonight, you're not gonna hear anything about this case until the court hearing."

It was my turn to take a stiff drink. I always saw myself as the lead detective, but she had a point. I agreed. She then answered my question about her next steps.

"We will continue to interview each beneficiary individually to see if we can find inconsistencies and try to determine why Ruth changed her mind so dramatically after the dinner party. Martha will finish searching through her household and personal belongings to get more background information."

"I would pay particular attention to the lawyer who drew up the new will. It seems strange that she allowed him to write himself into the will," I said.

"He's not an actual beneficiary, but he gets a hefty retainer for administering her assets. He's to liquidate all her holdings," Jackie said.

"It does seem obvious that he's key to cracking this case,"

Martha said. "Ruth must have found out something during the night of the party that made her distrust him enough to change her will again with a different lawyer."

We continued talking over a few more drinks. When we left the restaurant, I let them know I had to hurry or I'd be late for a meeting with O'Reilly at my uncle's joint. I walked them back to the apartment building and promised I'd stop by the office before leaving for Jersey in the morning. As I looked over my shoulder, they remained on the stoop of the brownstone looking a little stunned. For a minute I wondered what it would have been like if we all had wound up in the sack together tonight, but I quickly dropped that thought—not after what we just went through to get our relationships back on track.

Chapter 25

Luigi and Castellano had joined O'Reilly at his table and were waiting for me to arrive.

I sat next to my uncle. "Castellano has news," he said.

"Word's come down from the top that Stefano is a marked man for pulling me into his vendetta against you," Castellano said.

"He's gone totally underground, disappeared," Luigi added. "Even the Jersey mob bosses have lost track of his whereabouts."

"Who put out the contract?" I asked.

Luigi smiled, "Your uncle Torrio."

"If he could do that, why the hell did he wait so damn long?"

"Whether you like it or not, Stefano has a right to avenge his brother's death. Torrio could protect you, as I have, but the other syndicate members would resent his interference if he eliminated Stefano just because you're his nephew," Castellano said. "Attacking me, a mob boss, without provocation is an altogether different issue."

I hadn't known I had another uncle until I had become entangled with the Chicago mob in one of my cases last year. My parents seldom talked about their families or life in the old country, but many of their secrets had unraveled as my work brought me closer to the criminal underworld. Ma's brother—Johnny Torrio, head of a large Chicago syndicate—is ruthless and has significant influence outside Chicago.

My first reaction to this news was relief until Luigi gave me a dose of reality. "Stefano's more dangerous than ever. He has nothing to lose." Castellano and O'Reilly agreed.

"Why? I would think he's long gone, on the run," I said.

"Where can he hide? He has a bundle on his head, but more importantly, whoever takes him out is instantly made. Every punk in the city with Mafia aspirations will be gunning for him, not to mention the professionals. No, he's a walking corpse, and he knows it," Castellano said.

O'Reilly put his mug down and wiped his mouth with the back of his forearm. "The way I see it, Stefano has two choices: he can cower and wait for the inevitable or go out in a blaze of glory. My guess is he will simply walk up to Joey or into your brownstone and blast away. As Luigi said, Stefano has nothing to lose."

Now I had mixed emotions about Torrio inserting himself into my business. He'd actually made matters worse. O'Reilly was right; Stefano would now take more risks to avenge his brother before someone collected the price on his head.

* * * * *

Rather than hitting the sack after the meeting at my uncle's joint, I stopped at the office to think things over. I felt on edge and knew a sleepless night awaited me. Upon entering the dark room, I noticed a stream of light beneath the inner office door. I drew my piece and cautiously approached. In a crouched position, I flung the door open and went in low, ready to fire. Jackie swiveled in her chair, fell forward to use her desk as cover, and reached for the shotgun she kept at arm's length.

"Whoa! It's me, Joey."

"You scared me to death," Jackie said.

Sorry, I didn't mean to startle you," I said, feeling a little ridiculous.

She placed the gun back against the wall, still chambered with the round she had racked when Luigi first gave her the weapon.

"I didn't expect anyone to be here."

"I couldn't sleep, so I came in to jot down a list of questions I might ask the lawyer in the morning," she said.

"You should get some rest. Tomorrow could be a long day."

"What about you? Flushing out Stefano in his own territory won't be easy."

"Things have changed. Stefano's on the run, and O'Reilly thinks he's coming this way."

"What happened?"

I told her everything Castellano had reported. She agreed Stefano was more dangerous now that his days were numbered and didn't blame me for reacting the way I did when I saw a light in the office late at night.

We discussed how to anticipate Stefano's next move and ways to flush him out of hiding. We called it a night after it became clear we were both too tired to think clearly. Jackie came to me, and we embraced for a long moment. I thought I heard a slight sob, but if I did, she quickly brought her emotions under control and snaked her arms around my neck. She gently pulled me down so our lips would meet. If I hadn't bent her back slightly as we kissed, my head would have exploded. A bullet shattered the office window and grazed my scalp. We collapsed to the floor, still in an embrace. More rifle shots rang out. Moments later the sound of semiautomatic pistol fire followed. A gun battle raged on the rooftop across the street, but it didn't last long. My guess was that Castellano's men had closed in on the sniper.

Luigi and Pop rushed into the office low to the ground and helped Jackie and me slither to a safer position away from the windows. Suddenly, Martha came running into the main office wrapped in a bathrobe. Before she could utter a word, I lunged, driving my shoulder into her midsection as a barrage of bullets whistled past. Sprawled on the hallway floor, entangled in each other's arms, I pushed her out of the line of fire and yelled for her to stay put.

I didn't have time to explain what was going on; this was my chance to get Stefano. It had to be him taking those shots.

I leapt down the stairs and tumbled into Ma and Rosalie on the second-floor landing as they ran toward the commotion. I shuffled them to Ma's apartment and then ran out the back into a pitch-black alleyway. The street looked deserted, and the surrounding apartments had their shades drawn. Gunfire was no stranger in and around this neighborhood, so everyone knew to hunker down.

The shots had come from directly across the street, a building I knew well. The heavy steel door to the roof would stop a .45 with ease, so I used it to shield my left side as I peered into the darkness. A body lay in a pool of blood in front of me and another not far from the two-foot brick wall that lined the edge of the building. Castellano's men had been no match for Stefano.

Skirting around the various structures on the roof for cover, I assured myself that Stefano had gone. Rather than leave,

I sat behind a chimney, not far from the stairwell, which gave me a clear view of the fire escapes in case Stefano doubled back.

The night air swirled briskly, making it difficult to keep warm. I had just pulled the coat from the dead body that lay before me when Pop shoved the metal door open and stood silhouetted against the backdrop of the lit stairwell.

"Are you crazy? Get down," I shouted.

He dropped into a squat. "You need to get the hell off this roof. O'Reilly called; the DA will be here any minute."

We slipped into the alleyway that led to the back of our building moments before several cop cars converged from both ends of the street and screeched to a halt in front of Pop's shop. The DA emerged from his car once the area was secured. He had several of his officers take statements from bystanders congregated around our stoop, while he came directly to my office.

Rosalie was wrapping Martha's bruised ribs with thick gauze when the DA barged into her office.

"What are you looking at?" Martha snapped.

"Just tell me what happened?"

"Ask Joey, he's in the other room. He has the decency to give me some privacy while I'm getting patched up."

"So, he's alive. Too bad, I was looking forward to saying a few words at his wake. If I'd known, I would've stayed in bed."

I was digging several bullets out of the wall when the DA entered.

"Why am I not surprised to see you so soon after Joey and I almost got killed?" Jackie said.

"Too bad you didn't come by earlier, maybe one of these would be buried in your skull instead of the wall," I said, with my back to him, as the last slug popped into my hand. "But don't misunderstand me, we appreciate your personal involvement. Nice to know you're watching over us."

"I have to admit I was hoping for a different outcome. The switchboard is jammed with frantic calls about bullets ricocheting off buildings and hitting innocent bystanders. What happened?" the DA asked, looking down as his shoes pulverized the broken glass from the shattered window.

I had expected him to arrest me for some trumped-up charge long before now, which made me concerned because the more time he took to take revenge for what happened at the safe house, the tighter the noose would fit.

"Someone took a few shots at us from across the street," I said.

I dropped the mangled bullets into his outstretched palm. "You wouldn't happen to know anything about it?"

"I don't have a beef with the girls, just you. Anyone hit?"

"I had to tackle Martha to get her out of the line of fire. She has a few bruised ribs. Other than that, no one's hurt."

"You're bleeding," he said pointing to my head.

Blood trickled down my fingers when I touched the side of my forehead. "Just a flesh wound."

"I swear, Batista, you have nine lives. One of these days your luck's gonna run out, and I hope I'm around to enjoy the moment."

O'Reilly and two other homicide detectives came into the office.

"What did ya find?" the DA asked.

"Two bodies on the roof across the street, both shot with a .45. We also picked up a few shell casings from a rifle," O'Reilly said.

The DA ordered me to hand over my guns. Neither had been fired.

"Did you recognize the bodies?" he asked O'Reilly.

"I've seen them around. They both work for Castellano."

The DA put my guns on the desk. "Who's after you, Batista?"

"Bobby Stefano."

"I thought he was in the slammer."

"He got out several weeks ago."

"Now I remember, you shot his brother. I guess I'm not gonna have to worry about you much longer. I just love how life works out sometimes," he said with a nasty grin.

"You have a short memory. I didn't kill Tommy Stefano."

"Oh, that's right. Some mystery guy came along with a rifle and shot him in the back from across the street. I'm sure when you explain that to his brother, he'll just leave town."

The DA ordered his men out. "One of these days, Batista, an innocent bystander is going to get killed, and that's when I'll pull your PI ticket. That's if I don't get you for murder first. It's just a matter of time, just a matter of time."

Chapter 26

Torrio doubled the price on Stefano's head when he heard about the shooting. This had the negative effect of bringing even more wiseguys to the neighborhood, eager to make some easy dough and move up in the ranks of the syndicate.

Except for the gangsters, the streets remained deserted, which devastated the local shops. Their regular customers stayed inside or conducted their business elsewhere. To make matters worse, Castellano changed tactics in an attempt to safeguard his men. He had them hang out by the stores and stoops during the day and then move inside the buildings at night. Something had to give.

For two days we waited for Stefano to make his next move, a strategy that frayed everyone's nerves, especially mine. As Luigi had said, the army had trained me to go on the offensive and to be the aggressor under any and all circumstances. It was time to put that experience to use.

"This is ridiculous. We need to go find the bastard," I said to no one in particular.

O'Reilly was having lunch with the family and took issue with my statement.

"I know what you're thinking, but believe me, you won't stand a chance. He's watching and knows our every move. Be patient. Someone will drop a dime on him. He can't hide forever."

I got up and threw my napkin on the table. "I don't have forever. Someone is helping him and that someone is the same person who killed Kowalski and the others."

"What makes you say that?" Ma asked.

We hadn't told her everything we knew about Kowalski's killer, so I had to explain how we found Jackie's knife stuck in one of the dead fishermen, and that it was the same knife Jackie had used during our first run-in with Stefano.

"Let's assume Joey's right and that Stefano's hiding in the neighborhood. Where can he be?" Jackie asked.

"If Kowalski's killer and Stefano have hooked up, they could be hiding out together," Luigi said.

"Nah, the guy who killed Kowalski is too smart for that. If we found Stefano, we'd find him. Too risky," O'Reilly said, in between spoonfuls of minestrone soup.

"I agree," Martha said. "But we can assume he knows where Stefano is holed up. Let's go over what we know about the guy who killed Kowalski."

She didn't wait for anyone else to answer.

"We all believe whoever killed Kowalski and the others is out to bring down Castellano, but he doesn't want him dead, at least not yet. He was able to make contact with Stefano, so he must have mob connections. If you put those two facts together, then our fella either works for Castellano, is a member of his family, or is someone in the Mafia with a personal grudge against him."

"You've got one smart secretary," Pop said to me.

"Office manager. I'm an office manager, not a secretary."

"Sorry, but you still haven't explained to me exactly what an office manager does. A secretary I understand."

"I told you before, it sounds better than a secretary, and I do a hell of a lot more," Martha said.

Jackie cut the banter short. "I think Martha's onto something. If she's right, then whoever is helping Stefano is familiar with the neighborhood. So where would he hide Stefano, if not in his apartment?"

"It would have to be close by because Stefano can't risk being seen when he makes his next move," Luigi said.

Ma placed more food on the table and said, "An abandoned building would be a good spot."

Pop dug into his pasta and mumbled his thoughts. "We don't have that many vacant buildings in the neighborhood, and the few we have are overrun by street bums."

"I think the bombed-out union offices would make a great place to lay low. They've been fenced off for safety concerns, so no one can wander in without making a racket, giving him plenty of warning," Martha said.

"That's a possibility, and so are the two pier warehouses scheduled for demolition," I said, excited that we were breaking out of our protective shell and thinking more aggressively.

"Let's not forget that Stefano was sent up for a bank job and the dough was never found. I think we can assume he didn't leave Jersey without a stash and can use it to pay for a safe haven," O'Reilly said.

"That opens up a whole slew of possibilities. I suggest we check out the piers and union offices first and think about that angle later," I said.

O'Reilly agreed to meet Jackie and me at Pier 15, after his shift, to poke around the gutted union offices.

* * * * *

To the casual out-of-town observer, Jackie and I were

taking an evening stroll toward the waterfront, arm-in-arm. But those who lived in the apartment buildings and peered through their curtains or leaned over the railing of their fire escapes, saw a different sight. They knew no one walked the streets at night without a compelling reason. It wasn't safe.

They would notice that we each had a hand under our coats and the way our gazes constantly shifted from rooftop to rooftop and into alleyways, and the way we cautiously approached each corner. The neighborhood had a built-in sense about danger and could tell when the hunted were hunting and when all hell was about to erupt. By the time we reached Waters Street, most window shades had been drawn and the sound of door bolts ramming home cascaded down the street, followed by an unusual silence, a silence that would warn Stefano we were coming.

* * * * *

O'Reilly waved for us to join him in the shadow of a tugboat silhouetted by the glow of a full moon. The moonlight had transformed the waterfront into a weird array of distorted shapes that would normally reside in childhood nightmares. We moved cautiously, knowing that a stream of moonlight illuminating any part of our bodies could bring the shattering sound of death.

O'Reilly went around the back of the bombed-out union offices and motioned for us to take the front. I indicated to Jackie to cover me while I hopped the fence. I had reached the top metal bar and pulled myself up on the fence when Jackie noticed the locking arm of the padlock holding the gate shut had been sheared. She opened the gate and waited in the shadows for me to finish making a racket. The fence shook each time I shifted my weight to get a toe hold. If Stefano was in the building, I expected him to open fire any second, so I dropped to the ground and moved to take cover with Jackie. We listened for any movement—half expecting Stefano to run out the back—but all we heard was a scratching sound that came from deep within the buildings. The water rats had already taken possession of the structures.

Jackie moved to position herself next to the adjacent building. I reached for her shoulder, thinking it wasn't wise for us to separate. At that instant, a metal can tumbled to the ground and two alley cats flew at each other, screeching in the darkness. Jackie leaped back and stumbled into my arms.

"Let's stay together," I said.

She nodded and followed me into the first building. The bomb blast that went off during the union riots had been effective in obliterating everything in the room. Wooden slats hung from the ceiling where the plaster had been reduced to dust, and cabinets lay on their sides with drawers mangled and their contents strewn across the floor. Donnelley's desk resembled a pile of discarded scraps tossed into a corner. With each step, glass fragments crunched under foot.

The back rooms were relatively unscathed, except for the windows blown out from the concussion. Jackie pushed down on my shoulder, holding me back from entering the last room. There was a presence huddled in a far corner.

"Step into the moonlight with your hands up," Jackie ordered.

A hunched-over bum shuffled from the darkness toward us, bedroll clutched to his chest, weeping gently.

Spittle dripped from the old man's discolored beard as he stammered, "Please don't shoot. I'll leave. The gate wasn't locked. Honest, I didn't break in."

"Sorry, old timer. We didn't mean to scare ya. Have you seen anyone around lately?" I asked.

"Nope, just some rats, the four-legged kind."

O'Reilly joined us. "The other side's all clear. Doesn't look like our man's been around," he said, as we walked to the front of the building.

A thunderous boom fractured the sounds of the sea lapping against the pilings and the seagulls' never-ending feeding frenzy. O'Reilly and I reacted simultaneously. He threw himself against a wall, and I yanked Jackie to the ground. Bullets struck the floor not far from my face, sending fragments of concrete into the air. I shielded my eyes with my forearm, and when I looked up, I saw the bum lifted off his feet and thrown back from a bullet's impact. He landed hard on his ass, and then his head flew back, smashing onto the floor.

Jackie jerked loose from my grip and clawed over me toward the body. I caught her around the waist and rolled to my left, flinging her against the wall. More shots rang out.

I held her down with one hand and shifted to a crouched position close to her head. "He's dead. Stay here and give us cover."

O'Reilly and I started to move deeper into the building to exit out the back.

"Where is he?" Jackie asked.

"He's on top of the pier across the street. I don't have time to explain. When you hear me whistle, aim high and open fire," I said to her.

I was several feet behind O'Reilly. He turned left, so I

took the right side. When we were at the edge of the building by the fence, I gave Jackie the signal to shoot. O'Reilly and I made it across the street and into the covered pier without incident. The full moon provided some light, but faded fast behind a moving cloud. We cleared the front half of the building and waited for the moonlight to return. After a few minutes, O'Reilly decided to go on the prowl again. We had to act fast or Stefano would get away. In the darkness, the shipping crates grew larger with each step, and the sounds of the wharf melded together making it difficult to hear that scrape or bump that might save our lives. With each step deeper into the maze of disfigured shapes, I felt my survival instincts heighten my sense of awareness and agility.

O'Reilly made it to the night watchmen's utility shack at the end of the pier, while I stayed back in the shadows to protect our flank. Seconds turned into an eternity when suddenly I noticed a shadowy presence weave between crates near the entrance of the pier. I waited and listened, concentrating on the sounds. A pattern of movement emerged. I took aim where he would be next, steadied my arms on top of a small crate and inched back the trigger.

The moonlight broke through the clouds again and streamed through the skylights. Jackie froze. I eased up on the trigger. "Cops are coming from all directions," she shouted.

O'Reilly came out of the shack. "The night watchman's dead. We better scram."

"There should be a dinghy tied up at the end of the pier for the watchman to use," I said.

O'Reilly looked out over the edge of the pier. "My guess is that's how our friend got away."

"The DA's about to get his wish, two dead bystanders, and we're between both of them," Jackie said.

"I'll try to stall the cops. I suggest you two go for a swim," O'Reilly said.

He headed toward the entrance, leaving Jackie and me standing on the edge of the dock about to jump into the freezing water to swim to the next pier when we heard Luigi's voice. "You guys better get your asses in this boat and fast."

None of us knew where the hell Luigi came from, and we weren't about to ask with the cops closing in. Luigi and I each took an oar and rowed the small boat two piers over to where O'Reilly had his patrol car parked. He waited until all the police cars passed in the opposite direction and then drove with his lights out for a few blocks.

He dropped us off in front of our brownstone but held Luigi back for a minute. "How the hell did you know we were in a jam?" O'Reilly asked.

"You really think I would let these two go after that nut without me?"

"Where did ya get the boat?" I asked.

"A good customer of mine is one of the night watchmen on duty tonight, so I borrowed his dinghy. He took off running when he heard the first shot. I never saw an old guy run so fast."

O'Reilly drove back to the crime scene, but not before giving us some advice. "You better clean Jackie's gun. I'm sure the DA will show up on your doorstep."

Ma and Pop stood on the stoop with the front door open.

"When we heard the gunfire, we were worried you walked into an ambush. Tell us what happened. I have hot coffee and food on the table," Ma said.

Jackie followed them into the kitchen, and I wasn't far behind when Luigi nudged me past their apartment door.

"I know where Stefano's hiding," he said, and then joined Jackie, leaving me standing in the hallway wondering why he had left me hanging.

Chapter 27

Bad news travels especially fast in an ethnic community and has the effect of galvanizing support to deal with both external threats and internal needs. I soon discovered, though, the solidarity in our neighborhood had reached its breaking point with the death of the night watchman and the bum. It didn't make any difference that they were killed by Stefano. In the eyes of the neighborhood, Jackie and I were responsible.

Once we gave the details of our encounter with Stefano, Ma knew to expect a full house. The first thing she did was place several pints of whiskey in the center of the table. To my surprise, Jackie reached for a bottle first and threw back two shots without saying a word. She turned the glass over and gently placed it in front of her. Staring off, she swiped her hands across her cheeks to brush away several tears.

"He was a harmless old man who didn't deserve to die. That bullet was meant for one of us," she said to no one in particular.

I had seen many sides of Jackie during the past year, but never this one. She was passionate, aggressive, and surprisingly deadly—a product of poverty and the worst that Chicago had to offer. She was hard and normally kept her emotions locked down tight inside. Not knowing what to say, I simply put my arm around her shoulder and pulled her close.

I looked over to Luigi, and he shook his head. This wasn't the time to discuss what he'd seen at the pier. He picked up a bottle and filled everyone's glass.

"Let's not forget this life is part of a longer journey. Some will rejoice and some will suffer after death. My hope is that those who died tonight will rejoice." He lifted his glass, and we all did likewise, except for Jackie.

"What are we waiting for? We know Stefano's in the neighborhood. Why aren't we out there searching rather than makin' meaningless toasts?" she said.

"You and Joey tried that and look what it's gotten us. That discussion will have to wait until Castellano and O'Reilly arrive," Luigi said. "Now, I suggest we get some of Ma's food in our stomachs, or we'll drink ourselves into oblivion."

Not one to hesitate, he ripped the end off a loaf of Italian bread and stuffed it with homemade sausage.

* * * * *

Soon Martha and the rest of the household, including Frank, joined us, followed by Castellano and two of his bodyguards, who stood watch by the main entrance to the apartment building.

We had just moved into the living area when Tony the Butcher peeked into the room from the hallway. Pop greeted his old friend.

"Tony, come in. Nice to see ya."

Tony stood in the doorway and removed his hat, tightly gripping the rim with both hands. He looked around the gathering and stiffened when he saw Castellano.

"Maybe I shoulda come another time."

Tony had come alone, without his wife, so his dropping in

unexpectedly wasn't a social call. Since he had been recently elected president of the local shop owners' association, I suspected Tony had a message to deliver.

"You're among friends. If you have something important on your mind, we need to hear it," I said.

Pop offered him a drink and a stogie. He refused both.

"Joey, what I have to do is not easy. I've known you since a *bambino,* and it hurts me to say these things, but the neighborhood—she is afraid. Too much shooting, too many dead people, and now tonight, they are our own."

Ma brought him a glass of water, and he took two long gulps. "We, the shop owners, we got together."

Pop erupted. "What am I? Am I not a shop owner? Didn't I make those shoes you're wearing? Why wasn't I told about this big meeting?"

Beads of sweat formed on Tony's forehead. "Vito, please, you must understand. We talked about your son, and you would just argue. This is expected."

Pop plopped back into his seat. "Finish what the hell you came to say and leave."

"Don't you mind him," Ma said. "He's just a grumpy old man like the rest of you. Tell us what the shop owners want."

"They want that Joey should move his detective agency. All our businesses are down. People... they go to other streets to shop. We have hoodlums roaming the neighborhood, day and night." Tony glanced at Castellano. "These are not people we know who are here to protect us. We think Joey should set his business up in another part of town."

I leaned over with my elbows on my knees for support. It felt like a sledgehammer had slammed into my gut. I knew the shop owners were right, and that it was difficult for Tony to deliver such a message. I started to move toward him when I saw Ma stiffen and walk quickly into the kitchen. Before I could turn to see what had caused her reaction, I heard slow, rhythmic clapping.

"What a shame. The old neighborhood is no longer a safe haven, is it, Joey?" The DA came from behind my chair with a vicious smile. "In fact, some of your so-called neighbors told my men that you and Jackie were down by the waterfront tonight. You know, a few weeks ago no one around here would even speak to a cop. Thanks to you, all that's changed."

"How the hell did you and your minions get in here?" I said, tossing my chair aside.

Luigi grabbed my arms and pulled me back. "Easy, Joey. He'd like nothing better than for you to kiss him one."

"Your uncle's right. Striking an officer of the court would get you at least two years in the slammer. I suggest you take a seat and calm down. I'll answer your question. Castellano's boys made the wise decision not to stop us from entering the building. The rest was easy because your door was unlocked. You should be careful about that. You never know when Stefano might make another move."

He lit a smoke and pulled up a chair so we were face to face. "Now, unless you want to spend the night in a cell, I suggest you answer *my* question. Were you down by the waterfront tonight?"

"We took a short stroll. Is that against the law?"

"Only if you do something illegal, like killing a few people."

"Are you accusing us?"

"No, no, of course not, but you and Jackie need to hand over your guns. You see, having a permit in this town is a privilege, and since there are two stiffs not far from here, I'm obligated to check."

The assistant DA removed the iron from my shoulder holsters and then stood in front of Jackie.

"Mrs. Forsythe, your gun please," the DA said.

The color drained from Jackie's face.

"Mrs. Forsythe, did you hear me?"

"It's in my coat, in the kitchen," Jackie said.

One of the cops returned with the weapon, then took mine from the assistant DA and proceeded to disassemble them. We all waited in silence.

"They haven't been fired," he said.

"Have they been cleaned recently?" the DA asked.

"No, the oil isn't fresh and there's no powder residue."

A homicide detective entered the room and whispered in the DA's ear, and then he left.

"Batista, your luck continues to amaze me. Whoever killed your neighbors used a rifle and shot one of them from the roof of the warehouse across from the old union offices. We found the spent shells. They were the same caliber as the ones from the night you were grazed. Sorry to break up your little meeting, but I must say, I enjoyed every minute," the DA said. He led his men out.

Martha tapped the assistant DA on the shoulder. As he turned, she socked him with a wicked right-cross.

"That's for dumping me, you spineless creep."

The DA laughed. "A scorned woman is a dangerous enemy," he said and then turned to Luigi. "It looks like you've moved your speakeasy to this apartment. If you want to stay in business, it's now gonna cost you fifteen percent."

No one spoke until we heard the main door to the building slam shut. Luigi swore. I looked over at Jackie, and she shrugged. Seeing our confusion, Ma pulled her gun from her thigh holster.

"Jackie had mentioned she did all the shooting tonight. So when I saw the DA, I stepped into the kitchen and swapped guns."

Luigi went to her and planted a kiss on her forehead. "Vito, my brother, the reason I'm still a bachelor is because I could never find a woman like your wife."

Pop handed Luigi a drink and said, "The reason you never got married is because any woman like my wife would have sense enough not to marry you."

Tony shook his head and got up to leave. "Please, think about what I said before someone else gets killed."

* * * * *

Ma cleared off the plates and placed two more bottles of hooch on the table. Luigi looked to see how many she had left.

"We're about to run out," I said. "Would you mind if I come by your new drum and grab a couple of cases?"

"Guess until I pay you back, the speakeasy is technically yours."

I was surprised by his answer. "You don't think I was serious about that loan business?"

"Just making sure. Arguments over cabbage have broken up many a family. Take what you need. You don't have to ask anymore. I drink more than my share anyway."

While Luigi and I needled each other, another bottle made the rounds. We got down to some serious drinking, waiting for O'Reilly.

* * * * *

The women had staggered to bed long before O'Reilly arrived, except for Jackie. Determined to wait up, she fell asleep on the sofa before he joined us.

O'Reilly pulled up a chair and helped himself to two quick shots.

"The DA came back to the pier in one hell of a bad mood. What happened during his little visit?" he asked.

Pop made Ma sound like Jackie's guardian angel. I filled in the part about the store owners voting to banish me from the neighborhood.

"Your ma is a clever woman. I wouldn't want to match wits with her, or to be honest, with any member of your family."

"I think that's how Stefano will soon feel. My uncle has some news he's been waiting to tell everyone. Isn't that right, Uncle?" I said.

Luigi drew back a shot of whiskey and took his time putting the glass down. "I know where Stefano is holed up."

Castellano shot out of his chair and leaned across the table. "What the hell have you been waiting for? That son-of-a-bitch killed two of my men—men who were protecting you and your family."

"He's not going anywhere tonight, not with the cops swarming all over the waterfront."

Castellano smashed his fist down, and his face flushed. "What makes you so damn sure?"

Luigi shoved his chair aside and shouted back. "I saw him get into the watchman's dinghy and row out to a tugboat anchored a short distance from shore."

"For all we know that tug can be anywhere along the Hudson by now," Castellano shouted.

My uncle had his hackles up. "We've been through this already. With the bundle Torrio put on his head, Stefano's a dead man, and he knows it. His only thought is to kill Joey to avenge his brother before he gets his. He's not goin' anywhere, and the last thing we need is for you to send out your goons and get more innocent people killed."

"Luigi's right," O'Reilly said. "A tugboat gives Stefano a significant advantage. If he's still on it, it'll be difficult to surprise him, and there's no room to maneuver. Watch and wait, then take him out when he comes ashore."

Gino suddenly stood up, poured his shot of whiskey that he'd been staring at the entire time back into the bottle, and said, "I'll do it."

"Do what?" Luigi asked.

"Keep a watch on the boat. I'll get my bedroll and flop down at the end of the pier."

Gino, you don't need to get involved. We'll find a way to keep an eye on him," I said.

"I'm already involved. He killed a friend of mine tonight and almost killed you. I couldn't prevent the murder of my family years ago, but I can do this. What's more natural than a bum hanging around?"

Pop hadn't said a thing since the women left the room, but when he spoke, there was no arguing.

"Castellano, I hate to admit it, but I agree with Luigi. If you go after Stefano with your men, word will get out, and we'll have a whole flotilla of small boats converging on that tugboat. Every trigger-happy hood from Manhattan to the Bronx is itching to claim the reward on Stefano's head. They'll be shooting at their own shadows."

"So what should I do? Let that lunatic get away with

killin' two of my guys? And don't forget, it was Stefano's man who shot me in the shoulder."

"Joey," Pop said. "This is your problem. You need to show the neighborhood you can protect them from slime like Stefano, and you must help Castellano avenge his men."

Gino sat back down. All eyes were on me, including O'Reilly's. I could tell he agreed with Pop. There was only one way to solve this problem, and from the look on everyone's face, they had come to the same conclusion. Somehow I had to bring Stefano to Castellano so *he* could take him out, and do it without every wiseguy in town knowing what was goin' down.

"Castellano, can you take Stefano in a fair fight?" I asked.

"In my younger days, but I'm not in shape like your pop. But that's not a problem. No one expects me to dirty my hands. Butch can do it."

I turned to O'Reilly. "Is Pier 17 still a crime scene?"

"Nope, commerce has priority in this town."

I knew what I needed to do and how to get it done. I outlined my plan to capture Stefano and bring him to face Butch. Castellano agreed to have Butch at the end of the pier a half hour past sunrise, and Luigi committed to having everything I requested in less than an hour, while I got my gear ready to confront Stefano.

Now it was up to me to deliver the goods.

Chapter 28

The new night watchman avoided the utility shack, which was still streaked with blood. He mainly hung out near the front of the pier, sitting among some crates for shelter. Castellano struck up a conversation with the guy while Luigi and I slipped past. Anxious to estimate the distance I would have to swim, we went past the shack to the end of the pier. Luigi pointed toward the main shipping lane but didn't say anything.

"What's wrong?" I asked.

"More ships have dropped anchor since I saw Stefano row to his boat. I don't know which one he's on."

With so many ships silhouetted against the Staten Island shoreline, the situation looked hopeless. Castellano had been right. Luigi should have acted quicker. Frustrated, we reluctantly abandoned our plan. Halfway down the pier, Luigi turned and ran back toward the shack. He had remembered he'd seen a buoy a little beyond the stern of the tug. Looking out over the bay again we counted three boats near a buoy and only one was a tugboat. Once I had my bearings, we entered the shack to prepare for my swim.

Luigi helped me rub axle grease over my body. Although it's a terrific insulator in frigid water and great for night maneuvers, it has its drawbacks. If the grease gets on my hands and feet, I'll never survive hand-to-hand combat. It's also difficult as hell to remove. I wore a black pair of skivvies over the grease, a utility belt, and my military-issued rubber gloves and webbed socks to protect my hands and feet from the cold, and to provide the maneuverability I'd need to take down Stefano.

"You sure this stuff's gonna work? That water's pretty damn cold," Luigi said.

"Just be here to help scrub this gunk off when I return. I don't want to miss the fight between Butch and Stefano."

I descended the ladder attached to the end of the pier and was about to enter the water when Luigi leaned over the side. "Hey kid, don't take any chances. If you can't subdue Stefano quickly, kill the bastard."

I waved and then glided into the murky water. I had prepared myself to confront a full crew, but suspected I'd really only have to deal with Stefano and the captain. With a Mafia contract on his head, Stefano would be nuts to involve more seamen. My uncle didn't have to worry. I wasn't about to risk my life for the sake of Castellano's honor. I had several means available to take down Stefano or anyone else on board.

We had underestimated the distance to the tug, making the swim more difficult than I'd anticipated. To keep my bearings I had to tread water every few hundred feet. Each time I stopped, the cold penetrated the grease, and my limbs stiffened. By the time I pulled alongside the hull, my hands were numb, and I barely had the strength to claw up the towlines coiled along the length of the tug.

I crouched down in the stern against the hatchway that led below deck to the crew quarters. I then maneuvered my way to the base of the wheelhouse, where the captain likely had his berth. Resting against the cold steel, I took a swig from a flask Luigi had given me and immediately felt a surge of warmth careen to my extremities. Hot tea with whiskey was just what I needed. I had always suspected Luigi had an interesting past. As I sucked out the last few drops of whiskey, I wondered if he'd ever taken any clandestine, late night swims of his own in freezing waters.

I was hesitant to move again until I became familiar with my surroundings. I controlled my breathing and focused on the sounds of the tug. At first it was difficult to hear anything other than the humdrum of the city skimming across the water's surface. But soon those sounds faded into the background. My heart rate slowed, and with it, my hearing became more selective. The sound of the anchor chain grating against the metal-lined portal was replaced with the creaking of the boat's wooden structures and the sound of ropes shifting along the hull. Then I heard it. It was close, very close. I held my breath and waited. It came again—the low resonance of someone snoring. I made my move.

The hinges of the wheelhouse door groaned when I pushed down on the rusted handle and pushed against the massive metal door. I had to move quickly. The noise brought the captain out of a deep sleep. I can only imagine the thoughts that ran through his mind when a ray of moonlight reflected off the whites of my eyes. He froze long enough for me to reach his gun, which was lying on a side table. He was lucky—if he had moved faster, he'd be dead.

It didn't take long to immobilize the captain and begin my search for Stefano. The smart thing would've been to wait until dawn, but time was running out. At the first sign of sunrise, the waterway would come alive.

I made sure Stefano wasn't on deck and then descended into the bowels of the tug. With each step, I moved deeper into an intense darkness. As my pupils strained to adjust, my other senses sharpened. I grasped a wooden railing and cautiously moved along the narrow corridor, stopping at the entrance to the first cabin.

I held onto the frame of the door and pressed my ear against the surface, listening for any sound. About to push back from the next-to-last cabin door, I heard a click. Light streamed into the corridor from beneath the threshold. I slithered over to the adjacent doorway, pressed my back against the cold surface, and held my breath. Stefano's massive outline suddenly reflected on the wall, backlit by his cabin light. He entered the corridor and walked toward the head, which was directly opposite me. Sensing a presence, he released the handle to the john and flung his elbow back toward my face. I avoided the blow, slipped in behind him, and landed two punches to his kidneys. He spun around, grabbed for my chest, and came away with fistfuls of grease. In his confusion, I pummeled his gut with little effect, but it gave me the chance to deliver a foot thrust to his chest. He slipped on some grease, crashing to the floor. He lashed out wildly, kicking his bare feet, preventing me from getting close enough to restrain him. One of his kicks slammed into my shin, buckling my knee. He turned over and grabbed a handrail. The grease on his hands prevented him from getting a firm grip. Panicked, he stumbled along the corridor onto the stairwell, clawed his way up the steps, and disappeared into the night.

Not far behind, I hung close to the wall to avoid the streaks of grease he left behind. When I emerged from the opening, a grappling hook flew past and clanged down the stairs. I grabbed the attached rope and pulled with such ferocity that Stefano again lost his footing and fell flat on his face. I was on him in a second, grabbed the grappling line, and looped it twice around his neck. He jerked me off his back and groped for the rope. I yanked hard, pulling Stefano in my direction. I tried to keep the tension tight by backing away from the stairwell, but he was too strong. He tugged on the other end of the rope to get some slack and was about to unravel the last loop around his neck when the grappling hook caught on one of the steps. I pulled with every ounce of strength I could summon. He lost his balance, and his legs slid out from under him. The more he struggled, the more the pressure on his neck increased, cutting off his air supply.

I pounced, pressed my foot into the middle of his back, and coiled the rope several more times around his neck. In my haste I let up on the tension, giving him an opening. He gripped the rope with both hands behind his neck, but I had too much leverage. This time he blacked out. I cut the rope free from the grappling hook and hogtied his legs, preventing any movement. I secured his hands behind his back with a cord I had brought along. He wasn't about to go anywhere.

* * * * *

The captain of the tug had no loyalty to Stefano. He agreed to dock the boat at Pier 17 if I didn't turn him over to the police. Fortunately, the sun hadn't come up yet when we docked. I had time to remove the axle grease before Castellano arrived with Butch. Luigi and Pop helped tie up the boat and placed Stefano in the watchman's utility shack while I went below deck to shower. I was still struggling to remove the grease when suddenly the shower curtain pulled back, and I found myself facing Martha and Jackie.

I was speechless, but the girls had plenty to say. They

each brandished a scraper, yellow laundry soap, and a scrubbing brush.

Martha couldn't control her laughter. "Luigi said—he said you needed our help and some clothes."

Jackie ran her fingers across my chest, "What in the world is this stuff?"

Embarrassed, I turned to face the wall and told them to leave. I don't know why I expected them to listen. They went to work with a vengeance. Martha gave me a wicked slap on the rump. "Spread those legs," she ordered.

They stopped scrubbing and waited for me to turn toward them.

"You've had your fun, now get out of here. I can do the rest myself."

I tore the brush and soap from Martha's hands. "I promise I will get even some day."

When I thought they had both left, I removed the remaining grease. Jackie reached past the shower curtain, turned off the water, and handed me a towel.

"I just want to know one thing," she said. "Why bring Stefano back ashore? I thought we agreed if we got another chance, we wouldn't hesitate to drill the bastard."

"Things got complicated when Stefano killed Castellano's men. He has to show his crew and the other Mafia bosses that he will avenge any and all intrusions upon his territory and authority."

She wasn't satisfied. "What if Butch loses the fight?"

"Then it'll be up to me to kill Stefano with my bare hands."

Chapter 29

Word spread along the waterfront that Castellano had captured the man who'd gunned down two of his crew. Soon a throng of longshoremen gathered to witness the enforcement of street justice.

I saw fear and hatred in Stefano's eyes when I entered the watchman's shack and flipped open my stiletto. I leaned over, pressed the blade against his neck, and slid it between his skin and the rope. One slip and he'd be done for. I took my time freeing his bonds, except for the ones binding his hands. When I pulled him to his feet, he spit in my face. If his hands weren't bound, we would have ended his vendetta against me then and there. I was tempted to free him and let him try to do just that, but I had promised Castellano to deliver him alive. Instead I heaved him head first at the closed door.

The crowd erupted in a collective cheer as the door of the shack flew off its hinges, and Stefano tumbled out onto the concrete platform. I stood in the doorway wiping off his spittle. Stefano faced the crowd, no doubt wondering what to expect.

The swarm of onlookers parted to let Castellano and Butch through and then closed ranks behind them. Castellano turned toward the crowd and waved them back to create more room for the pending fight. There was a scurry of activity to get a better view. Some climbed crates, while others boarded the tug that was still moored alongside the pier.

I yanked on the cord that held Stefano's hands behind his back. "If you can take Butch, you'll get a shot at me." I cut his hands free and shoved him forward. Stefano and Butch stood apart, facing each other bare-knuckled and bare-chested, each understanding the rules: there were no rules in a fight to the finish. Stefano took a step back and glanced over his shoulder, "I'm going to enjoy killing you, Batista," he said with an air of confidence I didn't expect.

He should never have taken his eyes off Butch. When he turned back, a huge fist pummeled his face, followed by a swift kick to his midsection that sent him crashing against the shack. Dazed, Stefano groped for something to give him support. He pushed against the wall of the shack to stand upright. Once he steadied himself, he rubbed his jaw and spit two bloody teeth into his hand. Stefano looked confused and said something unintelligible. Butch quickly moved in, slapped his massive hands against the sides of Stefano's skull, and plunged his thumbs into both eye sockets. Stefano brought his arms up between Butch's forearms, breaking his grip. He then grabbed Butch's head and rammed his forehead into the bridge of Butch's nose. Butch stumbled backward. Stefano took the opportunity to rub his eyes to relieve the pain.

Blood poured from Butch's nose, which threw him into a ferocious rage. He thrust his massive arms in the air with fists clenched, swung his arms down in one swift motion, and let loose a fierce roar. Every muscle in his body tensed, poised for action. Instinctively, the onlookers took a step back.

Stefano charged with his head down and arms outstretched. Butch sidestepped and landed a crushing blow to the back of Stefano's neck, which flattened him onto the concrete. Butch kicked wildly at Stefano's ribs and was about to stomp the small of his back when Stefano rolled, grabbed Butch's foot, and twisted with such force you could see his arteries bulge. Butch landed on his shoulder and tumbled into a crate, sending it flying into the crowd. A crowbar flew off the crate and skittered across the ground. Both men pounded each other, scrambling for the potential weapon. Castellano picked up the crowbar and tossed it to Butch. Stefano backed off, but not before Butch caught him with a glancing swipe across his rib cage. Stefano had swayed with the blow, minimizing the impact.

Butch rushed at Stefano with the crowbar raised. Stefano deflected his arm and landed a solid punch to Butch's midsection while thrusting his knee upward to smash Butch's face. Butch anticipated the move, grabbed Stefano's leg, heaved Stefano off the ground, and tossed him over his head. The crowd let out a collective moan. Stefano landed hard, dislocating his shoulder and smashing his head against a support column. Butch didn't wait to survey the damage. He hoisted Stefano in the air, with one hand gripping his neck and the other his calf. Butch stepped one foot forward, bent his knee, and brought Stefano's outstretched body down with such force that everyone heard his spine crack over Butch's thigh.

No one moved. No sound was uttered. Butch let Stefano's lifeless body fall to the ground. Castellano patted Butch on the shoulder and handed him his shirt. The longshoremen milled around for a few minutes, then meandered along the pier to their cargo bays and got back to work. Stefano was no longer a threat, and Castellano had gotten what he wanted—respect.

I went over to the girls, who stood motionless, staring at what was once a human being who had threatened their lives. I'm sure they had mixed feelings after witnessing such a brutal death, but street justice had been delivered and was justified.

Sadie stood apart from us with her arms wrapped tightly around her waist. I walked up to her and held her close. "He's not the one," I said. "He didn't kill your father."

She pushed back, "I know."

I watched her walk away, a lone figure oblivious to the commotion around her. Suddenly, I felt overwhelmed with her sadness.

Jackie and Martha came over. They stood on either side of me, each gripping an arm. We watched and waited until Sadie turned onto Waters Street. Halfway down the pier, we were startled by a lone figure who stepped out in front of us from between two large crates. A fedora covered his eyes, and his hands were tucked inside the pockets of his overcoat.

I recognized Ronnie, Vic's uncle, from the scar on his cheek below the line of his hat. I nudged the girls forward, while I held back to talk to Ronnie in private, but the girls stiffened, sensing danger. Jackie reached behind her back for a chiv and stepped in front of Martha to give her cover as Martha extracted the .45 from her purse.

"It's OK," I said. "I need to talk business with this guy, so why don't you both head back to the office and I'll meet you there when we finish." Since they hadn't recognized Ronnie, I decided to keep it that way. They would only argue when they heard what he wanted. Ronnie would have come out of hiding for only one reason—to collect on Castellano's and my uncle's debt.

"Office?" Jackie said, replacing her knife. "I think after all that's happened these last few days, Martha and I need a few stiff drinks. We'll meet you at your uncle's joint, and if we're still standing when you get there, we'll buy you dinner."

Ronnie pushed up his fedora and let out a low whistle. "Damn, I gotta hand it to ya. That was impressive. Who would expect a couple of dames to be so deadly?"

I was tired and in no mood for exchanging niceties. "What do you want?"

"Hey relax, I just came to see the show," he said, flicking his cigarette into the water. "I sure wouldn't want to go up against such a brute."

"What's on your mind? You wouldn't risk being arrested just to see a fight."

"You get right to the point. I like that. So here it is. I'm getting reports that my organization is being torn apart in my absence. I can't wait any longer. Now that your main problem is solved, I figure you can head to Detroit and take care of mine."

"I still need to wrap up some loose ends. Why don't we meet at my parents' place tomorrow night with Castellano and my uncle? You can tell us what's really goin' on and exactly what you expect from me."

"Tomorrow night then. I'll be there. I hope you're as good as or better than everyone says. And lucky, too, because you're gonna need it in Detroit."

Ronnie pushed his collar up around his neck, pulled his hat down, and walked away.

Chapter 30

I needed to breeze off and get away from everything. After Ronnie left and some of Castellano's men removed Stefano's body, I headed toward the ferry terminal along Front Street. With no particular destination in mind, I stopped at a diner I hadn't been in before. It felt good to sit alone, sipping a cup of joe, not having to worry if anyone saw my hands quiver. I'd seen guys in my army unit get the shakes after coming down from an adrenaline rush, but I had never experienced it myself until now.

I wondered why. The war was relentless. With one assignment after another, it was much more intense than the PI business, even with all the Mafia issues. During the war, there was no time to think or dwell on the past. There was no one to rely on, and no one to protect. I just had to train and then complete my mission. Over and over again, train and complete the mission. Even, if necessary, at the cost of my life.

The answer was that simple. When I joined up, after Anita's disappearance, I intended to return home in a pine box. I didn't want to face the rest of my life without her. Now, things were different. I wanted to stay alive.

The waitress came over, sat across from me, refilled my cup, and poured one for herself. Taken aback, I glanced around. The place was empty.

"Looks like you need someone to lean on." She reached out and steadied my hands. "Spill it."

"It's not pretty," I said.

"Sonny, I've heard just about everything possible in this joint. I don't shock easily, not after all these years."

I looked deeply into her eyes and asked, "Have you ever killed anyone?"

"No, but I sure as hell wanted to. Especially my husband. May God rest his soul," she said, crossing herself. "I take it you have."

"More than I can remember."

"The war?"

"Mostly."

"That doesn't count. Bury that stuff, 'cause it'll eat your insides."

My hands had stopped shaking.

"I know all about you, Batista, and I have a damn good idea what's bothering you."

She sipped her coffee and watched for my reaction over the rim of her cup.

We sat in silence. I wanted to know more, and my guess is she wanted to tell me more, but neither of us would go first. She topped off my cup and got up to leave.

"How? We've never met," I said.

She sat back down. "O'Reilly. I took care of him from time to time when he was a tyke. He drops in once in a while, but he's not the only one. I also know your family, especially Luigi. We go way back. Then, of course, there are some regulars from the old days who like to gossip. You've certainly spiced up their lives since you returned home," she said with a smile. "You see, I lived in your neighborhood until I got run out."

"I'm tempted to ask why you had to leave, but that's none of my business. So tell me, what's my problem?" I asked hoping she could pin it down.

"You may not see it, but you're getting too involved with the Mafia. My guess is down deep you *do* know it. You're a war hero. You risked your life behind enemy lines. A guy like that wouldn't respect the Mafia and would want his independence. Get too close to the Mafia, and they'll turn you into a puppet with the syndicate manipulating the strings. I know how it works; my husband worked for Castellano."

"That's it?"

"What'd you expect for nothin'? Leave a big tip and next time I'll tell your fortune."

A customer entered and sat at the counter. She got up and leaned in close. "I hear that Castellano ordered you to head to Detroit to take care of business for Ronnie. Trust me, that Ronnie, he's a bad seed. Always has been, always will be. Watch your back."

I placed money on the table and left. Outside I lit a cigarette, wondering if I would ever stop in there again.

* * * * *

In the event that I would survive my nighttime swim and my encounter with Stefano, O'Reilly and I had agreed to meet for lunch close to police headquarters. He'd stayed away from the waterfront knowing what might go down and had asked some of his buddies to do the same.

When I walked through the restaurant door, O'Reilly grinned and raised his flask in the air.

"I had my doubts you could take Stefano alive," he said.

I grabbed his flask and took a long draw.

"I had enough of my own. You never know what will happen when an animal is cornered."

With Stefano out of the way, we didn't dwell on the subject. I told O'Reilly that Ronnie showed up after the fight and demanded I head to Detroit. O'Reilly was already aware that Castellano had asked me to get involved, so he had done some checking with a few of his contacts on the force.

"Ronnie has moved up in the world since he left town. He's a small-time hood with a few canhouses and several speakeasies. Not satisfied with those, he tried to move into one of the big boy's territories. That's when he ran into trouble."

"So you think he was framed for those murders?"

"More than likely."

"Why wouldn't they just take him out?" I asked.

"Guys like Ronnie aren't afraid of being rubbed out, and that makes him dangerous. If they messed up, and he survived an ambush, they'd have a mini-war on their hands."

"I still don't get it. Why frame him for murder?"

"To show everyone you can put a guy like that in the big house waiting to be fried. Sends a real message," O'Reilly said, taking a bite of steak.

Satisfied that I knew what I might walk into when I arrived in Detroit, I changed subjects.

"I ran into a waitress after the fight this morning who knows you and others in our neighborhood. She works at a small diner halfway between here and the ferry terminal. Do you know who I'm talking about?"

O'Reilly thought for a second. "Sure, that must be Molly Ferguson. She was a seamstress and made a few extra bucks watching kids when their mothers were sick or out of town."

"Why'd she move out?"

"I was pretty young at the time, but from what I heard,

she was giving more attention to some of the kids' fathers. After that, her business dried up."

I wanted to know if Molly was someone to be trusted. I dug a little deeper.

"It sounds to me that you go to her from time to time for advice."

O'Reilly put his fork down. "If Molly gave you advice, I'd take it."

"She said not to trust Ronnie. She also said he's a bad seed."

"She's right about that," O'Reilly said.

"What do you mean?"

"He doesn't have a conscience, which makes him extremely dangerous."

* * * * *

By the time I got to my uncle's joint, Rosalie was smoked and Martha and Jackie weren't far behind.

"It's not like you girls to drag Rosalie down with you."

"Don't blame us," Jackie said with a slight slur. "She figured now that Stefano's dead, she can go back to school. There was no stopping her from drinking."

"That's right," Martha said. "It's all her fault. She made us join in."

They were quite the sight. Rosalie was slumped back with her butt slowly sliding forward in the seat. In another few minutes, she'd be under the table. Jackie and Martha leaned on each other, shoulder-to-shoulder, slouched against the booth.

"You two stay put while I take Rosalie to her room,

and don't drink any more booze. We need to talk, so sober up." I removed the drinks from the table and ordered two coffees.

I grabbed Rosalie under the arms, dragged her out of the booth like a rag doll, and heaved her over my shoulder. On my way out, my uncle advised me to carry her in my arms.

"You bounce her stomach on your shoulder like that and you won't get to the hallway before she heaves."

I took his advice and gingerly made my way down the back stairs to the alley. It was a tough slog, but I finally made it to the rear entrance of my parents' apartment where Rosalie had a room. I didn't want Ma to see her smoked. Rosalie hardly ever drank because of the way her drunken father had treated her and her mother. If Ma saw Rosalie blotto, she'd assume I was to blame.

I had just placed Rosalie on the bed and taken off her shoes and was debating if I should remove her outer clothes, when Ma entered.

"I'll take care of her," she said.

I expected a scolding, reminiscent of my childhood, but instead, she gave me a crushing hug. "When Pop woke me last night and told me how you planned to get Stefano, I didn't think I'd ever see you again."

I didn't know what to say. It hit me how much grief I had caused my family since enlisting in the army without their knowledge.

She regained her composure and switched back to being the typical Italian mother.

"Now I hear from Pop that you're going to Detroit to get Ronnie out of a jam." She didn't wait for a response. "There are certain things worth dying for, and Ronnie's not one of them. You remember that. Now, get out of here so I can take care of Rosalie, and how many times do I have to explain to you how much Rosalie means to us? Getting her canned is unacceptable, and don't you ever take advantage of her feelings toward you!"

"Ma, why would you say something like that?"

"You're not the boy I raised. Since returning home, you're becoming more like my brother, gentle but also ruthless. Unpredictable."

Rather than arguing, I took her advice and got out of there. I couldn't deny she was right, but what she didn't realize was that she also had the same traits. I guess they run in the family, and in my case, the army had brought them to the surface.

By the time I got back to the girls, they showed some signs of sobriety. At least they were sitting up straight, each holding a cup of joe.

My butt hadn't hit the seat before Jackie launched into an interrogation. "Who was that guy at the pier and what did he want with you?"

"I take it you didn't notice the scar on his face. That was Ronnie, and he expects me to take care of his problem now that Stefano's out of the way."

Jackie leaned back against the backrest and shook her head. Martha, slower to react, pushed back when the message registered.

"Wait a minute. You can't leave with Kowalski's murderer at large and Frank's case hanging out there. We made commitments. Besides, who is this Ronnie guy anyway that you're expected to drop everything and run off to Detroit?"

Martha had a point, but it was hard to explain. Castellano couldn't turn Ronnie away, and I couldn't turn Castellano or my uncle down. What belongs to the father belongs to the son. Everyone in the family is obligated to everyone else. It's just the way things work.

"Given what happened to Stefano, Kowalski's killer will lay low for awhile, and at this point, he's only a danger to Castellano," I said.

"What if you're wrong?" Jackie asked. "There's still Gino. This guy might think Gino saw what went down that night."

"I don't believe that's a problem. If it were, Gino would be dead already, or at least an attempt on his life would have been made by now."

"You're willing to take that chance?" Jackie said, with a look that said I shouldn't.

"If it makes you girls feel better, I'll take him with me. He could come in handy."

"Sure, he'll be real safe in Detroit when you try to bribe city officials and go up against a mob boss. Don't look so surprised. The whole neighborhood knows what's goin' on," Martha said.

"Jackie will be there to help keep an eye on him," I said, as if it was assumed all along that Jackie would come along.

Martha took a deep breath and turned to Jackie, who shrugged. She turned back to confront me.

"In case you've forgotten, I'm not a private investigator or a partner in this business. How am I supposed to deal with Frank's case on my own, not to mention Kowalski's killer?"

"I filled O'Reilly in on your progress, and he reopened the investigation into Ruth's death. Keep Frank informed, listen to O'Reilly, and don't worry about Kowalski's murderer."

Martha brushed aside the coffee mug and ordered another beer. "Easy for you to say."

* * * * *

Ma expressed her displeasure to Castellano and Luigi for getting me involved with Ronnie by refusing to provide food or refreshments for the meeting I had arranged. This had never happened in my lifetime. Everyone was speechless. Jackie had gone into the kitchen to smooth things over with Ma when Ronnie entered the apartment from the back alley.

Ronnie ignored normal etiquette, plopped down into Jackie's spot, and launched into the details of what he expected me to accomplish in Detroit.

Ma came back in and tossed her apron on the table in front of Ronnie.

"You don't even have the decency to acknowledge your host or pay your respects to Mr. Castellano. You've been nothing but trouble your whole life and now you're sucking my son down your rat hole. I have a good mind to turn you in to the cops myself." She grabbed the apron from the table and stormed out of the apartment with Pop in tow.

Ronnie pushed back his chair to follow. I yanked him down.

"Relax, she's just upset," I said. Jackie poured everyone a cup of coffee and joined us.

"What's *she* doing here, and what is this crap? I need a shot of whiskey," Ronnie said.

Castellano smiled, "She's part of the team that's gonna pull your ass out of the mess you've created."

"I was framed. Why would I whack two mucky mucks in one of my own houses?"

"Whose territory have you been muscling in on?" Castellano asked.

"Nick's, but I didn't expand into his area. Some of his clientele shifted their business over."

"Who's Nick?" I asked.

"Where have you been? Johnny Torrio's your uncle—and you don't know Nick Bandini? What are you, a hermit?"

"I was fighting in the war so people like you could have the freedom to break the law."

"Oh yeah. I forgot. You single-handedly saved Europe."

"He did," Luigi said. "And if you want him to save your hide, I suggest you cut the crap and answer his question."

"Joey doesn't have to worry about Bandini. I'll take care of him. All he has to do is get the charges against me dropped."

"And exactly how do we do that?" I asked.

"It's simple. So simple you'll be back here in a few days."

He handed me a ring and an envelope. "The envelope contains two addresses. The first is to one of my canhouses. Just show the ring to the head madam and she'll give you a key. The second address is where the money is stashed. You'll need the key to get the dough."

"Then what?" Jackie asked.

"Make a deal with the police chief. He'll take it from there. He and the mayor are as corrupt as they come. Do me a favor and try not to give away all the cash."

Jackie and I asked a few more questions, and when we were satisfied, the meeting broke up.

Castellano pulled me aside afterward. "You remember the broad you asked me to place in a high-class house last year?"

"Sure, Shirley's sister, Debbie. For some reason you refused to tell me where you sent her. Is she okay?"

"Don't worry, she's fine. I didn't tell you because you didn't need to know. But I'm tellin' you now. She's in Detroit, working in one of Ronnie's houses."

Chapter 31

On the day we were scheduled to leave for Detroit, Martha continued to argue that it wasn't practical for her to work Frank's case alone, especially with the hearing date rapidly approaching. She shot down every point I made. But when Frank Galvano walked in on the discussion, she sang a different tune. Frank insisted we transfer all the information we had gathered to a rival detective agency, and emphatically stated he wasn't satisfied with the progress we'd made. He accused us of not giving his case the priority it deserved.

"First, you fire me as your secretary and now you're taking away my case. What is it about me you detest?" Martha barked at Frank.

He backed up. "I'm not taking anything away from *you*. Joey and Jackie are headed to Detroit, and my client is on the docket in a little less than a month. There won't be enough time to make progress if we wait until they return."

"See, what did I tell you? You don't think I can solve this case on my own. What's so damn difficult? There are only two lawyers, five beneficiaries, and your client involved. Either one of them is a murderer, or the old lady's death was an accident. How complicated can this be?"

"I can't afford to take the chance, and neither can my client. There's a lot of dough at stake here, and let's be honest, you're not a licensed detective."

I had complete confidence in Martha, especially now that she felt challenged.

"Frank, O'Reilly has reopened the investigation and agreed to work with Martha. Together I have no doubt they'll uncover the truth. Another agency won't have O'Reilly's cooperation, nor will they have time to come up to speed. Martha's your best bet," I said.

Jackie put her arm around Martha's shoulder and pointed at Frank. "She's your *only* bet. I suggest you grab it before we decide to take her to Detroit."

"You guys had plenty of time to work this case. At least get back before the hearing begins so we can agree on a strategy."

He didn't slam the door on the way out, but it was easy to see he wanted to.

* * * * *

Gino agreed to follow us to Detroit by hopping a railcar with his bindle, wearing the rags he had worn when he first came to work for Pop. The plan seemed simple enough. He knew the address of our hotel and the location of the house where Ronnie had told us to pick up the key to a public locker that contained the cash. Gino would keep track of our movements and listen for any street talk that might signal trouble headed our way.

Jackie and I caught the early morning train and reviewed what little information Ronnie had given us for the trip. Jackie clutched her handbag that contained her .45 and adjusted her knife harness several times while we talked.

"You seem on edge."

"What do you really know about Ronnie and the situation we're walking into?"

"Not much. Pop filled me in on how things were when they first arrived from Italy. All the neighborhoods were in chaos, with the shop owners taking the brunt of the abuse from ethnic gangs trying to grab control of adjacent streets to expand their territory."

"What's that got to do with Ronnie?" Jackie asked.

"Our section of town was particularly vulnerable since we were isolated from Little Italy. The shop owners and employees got together and formed a partnership to protect each other. Ronnie was the neighborhood enforcer. If anyone made trouble, he took care of things. According to Pop, Ronnie was ruthless; you might even say sadistic."

Jackie looked out the window. She didn't speak again until after she had handed our tickets to the conductor.

"Do you know about the Mafia wars that took place in Detroit while you fought overseas?" Jackie asked. She shook her head. "Of course you don't. How about since you've been back?"

"You might say I've been busy staying alive."

"Didn't you mention the hotel where we're stayin' is in the Wyandotte area of Detroit? That's where it all began. Vito and Savatore Adamo controlled the area until a rival Sicilian family opened up shop. The Gianolla brothers, Sam and Tony, eventually pushed the Adamo family out of Wyandotte, launching a bloody war resulting in the death of both Adamo brothers and many of their family members and associates."

"How do you know so much about Detroit? You grew up in Chicago."

"Did you forget that my deceased husband was the editor of the *Daily News*, and I was his assistant editor? The growth of the Mafia is big news no matter where it occurs. Every now and then we ran a special edition tracing the growth of the Mafia in different cities."

I hadn't noticed the conductor had stopped to listen to Jackie, and so had several passengers who leaned out of their seats, encouraging her to continue.

"Go on lady. Tell him what happened to the Gianolla brothers."

Noticing the crowd, Jackie turned so everyone could hear.

"The Adamo brothers were gunned down near the end of 1913. Relative peace followed with the Gianolla gang in control of Detroit's underworld, which included labor racketeering, gambling, loan sharking, extortion, hijacking, fencing, drugs, and prostitution. You know, just your typical Italian family enterprises."

"Hey, don't forget they had some legitimate businesses," someone shouted.

"Yeah, they ran the garbage companies, not to mention construction and food supplies to restaurants," added the conductor.

"The Mafia still does," another passenger shouted.

More and more passengers gathered around. Jackie continued her narrative. "Things were relatively calm for the next few years until John Vitale broke away from the Gianolla syndicate, igniting a new Mafia war more deadly than the Adamo era,"

"That's right lady. You couldn't walk down the street without stumbling over a dead body," a heavy-set man said without looking past his paper. "I know 'cause one of them was my cousin. Everybody wanted to be a wiseguy, but most didn't last long."

"So who won?" I asked.

"Nobody," Jackie said. "By the end of 1920, both sides were wiped out, including Vitale and the Gianolla brothers."

The conductor moved on. "Tickets, get your tickets out," he shouted.

With everyone's attention on the conductor, I drew Jackie back to the present. "I know Detroit isn't the city of peace and joy. What's goin' on now?"

"A guy by the name of Sam Catalanotte emerged to lead the Detroit Mafia by gathering together all the factions left over from the Vitale and Gianolla gangs. With the advent of prohibition, he formed a 'combine' focused around liquor, but he also controls all the other rackets. So far it's been successful because he's allowed each boss to run their territory under a loosely knit umbrella. Not too different than how Little Italy is held together back in New York."

All that Ronnie had said the night he divulged how we were to get access to his cash now made sense. Ronnie had small but growing enterprises that drew more and more customers away from one of Catalanotte's bosses, Nick Bandini. Rather than risk Ronnie joining the combine and the eventual encroachment into his territory, Bandini used his influence to frame Ronnie for murder.

It wasn't a bad strategy, except for the fact that Ronnie skipped town before he could get arrested. Given Ronnie's violent tendencies, Bandini had to be on edge, which complicated things. Bandini wasn't expecting us, but he knew that as long as Ronnie was on the lam he was a threat, so his guard would be up.

Chapter 32

Ronnie had recommended we stay at the Holly Hotel because it was within walking distance to the train station. The hotel catered mainly to traveling salesmen who appreciated the Victorian architecture, its excellent restaurant, and the "services" provided by some of Ronnie's nearby establishments. Jackie was all for taking advantage of the luxurious accommodations and shoved me backward onto the plush four-poster bed, but I resisted. Given the Mafia history she had rattled off on the train, I thought it best not to waste any time locating the woman Ronnie trusted with the key to his cash hoard. From my perspective, the less time we spent in Detroit the better. The last thing we needed was for Bandini to get wind of why we were in town.

The cab driver nodded when I gave him the address of the house and took several back roads to avoid traffic headed downtown. During the drive I noticed that the driver kept glancing at his rearview mirror.

"Is someone following us?" I asked him, looking over my shoulder out the back window.

"Nah, just never took a woman to this place before. She looking for a job? Because if she is, when we get there, I'm parking this heap and goin' inside with you guys."

Jackie knew we were headed for one of Ronnie's brothels, and she started teasing the driver until he lost focus and swerved into oncoming traffic. He jerked the car back in time to miss a delivery truck.

"You better keep your mind on the road. Besides, you're not my type," she said with a chuckle.

"Oh yeah, what is your type?" the cabbie asked.

"He's sitting next to me."

The guy looked confused, and then let loose a hearty laugh. "Now I get it. You two are looking to try something new. Well, you're goin' to the right place if you got the dough." He parked the cab in front of an elegant brownstone building.

After I paid the cabbie, he leaned out the window. "Some guys have all the luck," he said and drove away.

* * * * *

I recognized the gent who opened the door. He was one of the studs who had come for Debbie the day she left to enter the world of upscale prostitution. At the time it had seemed like a good idea to Debbie, since one of the requirements was to stay off drugs, a habit she had just kicked. Doctor Schwartz, who cured her of her drug habit, hadn't been as successful with her addiction to sex. According to him, she was a classic nymphomaniac.

"You got an appointment?" the attendant asked, blocking the entrance to the brothel.

"We're here to see Victoria, the lady of the house," I said.

"Maybe you didn't hear me. So I'll ask again. Do you have an appointment?" he said, unbuttoning his jacket.

"Ronnie sent us."

"Wait in the receiving room, and I'll see if she's interested."

The room was just off the entrance hall on the right-hand side. Down the center of the hallway ran a velvet runner, which led to an expansive parlor with an assortment of lounges and sofas occupied by some of the most beautiful women I'd ever seen. Several men in business attire moved from one woman to another trying to choose a companion for the evening.

I guess I had lingered a little too long taking in the sights because Jackie yanked my arm so hard that I stumbled over the threshold into the room. I regained my footing and pulled her close. "Don't tell me you're jealous."

"I promise after tonight you won't give this place a second thought," she said.

"Then I suggest we get the key and the heck out of here as quickly as possible."

Jackie was about to say something when we heard someone call my name. I had suspected this might be the place Debbie was working when I had recognized the brute at the entrance to the house. I released my grip on Jackie and stepped back into the hall. I saw Debbie rushing down the spiral staircase that led to the second-floor rooms. Her robe flung open, revealing a sheer silk nightgown. She ran into my arms and smothered me in kisses.

"Oh my God, I never thought I'd see you again," she said, hugging me so tight that it felt like I was in one of Uncle Luigi's bear hugs.

"Please get me out of here," she whispered and stepped back.

A shrill voice called out to her. "*Debbie,* that is *not* how one behaves in this establishment."

"Yes, madam, it won't happen again."

I looked past Debbie and saw an old lady walking toward

us using an ivory cane. Debbie regained her composure and departed with stately grace to the parlor.

* * * * *

The woman sat down in a Queen Anne chair, placed the cane across her lap, and directed me to a sofa, ignoring Jackie. Jackie sat next to me and quietly listened to our conversation.

"I'm told that my son sent you. How do I know you're telling the truth?"

"You're Ronnie's mother?"

She laughed, "Ronnie likes to hold back information. He says it gives him an edge. I don't know your relationship with Ronnie, but if I were you, I wouldn't trust him. I certainly don't."

Surprised, I handed her the ring Ronnie had given me.

She examined it closely. "How is Ronnie?"

"He's hiding in New York City and sent me to clean up his mess," I said.

"And exactly who are you?"

"A friend of Castellano's. My name is Joey Batista."

"I remember now. You turned Debbie over to me. She was quite the find. The girl has a voracious appetite, something you're aware of, no doubt, given the reception you just received."

I didn't correct her perception since I wanted some time alone with Debbie before we left.

"You should also remember my parents from when you lived in our neighborhood," I said.

"I do, and I have a vague recollection of you playing with Vic. How is Vic? I heard he took his brother's death in the war pretty hard."

"He's dead, which is how I ran into Ronnie. He paid his last respects at the funeral." I watched for a reaction—nothing, not even a twitch. Just by looking at her I understood how Ronnie had turned out the way he did. This woman, Ronnie's mother, had tainted blood running through her veins.

"Vic was his godchild. Damn foolish of Ronnie to take such a risk when he's on the lam. So tell me why my son would turn over his stash to you?" she said, examining the ring again.

"I'm not sure you need to know that," I said.

"I don't blame Ronnie for not trusting me with his dough. To be honest, I wouldn't give him access to mine either. Now, if you want the key, answer my question. Why would my son turn so much money over to *you*?"

"Ronnie's convinced that all it will take for the police chief to drop the murder charges is a hefty bribe. Once he's free to return, he plans on dealing with Nick Bandini."

"I'm afraid it's too late for that. Most of Ronnie's men have gone over to Bandini or skipped town. Mr. Bandini has given me two weeks to do the same."

"You seem calm, given the situation."

"I'm an old lady and don't scare easily. Besides, the mayor is one of my more frequent customers, and I have embarrassing information about him that will go public if I'm forced to leave town. I'm confident Bandini will back off."

Jackie, up to that point, had remained silent and still, but suddenly shifted positions in her chair. Both Victoria and I gazed in her direction.

"Young lady, do you have something you want to say?" Victoria asked.

"My name is Jackie. Why didn't you use this information

to get the mayor to have the charges dropped against your son?"

Victoria smiled, reached for a flask of whiskey that sat on an end table, and poured a drink. "Please help yourselves."

She returned her attention to Jackie, "I've learned over the years that it's best not to ask for too much when blackmailing someone. Besides, I've raised my son to be quite capable of handling his own affairs."

There was an uncomfortable pause in the conversation. Victoria took a sip of whiskey and stared at us.

"Ronnie didn't give us many details of the murders that took place. It would help if I knew more before approaching the police chief," I said.

Victoria grabbed her cane and stood. "It's getting late. Why don't you return in the morning to discuss an appropriate course of action? Once we agree on my cut, I'll turn over the key."

"Ronnie didn't mention giving you any of his dough."

"He's not here, is he?" she said.

Exiting the room, I noticed Debbie standing on the upstairs landing, imploring us not to leave. I turned to Victoria.

"It has been a long time since I've been with Debbie. Would you mind if we took advantage of her services?"

Victoria looked at Jackie and asked, "The both of you?"

Jackie reached her arm around mine and nudged me forward. "Forbidden fruits are the sweetest. Don't you agree?" she asked Victoria.

* * * * *

Debbie had a lavishly decorated attic room to herself that included ornate bathroom fixtures behind exotic privacy screens, a well-stocked bar, and an oversized circular bed positioned in the center of the room. Sofas surrounded the bed on three sides. Two wardrobes and a credenza made up the rest of the furnishings.

I went to the bar and fixed drinks while the girls sat on one of the sofas and talked.

"I can't believe Joey is here," Debbie said.

"Castellano wouldn't tell Joey where he sent you. According to him, it was for your own protection," Jackie said.

"Then how did you find me?"

"That's a long story," I said.

I handed out the drinks. "Why don't you tell us why you want to leave this place? Is anyone mistreating you? Are you in danger?"

Tears filled Debbie's eyes. "No, everyone's been nice. I've stayed off drugs and I get the highest-paying clients. I couldn't ask for more."

When Debbie broke down and sobbed, Jackie moved closer and put an arm around her shoulder. "Debbie, tell us what's wrong."

"I'm a prisoner. I can't leave without one of those big goons in tow, and I have no time to myself. I'm a glorified sex slave with no future."

My ma had been right again. I thought I was doing Debbie a favor; when in reality, she would've been better off taking her chances on the streets where she'd have some control over her life.

"If I could get you free of this place, what would you do?" I asked.

"I thought maybe Dr. Schwartz would take me back at the clinic. I could help the girls just like my sister did and continue treatments for—you know—my condition."

I told her I didn't think it would work. She'd have little contact with anyone outside the clinic and would still feel a sense of imprisonment. Debbie stood and paced the room, staring at the floor.

"I know I can control my desires. I can. I must. I want a normal life—to get married, have kids. I can do this. I just need another chance."

We agreed to take her with us to New York once we finished our job in Detroit, and I committed to talking with Dr. Schwartz. She broke down and cried again. By the time we got her settled, it was past two in the morning, so Jackie and I decided to spend the night. We each took a sofa.

We awoke an hour later to hideous screams and the smell of smoke.

Chapter 33

The screams intensified. "What's goin' on?" Debbie yelled.

"I don't know, but you both better get dressed," I said, heading for the door.

Jackie grabbed my shoulder holster off a couch and tossed it at me. "You might need this," she said.

I turned and caught the holster as I opened the door. Thick gray smoke billowed into the room, throwing me into a fit of coughing. I slammed the door shut. I looked around the room then ran past Jackie toward one of the gable windows. The roofline had a steep angle to the side of the building. There was no safe way down.

"Over here," Debbie screamed. "The roof at the back of my apartment by this window is flat."

When I backed away from the window where I stood, I noticed a small flame floating over the adjacent rooftop above the silhouette of a man, a sight I had seen twice in the war. He was about to toss a bottle filled with gasoline. I didn't hesitate and fired three rapid shots inches below the flame. The bullets hit their mark. The silhouette, drenched in gasoline, ignited, and lit up the skyline. The human torch flapped around in agony then disappeared over the side.

Victoria's house had been purposely set ablaze, and given the method, I knew not many would survive.

Debbie had exited out the only other window in the apartment and called for us to follow. The roof was five feet below the window ledge and led to a fire escape.

"Get Debbie over to the next building and out before it goes up in flames. They're connected," I told Jackie when she was on the roof.

"Why can't we use the fire escape?"

"You'll never make it down all the way. The ground floor probably got torched first."

Jackie looked back. "Where are you going?" she shouted.

"I have to try and save some of the girls on the floor below us." She reached out her hand.

"I'll see you later," I said.

"Send them up the escape ladder; I'll direct them off the roof," she called back with a determined look that told me not to argue.

Debbie yelled that the attic apartment across the hall from hers was empty.

I nodded, headed for the sink, soaked a cloth, and disappeared through the door into a cloak of thick smoke. Unable to see, I tumbled down the stairs to the third-floor landing and kicked in the first door on my left. A girl, no more than seventeen, was crouched in a corner shaking uncontrollably and clutching her robe. I dragged her into the bathroom, turned the shower on both of us, and then carried her to the escape window in the hall. The cold shower brought her survival instincts to life; she didn't hesitate to climb the ladder to the roof.

Two more girls made it out, but a third had been burned to death. Her room had exploded into a fireball when one of the gasoline bombs smashed through her window. She never had a chance.

Having cleared all the rooms on the third floor, I had one

foot on the fire escape when piercing howls from the floor below beckoned me back—that is, until I recognized the shrill screams for what they were. I'd heard similar piercing sounds before, and I still do in my nightmares. I'd witnessed whole families trapped inside buildings that had caught fire during intense shelling, and there wasn't anything anyone could do. Instinctively the occupants rushed to the basement for shelter, sealing their fate.

I pulled myself back onto the landing to head up to the roof, but then heard a yell for help. Someone was still alive on the second floor. Against my better judgment, I went back into the burning inferno.

* * * * *

If I hadn't hesitated before reentering the building, I would've perished on the stairwell when it suddenly collapsed. As I teetered on the edge of the precipice, a fountain of flames shot up toward the ceiling, singeing the front of my clothes. There was only one option left. I hurried back to the window, staying low to avoid the thick smoke, and descended the fire escape to the second floor. Shielding my eyes from the intense heat, I had the sense that Dante was daring me to cross the threshold of the blown-out window into his domain. Multi-colored flames consumed the walls, rushed across the ceiling, and collided in the center to form an eerie funnel to certain oblivion. I heard the cry for help again, put aside my fear, and entered.

The flames sucked the air out of the hallway in an effort to keep themselves alive, making it even more difficult to breathe with the wet cloth I held over my face. I was moving cautiously along the hall, listening, when a human flame ran toward me with a gaping hole of fire where a mouth should have been. She was dead before she hit the floor a few feet in front of me. Her hair was gone and her skull seared to the bone.

I instinctively reached out to touch her and that's when I noticed the skin on my hands blistering, which told me to get the hell out. Heading back toward the fire escape, I heard the weeping call for help again. I had passed her room. Without thinking, I plunged through the charred door, shoulder first, and rolled onto a blazing floor. She was in her bathtub, crying hysterically. On fire, I dove for the tub and landed on top of her. She went under the surface of the water still screaming. I rolled over and sat up, holding her in a tight embrace. She spewed up water, coughing and gasping for air.

I threw a soaked robe around her, heaved her over my shoulder, and skirted the edge of the room, concerned that the floor might collapse under our combined weight. Upon entering the hall, the flames that reached down from the center of the ceiling scorched the back of her robe, so I cradled her in my arms and ran toward the fire escape.

Once on the landing, I threw her back over my shoulder. The wet cloth I used to grip the railing hissed, and my shoes smoldered with each step on the hot, metallic steps. Jackie reached over and pulled the girl to safety. She then led us to the other building and down the stairs through streams of smoke that wafted up the stairwell.

Exiting the building, we were greeted by a chaotic scene. Fire trucks and police cars had converged on the street. The police were attempting to control the crowds while the firefighters dealt with the flames. Their primary focus was to save the two adjacent buildings, but it looked hopeless.

An officer rushed Jackie and me— along with Debbie

and one of the girls I had saved—to the hospital. Most of my burns were minor, but it would take time for my hair to grow back. The doc had to shave off what was left to treat several patches of burned skin on my scalp. He also bandaged my hands, after applying a healing salve.

Jackie never left my side at the hospital and managed to convince the cop who drove us there that we were passersby, who had tried to help when we saw the building erupt into flames. The cop went back to the scene to help bring others for medical treatment, but first told Jackie to wait for him to return so he could take our statements. She agreed, but as soon as I was bandaged, she hailed a cab and got Debbie and me back to the hotel where we stayed secluded for three days. During the time while I recovered, we concluded that Nick Bandini had ordered his men to burn down the building. We agreed he had to pay. This was no longer about Ronnie; Bandini had to answer for this atrocity.

On the third day, Gino showed up and dumped the contents of his bedroll. Two Tommy guns and a pair of 9 mm automatic revolvers tumbled onto the bed by my feet, along with extra ammunition.

"Your uncle said you might need these."

Seeing that I couldn't handle the Tommy gun, Jackie rewrapped the bandages on my hands to free my fingers. When I was still unable to effectively hold any of the weapons, she adjusted the bandages again without success. "I guess these guns are mine for this job," she said.

"I always wanted to shoot a Tommy gun," Gino said.

The odds of taking out Nick Bandini and surviving were close to zero, yet even Debbie wanted in on the action.

"The both of you need to stay out of this," I said to Jackie and Debbie. "No sense all of us getting killed. If I don't avenge those girls, I'll never get the horrific sights and sounds out of my head."

"Partner," Jackie said, "we're doing this together or we're leaving town together, right now. Which will it be?"

I didn't like either choice and was about to insist she and the others leave when the door to our room flew open. Pete Fitzpatrick, the sergeant the DA had assigned to keep tabs on me, stood in the doorway sporting a big grin.

"I'm with Jackie," he said.

"What the hell are you doing here?"

"Hey, we had a deal. You keep me informed, and I stay off your back. Then I discovered you skipped town. If I didn't know better, I'd say you're tryin' to get me fired just before I retire from the force. The DA said to follow your every move, no matter where you went. He'd do anything to get the chance to put you away for good."

"Do you know what happened?" Jackie asked.

"I saw who torched the house and followed them back to their hangout," Pete said.

He then took the Tommy gun from Gino and racked the slide. "Most of them stumbled out of the joint hours later drunk, having celebrated a job well done. Scum like that don't deserve a trial."

I looked from Jackie to Pete and saw that it would be useless to argue with them, and to be honest, I was in no shape to go it alone. "Do you know how many girls were burned to death?" I asked Pete.

"They pulled out nine charred remains. Two died clinging to each other."

"That'd be Ronnie's mother, Victoria, and Cynthia. They shared a room," Debbie said.

"You have a car?" I asked Pete.

"Yep, borrowed one from the local police chief."

That settled it. Driving up in a police car with a copper and a badge would get us inside Nick Bandini's hangout. Once in, the rest would take care of itself. The only remaining problem was Gino and Debbie. Their inexperience would get in the way. They had to leave.

"Gino, I want you to take Debbie back to New York on the next train."

"Come on, Joey, I just got here."

I tossed Gino a wad of dough to buy train tickets and some decent clothes. Jackie told Debbie to take what she needed from her suitcase.

"Gino, don't argue. Tell my family to take care of Debbie. They'll see us in a few days or read about us in the papers."

Jackie strapped on the shoulder harness that held the automatic pistols, several extra clips, and two chivs and then slipped on a light jacket. Pete tossed me an overcoat, and we were out the door before Gino or Debbie could respond.

O'Reilly once said revenge was sweet; this was a fact I already knew from the war and was about to taste again.

Chapter 34

Pete pointed out Bandini's hangout in a ritzy area on the outskirts of Detroit.

"This guy lives like there's no tomorrow," Pete said. "Which, when you think about it, isn't a bad philosophy. The life expectancy of a Detroit mob boss is pretty damn short."

"Jackie gave me a history lesson on the train. Until then, I thought New York City was a tough town."

"Don't kid yourself. The only difference is how things are done. In New York, you get taken for a ride. Here you get blown away anytime, anyplace," Pete said.

We drove past Bandini's two-story house and stopped at a downtown speakeasy to have a few drinks and plan how to take Bandini and his boys down. Pete had already spent a few late evenings at the joint, so we didn't have trouble getting in once he slipped the doorman a fin. He had found a convenient spot to park his police car out of sight; no one at the speakeasy suspected he was a cop.

The food was decent and the beer locally brewed. We stayed away from the hard stuff and took it easy on the beer while Pete laid out the information he had gathered.

"I've been watching Bandini's hangout for the last three days since the fire, and I know some of the routine. But once inside, when the shooting starts, it's gonna be all instincts and luck," he said.

When we had driven past Bandini's place, there had been

so many parked cars it looked like a convention hall. "How many men are we goin' up against?" I asked.

"Don't worry, it's not as bad as it looks. Bandini likes to throw parties for his cronies from City Hall and other influential men. Most everyone clears out by three in the morning. I suggest we go in an hour later. There are four guards walking the grounds at all times, two in back and two out front. It should be easy to get past them in the police car. Just be aware that once shots are fired inside the house, the four outside guards, if they're not cowards, will storm both ends of the building."

"How many inside?" Jackie asked.

"That's hard to say, but there's at least five, and as many, if not more, dames. The place reminds me of the old saloons out west that catered to the miners—one-stop shopping for all your manly needs. By the way, the police chief supplies most of the broads."

"That's a new twist. How does he do his recruiting?" Jackie asked.

"Easy, when a good-looking dame gets busted and faces hard time for a serious crime, he gives her an option—years in the hoosegow or a good-paying job."

"Seems like an obvious choice," Jackie said.

I thought it best not to ask her what she meant and got back to the business at hand.

"It'll be difficult to use the choppers," I said.

"Why's that?" Pete asked.

"Too many woman. Chaos will erupt when the first shots are fired. The dames will panic and get in the way."

"That's a problem. Once the goons realize we're immobilized for fear of hitting the skirts, they'll try to catch us in a crossfire," Pete said.

He pulled his rod and chambered a round. "Wish I was better with this thing. Last time on the range, I barely qualified. Good thing I'm retiring soon."

"Normally, I'm pretty damn good," I said.

I took his heater and tried to get a decent grip, but the bandages were too bulky. Jackie knew what I was thinking and removed the bandages. I gripped the rough metal and grimaced. Jackie wrapped the handle of the gun with two layers of gauze, and I tried again. The pain was tolerable, but not good enough to assure the accuracy I'd need to pick off the hoodlums without hitting the dames. A thin bandage around each of my palms combined with the wrapped gun handle did the trick.

Jackie headed for the ladies' room. When she returned, she handed me the shoulder holster under the table. I checked the guns and shoved Pete's in my waistband.

"It's settled then," Pete said. "Jackie and I will use the choppers the best we can and the rest is up to you."

Jackie got out of the booth and finished the last of her beer. "It's half past three. I suggest we get this over with," she said and led the way out the door. We followed.

"That's one hell of a broad," Pete said.

* * * * *

Pete drove up to the front of the house and parked off to the side of the porch steps. One of the guards approached, shouldering a shotgun.

"We're shut down for the night."

Pete opened the back door of the car and roughly pulled Jackie out of her seat.

"I've got a present for Nick," he said, shoving Jackie forward.

I got out the other side and walked to the front of the car.

"Who's he?" the guard asked, pointing the shotgun at my chest.

"Her husband. He's here to make sure she cooperates or they both go to the slammer for a long time."

"Nice guy," the guard said, as he walked over to Jackie and brushed aside the front of her jacket.

Pete pushed the guard back. "Hands off the merchandise," he said, and then pulled Jackie up the stairs. I kept my trap shut and walked behind Pete.

The guard put his shotgun over his shoulder and laughed. "That's alright. I'll get my turn sometime tonight."

Pete pushed Jackie through the front door that was held open by another bozo who had overheard the conversation. He was so interested in Jackie that he didn't notice my bulging overcoat. Once inside, both Jackie and Pete turned to face me, and I handed them their Tommy guns. They opened fire on the downstairs, shattering mirrors, chandeliers, and the French doors leading to various sitting rooms. They aimed high to avoid hitting anyone who might not have gone to bed. But as we had suspected, everyone was in the upstairs chambers.

The guard, who had closed the door behind me, pulled his revolver, but not before I pivoted around and caught him in the throat with the edge of my hand. He flew back against the door, gripping his neck, and leveled his gun at my chest. I dove to the right, firing, but it wasn't necessary. A shotgun blast from outside blew a hole in the door, piercing his back with slivers of wood. Stunned, he looked down in dismay at a large piece of wood that protruded from his stomach and then fell forward and slammed face-first onto the floor.

Jackie and Pete turned to the front of the entrance. When the outside guard who had fired the shotgun kicked in what remained of the door, they riddled him with bullets before he could get off another shot.

There was screaming coming from upstairs and the sound of glass breaking. Pete rushed outside, took out the remaining front sentry, and then blasted at the upstairs windows. Jackie moved to the back of the house to deal with the other two outside guards in case they were stupid enough to enter the house. I stood in the middle of the foyer with both guns ready, waiting for the inevitable.

The women emerged from the upstairs rooms; some ran down the stairs, while others flung themselves on the landing to get out of the line of fire. A sudden burst of Jackie's Tommy gun—followed by a round outside from Pete, who was shattering more of the upstairs windows—scared Nick's men enough that they rushed out of the bedrooms, blasting away at their own shadows. I dropped two who had leaned over the banister to see what the hell was going on. A third grabbed one of the girls off the floor and shielded himself while firing indiscriminately. When he reached midway down the stairs, the girl fainted and slumped in his arms. I stepped out from my cover and caught him in the leg, then between the eyes. They both tumbled down the stairs. The dame was out cold, but alive.

Jackie returned to the main hall and indicated she'd cut down the two outside guards who had rushed through the kitchen door with their backs turned to fire at Pete. Jackie stayed out of sight on the ground level while I went upstairs. There were a few girls huddled together in a corner. I waved for them to go down the stairs. I stopped the blonde who had encouraged the other girls to move.

"Do you know what these guys did?" I asked.

She nodded. "They were bragging about the fire."

"Any left in these rooms?"

"There are usually five up here, one downstairs and four outside. The other girls said two jumped out of the bedroom windows."

"Where's Bandini?" I asked.

She looked at the bandages on my hands and the patches on my shaved head. I hadn't realized until then that I'd lost my hat. "Were you there?" she asked.

"I saved as many as I could."

"He's turned the basement into a plush apartment and office. The place is a fortress. No way in or out except through a steel door."

"Anyone with him?"

"Usually he takes one of us for the night, but he's been on a binge these last few days. He's alone." I let go of her arm. She turned to leave, but then leaned back and gave me a kiss on the cheek. "Thanks. I never thought I'd get out of this hell."

* * * * *

Sirens sounded off in the distance, so I gave up any thought of trying to get Bandini. Jackie and I ran out the front door and saw Pete slumped over in the passenger seat of the police car. He'd been hit in the chest and was having trouble breathing.

"Don't worry, pal. I know where the hospital is located. You made it to the car; you can make it all the way," I said.

Jackie reached from behind the front seat and tried to keep his mouth clear of blood while applying pressure to his wound. Pete was unconscious when we drove up to the hospital.

The doctor who came out of the operating room was the same one who had patched my head a few days before.

"You're having a rough week," he said. "Your friend's gonna pull through, but he'll be laid up for at least a few weeks, possibly a month or more."

"He's a cop from New York on a special assignment for the DA. If anybody asks, he heard a gun battle goin' on and went to investigate. Do me a favor. When he wakes up, make sure he tells the same story."

The doctor yanked off his surgical cap, threw it into a bin, and pulled me aside. "Did you get the creeps who burned those girls to death?"

I was about to tell him I didn't know what he meant when I saw tears in his eyes.

"Not sure, but I think we got all but one."

"You better get out of town. I'll take good care of your friend. My sister died in that fire. She was no damn good, but she didn't deserve to die like that."

We walked out of the hospital, not sure what the future held, except that we had unfinished business to complete. Jackie put her arm around mine and held on tight.

Chapter 35

We abandoned the police car in the back parking lot of the hospital, walked a few blocks, and hailed a cab to our hotel. Jackie took a long bath, while I stripped and hit the sack. The next morning I woke to the smell of coffee.

"Room service in this place is top notch. You better get over here before I eat your eggs," Jackie said.

I stumbled out of bed in my skivvies, sat across from her, and dove into my food. "You wanna know somethin'? Pete was right. You're one tough bitch," I said, thinking back to how she had handled that chopper.

"The instinct to survive chips away at your humanity when you find yourself deserted as a kid. Fear kept me safe."

I looked up from my plate. "You expect me to believe you were afraid?"

"I was never afraid. I learned how to make others fear me."

"You have your gentle side too."

She put her hand on top of mine. "So do you. We're the same, you and I. We each have a foot in two worlds and feel comfortable in both."

It felt good to be with someone who understood. Life had made her who she was, and the army had transformed me from a decent kid into an assassin, a skill I had carried over into my civilian life. Together we were unstoppable, at least so far. I knew our luck couldn't hold out forever.

"You know we have some unfinished business."

She nodded. "We should get it done tonight before Bandini has time to gather a new crew."

"Exactly what I was thinking. What do you suggest we do while we wait for nightfall?"

She pushed me toward the bathroom. "First, I suggest you take a bath."

* * * * *

The house was dark except for the downstairs level and two dimly lit porch lights. It looked like Nick Bandini had gotten the message and planned on leaving town. The front door stood open, and a black touring car parked by the foot of the stairs had several boxes stacked in the back seat.

We split up and skirted the wall that enclosed the property. Jackie stumbled over something a few feet from the entrance. She struggled to stand, groping for the wall in the pitch darkness for support. I had rushed to her side and found one of Bandini's few remaining goons sprawled on the ground with his stomach bleeding and his throat slit.

"This guy knew his attacker and didn't sense a threat," I said.

"How do you know?"

"There would be no need to plunge a knife into his gut after you slit his throat. Whoever did this got real close, drove the chiv home, and then slit his throat to keep him from alerting others."

"If you ask me, one of the women from last night came back to settle a score," Jackie said.

"Likely more than one dame. I bet there's a few other bodies littered around this place."

We stayed together and moved cautiously toward the side of the house. Jackie pointed to another stiff near the rear of the car, and then she hit the ground when two gunshots sounded from inside the house. I bent down with one knee on the ground next to Jackie, ready to return fire, but none came. After a few minutes, we continued toward the house.

We were standing on either side of the front door, ready to go in, when we heard what sounded like wild animals attacking their prey. I went in low with both guns ready, and Jackie followed. Three women splattered in blood and wielding butcher knives turned to face us. Another dame lay in a pool of blood at the foot of the stairs. The blonde I had talked with the night before was poised to attack until she recognized me. The two women behind her let go of their mutilated victim. He fell with a loud thud, face forward onto the wooden floor.

The blonde relaxed, dropped her knife, and joined the other girls who were now kneeling around the brunette who had been shot in the head.

"She's dead," the blonde declared. "She knew the risk of coming back with us. We better go upstairs to change and get the hell out of here."

She looked down at us from the landing. "Last night you said you wanted Bandini. There he is," she said, pointing to the body on the floor. "He's all yours."

"Let's go," Jackie said.

"Not yet, I want to check out Bandini's room."

The unlocked door yielded to a gentle push. The room had been ransacked. Desk drawers had been pulled out with their contents strewn about, and an array of books were scattered on the floor. Two empty wall safes in the book cases caught my attention, as well as a lone box on an untidy bed. Bandini had come back to gather everything of value that he hadn't been able to clear out the night before after the cops had swarmed the building to gather evidence.

While I rummaged through the box, Jackie came in carrying a valise.

"I suspect Bandini hid this behind the stairwell when he saw the women and went to confront them. It's loaded with money," she said.

I was more interested in the pictures I found in the box and the handwritten notes on the back of each. They looked like crime shots of murdered victims that Bandini had snuffed out or had ordered killed. Chances were that two of the pictures were of the murder victims pinned on Ronnie, which was all the proof I'd need to get the charges against him dropped.

We were about to leave when the blonde appeared in the doorway. "You found some of his pictures," she said.

"I don't understand. Why leave such damming evidence around?" I asked.

"What can I say? Bandini was nuts. He had a bloke whose only job was to take pictures. Sometimes the guy was in this room taking pictures of Bandini in bed with one of the girls."

"You got a name?" Jackie asked.

"Margaret."

"Where are the others now?"

"They'll let us know if anyone comes snooping around."

"What happened upstairs?" I asked.

"We had split up. Bandini surprised Dolores and shot her.

One of the other girls came from behind and stabbed him in the back. Then the rest of us went crazy."

Cleaned up and dressed in a fresh outfit, she didn't look the type to commit a major crime, but she must have been accused of one to end up under Bandini's control.

"Why take the risk and come back to the house today?" I asked.

"Money. But it looks like he moved his dough earlier in the day," she said, pointing to the open wall safes. "But there's still a chance. There's another safe hidden behind that dresser."

"I'm not a safe cracker by profession, but I have some experience." We moved the dresser, and I got to work.

Since three-fingered Malone gave me a crash course last year, I've practiced several times on my uncle's safe. To Luigi's dismay, I was able to open it each time he changed the combination. He finally gave up and let me have the new combination, so I could get to the dough he held for us whenever needed.

It took twenty tense minutes before I got the safe open. We were disappointed with what it contained. Bandini was apparently a serious gun collector. I grabbed the valise Jackie had found upstairs and dumped a handcrafted pearl-handled revolver that caught my attention and several other guns on top of the money that was already in the satchel. That way Margaret wouldn't ask questions about the valise when I left with it. Jackie picked up the box of photos, and the three of us headed upstairs. The other girls had put out the lights and stood by the front entrance.

The five of us rummaged through Bandini's car and dumped out several boxes of papers. We piled into the car and headed out of the driveway to the girls' hotel in downtown

Detroit. Margaret cursed Bandini nonstop for not having scratch in his safe. They had counted on finding some dough to get a fresh start. I caught Jackie's arm as she reached for the bag. It was obvious what she had in mind, but until I knew how much dough we had, I wasn't about to give any away.

Back at our hotel, after abandoning the car, Jackie dumped the contents of the valise onto the bed. The final tally was one hundred and fifty-one grand. For a local boss, Bandini had done okay for himself. There was enough to pay off the police chief, help out the girls, and have some left over for our trouble.

Jackie wanted to go back and give the girls their cut, but I had other ideas. It didn't take much to persuade Jackie they could wait until morning.

* * * * *

The police chief was a regular customer of Margaret's at Bandini's house, so she knew his daily routine. After we handed out ten grand to each girl, Margaret willingly shared how best to approach him.

We found the chief eating breakfast in the local diner Margaret told us about.

Jackie caught his attention, and everyone else's, when she bent over to pick up her purse that she had intentionally dropped by the chief's table. He got down to help gather the contents and invited her to join him for breakfast.

Ten minutes later, I entered and sat next to Jackie.

"Sorry I'm late, honey. I had trouble cranking that old flivver of mine."

"I understand, Danny," Jackie said. "I'd like you to meet

the local police chief. He was kind enough to invite me to join him."

I extended my hand. "Nice to meet you, Chief. I'm Danny Riccio."

The chief took a sip of coffee, put down his cup, and took his hand off the table. "How long you two gonna keep up this charade?" he asked.

I reached for my inside jacket pocket.

The chief pointed a revolver at my chest. "I wouldn't do that if I were you, son."

I opened my coat to show I was unarmed and slowly pulled from the inside lining five of the pictures I had found in Bandini's room. Two were of the men Ronnie was accused of killing. Margaret had identified them for us, along with three deceased members of the chief's police force.

"Where'd you get these?" he asked.

"Nick Bandini's private collection of his victims."

"How do I know you're telling the truth?"

"Read the backs."

The chief's brow wrinkled as he flipped over the pictures. When he put the last one down, he ran a hand over his bald head.

"You have more of these?" he asked.

"You're looking at a sample, a small sample."

"Why shouldn't I arrest the both of you right now for Bandini's murder, because that's the only way you could've obtained these pictures?"

"Maybe. But we didn't kill him or the others you found at his hangout this morning. I don't think you'll slap the cuffs on us," I said.

"Why's that?"

"Nick seemed to have a passion for keeping records, as

you can tell from the information on the back of each picture," Jackie said. "I guess you can solve quite a few murders now that you know who the button men were and how much they were paid."

The chief leaned back and tried to push away from the table, but his large girth had him wedged in tight.

"What do you want?" he asked, with his hand resting on his gun.

"It's not what we want, it's what Ronnie Ligotti wants," I said. The chief relaxed and moved his hand away from the gun. "He wants the murder charges against him dropped and for you to look the other way. He needs to rebuild his businesses."

The waitress came over, filled our coffee cups, and removed the chief's plate. "You need anything else before I write up the check?"

"That's it, Alice, and give them the bill," the chief said. He then turned to us with a more serious demeanor.

"For my cooperation, I get *all* the pictures."

I pulled out a thick package from my inside pocket and slid it across the table. "You get more pictures and a bonus," I said. "There are a few pictures that stay with Ronnie to assure the continued success of your new friendship."

The chief counted the dough. "You may not know this, but Ronnie worked for Bandini when he first arrived in town. He eventually became his top enforcer. My cousin held that position before he was gunned down. I always suspected Ronnie did the job, but could never prove it. Now you're asking me to let him run loose in this town again. In some ways, he's worse than Bandini ever was."

"That's hard to believe, given that Bandini gave the order to burn down Ronnie's canhouse. Eight of his girls, plus his mother, died that night," I said.

"You'd be surprised about Ronnie."

"I'm sure you will both find a way to compromise. There's no reason for Ronnie to go public with the pictures that show you as a hit man for Bandini in your younger days. That is, unless his life's in danger," I said.

I helped Jackie out of the booth and picked up the bill. "One more thing," I said. "There's a New York City cop in the hospital. I'm sure Ronnie would appreciate it if you made sure he got the best of care."

The chief grabbed hold of my wrist. "Tell me something. How did Ronnie pull this off? I thought all his boys skipped town or went over to Bandini."

"I guess that's something that'll keep you awake at night."

Chapter 36

Jackie and I hung out at the hotel until the Bandini story broke to make sure the charges against Ronnie were dropped. It didn't take long. Two days after meeting with the police chief, every newspaper in town had Bandini's picture plastered on the front page. We skipped breakfast, grabbed our bags, and headed for the train station.

On the way, I noticed we had picked up a tail. It took him longer than I had expected to figure out we were heading out of town. Our bags should've been a dead give away, but he waited until we got to the train station to call his boss.

A porter carried the bags and escorted Jackie to our private compartment while I bought an extra newspaper from a kid outside the ticket office. Using a cascade of superlatives, he hawked the names of those Bandini and his gang had murdered. The kid knew how to get people's attention. I had to wait in line to get my paper. It turned out Ronnie wasn't the only person Bandini had framed for murder. Pictures of two men on death row, as well as Ronnie's picture, appeared below Bandini's. In the same article, the mayor heaped praise on his police chief for capturing several torpedoes hired by Bandini to take out his opposition and several public officials. One of the arrested goons turned stool-pigeon and fingered a guy who helped torch Ronnie's business.

I turned toward the train, still reading, wondering if anyone else involved in that horrendous act escaped or wasn't around the night we had attacked Bandini's hangout. The kid brought me back to the present when he yelled, "Hey mista, pay up!"

I flipped him two bits to make up for my negligence, tucked the paper under my arm, and headed toward the train.

It felt good to feel the rumble of the engine roar to life and to hear the conductor yell, "All aboard," and the screech of two long horn blasts. There was a sudden jerk, and the train inched along the platform, followed soon after by another jolt. The train had stopped.

"What's goin on?" Jackie asked.

"My guess is we're about to have some visitors," I said, my head buried in the newspaper.

Jackie opened the compartment door to look down along the corridor. She was abruptly backed into the room by the police chief and two of his officers.

"Leaving town so soon?" the chief asked.

"Is that a crime?" I responded.

He handed me an arrest warrant for the murder of Nick Bandini. "No, but murder is."

"I take it this means you've decided to go straight and turn yourself in for murder or have you forgotten about our little deal?"

"That's why we're here," the chief said, ordering his men to search our bags.

They frisked me and then proceeded to dump our belongings on the compartment floor. They were disappointed until they got to the valise. The chief pulled out the pearl-handled revolver.

"Did I mention Bandini was a gun collector and that many of his best guns were stolen? My cousin, the one I had suspected Ronnie iced, owned this beauty. Nice to have it back," he said and tucked it into his waistband and continued to search through the valise.

"What are you looking for?" I asked.

"My cousin had two hand-crafted pieces, and both were missing when we found his body."

"There was only one in Bandini's safe," I said.

"I guess I owe Ronnie an apology for suspecting he had taken out my cousin. Bandini probably sold this gun's twin to another collector."

Other than the rods, there wasn't anything of interest in our baggage.

"You know what I think? I think that whole bit about having incriminating pictures of me and some of my men was a bluff. Bandini told me he burned those pictures when I became police chief."

"And you believed him?"

He turned to his men and told them to cuff us both.

"I suggest you lift up the bottom support in the valise," I said to the chief.

The color drained from his face as he pulled free a picture. He ordered his men outside, closed the compartment door, and removed our handcuffs.

"I don't know where you hid the rest of this crap, but if any pictures like this one ever go public, I'll make sure you're both hunted down."

"Just keep our little deal and you have nothing to worry about. Well, that's not exactly true," I said.

"What the hell is that supposed to mean?"

"We didn't kill Bandini. But we know who did, and they're not happy with the way you treated them."

Jackie pulled a chiv from behind her back. "You shouldn't

assume women aren't as violent as men. Some are more deadly than you would ever suspect," she said, backing him out of the compartment.

She laughed and then turned on me, waving the knife in my face. "What happened to all the pictures and the dough that was in the valise?"

I pushed the chiv aside, grabbed her about the waist, and pinned her to the floor. "I had the hotel mail several packages addressed to my uncle. I anticipated we'd be searched on the way out of town."

I released her as the train departed. She shoved me down onto the cushioned seat, lowered the window shades, and closed the curtain over the door.

The train ride home, in a private compartment, proved once again that having a female partner provided some distinct advantages.

Chapter 37

Every organism pulsates with the energy of each of its cells, giving it the ability to sense its inner workings and deal with threats to its well-being. Likewise, city neighborhoods are alive, forever changing, interconnected and vulnerable. Their streets enable residents to move from place to place, send information with lightning speed, and allow police to swarm to trouble spots. In reality, a neighborhood is also no different than a small town. There are no secrets.

Famished, Jackie and I hustled out of the cab from the train station, both anticipating whatever Ma could throw together on short notice. To our surprise, my parents' apartment was jammed with bodies consuming copious amounts of food. When we entered, all motion stopped, the chatter that had echoed down the hallway ceased, and then, as if on cue, the room erupted into cheers.

Ma dropped a plate and lunged toward us. She embraced me and then Jackie. When she backed away, the onslaught began. Uncle Luigi assaulted me with a crushing hug followed by a hardy slap on the back from Castellano. The crowd parted as Ronnie approached. He grabbed my head in both hands and kissed me on each cheek, a sign of respect. Pop shook my hand and pulled me in close, a show of affection rarely given. O'Reilly sat in a corner sipping a beer. He nodded. Martha embraced Jackie, and Sadie did the same.

Rosalie brushed aside Frank Galvano, who had hold of my hand, jumped into my arms and planted a smothering kiss on my lips. She turned red as she slipped out of my embrace, conscious of the raucous yells. She was moving back trying to blend into the crowd when Ma gave her a slap on the rump that once again ignited a chorus of laughter.

It took several hours for the flow of neighbors, eager to hear how Jackie and I had rescued dozens of young women from a raging inferno, to die down. Tony the Butcher had heard that we saved over fifty women and children and that I was covered in burns. I don't know if Gino, who had arrived home with Debbie before us, had embellished the story or if the exaggeration occurred as the story spread from brownstone to brownstone.

It wasn't until midnight that we got down to a core group and into the details of what really happened in Detroit. Ma and the girls went into the kitchen to clean up the mess, and I sat with the men around the dining room table.

"Sorry, Ronnie, that I wasn't able to save your mother. The first floor had been consumed by the time I knew the place was ablaze."

"If you ask me, she got what she deserved. The bitch never cared about me or anyone else. Did she turn over the key before she died?"

Neither Luigi nor Castellano reacted to Ronnie's comment, validating his assessment of his mother.

"She never had the chance."

Ronnie pushed back from the table.

"Then how did you get the dough to bribe the police chief? He never misses a chance to make a deal."

I didn't like his innuendo, but I kept quiet. I rose from the table in a threatening manner to let Ronnie know he needed to be careful. I retrieved a copy of the Detroit paper we had brought back. I threw it across the table at him and then sat down.

"Your friend Nick Bandini was in the process of emptying his safe when Jackie and I dropped in unexpectedly. He had survived the previous night's raid of his hangout and decided to skip town. When we got there, he was in no shape to use his dough, so we took it for safe keeping."

"The way I see it, that scratch belongs to me. Bandini had my speakeasies shutdown and torched my building. I need that dough to rebuild," Ronnie said, looking to Castellano for support.

I cut Ronnie off so Castellano wouldn't get dragged into it. I wasn't sure whose side he would take.

"If you can't get to your money, it's your own damn fault. Why the hell would you entrust that key with your mother when she didn't give a damn about you?"

"Hey, leave that bitch out of this. What we're talking about is Bandini's dough, and I want a cut."

"You got your damn cut," I said. "We paid off the chief to drop the charges against you and gave a chunk of the money to the dames Bandini and the police chief enslaved, and the rest we're keeping for our trouble. If you have a problem with that, I suggest you think twice before bringing it up again."

"Don't expect me to forget about it. We'll have this conversation again once I get things established back in Detroit. That's a promise!"

"You need to face reality," I said. "You have nothing to go back to. Most of your guys either skipped town or are dead. Your speakeasies are shut down, and your whore houses are all out of commission with the dames scattered."

"Listen you son-of-a-bitch, you don't need to worry about my interests. Worry about your back. With Debbie, it won't take long for the dough to be rolling in again."

Hearing the commotion, Ma and the girls moved out of the kitchen, still gripping the pans they were drying, and stood in the doorway.

"What the hell are you talking about?" I shouted.

"Now that Bandini's out of the way, I'll work a deal with the police chief to reopen my speakeasies. My whore houses will be up and running in no time. Dames are easy to come by, and Debbie will attract my best customers back. Before you know it, I'll be on top again."

I'd had enough, so I pulled my rod and slammed it down on the table. "Debbie's not goin' anywhere with you."

"The hell she is. I own her," Ronnie said, reaching for his gun.

Ma hit him in the face with a cast iron skillet, shattering his nose. Pop grabbed his wrist, and in one quick motion, snapped it back until it broke. Ronnie's gun flew across the room as he yelped in pain. He reached for his other gun with his good hand.

Castellano and Luigi threw him against the wall and held him there while I removed his weapon.

Castellano snarled in Ronnie's face. "You better listen and listen good. Joey paid the old debt we owed you, so it's time for you to get the hell out of town."

They led him out the door, shoved him along the stoop, and watched him stumble down the stairs to the sidewalk. Back inside, Pop went to help Ma clean the blood off the floor while Castellano came over to Jackie and me and nudged us aside.

"We haven't seen the last of that rake, so be careful.

Under normal circumstances he's dangerous, now he'll be obsessed."

I wasn't worried about Ronnie at the moment. By morning, every street kid would know Castellano wanted Ronnie out of town. He only had one choice: crawl back to Detroit and reestablish his business endeavors.

"I don't think we'll hear from Ronnie for some time. He might try to take a potshot on the way out of town, but he knows if he does, you won't let him get far," I said to Castellano.

"Speaking of potshots, did you hear what happened to Gino?" Castellano asked.

"No!" Jackie and I said in unison.

"I think its best I get goin' and have Butch make sure Ronnie gets on the morning train to Detroit. Why don't you have your pop or Martha give you the details about Gino?"

"Is he hurt?" Jackie asked.

"He was lucky," Castellano said, heading for the door.

In all the excitement, I hadn't noticed that Gino and Debbie had never shown up to greet us.

Chapter 38

Ma and Pop retired for the night, and O'Reilly left soon after Castellano, leaving Martha and Rosalie to give us a rundown on Gino's brush with death.

According to Rosalie, after Gino returned from Detroit, someone fired two shots through the front window of Pop's repair shop. The first grazed Gino's cheek, and if he hadn't ducked, the second bullet would have splattered his brains on the wall behind the counter.

Martha took over the story and made it clear I had been wrong in thinking Gino's life wasn't in danger. Somehow the killer now knew that Gino was hanging around the docks on the night Kowalski got bumped. Martha reasoned that, in the killer's mind, Gino had to be eliminated.

Once Martha got going, there was no stopping her. "Not only were you wrong about Gino, you also made the mistake of leaving me to solve Frank's case."

"We still have time," I said.

"Not according to Frank. He hasn't missed an opportunity to drive home the point that O'Reilly and I haven't made much progress."

It was late, and after Martha's emotional dump, sleep was no longer an option. I suggested we retreat to my apartment so Ma and Pop could get some rest.

* * * * *

Rosalie had grabbed medical supplies from her room and, upon entering my apartment, insisted she change my bandages. She removed the gauze from my hands while Jackie attended to my head.

Jackie pulled the gauze off my scalp, rupturing several blisters. Yellowish-green pus oozed over the side of my head, filling the room with a fetid odor. She stepped back to catch her breath, holding the putrid bandage at arm's length. Rosalie took the gauze and flushed it down the john. She placed a mask over her nose and mouth and proceeded to clean and disinfect the offensive areas. She directed Jackie to apply a salve to my hands and told her not to wrap them again until morning. They showed signs of healing, unlike the burns on my scalp that were clearly infected.

Martha opened a window and busied herself in the kitchen, rummaging through the cupboard for the pieces to my coffee pot. She pulled open all the drawers, making a racket while moving everything around.

"Where's the glass dome that fits into the lid?" she asked.

"Look in the cup on the counter next to the icebox," I said in a high-pitched voice as Rosalie dabbed peroxide on the infected areas.

"You need to see a doctor first thing in the morning," Rosalie said.

I didn't want to waste time in a doctor's office, not with Kowalski's killer still on the prowl. I convinced Rosalie to continue treating the infected blisters for at least the next few days, but only after I agreed to take her advice and seek medical help if the sores deteriorated. Satisfied, she left the apartment, eager to get some rest. She had an early morning class.

With Rosalie gone, Martha, Jackie, and I—each with a fresh cup of joe—got down to business.

"Where's Gino now?" I asked.

"Doctor Schwartz hired him at the clinic," Martha said.

She went on to explain that when Gino and Debbie arrived home from Detroit and told Ma that Debbie wanted to return to the clinic on Staten Island, she suggested that Maria, the owner of La Cucina Restaurant, go along to see Dr. Schwartz. Maria had sold the clinic to him after her husband died, and the doctor still owed her money. Dr. Schwartz didn't hesitate to take Debbie back as a patient, and when he heard Gino's tragic story, he offered Gino a job caring for the girls' minor illnesses and complaints. At the time, Gino turned down the position, but soon after the attempt on his life, reconsidered.

We agreed that Debbie and Gino were safe for the time being, so we shifted our focus to Kowalski.

"Did O'Reilly make any progress while we were gone?" Jackie asked.

Martha said the DA had closed the books on the waterfront murders, including Kowalski's, and tied O'Reilly up on higher profile investigations. On his personal time, O'Reilly had helped Martha the best he could with Frank's case. Martha thought she might have found a break when she recently went through the Kowalski file again after the attempt on Gino's life and found an old lead that we had failed to follow up on.

"You might recall that Toby Tobias is the guy who got passed up by Kowalski for a foreman position. He's also the one who got the job after Kowalski's death. I asked your pop to check around, and it's fair to say, Toby wasn't happy with Castellano or Kowalski when he initially didn't get the job," Martha said.

I committed to tracking down Tobias, and Jackie and I

agreed to visit the clinic to see if Debbie and Gino needed anything. Martha then launched another salvo at both of us.

"Didn't I tell you not to leave for Detroit before Frank's case was resolved? Now we're gonna lose another day as you traipse around looking for Tobias and traveling to the clinic? Why didn't you agree with Frank and have him hire another flatfoot? The hearing is a little less than a week away and the old lady's actions before she was run down make no sense. In my opinion, the only things I know for certain are that her nephew is a creep and her lawyer's a shyster."

It had been a long day and the last thing we needed was to rehash the past. I knew I should avoid a confrontation with Martha because things would quickly get out of hand. But for some reason, I couldn't resist.

"You were the one who told Frank not to give the case away, so why blame me?"

"You know damn well I didn't want to give him the satisfaction of pushing me off the case. If you were sharp, you would've found a way to agree with him without implying that I couldn't handle things. If you had, we wouldn't be in this mess, and I could've gone to Detroit with you guys. Or was that the plan all along? Leave me here to be the fall guy while you two get to be alone without me hangin' around."

Seeing that I'd had enough, Jackie stepped into the fray and calmed down the rhetoric. "We're familiar with your ability to gather facts, so tell us what you've learned. We'll work together to get Frank what he needs to defend his client's interests," she said. "Let's start with why you say Frank's client is a creep?"

Martha stepped back and took a deep breath. "According to Frank he's a reputable book dealer, but when I entered his shop, I couldn't stand the musty odor that permeated the place. I can guarantee you if he's dealing in rare books, he wouldn't have mildewed books stored anywhere on the premises. Besides, he just gives me the heebie-jeebies."

Martha then went on to give a brief impression of each beneficiary. The priest and rabbi appeared to be on the level; neither would benefit from any inheritance money. She accused the chauffeur of making a deal with the grim reaper because in the last six years, four of his employers had died of natural or suspicious causes. Coincidently, he was in the wills of three of them for compensation equal to a year's pay or more. Next she described the old lady's companion—who did most of the domestic work for Ruth—as a lonely spinster who glommed on to the first man who had made a proposal. Who, according to Martha, just happened to be a known swindler. She speculated that he could've gotten wind that the companion was in Ruth's will and saw an opportunity to cash in. A car accident, followed by a quick divorce, and he's in the dough.

Martha became really animated when she got to the lawyer.

"I don't think I saw a client come or leave his office who wasn't over eighty. His whole practice is built around fleecing the elderly on the way to their graves."

"Is that an opinion or a fact?" I asked.

"I checked court records, goin' back two years for probate cases he brought before the bench. In every instance, his clients wanted their assets liquidated before distribution. As the executor, he received a percentage of all sales. Some of the estates—Ruth's is a great example—were extraordinarily valuable."

With that statement, we parted and agreed not to show up for work until noon at the earliest.

Chapter 39

Upon waking the next day well past noon, I opened the apartment window to fill my lungs with the breeze blowing off the bay. I was struck by the sights and sounds that didn't exist ten days ago, prior to leaving for Detroit.

I gazed up and down the block as I did as a kid, still amazed by how quickly life in the city changed between seasons. The gloomy cloud cover and constant threat of rain in April and May often washed away any sense of spring, leaving only three seasons. With the emergence of summer, however, the local vitality—characteristic of New York—returned virtually overnight.

The once nearly empty street was now besieged with a horde of vendors hawking their wares from two-wheeled carts. Merchandise lined the front of Mom and Pop shops, and the concrete stoops leading to each brownstone swelled with old timers hungry for the latest gossip.

Pop had told me the night before that all concerns about the danger my detective agency brought to the neighborhood had disappeared. The stoops were abuzz with exaggerated details of how I had rushed into a burning building to save helpless women. Once again I was the local hero who had returned home with more war medals than the entire neighborhood. The person who single-handedly brought a crazed mobster, Bobby Stefano, face to face with the type of justice everyone from the old country understood—an eye for an eye, death for death.

While I was still frozen in time, reflecting on my childhood, Luigi marched into my apartment waving two tickets for a Yankees-Red Sox game. I turned down his offer. I already had my mind set on finding Toby Tobias, the longshoreman who had taken over Kowalski's foreman position. Luigi didn't give up easily.

"Kid, I'm telling ya, you need to take a break. Didn't you hear what I said? Babe Ruth is going up against his old team. I bet he hits at least three out of the park."

"Maybe some other time. I have business to take care of that can't wait. Tell you what. I'm gonna see Gino and Debbie today so why don't I give them the tickets," I said, snatching them from his hand. "I bet it's been years since they've seen a game."

"Why the hell not? It wouldn't be any fun goin' to the game with you anyhow. Since you went off to war, you're not the same. You just don't know how to have a good time anymore. Do yourself a favor, take a day off and get blotto."

I promised to follow his advice when Kowalski's killer was either dead or in the clink.

* * * * *

The girls were nowhere to be found when I got to the office, so I headed down to Waters Street to find Toby on my own.

The docks bustled with activity, making it difficult to walk along the waterfront. Five freighters were in the process of unloading cargo, and several more waited offshore for slots to open up. Flatbed trucks rolled in and out of the wharfs, often cutting corners or jumping onto the sidewalks. Some double parked, which routinely resulted in fist fights between the truckers, attracting onlookers.

I shoved my way through the chaos and asked one of the foremen if he knew where Tobias and his crew were working. He said Tobias wouldn't be hard to find, "cause you can hear him chewing out his men before you get close enough to see him." Five minutes later I had no doubt I'd found my man.

"What the hell is wrong with you bums?" Tobias yelled. "You move like a bunch of old ladies with piles. We need to have this load out of here before the next ship docks."

He pushed two workers aside and hurled hundred-pound sacks of grain onto a truck as if he were tossing feather pillows. I was about to tap his shoulder when he pivoted and knocked into me.

"You looking for work? If you can do what I just did, you're hired," he said walking past me, but then he turned and stared. "Wait a minute. I know you. You're that Batista fella everyone's talkin' about."

"That's right."

"Whatayadoin' around here?"

"I'm looking into Kowalski's murder and I'm told you went half crazy when he got bumped over you."

We walked toward each other. He smashed an open palm into my chest, shoving me back a step. "You're damn right. I didn't know who I hated more, Castellano or Kowalski, and I said as much."

"Enough hate to kill Kowalski?"

"Enough to kill them both. You can't run these docks with old men in charge, and that includes Castellano," he said, moving closer.

"Tough talk for a guy about to get pasted if you try pushing me again."

He backed off. "I heard all about you, Batista. You're some kind of war assassin who sneaks around in the middle of the night. I wonder how you'd fare when Butch isn't around to do your dirty work."

"You know somethin', Toby? You just made the top of my list of suspects."

"You put the screws on me and we're gonna find out just how tough you are."

I picked up one of the sacks of grain and tossed it in the air. As he reached up to catch it, I hit him in the chest with another.

"I'm lookin' forward to it," I said.

I left him sprawled on the ground cussing when two more sacks came out of nowhere, knocking him unconscious. I looked back and saw several of his longshoremen grinning.

The course texture of the grain sacks had scraped the freshly healed skin on my palms, but the bleeding was hardly noticeable through the thin layer of gauze. A small price to pay to put Tobias on notice.

* * * * *

I turned onto Market Street and was heading home when Pop slipped out of the shadows and walked beside me.

"If I didn't know better, I'd say you still have a death wish," he said.

"Is there something I should know about Toby?"

"He was once one of Castellano's bodyguards, but then he messed up."

"How?"

"He beat a couple of guys to death without orders."

I needed a moment to think. I leaned against the side of a stoop to block the wind and lit a cigarette. Pop didn't usually say much, but when he did, he chose his words carefully.

"There's a lot you don't know about Castellano," he said, reading my thoughts.

"I don't remember seeing Toby around," I said, and then took a deep drag and continued walking home.

"He showed up during the war, not long after Butch."

"What's he doin' workin' the docks?"

"Beats the hell out of me. You'll have to ask Castellano that one."

Half way up the stairs to my office, I turned and asked Pop what he was doing down by the docks.

"Martha told me this morning that you might confront Toby. When I saw you leave, I followed."

"Thanks," I said, remembering that for an old man he could still handle himself in a fight.

Chapter 40

It was late afternoon by the time I got back to the office after dealing with Tobias. I had expected to see Martha and Jackie working together to review Frank's case and laying out a plan of action. Instead, I was greeted with the aroma of a Cuban cigar and angry voices coming from the inner office. Jackie had a visitor.

"Listen you son-of-a-bitch, I'm gonna tell you one more time, then I want you to get the hell out of this office and never come back without a warrant," Jackie said. "I don't know where Joey went. We had a late night, and I arrived minutes ago to an empty office. Now get out."

I stood to the side of the glass panel that separated the two rooms and watched Jackie argue with the DA. I was about to enter and confront him before Jackie did something drastic when O'Reilly noticed me and moved nonchalantly toward the doorway. He stepped into the waiting area and whispered that a crabber had fished Stefano's body out of the bay. Before O'Reilly could say more, the DA pushed him aside and came toward me, pointing his cigar in a threatening manner.

"You're not gonna get away with this one, Batista. Everyone knows Stefano wanted you dead."

"That's true. But I suggest you save yourself the embarrassment of losing another case. If I were you, I'd take Jackie's advice and get out of here while you still can," I said, nudging past him to give Jackie a good- morning hug.

"So, you admit to killing him," he shouted.

"I didn't have to kill him. Every hit man from here to Chicago had flooded the city to collect the bounty on his head. Why don't you wise up and spend your time chasing real criminals, or are there none left that don't have you on their payroll?"

"Sooner or later, Batista, I'm gonna get my hands around your throat. If not for this murder, then another; corpses are littering the streets since you arrived back from the war."

"Why the hell wouldn't you expect murders to increase in this town? Thousands of unskilled troops came home with the stench of blood still in their nostrils and only the Mafia hiring."

"Nice try, but not all the soldiers enjoyed killing the way you did. You know damn well the docs at the sanitarium where the army held you debated whether you were fit to return to civilian life. If you ask me, they blundered big time."

I glanced at Jackie and O'Reilly to catch their reactions.

"So you didn't tell anyone about your 'mental evaluation,' huh?" The DA said. "Well, don't worry; it won't make any difference to them. Everyone around you knows you're a killer. How could they not?"

"Something you might keep in mind before coming around here accusing me of murder every time you find a floater."

"Is that a threat?"

"Take it any way you want. But I'll tell you this, if you pull another stunt like you did kidnapping Jackie, you're gonna join Stefano as fish bait."

"O'Reilly, arrest this bastard," he shouted.

"What for?"

"You heard him, threatening an officer of the court."

O'Reilly pulled out his cuffs, but then put them back. "Sorry, sir, I wasn't paying attention. It'll be your word against theirs."

"What the hell are you talking about? You're standing not more than five feet away."

"Well, Jackie's an attractive woman, and I guess I was a little distracted," O'Reilly said with a shrug.

Jackie smiled and crossed her legs.

The DA turned away from looking at Jackie and got into O'Reilly's face. "I'm gonna have you busted so low you'll be patrolling the sewage system," he said and shoved him aside and stormed out.

* * * * *

Jackie closed the door and leaned against it with her arms folded against her chest. "Why is it when we make progress in one area, another problem gets bigger or a new one pops up?"

"No different than any other business," I said. "Pop goes from one problem to another, and he simply sells shoes and repairs them."

"There *is* a difference."

"What's that?"

"People don't get killed in the shoe business."

I couldn't argue with that.

"Why don't we take a few minutes and write down everything that's goin' on," I said, while searching my desk drawers for an ink bottle and a pen. Jackie handed me some paper.

"You start," I said. "What's first?"

"Kowalski's murderer. He's the most dangerous. Our only lead is Toby Tobias."

"I took care of Toby this morning."

"I thought we agreed to do that together," Jackie said.

"I tracked him down on my own since you weren't around this morning. Everything turned out okay, but you might say I added another person to the list of thugs who hate my guts."

"If he's our killer and felt cornered, he would have turned on you. You should've taken me along, or did you forget we're partners?"

She had a point. I certainly wouldn't want her to take such a risk.

"Pop was hanging out nearby in case things got nasty."

I didn't think she needed to know that I wasn't aware of his presence until after I had confronted Toby.

"So, what do you think? Can he be our guy?" she asked.

"He's a bully who hates Castellano and disliked Kowalski. That makes him a suspect. What's next on our list?"

"Frank's case, which we can't afford to mess up. We need his business."

"True. And I don't think we've heard the last from Ronnie," I said, jotting down his name below Frank's.

"Don't forget Gino and Debbie," Jackie added.

I looked at the list. It would have been nice if a few more of our clients were the paying kind. "Looks manageable to me," I said.

Jackie took the pen from my hand and scribbled Martha's name on the list. I thought she was kidding, so I scratched it out.

"Didn't you wonder why she was so upset last night?" Jackie asked.

"She wasn't able to solve Frank's case on her own."

"Sometimes I think you're a real flat tire. We had a long talk after we left you, and she wanted to know if things had changed between you and me."

"Like what?"

"Think about it. We spent almost two weeks together in Detroit. She's jealous, and I don't blame her. I would be if the situation were reversed."

"How many times do we have to go through this?" I asked.

Jackie sat on the desk and pushed back my swivel chair with her foot. "As many times as it takes, or until the dynamics in this office change. So, we're both asking you if anything has changed?"

I wasn't ready for this. "I'm not sure what you mean?"

"Well, then I guess Martha has nothing to be jealous about," Jackie said and abruptly got off my desk to go back to hers.

I grabbed her arm. "Wait, just wait. I'm not as much of a flat tire as you might think. But we had already agreed that neither of us is ready to settle down."

"What makes you say that? You don't know how I'm feeling, although you should."

"Do you really think you're ready to quit your job?" I asked.

Jackie gave me a queer look. "Why would I have to quit my job? I've been married before and held an important position at the *Daily News*. Staying at home wasn't a requirement, nor would I have ever agreed to such an arrangement."

"It's the way it is here, though. It's the way it's always been in my family," I said.

"If that's the case, I'm just wasting my time waiting for you to decide when you're ready to get serious about our relationship."

I didn't like where this conversation was going. "Maybe we should talk about this some other time."

"That's fine with me, but let me make something crystal clear. I'm a private investigator and I like my job. If I can't do it with you, I'll start my own business or join another agency. So get the idea of my quitting out of your head just because you have some antiquated concept of how married woman should behave."

We turned toward the office door as Martha entered.

"What are you two yelling about? I could hear your voices out in the hallway," she said.

"Nothing important," Jackie said. "I think we both just realized that you have the right approach and that *I* should also be dating other people."

I don't know who looked more surprised, Martha or me, but Martha didn't miss the opportunity and quickly changed the topic.

"I'm glad you two agree with me on something because we need to make faster progress on the issues facing us."

I crumbled the paper Jackie and I had been working on and tossed it in the waste basket. I didn't want Martha to see her name on the list. Martha went to Jackie and sat beside her on the office couch. That's when I realized, in spite of all our personal tensions, the two of them had become good friends.

* * * * *

We agreed again that Jackie and I should head over to Staten Island and check on Gino and Debbie before we got immersed with Frank's case.

Jackie had called ahead, so when we arrived, Dr. Schwartz interrupted one of his counseling sessions to give us a quick rundown on how things were going.

"Debbie's living in one of the cottages on the grounds, and Gino has the guest bedroom across the hall from my office. He needs to be close by to have easy access to the patients."

"How's it working out?" I asked.

"To be honest, I don't know how I ran the place without them. At first I was hesitant to give Debbie a job, but the girls instinctively knew she understood their internal turmoil and openly share their lives with her. Debbie's insights have already helped me make progress with some of my more difficult patients."

"What about Gino?" Jackie asked.

"I have more time to spend on therapy now that he takes care of their general ailments."

"Can you spare them for a few minutes? We need some information, and I have a couple of tickets to the Yankees game I'd like to give them," I said.

"Sure, Debbie's walking the grounds with a patient, and Gino's having lunch in his room. I thought that game was sold out."

"Are you a fan?" Jackie asked.

"Isn't everyone? Just don't have time since I took over this place," he said, pointing to a stack of patient folders on his desk.

Jackie left to find Debbie, and I was about to knock on Gino's door when I decided to go back into the doctor's office.

"Why is Gino eating in his room? Doesn't everyone have meals together?"

"He's been doing it since he arrived. Breakfast and dinner he joins the rest of us and seems fine. I suspect he still needs a drink to get through the day."

"Has that been a problem?" I asked.

"Not yet. I've decided to give him another week, and if his behavior doesn't change, I'll confront him."

* * * * *

Gino didn't have the chance to disguise the smell of cheap whiskey on his breath.

"No lectures," he said. "I know I'm risking everything now that I'm drinking again."

"You're lucky it's just me. Pop would try to pound some sense into you."

"I don't think he'd give a damn," Gino said.

"You're wrong about that. Everyone cares, the whole neighborhood. This time, they'll not stand by and watch you destroy yourself."

Gino slumped on the side of his bed. "I thought I'd put my family's slaughter behind me, but the attempt on my life last week brought the nightmares back more vivid than ever."

"Why don't you talk with Dr. Schwartz? Maybe he can help you through this."

Gino poured himself a drink. "The only help I need is to see the scum that killed my wife and daughter dead."

I yanked the bottle out of his hand and dumped the whiskey down the bathroom drain.

"I know Jackie and Martha promised we'd investigate,

but it happened so long ago. The chances of finding those guys are slim."

Gino lifted his head and wiped his sleeve across his eyes. "If you don't try, there's no chance. I need hope more than this shot of whiskey," he said, putting the full glass on his nightstand.

"If that's all it takes to keep you sober, let's start."

Gino leaned back against the headboard and closed his eyes.

"How many men attacked you?"

"Two. They were young, no more than twenty years old."

"How did they get into your apartment?"

"They must've followed me into the building. When I turned the key, they shoved me through the door."

"What happened next?"

"My daughter screamed, and the short, stubby guy slapped her hard and told her to shut up. My wife grabbed Jenny and tried to comfort her.

"By stubby, you mean he was fat?"

"No, all muscle, too much for his size."

"What happened next?"

"The other guy threw me up against the wall and shoved a chiv in my back. I felt the tip of the blade pierce my flesh. He demanded money. I had two hundred and twenty under the mattress. I begged them not to hurt my family. They wanted more. I told them it was all we had. They didn't believe me. The stubby guy punched me in the gut and then pounded my head. Jenny screamed again. He turned on her and snapped her neck. In that instant, time seemed to slow down. I saw her face twisted in pain and her neck flop to the side as she floated to the floor. My wife yelled, and I saw the knife slit her throat. Blood squirted everywhere, but what I can't forget is the image of the hand that gripped the blade drenched in blood. Then there was a loud noise like an explosion had gone off in my head. I don't know how long I was out. Blood had soaked my hair and had formed a puddle by the side of my face where I laid. They must have thought I was dead. I wish I had died. There *was* more money in the house. I had more money," Gino sobbed.

I handed Gino his shot of whiskey. I could've used one myself.

Once he downed his drink, I continued to probe.

"I need a better description. What did they look like? Did they have an accent?"

"Italian, they were both Italian. The one who killed my daughter was hairy, like an ape. The other one was almost a foot taller than me, closer to your size."

"Do you remember anything else? Give me more to go on."

"It happened so quickly. I keep hearing Jenny's screams and I see the knife slicing through my wife's throat. There are no faces. There's nothing but a hand gripping a bloody knife. Each time I close my eyes at night, I hear and see it all again. Over and over again."

Gino wept, but I persisted. I knew it would be difficult to get him to speak again of that night.

"Gino, there's a person connected to that hand. See *him*. Focus on his face. What does he look like?"

"I've tried so many times. There's just a hand and a long blade… wait. My God, Joey, what have you done to me? I can see it now. I *never* see it during the day."

Gino jumped off the bed, his eyes bulging. He gripped his stomach. The sound of him retching in the bathroom tore my heart out. He stood in the doorway with a crazed look and then lunged for his desk.

"Until now all I clearly saw was the blade. The hand was just a hand, any hand. But it's not!" he said. He handed me a piece of paper with a ship's anchor hastily drawn.

I looked up from the drawing, confused.

"It's a tattoo; he had a tattoo on the back of his hand. Those droplets of blood are not my wife's; they're part of the tattoo."

Gino had finally admitted his guilt over holding back money, and in doing so, he freed a memory that I was confident would eventually lead to his family's killers. If they were alive after all this time and still in New York, I'd find them.

The real question in my mind was if Gino would have the patience to wait until we could actively pursue his case, or would he once again set out on his own to seek revenge?

"Gino, you have an opportunity for a new life here at the clinic. Are you gonna take advantage of it or throw it away?"

"Will you bring them to justice?"

"One way or another I will."

"That's good enough for me. I've spent enough of my life wallowing in the past. I think it's time to move on," he said. He handed me his empty whiskey glass. "I won't need this."

Leaving his room, I realized the burden had shifted from his shoulders to mine. His nightmare was now mine until I found the creeps that had killed his wife and daughter.

* * * * *

I assumed that by the time I had finished with Gino, Jackie

would have found Debbie somewhere on the clinic grounds. Unable to locate them, I headed toward Debbie's cottage. On the way I stopped at the spot where Shirley, Debbie's sister, had admitted to me she had shot and killed Castellano's brother. That had been my first real case, but I hadn't turned Shirley over to the law or to Castellano because his brother got what he deserved. In the end, it didn't do Shirley any good. She died a horrific death. I had promised Shirley that I would look after Debbie, a promise I intended to keep.

I knocked on Debbie's cottage door. Jackie opened the door, and Debbie flew into my arms.

"I don't know how to thank you, both of you," she said.

"The doc tells us you're doing wonders with his patients," I said.

"Now I know why my sister was so happy here. She felt a purpose in life."

Jackie closed the door behind us. "Do you still have the tickets to the baseball game?" she asked with an impish smile.

"Gino's in no shape to take Debbie to a game. It's a shame to waste these," I said, holding them in my hand.

Debbie snatched the tickets. "All the doc does is talk about baseball. I think it's time I ask him to teach me about the sport."

Jackie smiled and Debbie blushed.

Chapter 41

I waited until we were on the ferryboat headed back to Manhattan before telling Jackie about Gino's revelation. Her immediate reaction was to have Martha investigate if there was any meaning to the tattoo on the killer's hand. I wasn't surprised that she would want to delve into Gino's case now that we had a potential lead. But this wasn't the time to have our attention diverted by murders that took place more than twenty years ago.

"I suggest we stick with our current priorities and pay Frank's client, Mathew Capelli, an unexpected visit. There'll still be a few hours of daylight left by the time the ferry docks."

"You're right. Once we get Frank's case and Kowalski's killer off our backs, we can concentrate on Gino."

A long silence followed Jackie's comment. Normally we discussed many different topics, but since we'd left for Staten Island, we had only talked about business matters. I'd been so disturbed by the way Jackie and I ended our discussion about our relationship that I didn't know how to bring the subject up again. I suspected Jackie felt the same way. At least I hoped she did.

I took Jackie's hand and led her to the boat railing to gaze out over the water at the Statue of Liberty. I needed to say something to make things right between us.

"I realize I was out of line earlier. I don't know what the

future holds, but I do know I want a wife who values her independence."

"That's quite a change from what you said."

"We have a dangerous profession, and I worry about your safety. It would be even worse if we were married, but I wouldn't expect you to quit your job."

"That's good to know, but it's a little late. You made me realize I had narrowed my life down to the agency and you, which puts me behind the eight ball."

"What does that mean?"

"That I meant everything I said. You have a right to be with Martha or anyone else. And so do I."

The ferry docked, hitting the pilings and jolting the passengers. Jackie fell into my arms.

"I do love you," I said.

"I know, but it's not enough for me to put my life on hold waiting for you to make a real commitment. Our time in Detroit made a difference to me, but apparently not to you"

"You're not leaving?"

"No, I like my job. Like you said, let's not waste daylight. It's time to pay Capelli a visit."

* * * * *

Capelli's book store was situated in the middle of an exclusive row of shops near Broadway. His building looked rundown compared to his neighbors, which showcased expensive jewelry or the latest clothing fashions. In contrast, a simple wooden sign announced Capelli's profession, "Rare Books."

A guttural voice, devoid of emotion, responded to the sound of a small bell attached to the door.

"Feel free to browse, and let me know if you have any questions. My rare books collection is located upstairs in the loft, but no one is allowed in that section. If you're interested in a specific title, I'll fetch it for you."

Jackie pointed to an old desk in a dark corner where Capelli sat hidden, nothing visible except for his bald head peeking above stacks of haphazardly placed books.

"We're here to ask a few questions about your aunt's death. Frank Galvano sent us," Jackie said, holding a handkerchief over her mouth and nose.

Martha had understated the musty odor that permeated the store. Coughing, Jackie brushed up against a bookcase and inadvertently touched several books. Her hand immediately began to swell and become itchy with red welts.

I'd seen a few soldiers during the war break out in hives when they entered the basements of bombed-out buildings. Mold that had been undisturbed for decades irritated their skin and lungs. Jackie needed to leave.

"You're having a reaction to the air in the store. Wait outside," I said, opening the door.

Capelli unraveled his gangly legs from behind his desk and extended a skeletal-hand with exceptionally long fingers. His face was even more emaciated with eye sockets deeply set next to a long, boney nose and sunken cheeks.

"I see your associate has left," he said. "Will she return?"

"To be honest, Mr. Capelli, the musty odor in this place is overwhelming. It's nearly dinner time; I suggest we find a local diner to conduct our interview."

"I understand. Many of my books come from estate sales. Some have been stored improperly for years. I just don't have time to sort through the endless supply of boxes

I impulsively buy. I assure you, however, that all the books upstairs are of the highest quality."

"If they weren't, I don't think you'd be able to afford a shop in such an exclusive section of the city."

"I've been fortunate to make a number of lucrative finds over the years," he said.

"Still, I'm surprised you don't take better care of your premises," I said, letting him know to expect a tough interview.

"I make my living being an expert in my field and that requires research. I don't have time to be fastidious, and besides, it's not necessary. A true collector will overcome any obstacle to track down a unique book."

I took a step back, glanced around, and caught an interesting glimpse of Capelli framed within the background of his disarrayed book store. I was reminded of Martha's description of him. He would give the average bloke the heebie-jeebies.

"Not being a collector, I'll wait outside with my partner until you join us," I said, anxious to take in a deep breath of fresh air.

* * * * *

Once we had finished eating, I dispensed with small talk and hit Capelli with a question I believed would either end the conversation or reveal what was going on in Ruth's life prior to her death.

"Frank told us you and your aunt had a falling out and that you refused to give him any of the details. Why would you hold back information from your lawyer?"

Capelli took a long sip of coffee, draining his cup, and then methodically turned it upside down on the saucer.

"It's not germane to your investigation."

"You should let us make that determination," Jackie said.

"If we're gonna uncover a reason to invalidate your aunt's will, you need to tell us everything you know about what was happening in her life, including the details of your relationship with her," I said.

"And if I don't?"

I waved the waitress over for the bill. "We'll recommend to Frank to drop your case. It's your decision."

Frank was Capelli's only option at this late date, and he was shrewd enough to know we were aware of that fact.

"Aunt Ruth accused me of stealing the rarest book in my uncle's collection. She wouldn't even consider the fact that any member of her domestic household had easier access to his collection than I did."

"How valuable a book?" Jackie asked.

"Priceless. The first book ever printed—the 1455 Gutenberg Bible. Slightly less than two hundred were produced and an unknown quantity still exists."

"Certainly a temptation for any book dealer. I can see why your aunt suspected you," I said.

"My uncle introduced me to rare books at an early age, and it has turned into a profitable livelihood. I fully expected to inherit his collection when my aunt died. I had no motive to steal it."

"Unless you had a buyer," Jackie said.

Capelli ignored her statement.

"Was there an investigation?" I asked.

"No, my aunt didn't want a family scandal made public."

"Since you weren't invited to the beneficiary party your

aunt gave after she signed a new will, can we assume she continued to suspect you?" I asked.

"That's the strangest part of this mystery. The morning after the party, Aunt Ruth called, apologized for her behavior, and said she planned to change her will back to what she and my uncle had agreed upon."

"Does that mean she intended to reinstate your inheritance?" Jackie asked.

"Yes."

"Did she say what changed her mind?"

"No, the conversation was brief. Someone came into the parlor and she disconnected."

I thought it was convenient that Ruth had undergone a change of heart with no witnesses available to confirm Capelli's version of her intent.

"Tell us about the beneficiaries," I said.

"I don't know a whole lot. I didn't spend much time with my aunt. It never occurred to me my inheritance was at risk or I would have."

Jackie's facial expression changed to one of disgust.

"Do the best you can," I said to keep Capelli engaged and give Jackie time to regain her composure.

"Althea, her house maid and companion, had been with Aunt Ruth for many years and had recently married. She occupied a flat next to my aunt's. The chauffer is relatively new, maybe with her six months or so. My aunt and uncle honored each other's religion, so her rabbi and his priest have been around for a long time. Ruth spent considerable time after my uncle's death trying to reconcile both religions. I know even less about the lawyer. The family solicitor died months ago. I don't understand how she ended up with this shylock. Have you ever heard of a lawyer putting himself in a client's will?"

"Not being a lawyer, I can't say."

I asked Jackie if she had any more questions.

"I do. Mr. Capelli, I believe you estimated your aunt's estate at five hundred thousand. Is that correct?"

"That was a rough guess. My aunt and uncle accumulated an impressive array of investment properties over the years."

"How did they make their money?"

"My uncle was a builder. He financed many of the exclusive apartments on West Fifty-Ninth Street between Broadway and Seventh Avenue. In fact, they lived in one of his more expensive flats."

"An associate of ours has been going through Ruth's apartment, with Frank's permission. The details from the early Victorian period, especially the exquisite tin-engraved ceiling tiles and imported antique furniture, impressed her. And strangely, she didn't find any modern clothes in Ruth's closets. Would you say your aunt was obsessed with that time period?" Jackie asked.

"The older she became, the more money Ruth spent on reproducing the era of her childhood. She spared no expense. I guess you could call it an obsession."

"Was she generous with her money?" I asked.

"How do you mean?"

"Did she have some favorite charities? Did she support your business before you had your falling out?"

"My business doesn't need to be subsidized. I'm a well-known and respected dealer in rare books."

"I didn't mean to imply differently, but I'm interested in knowing how you got started in the business," I said.

Capelli hesitated. "If you must know, my uncle financed my venture many years ago with a portion of his personal collection."

"Ruth's library is bare. What happened to your uncle's books?" Jackie asked.

Capelli got up to leave. "I must attend to my business," he said. "I took them for safe keeping. If you're wondering, the police have a list of the books in my possession."

"If your aunt's will is upheld, who would inherit the collection?" I asked.

"That's not going to happen," he said.

"And if it does?"

"Her rabbi. He's a collector of rare books."

When he left the restaurant, I asked Jackie for her impression.

"He's not telling the whole truth. I agree with Martha. His business isn't doing that great. No reputable dealer would allow mildewed books in his store."

"Ten to one he stole that Bible," I said.

"So what's our next move?"

"We'll have Martha stay focused on Ruth's apartment to see what more she can find while we visit the two lawyers."

"You realize we're retracing Martha's steps, and she didn't find anything useful."

"Something will turn up. It always does," I said with more confidence than I felt.

* * * * *

In the stairwell leading to our office, we heard Martha pounding on her typewriter. Jackie pulled me back from the landing.

"I have a date tonight and need to get ready. Why don't you fill Martha in on the information you got from Gino and our discussion with Capelli."

Stunned, I was unable to respond before she continued down the hallway. I stood watching until she entered her apartment.

The noise from the typewriter had stopped, and the door flew open as I reached for the knob. Both Martha and I stepped back.

"I was just calling it quits for the day," Martha said, holding the door open for me to pass. I didn't budge.

"Where's Jackie?" Martha asked, looking past me.

"She's getting ready to go out," I said, still in a fog.

"That's right, Jackie told me she had a date with one of her old co-workers at the *Daily News*. He's been pestering her for some time and he called before you guys left for the Island," Martha said. She headed up the stairs. "I'm eating in my apartment tonight. Why don't you join me? You look like you could use a stiff drink and a good meal. I can arrange for both."

* * * * *

Martha added some fresh spices to the spaghetti sauce simmering on the stove while I filled a large pot with water.

"Why did you take me up on my invitation?" she asked, as she tasted the sauce from a wooden spoon and added more oregano.

I didn't answer right away. Jackie had set the stage for this encounter by laying down new ground rules for our relationships and it felt like both women were taking quick advantage of them. So I decided to do the same.

I poured two glasses of wine and placed them on the table. Martha took her seat and watched while I set the table and added salt to the boiling water. Martha sipped her wine and placed an elbow on the table, resting her chin in that hand, and waited patiently for a response to her question. We both knew my answer would determine how the night would go.

"I want to say I was wrong for leaving you alone to work Frank's case. I left you in a dangerous situation with an impossible task."

"So, you don't have confidence in me?"

I smiled.

"What's so funny? Do you or don't you?"

"I'm not going to answer. You like to argue. No matter what I say, there's gonna be tension between us. You'll either shove me out the door or we'll end up in your bed."

She smiled, which confirmed that truth was the best way to deal with Martha. Choosing words carefully to avoid conflict made things worse.

I got up from the table to add the spaghetti to the boiling water. "Do you think Jackie and I are good private investigators?" I asked.

Martha took another sip of her wine. "I haven't given that much thought. I guess that's a good sign."

"We both got our credentials from mail order courses, and since I started the business a year and a half ago, I've been fighting to stay alive, dealing with hoodlums and the Mafia. And taking Jackie on as a partner hasn't changed that dynamic. We haven't solved a single legitimate case."

"That's not true! You found a mass murderer and proved Castellano's brother didn't commit suicide. Don't forget how we met; you helped Tony the Butcher out of a jam."

"Kowalski's murderer is still a threat to us all and even

Frank's case is beyond me. To make matters worse, I find it boring. I know Ruth Capelli was probably murdered, but it's not a dangerous case."

"That's the business we're in; you should see some of the clients I've turned away. Trust me, you should be grateful you cross paths with the Mafia every now and then, and that the DA hates your guts."

While we talked, I got up a few more times to stir the spaghetti. When it was ready, I served two heaping dishes smothered in tomato sauce that was seasoned to perfection. I had no idea Martha could cook.

She spent the meal drilling me about Detroit and Ronnie. We cleared the table and then sat on the sofa to finish the remaining wine.

I felt pleased I had skillfully eliminated the friction that had separated us since Jackie and I returned from Detroit. That is, until Martha knocked off her fourth glass of wine and got personal.

"Do you love Jackie?" she asked.

"I do."

"What about me?"

"It's different."

"How?"

"Hard to explain," I said.

"Give it a try."

I stood and pulled her off the sofa into my arms. "As I said once before, I would give my life to save you both without hesitation, and I'm attracted to you. But I can't deny that with Jackie I'm feeling something different."

Martha broke my embrace and led me toward her bedroom.

"I'm not gonna shove you out the door, not yet anyway.

But when you and Jackie get serious or I find who I'm looking for, it'll be a different story."

"You told me that once before, and it got me into big trouble," I said.

"That's because you dropped me just because I dated someone else. I'll let you know when it's time to end our intimacy."

"What about Jackie? Does she feel the same way?"

"I'm taking you into my bedroom and you're asking about Jackie?"

I had a lot to learn about women, but I knew what I had to do. I swept her off her feet, kicked the bedroom door shut, and never gave Jackie a second thought.

Chapter 42

The next morning when I entered the inner office, the girls were sitting opposite each other discussing whether Ronnie would create problems down the road. I took the chair between them, and Jackie abruptly changed the subject.

"I thought you were goin' to tell Martha about our discussions at the clinic and with Ruth's nephew," Jackie said. "She doesn't know anything about what Gino recalled regarding the killers of his family."

"You were gone a long time in Detroit. Joey and I had a lot to catch up on," Martha said.

"I hope Joey was able to satisfy your *need* for information."

There are no words to describe the look Jackie gave me. It was a blend of curiosity and jealousy. But thankfully, it wasn't hate.

I must have looked panicked, because they both broke out laughing. It was time for me to relax and realize the three of us had interwoven our lives in a way that was acceptable to everyone. We knew where we stood with each other.

"Please don't do that again," I said.

"Just remember, we are as free as you," Jackie said.

Her message was clear. The longer our arrangement continued, the higher the risk of my losing both women. A risk I wasn't sure I wanted to take.

* * * * *

Jackie and I had just finished giving Martha our impressions of Mathew Capelli when O'Reilly showed up. He wore street clothes, which either meant he had resigned from the force or the DA hadn't been able to follow through on his threat to have him busted back to walking a beat. He didn't keep us wondering.

"The chief told the DA to quit meddling in his department's business and promoted me back to lieutenant, on the spot," O'Reilly said, with open arms.

The girls each gave him a hug and I shook his hand.

"Since when did the chief get a backbone?" I asked.

"My guess is both City Hall and the mayor have turned against the DA. Just too much bad publicity. The body count from his botched attempt to get hold of Jackie's ex-husband's book of names was excessive. Besides, I wasn't the only one the DA had the chief demote because they wouldn't cooperate with his corrupt sense of justice. If you ask me, the chief was also losing credibility within the ranks and needed to reestablish his authority."

O'Reilly sat down, and we continued our discussion about Ruth's death.

"Mike, did you come up with any new leads since you reopened the file on Ruth Capelli's death?" I asked.

"Martha's been doing all the interviews with people involved in the estate, and I'm sure she's already given you her impressions. I've been goin' over the evidence from the scene and talking to eye witnesses. All we know for sure is that the driver was a white male in a Model T."

"Was she killed instantly?" Jackie asked.

"The coroner's guess is she died when her head hit the

road, but he's not sure. She had multiple head injuries and massive internal bleeding."

"I know the driver didn't stop, but did anyone go to her as she lay in the street?" I asked.

"Sure, but she was dragged for almost a city block before she rolled out from under the car into traffic. By the time anyone got to her, she was dead."

Silence fell over the room. I'm sure we all had the same image of Ruth's body bouncing under the car over the cobblestones, each hoping she had died instantly.

Martha broke the trance when she mentioned she had met with Ruth's new lawyer, a Vincent Rivisi. Ruth never made it to their first appointment because she was run over on the way to his office. Martha had a follow-up meeting scheduled just in case he might have remembered something critical after having thought about it for a few days.

Martha reluctantly agreed that Jackie and I would keep her appointment with Vincent Rivisi while she went through Ruth's apartment one more time. She had initially argued her presence was important since she had established a rapport with Rivisi. I disagreed. I had already arranged a morning meeting with Ruth's solicitor, a Mr. Doyle, who'd written the contested will. By meeting the same day with Rivisi, Jackie and I would have a good feel for both lawyers. O'Reilly said he'd be available if needed, but he had higher priority cases to work on.

With that settled, O'Reilly mentioned he'd had some of his contacts check on Ronnie's progress in Detroit.

"Ronnie has reopened two of his speakeasies and hired several well-known torpedoes for protection. He is successfully rebuilding his organization."

"How long before he's back at full strength?" Martha asked.

"That's hard to predict, but given that the cops are looking the other way, I'd say another month."

"Unless one of the local bosses decides he's getting too big," I said.

O'Reilly got up to leave. "Word on the street is that Ronnie took out Bandini while on the lam, an impressive feat. With respect like that, he'll be allowed to expand."

We put concerns about Ronnie aside since the hearing for Ruth's will was quickly approaching, and Frank needed a day or two to prepare. Time was running out.

* * * * *

We entered the law office of Doyle and Son at the appointed time only to find the elder Doyle with a client. While I tried unsuccessfully to engage the receptionist in a conversation, Jackie sat next to the only other person in the waiting area.

"She's not friendly at all," the woman loudly whispered.

"Have you been waiting long?" Jackie asked.

"Oh, don't worry dear. I always come early. Something to do you know?"

"I couldn't help noticing the beautiful broach you're wearing. Aren't you afraid someone might try to rob you?"

"My dear girl, if you were my age, you would welcome that kind of excitement in your life. Besides, no one pays attention to an old woman."

Mr. Doyle entered the waiting area from his office, escorted his client to the door, and handed him his cane. "Don't worry. My secretary will call when the papers are ready for your signature."

The receptionist handed Doyle a slip of paper. He turned,

greeted everyone, and invited Jackie and me into his office. Jackie stood by his corner windows, mesmerized by the spectacular harbor view of tugboats maneuvering huge ships around and sky boys crisscrossing steel beams calling up more girders to complete the steel skeleton of a nearby skyscraper. Everything about Mr. Doyle oozed success, from his tailored suit to his diamond-studded ring to the thick, gold, pocket watch chain that spanned his considerable girth.

"How can I help you, Mr. Batista?"

"We're investigating the death of one of your clients, a Ruth Capelli."

"I didn't realize the police department had women detectives," he said, glancing at Jackie.

"Mrs. Forsythe and I are private investigators. Sorry if we gave your receptionist the wrong impression."

"I see," he said, as he pulled open a drawer and placed a bottle of scotch and two shot glasses on the desk. "Would you care to join me?" he asked.

"I imagine the quality of your whiskey matches that of your office decor, so we would be foolish to turn down such an offer," I said, handing Jackie my glass and picking up his.

"Oh, I'm sorry, Mrs. Forsythe, I should have known better," he said.

He found another glass and filled it for himself.

"Mrs. Capelli's accident happened some time ago. Why the sudden interest?" he asked, after tossing back his drink.

"I know you're aware an injunction has been ordered against executing the new will you penned for Mrs. Capelli. Our firm has been hired by Mr. Mathew Capelli's attorney," I said. "You may recall, Mathew Capelli is Ruth Capelli's only living relative."

Doyle poured himself another drink without offering to refill ours.

"I do have a client waiting, so how can I help you?"

"I'll get to the point. Don't you think it's unprofessional to write yourself into Mrs. Capelli's will?"

"I'm afraid you have been ill informed. I'm not a beneficiary, only the executor. Any other questions?"

"I disagree with your assessment, especially since you will receive much more than some of the beneficiaries. Isn't it true that the will states, as executor, you have complete control over the liquidation of all assets and receive a sizable commission with each sale?"

"Rare, but not unusual. Is that all?"

"Her new will also stipulates that all assets will be liquidated prior to settlement."

"Like I said, rare but not unusual."

"Didn't you think her choice of beneficiaries is odd given her prior will?"

"Not at all. It was nice meeting you both, especially you, Mrs. Forsythe, after reading so much about your murder trial last year. Please call again if I can be of assistance."

Doyle was giving us the bum's rush and had lied about not knowing who we were. Jackie took advantage of the moment.

"We certainly will," she said. "But in any event, we'll see each other at the hearing. I'll be glad to answer any lingering questions you might have about my trial at that time. Isn't it gratifying to know that when the truth comes out, justice prevails?"

Doyle wasn't about to give Jackie the last word.

"I've found, and I'm sure you have as well, that in the

courtroom truth is subjective, and it is dependent on the skill of your solicitor. Good day, Mrs. Forsythe."

Leaving Doyle's building, I hoped our next meeting with the lawyer Ruth Capelli had called on the morning of her death would be more cordial.

* * * * *

The minute I met Vincent Rivisi, I knew why Martha had looked disappointed when we took over the interview. He had all the attributes Martha looked for; he was a young, tall, handsome professional with the potential to provide financial stability. I had the feeling we would be seeing a lot more of Rivisi, even after this case was long over. From Jackie's reaction, I think she had the same thoughts, but not necessarily for Martha.

"Mrs. Forsythe, are you okay?" Rivisi asked.

"Sorry, something crossed my mind that distracted me. Please continue."

"As I was saying, I don't think I can help with your investigation. Mrs. Capelli and I never actually met."

"There's a good chance you were the last person she spoke with before her death. Did Mrs. Capelli say why she selected you to alter her new will?" Jackie asked, ready to take notes.

"I did ask who referred her to my office. Her response was not what I expected. I'm apparently the closest lawyer within walking distance to her apartment."

I thought that was an odd reason since Ruth had her chauffeur take her everywhere, even to the local stores. "Were those her exact words?" I asked.

"The best I can remember."

"When did you agree to meet with her?" Jackie asked.

"The same day. She died not ten feet from my office. She had insisted I rearrange my schedule so we could meet that very afternoon. To be honest, I'm new to this area and don't have many clients. It was easy to oblige her."

"Did she sound angry or distraught when she called?" I asked.

"Agitated would be a better description. She certainly expressed a sense of urgency. Maybe she'd had a premonition."

I wished I had a way to discover what had happened at the party on the night before Ruth's death. Whatever it was, it had a dramatic effect on Ruth and possibly prompted someone to commit murder.

Jackie turned on the way out of the office door and asked if she could return as the investigation progressed.

"Certainly, anything I can do to help," Rivisi said with a smile.

"I'm sure we'll send Martha, our assistant, if it becomes necessary. Thanks for your time," I said, ushering Jackie out the door.

Jackie didn't say anything until we got in the car.

"What was that all about?"

"What?"

"You know what I'm talking about. I'm perfectly capable of doing a follow-up interview."

"That's not your job," I said.

"Then what is?"

"Your job is to track down leads, not to pick up strangers."

"Now you know how it feels," she said, turning to look out the window.

She was referring to Gloria, and Jackie was right. I did now know how it felt.

*****

Jackie joined Martha at Ruth's apartment, and they spent several days locating and sorting through years of papers and documents that Ruth had kept in various hideaways throughout the flat.

I had spent much of that time reassuring Frank we would have something for him by the hearing date. When I wasn't consoling Frank, I was digging into Ruth's nephew's financial background and checking out Vincent Rivisi's story. The only justification I had for my actions was that Mathew Capelli gave me the creeps and that Rivisi was a potential rival for Jackie's and Martha's affection. As it turned out, based on Capelli's recent spending habits, he had either come into a considerable amount of dough or was running up huge debts. Rivisi, on the other hand, had simply lied. There were plenty of experienced lawyers closer to Ruth's apartment than his office.

Frank found both facts interesting. Where did Capelli get his money? And did Ruth lie to Rivisi or did Rivisi lie to us? Frank quit bothering me and followed up on both leads.

On the last day of the girls' search of Ruth's apartment, the coroner's office dropped off Ruth's personal effects that had been removed during the autopsy. O'Reilly had released the contents since there wasn't anything germane to the investigation in Ruth's possessions at the time of her death. Jackie and Martha had hoped they'd find something, but there was nothing of interest. Her tattered coat reminded the girls of the awful death Ruth had suffered and made them more determined to uncover the truth.

We were all convinced, including Frank, that finding out why Ruth had suddenly wanted to change her will again was key to discovering the truth about Ruth's death.

Chapter 43

The three of us gathered in our main office, and I listened while Jackie and Martha laid out the background of Ruth's life. They emphasized their impressions of the circle of characters who influenced Ruth after the passing of her husband. After they had dissected each beneficiary and his or her motivations, I thought maybe the real threat in our city didn't come from the criminal underworld, but from those we trusted.

Finished, they waited for me to comment.

"You've succeeded in convincing me that almost everyone around Ruth had a motive to kill her *if* they knew she had intended to revert back to her previous will. But I'm afraid, until we understand Ruth's motivation, it doesn't get us any closer to finding who actually killed her."

"So you concur that it wasn't an accident," Jackie said.

"You've built a strong argument for that conclusion. I agree that the night before Ruth died she saw or overheard something that made her distrust everyone at the party. I say that because she didn't ask any of them to drive her the next morning to a well-known solicitor. Instead, she chose to walk to a novice lawyer, several blocks from her apartment."

"I'm not sure where this leaves us," Martha said. "How do we find the killer?"

I felt Martha's frustration, but I wasn't ready to give up on the investigation. "There are still a few unanswered questions," I said. "What happened to Ruth's husband's rare Gutenberg Bible and how did Ruth get dragged under the car for such a distance?"

"That never occurred to me," Jackie said. "The car should have rolled over Ruth where she was hit. The Model T has a high road clearance."

"I know why she was dragged—" Martha said, stopping in mid-sentence as a sudden commotion erupted in the hallway.

We stumbled out of our chairs and rushed into Martha's office to investigate. First Pop, then Luigi, were flung through the door and landed at our feet. Butch stood in the doorway with his shirt ripped open, drenched in perspiration. Two old men were no match for Butch, but they were no pushovers either.

"You need to come now," Butch said, lurching toward me.

I stepped back, pulled my rod, and jammed it against his stomach.

"Back off," I yelled.

Butch wiped his brow and plopped down on Martha's desk.

"There's no need for a gun. I'm not here to hurt anyone."

The desk slid back, and papers scattered when Butch pushed himself off and headed for the door. "The Boss sent me to get you. Castellano's son, Carmine, has vanished, along with his wife and kid. Carmine's bodyguards were found dead outside their home. Hurry, my car's out front," he said, then stomped down the stairs.

Martha and Jackie helped Pop and Luigi off the floor.

"What a big, dumb brute," Pop said. "All he had to do

was say why he smashed through the front door and ran up the stairs. Would have saved us a few bruises trying to stop him."

"All brawn and no brains," Luigi said. "How the hell could he not realize we'd be at Castellano's side at a time like this?"

Pop left to tell Ma what was happening and then to join Butch in his car. Luigi ordered me not to leave without him and rushed to his apartment. I pulled the girls back as they headed for the door.

"Stay here. If I need your help, I'll let you know. Frank's counting on us to find who murdered Ruth."

"You know damn well that Kowalski's killer kidnapped Castellano's family, and if I'm right, you'll need us," Jackie shouted, yanking her arm free of my grip.

Frank entered the office with Sadie close behind. "What's all the commotion about?"

"Frank, I'm gonna be gone for a while. The girls will find who murdered Ruth."

Ignoring Frank's protests, I took Jackie, Martha, and Sadie into the inner office and shut the door.

"Sadie, it looks like your father's killer has made another move against Castellano. It has to be obvious, even to you now, that everything that has happened on the waterfront has been about Castellano. I'm sorry, but your father's murder was the means of some demented plan to destroy him. I promise when this is over that your father's death will be avenged."

"You'll have to trust me and do what I ask," I said to Martha and Jackie. This is now personal. My godchild and close friends are in danger, if not dead already. One way or another, this is gonna end soon. It's my life or this lunatic's."

I grabbed my hat and left the room.

* * * * *

Pop was already in the car waiting. Luigi rushed down the stairs, threw a heavy vest at me, and shoved me into Pop's repair shop so Ma couldn't hear.

"Get rid of your shoulder holsters and put this vest on. It can hold both rods and has three razor-sharp knives, one behind the neck and two above the guns," he said.

Luigi then bent down, lifted his pants leg, and removed a leather ankle strap that held a switch blade and slapped it against my chest.

"You wear these day and night. Sleep with them, *capisch*?"

Luigi had taught me how to fight when I was a kid, later how to handle a stiletto, and then a gun. Now he was telling me I would need everything I had learned from him, and from the army, in order to stay alive.

He had said the same thing last year during one of my cases, without realizing he was one of the reasons I had survived the war. He'd already taught me how to handle myself. As a kid Pop had told me that in the old country, when in a fight, Luigi never gave up. No matter the odds, he always found a way to win. So did I.

"If you're gonna help Castellano, show no mercy when you find this guy. Don't flinch, because if you do, you'll die. You *know* who did this!"

"Kowalski's killer!"

"That's right, and he's one sick son-of-a-bitch, whoever he is. Trust me, he knows you'll be coming for him."

*****

Ever since I ran numbers for him when I was nine, Castellano had stood bigger than life. He was the Boss, the Godfather of our neighborhood, but on that night, my image of him changed forever. He reacted like everyone else when life crumbles at your feet—scared, confused, and humbled.

He picked up a scrap of paper from a table and handed it over with an unsteady hand.

"You and your family are the only ones I trust, Joey. I need your help. Someone's got Carmine, his wife, and kid," he said.

The note was written in blood. *You took my family. Now I take yours.*

"Find them," he said. "You know these streets; they talk to you. Find them."

The pounding in my chest throbbed in my ears. Carmine was a close friend growing up. Angela, his wife, had been my first childhood sweetheart, and their son, Antonio, was my godchild. No one, nothing, would stop me from finding them.

Castellano said he already had his men out working the streets, roughing up everyone who'd ever held a grudge against him or his son. They even rousted all the street bums from the waterfront to Little Italy to see if they saw or heard anything. So far, nothing!

O'Reilly arrived shortly after we did and gave an update on the investigation. Blood stains splattered the entry of Carmine's house, indicating his attacker struck as soon as the door was opened. O'Reilly believed Carmine knew his assailants, since there wasn't any sign of a forced entry. His two bodyguards found outside the house had their necks snapped. I knew those men and couldn't believe anyone could kill both without a struggle, but according to the investigator's report, that's exactly what had happened. There wasn't much to go on.

I was about to leave and check my sources around the neighborhood when Castellano pulled me aside.

"I called a sit-down with the other bosses. I want you to represent me. I must wait here. If my men get a break, I need to act fast."

I couldn't believe what I was hearing. Luigi had once told me that Castellano was considered an outcast by many of the other bosses because he refused to milk his territory for all it was worth. They felt he could add more to the syndicate's coffers if he opened the neighborhood to drugs, prostitution, gambling, and extortion. This, combined with the fact that Castellano almost allowed a union to gain a foothold along the docks, didn't bode well for winning their cooperation.

"They'll never listen to me. *You* have to go," I said.

"You listen to me," Castellano said. "If I face them in this condition, it'll be the end of me and this neighborhood. In six months you won't recognize the place."

He gripped my lapels with quivering hands. "You walk into that room as my *consigliore*. They'll listen, because when you speak, you're speaking for me. Tell them they have two days to locate my family. After that, if I find out someone in their organization did this, I will hold them personally responsible. You make them understand! Tell them for every drop of my family's blood, I'll take a liter of theirs. You tell them, and then you find Carmine and his family."

At that moment I knew if I didn't walk away and refuse to confront the syndicate on his behalf, I would be heading down a path with no easy way back. When I'd been old enough to truly understand, I'd grown to detest everything about the Mafia. It offered a veil of protection, but at too steep a price, corrupting all those caught within its embrace. Castellano was the exception, but *he* was corrupt and at times deadly.

Once I passed the threshold of that meeting as Castellano's consigliore, I would be willingly entering the Mafia's inner circle.

In reality, I had no choice. Castellano had deep ties to my family. And he had risked his life over the years protecting our neighborhood from the slime that infected others. Too many lives would be impacted if I didn't act on his behalf.

Pop and Luigi sat with Castellano and watched silently as I left the house and took that first step. They understood the significance. The oath they had taken to protect each other so many years ago was now my oath. Castellano's family was, and always had been, my family.

Chapter 44

The bosses who sat around the table knew my Uncle Torrio, and I was confident they'd heard of my reputation. They weren't pleased, however, that Castellano had sent a representative.

"This is a sign of disrespect," one shouted. The others grumbled their agreement.

"Is it disrespectful to search for your family, who are in the hands of a madman? Is it disrespectful to ask your colleagues for help?" I asked.

"He called this emergency meeting and he should be here. What can he do? He's not out searching. He's waiting for his men to report. If he wants our help, tell him to ask us himself," Big Ben Napoli said. Napoli was a long time nemesis of Castellano.

The others seemed to agree with Big Ben. I needed to gain control before they walked out.

"You have two days," I said.

"Two days to do what? Do you know who we are? Any one of us could have you snuffed out with the snap of our fingers," Big Ben shouted.

"I know who you are, and you know who I am. I'm only gonna say this once. Sweep your territories. If you find Carmine and the others, no questions asked, no repercussions. But after two days, if they aren't found, and it turns out your men or associates are in any way involved, *you're* involved, and you will pay a steep price in blood."

Big Ben spoke up again, emboldened by the support he sensed from the others. He ran the docks on the West Side and had coveted the East Side waterfront for years.

"Who's gonna extract this price? Castellano? He doesn't have the backbone. The way he runs his territory is a disgrace to us all. He even backed down when some young skirt threatened him in public. She should be in a cement block at the bottom of the bay. Instead she's still badmouthing Castellano, and he does nothin' about it."

"Castellano gave an ultimatum, and *I* will enforce it. If any of you are involved in his family's kidnapping, there will be no place to hide, and there will be no one able to protect you. You will die!" I said, looking around the room. "If it comes to that, and if any of the rest of you tries to stop me, the next time you meet, there'll be a slew of empty seats around this table."

"What the hell makes you think you're gonna get out of here alive?" Big Ben shouted.

Silvio Vigliotti, the head of Little Italy, stood. "Enough of this nonsense. Someone has attacked the family of one of our members, and we're arguing because he sent a representative to seek our help. Imagine if you were Castellano, and that we were talking about your son and grandson. What would you do? What would you say to us? The offer is fair, the consequences just. I suggest we adjourn and get our men on the streets, if not for Castellano, then for ourselves. We don't know what's goin' on, so any one of our families could be next. Castellano has given us an ultimatum, and I have no doubt that Batista is capable of following through on the consequences."

I expressed Castellano's appreciation and asked them to extend the same offer to the other ethnic sections of New York. Vigliotti agreed they would spread the word.

Vigliotti pulled me aside after the meeting broke up.

"Batista, you seem to have no fear."

"I don't fear dying, if that's what you mean."

"What then?"

"That there's a God and he's not forgiving."

Vigliotti smiled, but quickly changed his expression. "That's a good answer if you're fighting a war, but that's behind you. You live here in New York City and you don't live alone. If I were you, I'd give that some serious thought. You wanna play tough with the big boys then you need to become one of us. If you don't, you're putting everyone close to you at risk."

He saw I didn't like what he had said.

"I suggest you keep your trap shut and listen. I'll try again to get through that thick skull of yours. If you're one of us, then family and friends are off limits. If not, they're not—uncle or no uncle. You get my meaning now?"

I'm not sure I would've had the guts to speak up if I didn't know he feared Johnny Torrio. But he did and we both knew it.

"Do you think I want to live like you?" I said. "When I looked around this table I saw a bunch of overweight, greedy old men with crabby faces who'd sold their souls for thirty pieces of silver. I saw anger and fear eating away at their insides because they want what the other guy has and they don't know who around this table will someday put a bullet through the back of their heads. Become one of you? Not a chance."

Vigliotti snickered.

"Then why did you agree to come here and speak for Castellano?"

"For the same reason *you* stood up for him, he's family. In your case, you lose your power if the inner circle crumbles. In my case, if Castellano is brought down, I lose my neighborhood to a cretin like Big Ben. That will never happen."

Chapter 45

The note left behind by the goon who attacked Carmine and his family was my only clue, and I had a hunch Pop and Luigi held the key to unlocking its secret. They had roamed the streets of Sicily with Castellano as children and settled in the same New York neighborhood. Uncle Luigi remained closer to Castellano than Pop and operated in his shadow, never directly involved in the business, but under Castellano's umbrella of protection. Altogether, there were five who had sworn allegiance to protect one another, including Uncle Torrio and another good friend who had passed away last year.

Pop and Luigi waited for me at the speakeasy to hear how the meeting went with the Mafia bosses. They knew that without the other bosses' cooperation, Castellano's family didn't stand a chance. Whoever took his family couldn't afford to let any of them walk away. Every second counted.

O'Reilly, sitting at the bar, joined me on the way toward Pop's table.

"Glad to see you still have both kneecaps," he said.

"There were a few tense moments."

"I'll say this for ya, kid, you've got moxie."

"More like stupidity. To be honest, if it wasn't for my family's connections to the Chicago mob, I don't think I would've made it out of that room alive."

"Call it what you want, but I still say it took courage."

Pop grabbed two extra chairs.

"So, what happened?" he asked.

"Big Ben tried to take advantage of Castellano's absence and turn the other bosses against him. He sensed weakness and would like nothing better than to take over Castellano's territory."

"That's nothing new. I told Castellano years ago to take that bum out. Someday it's gonna come down to that," Luigi said.

"How did it end?" Pop asked.

"Vigliotti got things under control and agreed with Castellano's position. Vigliotti wants to avoid a blood bath within his organization. I guarantee you his organization will turn this town upside down over the next few days, including all the other ethnic parts of the city."

"They damn well better. For all he knows, their families could be next."

"Relax, Pop. They understand the consequences. What I need now is for you and Luigi to make sense of this bloody note."

I took the crumbled paper from my pocket and smoothed it out on the table.

"I've been thinking hard about that message, and I'm telling ya, Joey, those scribbles are meaningless. Sure, in the old country we needed to be tough, and maybe Castellano acted crazier than the rest of us and had to defend himself a few times. But he never killed nobody's family."

"What about since he became boss? Did anyone's family ever get wacked?"

"You listen to me," Pop said. "Castellano's different

than the other bosses in this town. Nothing like that has ever happened here."

"You told me yourself that Toby Tobias killed two men without Castellano's approval. He can't control everything his men do, but in the eyes of the neighborhood, he's held accountable for their actions."

"I'm telling you for the last time," Pop said. "There's never been a family wiped out in this neighborhood."

"That's not true. What about Gino's? He told me the details the other day, and even after all these years, he still wants revenge. The pain and hatred don't go away with time; they smolder," I said.

"Why the hell are you bringing up Gino? Castellano had nothing to do with the murder of Gino's wife and child," Pop yelled. "And nothing like that has happened since. You wanna know why? Because Castellano does his best to keep scum like that out of our neighborhood. You should spend time in Little Italy; maybe then you'd appreciate Castellano more."

O'Reilly came to my defense. "Look, we don't have time for all this emotional crap. Think back, was there ever a fire or a car accident where a family was lost? Anything can be made to look like an accident."

"These streets hold no secrets," Luigi said. "Sure things are violent, and I'm not saying no one dies, but we would have heard if we lost a whole family. Even if it was due to an accident, it would have been big news."

* * * * *

It was four in the morning. We were tired and a little drunk when Pop remembered something.

"The boat."

"What boat? Pop, what about a boat?"

"The trip from Italy to here was one hell of a voyage. The boat was overcrowded, the food wasn't fit for pigs, and tempers were shot. To kill the boredom, fighting became a form of entertainment. We were in the middle of nowhere, halfway to America, sleeping on the top deck to get away from the stench that permeated the lower decks. At the crack of dawn, Castellano got into one hell of a fight. Blood was flying everywhere, and most of it his. He was outmatched—the guy was a giant—but we didn't call Castellano "The Rock" for nothin'. When it looked like he was done for, he lunged and caught the brute under his ribcage, lifted him in the air, and sent him flying backwards. The guy hit the ships railing with incredible force and flipped over the side before anyone could react."

"By the time your pop and I got to the railing and looked over the side, there was no sign of him," Luigi said.

"What's that got to do with this note? Sounds like a fair fight and an unfortunate accident," I said, grabbing the wrinkled paper off the table.

"You're right, but we couldn't take the chance that the captain might see it differently, so we didn't report what happened, especially since Castellano had had a run-in with this guy a few weeks before. When the brute showed up missing, the captain logged his death an accident. He figured he was drunk and fell overboard," Luigi said. "But it didn't end there."

"No," Pop continued. "About a week later the guy's mother had a heart attack from grief and croaked. That same night, his old man killed himself, blew his brains all over the cabin. They were buried together at sea."

I couldn't believe what I was hearing. I asked if any family members survived the trip.

"Yeah," my uncle said. "The guy had a younger brother who saw him plunge to his death. Castellano grabbed the kid and held him out over the side railing where his brother had fallen. He told him if he squealed, he'd kill him and his family."

"It was a rotten thing to do, but he was worried about his own hide. He had no way of knowing the kid's parents would actually die," Pop said. "Who knows what went through the kid's head when he found his parents dead."

"Did he have any other relatives on board?"

"No, they had left everyone behind for a better future. We all did," Luigi said.

"What about Ma? Did she take care of the kid?"

"We never told her what happened. There was no way for her to know because there were a lot of orphans on that trip due to a flu outbreak," Pop said.

"After the kid's parents croaked, he sorta melted into the ship. Never saw him again. When we landed, it was a free-for-all. None of us gave him a second thought," Luigi said. "Until now."

* * * * *

Exhausted and a bit canned, I somehow made it to my room without stumbling back down the stairs. I didn't bother to flip on the light. I undressed, pulled back the covers, and flopped into bed. The fog of sleep that held me in its embrace was nudged by a gentle hand that slid down my chest. I was pleased that for once a nightmare wasn't dragging me back into the war. I thought of the warm touch of Jackie and Martha and wondered if I would ever love anyone as deeply as I had Anita, who was taken from me so many years ago.

As the shroud of sleep continued to engulf me, my dream took on a sense of reality. Jackie's voice floated in the air. Her body slid over mine, and her hair brushed across my face. Feeling myself slipping deeper into slumber, she tenderly kissed the nape of my neck.

"If you don't wake soon, I'm gonna scream," Jackie whispered in my ear.

Startled, I sat up and tossed her to the side. Jackie laughed and reached for me again. This time I knew I wasn't dreaming.

"How did you get in here?"

"I have my ways."

"Remind me to thank my uncle."

"Maybe you should thank your ma," she said with a smile. "She thinks you're under too much stress."

There was a low knock at the door. "Joey, it's me, Martha."

Jackie nibbled at my ear. "You gonna answer the door?"

"Why don't you hide in the bathroom?" I said.

"I'm not gonna hide," Jackie said, grabbing my robe and putting it on.

Martha stood frozen in the doorway. Jackie pulled her into the room and closed the door.

Jackie looked at Martha. "Have you ever done this before?" she asked.

By this time I was sitting up in bed.

Martha looked at me and then back to Jackie. "No, have you?"

"When I was young. I didn't have much of a choice if I wanted the protection of the leader of my street gang. Do you think Joey's ready for this?"

"Let's find out," Martha said, walking toward the bed, stripping off her clothes.

I *had* to be dreaming.

Chapter 46

I awoke at sunrise alone. The only sign that something unusual had happened during the night was that the bed was a shambles. Exhausted, I tried to stretch the soreness from my back and limbs and wished I hadn't gotten so damn smoked before hitting the sack.

I took a cold shower and downed a cup of java, all the time thinking of the implications of the previous few days. By her actions, Jackie had firmly declared that any unique relationship or expectations either one of us had toward each other were gone. The three of us were starting over, still friends, focused on establishing a successful PI business. The interaction of our personal lives would no longer interfere with our business.

It all sounded ideal, but for some reason, I felt a churning in my gut.

I skipped breakfast and went straight to the office to test if my conclusion had been correct. I also wanted a brief update from the girls on Frank's case. After that, I intended to head over to Castellano's to follow up on the lead Pop had given me the night before.

Martha sat at her desk, sorting through a pile of documents. She greeted me with her usual smile and stepped out from behind her desk to plant a kiss on my cheek.

"Morning, boss. We've been waiting to hear what happened after you stormed out after Butch yesterday," she said, not mentioning anything about last night.

She grabbed my hand and led me into the main office. Jackie had heard our conversation and was already walking toward us when we entered the room. She gave me a warm embrace.

"We were both concerned when we didn't hear from you. Is it true that Castellano's family was kidnapped?" she asked.

The way they were acting didn't make sense. I decided not to say anything about our encounter last night, thinking they might be embarrassed and hoping I was too drunk to remember.

"O'Reilly believes they knew their attackers."

The girls asked more questions, and I filled them in on the bloody note, my meeting with the Mafia bosses, and the incident my pop described that took place decades ago on a boat ride from Italy to New York.

Once their curiosity was satisfied, I got them refocused on Frank's case.

"Martha, you said you know why Ruth was dragged by the car, but you never had the chance to elaborate."

"That's right. O'Reilly had the coroner's office drop off Ruth's belongings at her apartment, and the package contained a plush overcoat that was badly damaged. I didn't think anything of it at the time until you mentioned you were surprised she had gotten dragged for such a long distance. I went back yesterday to Ruth's apartment and double checked the overcoat. A portion of one cuff was torn off. The coat was badly damaged, but that was the only part of the coat with a complete tear. I believe the cuff got caught in the undercarriage of the car, and that is why she was dragged.

I couldn't believe our luck.

"Ask O'Reilly to have his men check the undercarriage

of everyone's car who is even remotely connected with Ruth," I said.

Jackie walked over to Martha, and they both sat on the front of my desk looking a bit devilish as they crossed their legs.

"Of course Martha has already talked to O'Reilly," Jackie said.

Ignoring her bit of sarcasm, which was deserved, I asked Martha if she was able to locate Ruth's original will.

"I only found one copy. Frank said there should have been two, one each for Ruth and her husband. Her nephew was right—except for a few charities, he inherited everything. We also found a box full of deeds and a record of rents she received monthly. The old lady was loaded," Martha said. "The estate is worth considerably more than what her nephew estimated."

"Great, now we have proof that all of the new beneficiaries had a motive to kill her if they knew she was about to revert to the original will."

They both nodded.

"Any guess why she became upset during the party?"

"Not yet," Jackie answered.

I had to get over to Castellano's and told them I'd do my best to keep them updated. I was about to leave the outer office when I heard them whispering, so I went back.

"Did you girls get a good night's sleep?"

They looked at each other and answered simultaneously, "We did."

"Why?" Jackie asked.

"You both look tired."

"So do you," Martha said.

"I had a rough day yesterday and a little too much to

drink last night. I went to bed late. I have a feeling I'm gonna be gone for a few days. If you need me, get a message to Castellano."

Martha turned away and fiddled with some papers on my desk. Jackie nudged her in the ribs. "Don't worry. We will, and let us know if you need our help," Jackie said.

I had trouble concentrating during the drive to the ferry terminal to catch a boat to Staten Island where Castellano had his main residence. I still wasn't sure what happened last night, but the one thing I did know was that I had to get those broads out of my head and focus on finding Castellano's family.

Chapter 47

I walked in on a meeting between O'Reilly, Castellano, and some of his crew. Since none of his men had anything useful to say, Castellano turned toward O'Reilly.

"I hope your cops are better at this than these goons. What have you found out?"

"Not much. It looks like Carmine was taken out as soon as he opened the door. Angela was—"

"Wait, wait, are you sayin'? Carmine's dead?"

"We don't think so. There would've been more blood. All I'm sayin' is that he was taken by surprise and probably knocked out as soon as he opened the door."

"What about Angela and my grandson?"

"It was late, so Angela was likely asleep when attacked. She, however, put up one hell of a fight."

"How do you know?" Castellano asked.

"The bed had collapsed and was practically torn apart. There's not much I can say about Antonio; being so young, he didn't have a chance."

Castellano leaned forward in his chair and rubbed his face.

"That's it? That's all you got? For this you stopped me from entering my son's house, afraid I would destroy some evidence. What evidence?"

"There's more, but Joey has something you should hear."

"No, you tell me everything, and then we'll hear from Joey."

"There was a brief rain shower the night this happened, so the ground was damp. We couldn't account for one set of footprints outside the house. They were huge. Whoever did this was big and heavy."

Castellano looked around at his men, and half of them fit that description. He turned to me. "What about you?"

If we were going to make any progress toward finding this lunatic, I felt Castellano needed to remember the details of the fight, without me repeating what I was told by Pop and my uncle.

"It's clear from the note that whoever did this is obsessed with your destruction and has been waiting for the right time to avenge the death of his family. Kowalski's brutal murder, and then Donnelly's, were all part of a personal vendetta to destroy your credibility with the longshoremen and the syndicate. He killed the fishermen to eliminate any potential witnesses, but that also put pressure on you. Having failed, he's now goin' for the jugular—your family."

"Let me tell you somethin', Joey. What you just said is pure speculation. I never killed nobody's family. If you ask me, this guy is some kinda nut and it has nothin' to do with me."

"How about your men? Could they have done something without your knowledge?" I asked, looking over to O'Reilly. He nodded, understanding what I was doing.

"What? You think I've been sitting here all these hours feeling sorry for myself? Of course I've been thinking back, but nothin' ever happened that would've caused someone to want this type of retribution. Sure, I'm in a rough business, but I'm strictly small time. I don't covet other bosses' territories.

Never have. If I get pushed around, I'll stand my ground, but I don't do the pushing. I look after the neighborhood, stay out of the way of the big guys, and pay my dues. My men don't go around knocking off innocent people, and if they did, I would hear about it. In fact, everybody would hear about it."

It was time. I let him have it without warning.

"What about on the way over from Italy? You had a fight on the boat and killed some guy. Pop said his mom and dad died soon after."

"What are ya talkin' about? Fighting was the only pastime we had. I hit a guy and he fell overboard. What's the big deal? People were dying on that ship every day. There was no sanitation, the food stunk, and it was overcrowded. I bet your pop didn't tell ya he hit a guy so damn hard his head split open. That guy didn't last long, and no one's after him. This makes no sense. Why would anyone hold a grudge this long? Besides, I had nothing to do with the parents' deaths."

It was obvious from his rambling and rapid speech that Castellano was reliving the trip. Perspiration stained his shirt and sweat beaded on his forehead.

"Shit, there was a kid no more than ten years old. He saw his brother flip over the side. I yelled that I would kill him and everyone in his family if he ever squealed." Castellano collapsed back into his chair as he recalled the details of that day. "The kid had a look of terror on his face. What a jerk I was."

Time was running out for Carmine and his family, so I bombarded Castellano with questions. I hoped that if he answered without time to think, he would give us the clue we needed.

"Who was the guy you fought?"

"I don't know."

"What did you fight about?"

"It was a long trip. It could have been anything. I was bored, he was bored, we both liked to fight."

"Could the kid now be one of the other bosses?"

"Nah, they're too old, and besides, this kid was big for his age, like his brother. They were probably from northern Italy, looked more German than Italian."

I suddenly knew who the brother was, and if right, I also knew who took Castellano's family. There was only one person who fit that description in the neighborhood. One person who Carmine would trust enough to open his front door to in the middle of the night. Only one who could kill Carmine's bodyguards with his bare hands without a struggle and who had the strength to operate the crane manually on the pier where Kowalski's body hung.

"How did Butch become one of your bodyguards?"

Castellano looked at me in disbelief, then hurled whatever he could grab at his men, and chased them from his house, shouting.

"What the hell are you doin' standing around? Find that son-of-a-bitch and bring him to me alive. Do you understand? I want Butch alive!"

* * * * *

A sense of relief descended at lunch when I informed everyone that Butch had killed Kowalski and taken Castellano's family. They no longer had to face the unknown, even though Butch would be a dangerous adversary.

Pop and Luigi took the responsibility of alerting the

local residents and merchants to be on the lookout for Butch. Jackie and Martha recommitted to stay focused on Frank Galvano's case, but only after I promised to pull them off if needed. Rosalie offered to help in any way she could and Ma agreed to run Pop's business while he and Luigi worked to locate Butch.

I was upstairs packing my gear to bring over to Castellano's when Sadie burst into the room and flung herself at me. She had heard from Ma that I finally knew who killed her father. She caught me off balance, and we tumbled onto the bed. It was an awkward situation but one that broke the tension that had existed between us when I had agreed to work for Castellano on her father's case. As we stood laughing, we realized Jackie and Martha were in the doorway frowning.

"How many women do you need in your life at one time?" Jackie asked.

Martha turned away, but before she could get too far, I pulled both her and Jackie into the room.

"Hey, you two are overreacting. Sadie and I have been friends since before we could walk. You know we've been on the outs lately."

"I'm sorry if I caused a problem. I just wanted to thank Joey for finding who killed my father and warn him to be careful. Butch is so strong, and he must be deranged to do what he's done. This was an accident," Sadie said, pointing to the bed. She left and Martha followed. I caught Jackie's arm and pulled her around.

"I think you need to understand something. Sadie is a friend of mine, just like any other kid I grew up with. The girls were always around, either watching or participating in some of our games."

"I wouldn't know about that," Jackie said.

The anger that showed in her rigid posture had changed suddenly to sadness. Even her shoulders stooped. I had unintentionally brought her thoughts back to her childhood.

"I know, Jackie. Not many young girls are abandoned to survive on their own. You had to grow up too quickly."

Her eyes glistened with moisture. I pulled her in closer, and we embraced in silence. Eventually, she let go, turned, and walked away.

I watched Jackie leave and wondered if I would ever see her again. Soon I would have a deadly confrontation with Butch and I wasn't sure I could survive such a fight. Jackie must have had the same thought. She stopped at the threshold and leaned against the doorframe with her back to me.

"You saw what Butch did to Stefano. He will try to kill you," she said.

"I have an advantage over him."

She turned and wiped the tears from her cheeks. Her eyes begged me to explain.

"He's been consumed with hatred for over twenty years, and now that he's taking his revenge, Butch has nothing more to live for. I do."

Chapter 48

I had just thrown my gear into the rumble seat of my flivver when a black Pierce-Arrow pulled up behind me, and two men got out. One ran up the stairs to the front stoop and positioned himself to have a commanding view of the street. The other guy waited by the car until his buddy gave him the go-ahead to open the back door. Silvio Vigliotti, head of Little Italy's Mafia, stepped out.

His presence in our neighborhood was unprecedented. He seldom left the protection of Little Italy, even though a significant portion of his financial resources originated from controlling the docks that moved all the commercial goods in and out of the city.

Excited that Vigliotti might have information about Castellano's family, I walked toward the car to greet him. His bodyguard stepped between us and shoved me onto the hood of the car. I was wise enough to allow him to pat me down.

"Give back his rods," Vigliotti ordered. "Batista, you got a place we can talk?"

"My parents' apartment," I said, leading the way. Both of his bodyguards remained on the stoop to prevent anyone from entering the building.

I was surprised they didn't go inside to check the place out to assure Vigliotti's safety. And I would have thought they would guard both the front and back entrances.

"There is a back alleyway—"

Vigliotti cut me off. "I'm well protected. Other men have been posted in the area for the last several hours. Let's go. I'm anxious to see my old friends."

No one even looked up from their food when I entered the apartment, but when Vigliotti followed me in, Ma and Pop leapt from their chairs to greet him. Luigi turned and did the same. It was as if the prodigal son had returned. After she gave him a hug, Ma walked past Vigliotti and looked down the hall toward the main door.

"Silvio? Is it your wife? Is she…"

"She's fine, just fine, Carmella. She regrets she couldn't come along. I explained to her that this wasn't a social call. There's no time for small talk," Vigliotti said, accepting a glass of wine from Luigi. "We have located Carmine's wife, but my men can't rescue her without igniting a gangland war, and that means Castellano can't act either. That's why I'm here," he said, looking at me.

"What the hell are you talking about? Where is she?" I shouted.

Vigliotti ignored my outburst and laid a note on the table.

"We executed Castellano's request to scour our territories for any sign of his family, and we did so with a high level of brutality, even by our standards. When broken bones weren't working, we decided to offer a reward for information. An informer handed this to one of my men this morning.

The white slut's at the Bayou, entertainin'.

"You can understand why we're helpless," he said.

"No, I can't. What difference does it make where she is? We need to get her now!" I said.

Ma read the note. "This can't be happening to Angela.

Who would sell her into prostitution?" she said, crumbling the note in her fist.

I took it from her before she tore it to shreds.

"Easy, everybody, just take it easy," Luigi cautioned. "The Bayou is a joint in the middle of Harlem. Silvio's right. If we tell Castellano, he'll go in with an army."

"Damn well he should," I shouted.

"Try to understand," Vigliotti said. "Since prohibition passed, discipline within my organization has deteriorated. Your observation was correct. There's a lot of in-fighting, with everyone positioning themselves to develop new ways to rake in dough. The last thing I need is to galvanize a loosely knit group of black gangs—fighting among themselves over the numbers racket—into a powerful rival. On the other hand… doing nothing would be a sign of weakness."

Vigliotti finished his wine, gave Ma a hug, and walked out of the apartment.

I turned to my uncle. "What the hell just happened?"

"He gave us permission to get Angela. If an individual rescues a friend, Vigliotti stays out of the line of fire and saves face."

"We can do this without his help," I said to Luigi.

He smiled. "Like you said, what the hell are we waiting for?"

"I'm going with you," Pop said.

"No, Vito. Let's not risk everything. You have to think of Carmella."

Pop looked over at Ma. She picked up his shotgun that was leaning against the wall in the kitchen and tossed it to him.

"Obviously, Ma's ready to take care of herself," Pop said. "Besides, the way she cooks, she'll have a man around in no time if something happens to me. I'm goin'."

"You're wasting time," Ma said, shoving us out of the apartment. "Bring Angela back!"

*****

Luigi positioned himself by the front door of the Bayou, while Pop kept the car running outside. I went over to the bartender and passed him the note Vigliotti had given us, along with a couple of C-notes.

"What do ya want?"

"She's family."

"Look around, white boy, if ya wanna see family. No deal, I forked over a hell of a lot more than that for the bitch."

I didn't have to look around. I already knew everything I needed to know when I took the first step over the threshold. There was a flight of stairs in the back of a large open room that led to six doors along a narrow landing. Beneath the landing were a back exit and two bathrooms, along with a possible storage area. A mop stood in a bucket to the side of the door. The main room had fifteen to twenty circular tables separated from the bar by a ten-foot pathway that led to the staircase. The bartender's illegal supply of booze was behind the bar in a room with a padlocked door. The clientele was what I'd expected: young men in their twenties or early thirties, out of work, out of hope, and willing to slit your throat for a quick sawbuck.

"How much will it take?"

The bartender leaned across the bar. "Now listen closely, if you and your pal wanna get out of here alive. She's not for sale. She's a great earner and good for business."

Bile rose from my gut at the thought of Angela enduring

the atrocities happening to her while I wasted time talking to this slime.

"If she doesn't leave with me now, you're dead. I'm not gonna' ask again. Where's the girl?"

His laugh was short lived. I reached across the bar, grabbed the back of his head, and slammed his face onto the wooden surface. When he lifted up his head, I jammed my rod into his mouth and cocked the hammer back.

"I'll *not* ask again," I said, pulling the gun barrel out of his bloody mouth.

"Joey," Luigi shouted.

Massive hands grasped my neck and lifted me off the floor. I dropped my gun and struggled to loosen the grip, to no avail. I took a deep breath before my airway was completely shut off and pulled two knives from my vest. I reached behind and buried them into the sides of my attacker. Freed, I gasped for air. The bartender took advantage of my predicament, ducked down behind the bar, and came up with a bat. I twisted it out of his hands, turned, and took a wicked swing at my attacker as he yanked the short knives from his rib cages. The bat bounced off the side of his head, splitting open his ear and shattering his collar bone. He crumbled to the floor unconscious.

Luigi had lifted one of his Tommy guns from under his overcoat and had the place covered. I retrieved my piece and knives and confronted the bartender again. He had become mesmerized by the fight and leaned over the bar looking at the bloody heap that was his bouncer. Before he could back out of my reach, I grabbed the front of his shirt, yanked him forward, and shoved a chiv under his chin.

"Where's the girl?"

"Upstairs, last door on the left," he mumbled through a

mouthful of blood from his busted teeth. I shoved the damp cloth he'd used to wipe down the bar into his mouth and slid my chiv away, drawing a trickle of blood.

From that moment, I paid no attention to what was happening around me. I knew Luigi had my back, so my focus shifted to rescuing Angela, and nothing was going to stand in my way.

* * * * *

From outside the door to her room, I could hear Angela moaning. The next thing I knew, I was facing two startled men as they stumbled over each other to get away from Angela. I don't know what I said, but one ran toward me clutching his clothes. I shoved him against the wall, kicked him in the groin, and heaved him through the window onto the fire escape landing. The other guy was bent over, reaching for his clothes, and that's when I saw a glint of metal. Rage and self-preservation took control. He lurched across the bed, firing two bullets. One grazed my shoulder. Before he landed on Angela's legs, I had pumped four shots into his chest.

Angela pulled desperately on the bonds that held her to the bedposts, trying to shake his body off her legs. I dragged the stiff from the bed and threw his carcass into the hall to discourage anyone in the other rooms from interfering.

"Angela, it's me, Joey. Angela, it's Joey."

I stroked her cheek and brushed aside damp strands of hair. "I've come to take you home."

I saw recognition in her glazed eyes.

"Joey, oh my God, he took Antonio."

"I know, Angela. I've come to take you home."

Released from her bonds, she tried to stand, but her legs quivered, and she collapsed in my arms. A sudden burst from a Tommy gun downstairs brought me back to my surroundings.

Angela dug her nails into my arms, as I helped her back onto the bed. "What's happenin'?"

"Don't worry." I said. "Vito and Pop are with me, and they have things under control."

I noticed her clothes tossed over a chair and placed them in her lap. "Try to get dressed. We don't have a lot of time. I promise, I'll be right back."

I entered the hall with both guns drawn and leaned over the banister. The place lay in shambles. The chandeliers had fallen to the floor and nothing remained of the mirrors behind the bar. Luigi now had both his Tommy guns raised and was ordering everyone to remove their jackets, toss their weapons up against the bar, and drop their pants. I was about to return to Angela when I noticed a short, fat guy—hidden behind several others—take aim at my uncle. I was trying to get a clear shot when, suddenly, Pop kicked open the front door and rushed in with his shotgun raised.

"Nobody move," he shouted.

Everyone, in some fashion, reacted to Pop's unexpected entrance. Most of them ducked. That's when I fired and dropped the short guy, who was about to take out both Pop and Uncle Luigi. All it took was one shot to the head. At that point everyone did what my uncle had ordered. Guns, knives, and blackjacks soon littered the floor in front of the bar.

Satisfied that Luigi and Pop were in command of the situation, I holstered my guns and turned back toward Angela when the door to the adjacent room flew open. A naked woman was shoved at me by a crazed-looking brute. I brushed the woman against the wall and took advantage of the guy's forward motion. He stumbled over the dead body at his feet. Off balance, I easily yanked him over the banister.

I didn't bother to look at the damage. I knew from the sound of him hitting the floor below that he was no longer a threat. I fired two shots in the air and ordered everyone out of the rooms, but the doors remained closed. Luigi opened fire, raking the tops of the doors with a barrage of bullets. Moments after the bullets stopped, there was a mad rush from the rooms. Satisfied that it was safe, I pulled the young girl off the floor. She broke free from my grip, grabbed some clothes from her room, and rushed downstairs to join the others.

I helped Angela finish dressing. Still too weak to walk, I carried her to the stairs, where we saw a strange but comforting sight. My uncle had pulled the shades down on the entrance doors and was holding his Tommy guns, ready to fire. Everyone in the room stood with their hands in the air, and their trousers around their ankles. Pop was nowhere to be seen.

Satisfied it was safe, I carried Angela down the stairs. The only sounds in the entire place were the creaking of the steps under our combined weight and Angela sobbing Antonio's name.

Pop came out of the shadows from under the landing and walked alongside me, facing the hostile group of young men who were looking for an opportunity to make their move. Luigi waited until we were in the car and then backed his way out of the dive, blasting the weapons that had been tossed on the floor with several rounds from his Tommy guns.

* * * * *

We took Angela to Ma's, who bathed her with vigor, as if she was trying to wash away everything that had happened. She then bandaged Angela's rope burns, weeping the entire time. Angela and I had been close friends at a young age, and when her mother died, she had become attached to Ma. Their relationship had grown over the years.

"Joey, you gotta find Butch before he does something horrible to Antonio and Carmine."

"I'm tryin', Ma. I'm tryin'."

"You know what's expected of you."

"Don't worry. O'Reilly will be with me."

Still holding Angela's hand, she turned to me with a stern face.

"This is family, Joey. *You* take care of it. This monster doesn't deserve a trial."

I looked over at Pop, who was standing in the doorway smoking a stogie. He smashed the cigar out in his palm, straightened up, locked eyes with me, and left the room. Although he never said a word, his message was as clear as Ma's.

Chapter 49

When Angela was strong enough, Rosalie and I took her to Castellano's. Upon entering the house, Angela flung herself at Castellano, imploring him to find her family. He assured her everything possible was being done and tried to convince Angela to get some rest, but she refused. Concerned, he called her doctor, who administered barbital to help her relax. It took several painful hours for the sobbing to stop and sleep to creep in.

Once he got Angela settled, Castellano wanted to know how I found her. I initially told him about Vigliotti's desire not to get the Mafia directly involved, and I left out some specific details. Castellano insisted on knowing everything. He didn't give a damn about what Vigliotti wanted.

"Forget about Vigliotti. You think I don't know what those rope burns mean? You tell me who's responsible."

I handed him the note Vigliotti had given me.

"Luigi, Pop, and I went into Harlem and rescued Angela. None of us got hurt," I said.

"Is he dead?"

"Who?"

"The owner of the joint. The one who did this to Angela."

"No, not yet," I said.

Satisfied he had enough information to later deal with those involved, Castellano shifted his focus back to Butch.

His questions were relentless and useless. Nothing I hadn't asked myself many times over.

Exhausted, I went upstairs to check on Angela and say goodbye to Rosalie, who had agreed to stay with her until this ordeal ended. Angela had finally fallen asleep.

I'd told Castellano I needed to head back to the office to get some rest and find time to think. As I was about to open the door, gunshots rang out, shattering the living room window. After the bullets stopped, all we could hear were Antonio's cries for his grandpa. Raw emotion overrode our instincts to take cover. We both rushed outside to help Antonio and confront whatever danger awaited.

When we opened the door and stepped onto the porch, darkness and the pungent odor of gasoline overwhelmed us. At first we heard only Antonio's screams and couldn't see what was happening. Once our eyes adjusted to the dark, we saw one of Castellano's bodyguards sprawled at the foot of the porch steps in a pool of blood. Antonio was bound and kneeling in front of Butch behind a small section of stomped down hedge. The hedge looked out of place among the perfectly manicured green space in the center of the long horseshoe drive that led to the house.

Butch stood there with a lit cigar in his mouth, drenching Antonio in gasoline. He threw the gas canister aside, and from the sound, it hit several other empty cans. He then picked up another canister and slowly backed toward his car at the entrance to the drive, pouring gasoline along his path. I knew I could get off a clean shot, but if the cigar fell and ignited the gas, Antonio would go up in flames.

"I had a change of heart," Butch shouted, holding the lit cigar in the air. "You can have the damn brat, but if you move or shoot, the kid dies."

We were helpless to do anything but listen to Antonio's howls beseeching his grandfather for help. Each step Butch took toward his car lasted an eternity.

Butch opened his car door, laughed hideously, and dropped the cigar. Flames roared toward Antonio, igniting the entire green space before we could reach the bottom of the steps.

We both raised our arms to shield our eyes from the roaring flames and took several steps back from the intense heat. Antonio's screams intensified. His features took on distorted shapes through the multicolored flames that danced across his face. We stood, frozen by the horror of the sight.

Something wasn't right. I had heard the torturous sounds of people incinerated during the war and smelled the stench, but this was different. These were screams of panic, not agony. The smell of burning flesh should have overpowered the sweet odor of the burning bushes and trees. In that moment of my hesitation and recognition, Castellano grabbed a gun from my harness, yelled Antonio's name, and fired into the flames. The screaming stopped when the blurred image of Antonio slumped to the ground. Castellano dropped to his knees and put the gun to his head.

I yanked the gun from his hand and put it back into my holster. "Killing yourself won't help Angela or save your son," I said. "I suggest you get back in the house. I'll get Antonio. It's best if you don't see him now."

I ran down the driveway to where there was less foliage on fire and stopped short of the flames surrounding Antonio. There I looked into the heart of Butch's demented soul and saw the true meaning of evil. Antonio's body lay in a puddle of blood, encircled by a ring of burning branches; a fire within a fire. Butch had doused Antonio with water, not gasoline, setting up the illusion that Antonio was being burned alive. Butch had intended for Castellano to kill his grandson by making him think he was putting him out of his misery.

I kicked aside some of the branches to make a space, but in so doing, the heat and flames surrounding Antonio's lifeless body intensified. I knelt down and held him in my arms. He was shot in the head and chest. I had no tears, just memories of a sweet kid.

As the circle of fire continued to consume the branches laid down by Butch, I made the toughest decision of my life. I placed Antonio into the flames to spare his grandfather the knowledge that he had needlessly killed his grandson.

The next few hours were chaotic. The cops and fire department responded to the carnage, followed by reporters eager to get headlines for their morning editions.

I called my father and uncle, who tried to ease their friend's pain. Nothing helped, so they brought out the hooch and got smoked together.

Castellano was in a state of shock and, with the amount of booze he had consumed, incapable of making a decision. Given the fact that he had lost three additional men and the rest were out searching for Antonio and Carmine, his compound was no longer safe.

I decided to move Angela back to my parents' apartment in New York, while she was still under the influence of the sedative and unaware of what had happened to her son. There I figured Ma and Rosalie could care for her while Pop and Luigi provided protection. The apartment had been fortified against attacks when Bobby Stefano was on the loose. Plus Butch wouldn't have the maneuverability he had at Castellano's compound. The entire neighborhood was on the lookout for him.

I stayed behind with Castellano, who refused to leave in the hope that some of his men would return with information about his son. He was convinced that Butch was holding Carmine somewhere on Staten Island, but I thought differently. There were plenty of lowlifes Butch could hire to help him transport Castellano's family to a hideout in the city. That's where Butch would feel the safest, and that's where I intended to look for Carmine.

* * * * *

Emotionally drained and inconsolable, Castellano eventually fell asleep in a high-back chair in his den. I encouraged him several times to go to bed, but he refused, afraid of the nightmares waiting to tear at his soul. Rather than disturb him, I covered him with a blanket and turned out the lights. I sat in the darkness so I could be there when he awoke. Finally, I had time to think.

In reality, I had been tracking Butch for months. He had killed Kowalski, he had killed the three fishermen, and he had killed Donnelly. It seemed impossible that Butch didn't leave behind a clue, something that would lead to his whereabouts. If I found his hideout, I was confident I'd find Carmine.

I can't remember when I fell asleep, but I woke before Castellano, feeling surprisingly refreshed in spite of everything that had happened. I'd been able to push the sights of the previous night aside, as I did so many times during the war in order to stay focused on the mission. This time my assignment was to find Butch.

I went upstairs to shower. While I stood under the stream of hot water, something kept nagging at me, something I had dreamt about or thought of during the night. The harder I tried to remember, the further it slipped away. I finally gave up and hoped it would come to me later.

By noon there was a strange array of bedfellows in Castellano's den. O'Reilly came with the police commissioner, followed by Silvio Vigliotti, the head of Little Italy, and his bodyguards. Then my pop arrived to stay with Castellano so I could continue searching for Butch.

The doorbell chimed again, and I half expected the DA, but instead, a scruffy kid delivered a package. He said some big guy gave him a sawbuck to deliver the package and told him he'd be watching to make sure he made the delivery.

The message was simple and to the point. The package contained a gun and a note that read: *Your life for Carmine's.*

Castellano reached for the gun. I swiped the package from his lap and shouted, "You can't trust this guy! We all saw what he did to Antonio. As soon as you kill yourself, Carmine's dead. He can't keep him alive after what he's done to Carmine's family."

"He's my son. If we don't find Butch soon, I'll do what he asks."

Seeing the effect the gun had on Castellano, I found myself thinking like Butch: a kid who saw his family wiped out, a kid who hid in the bowels of a steamer for weeks, a kid who arrived in a strange land and had to fend for himself, a kid—now a man—who had bided his time to exact revenge. Why? Why did he wait so long when he had ample opportunities to kill Castellano?

In that reflective moment, I understood the rationale behind everything Butch had been doing, along with his next possible move. It was a crazy plan by an insane man driven to madness by events he had witnessed and experienced over his short lifetime.

I turned to my father to confirm my suspicions.

"Pop, tell me again how Butch's brother died."

"I imagine he drowned. We were on the first deck when he went over the railing."

"What about his parents?"

"Like I said before, his mother was grief stricken when she heard that her son fell overboard and she died of a heart attack. His father killed himself that same day."

"How did the father commit suicide?"

"Shot himself in the head."

I faced Castellano to make sure I had his attention.

"Butch is putting you through what his family suffered."

I didn't have much time to explain.

"This was a family on the verge of realizing their life-long dream of immigrating to America. Then it was all taken away by you. The parents suffered both emotional and physical pain before they died. Butch had lost everything and, most likely, was the one who found his parents dead. He hid, terrified he'd be next. Somehow he survived and now is extracting his revenge, just when you have everything you ever wanted." I looked around and saw that Pop and Luigi understood. The police commissioner and Vigliotti looked confused.

"Can you imagine the sacrifices Butch's parents made to afford passage to America and to create a new life for their family? Butch is making Castellano suffer the way his parents did. He wants him to lose everything, including his life.

"Unless I'm mistaken, if Castellano doesn't kill himself,

Butch will, and he'll do it after he makes him watch Carmine die."

"How can you be so sure?" Vigliotti asked.

"It all fits. Butch watched Castellano kill his brother."

"If you're right, then Butch's next move will be to kidnap Castellano," the commissioner stated.

There was only one place Butch couldn't get to Castellano, and that was the hoosegow. The commissioner agreed to arrest him, and O'Reilly slapped on the cuffs before Castellano could object.

"What are you doing? I haven't committed a crime. You have no right to do this," Castellano shouted. He pleaded with O'Reilly. "Mike, you're condemning my son to death. I'm an old man. I don't care what happens to me, but I can save my son."

"Sorry," O'Reilly said. "Joey's right. Killing yourself won't help Carmine."

Vigliotti pulled me aside and offered me whatever I needed. He quickly left with his men. Pop went with Castellano in O'Reilly's car.

I planned to head home to check on Angela before continuing the search for Carmine. To get to my car, I passed where Antonio had died and looked down at the blood stains. Ma was right; I was in a life and death struggle with Butch, and one of us would soon die.

Chapter 50

When I entered my parents' guest room, Rosalie got up from Angela's bedside and nudged me back into the hall.

"She just fell asleep. When you do talk with her, I think it best you give her some hope that you'll find her husband alive."

"Does she know everything that's happened?"

"No, only that her son is dead. We didn't give her the details."

"How's Ma taking Antonio's death?"

"You should go to her."

In the dining room Pop and Luigi sat on either side of Ma trying to console her. Given how vigorously she was crying, they weren't having much luck. When I entered, Ma asked Luigi to move over so I could sit beside her.

"Joey, how could anyone burn a small child to death? The thought of the pain Antonio suffered is killing me."

I didn't know if any of them would approve of what I did, but they needed to know. I put my arm around Ma and pulled her toward me.

"Ma, Antonio didn't burn while alive. It was all an illusion set up by Butch. Antonio died instantly when Castellano shot him."

When I uttered those words, all sound and movement

stopped. The silence broke when Angela, who was standing in the doorway behind me, collapsed.

"She woke up, Joey. She heard your voice and insisted that I take her to you," Rosalie cried out.

Pop and I carried Angela to the sofa, and Ma went to get a damp cloth. I knelt next to Angela, and when she sat up, she wrapped her arms around my neck and sobbed.

"Please tell me what happened. I can't believe Castellano would shoot my baby, his own grandson."

"Do you trust me?" I whispered.

She lifted her head off my shoulder. "I do, more than anyone."

I picked her off the couch and carried her back to her room and asked Rosalie to wait outside. I didn't hold anything back.

"Are you telling me he didn't have to die? He wasn't being burned," she shouted.

"Angela, try to calm down and listen to me. Antonio was screaming, and it looked like he was engulfed in flames. Butch wanted Castellano to kill his own grandson."

"You're sure he didn't suffer."

"I'm sure. I didn't want Castellano to know what he'd done. That's why I placed Antonio's body in the fire after he was dead. I know I defiled his body, but I had to make a quick decision. It would kill Castellano if he knew. There was nothing else I could do."

Angela wiped away her tears. "We're suffering the acts of a madman. Carmine and his father do not need any more torment. Joey, you did the right thing."

She took hold of my hands and then kissed them. "Please find Carmine, and may God keep you both safe."

I suggested to Rosalie that she give Angela another sedative to help her rest, and I went back to the dining table to finish telling my parents and Luigi what really happened to Antonio.

Ma drew blood as her nails dug into Pop's arm. Unable to utter a word, she covered her mouth with her other hand. To her, such an act of desecration was unthinkable, no matter what the reason. We agreed that Castellano and Carmine should never know the truth.

*****

I went to my apartment to change and then entered the office to check on the girls. Martha sat at her desk reading the *Daily News.* Jackie and Sadie, Frank's secretary, were standing on either side of her, leaning over. The front page showed the carnage outside of Castellano's home and a montage of other mangled bodies found along the waterfront and back alleyways. Some had their necks broken, others were gushing blood from slit throats, and two were impaled on wrought-iron fences. Butch had sent a clear message; he was hunting those who were after him, and this was going to end his way. In hindsight, Castellano should have pulled his remaining men off the streets and hunkered down until I found Butch. Now, Castellano's men were either dead or had deserted him when he was arrested.

At that moment, I realized I didn't have to find Butch. He would come for me.

Jackie grabbed my hand and led me to our inner office and closed the door. She held me close.

"I'm so sorry about Antonio. I can't imagine how horrible it was for you and Castellano to see him suffer so."

I explained what really happened and that Castellano had been placed into protective custody.

"I'm going with you to find Butch," she stated.

"I'll take care of Butch. You agreed to work with Martha."

"We're done. Frank has everything he needs for the hearing. I'm coming with you."

"Who murdered the old lady?"

"Sorry, it's Martha's case, and she said you'll find out during the hearing. Don't try to get it out of me because I'm sworn to secrecy."

Frank's case was the least of my worries, so I dropped the subject.

"Have you heard from O'Reilly?"

"He called an hour ago and said all he's finding are dead bodies. Everyone's scared to death and won't say a word about Butch, especially where he might be hiding out.

"I also heard from the editor of the *Daily News*, reminding us that you're on his payroll and he expects an exclusive story when Butch is taken into custody."

Jackie's husband had retained me last year as a special investigator for the newspaper. Given that her husband was now deceased, and we'd never received a new case since I solved my original assignment, I'd forgotten all about our arrangement. It turned out Martha had been putting the paper's monthly checks into our bank account.

"If I get out of this mess alive, he can have whatever he wants."

"What's our next move?" Jackie asked.

I knew we were about to have another fight.

"You can't go. It's too dangerous."

"You're no match for Butch."

"That is why you're not coming along. I can't worry about you."

"Why should you worry about me any more than you would a male partner?"

"You don't understand," I said.

"Of course I understand. Don't you think I have feelings for you? Don't you think I worry about you every time you leave the office? But I don't stop you from doing your job, and I expect you not to stop me from doing mine."

"Where are you going?"

"To get my knife harness and shoulder holster. You'd better not leave without me."

I stood there wondering why I had ever agreed to a female partner. Martha came over and put her arm around my waist.

"You need to forget she's a woman and that you're in love with her, or you'll both end up dead."

"That's not gonna happen," I said.

"It better not, because I need this job."

I couldn't help but laugh.

Jackie entered the office.

"I'm ready. Where are we heading?" she asked.

"Castellano's. To wait for Butch."

Chapter 51

The setting sun brought with it childhood fears of someone lurking in the darkness, ready to pounce. We sat on the floor in silence, listening for any sound that did not match those of Castellano's deserted house. Jackie had a clear view of the upstairs staircase and the hallway that led to the back of the house, and I positioned myself across the room from her, focused on the front entrance and Jackie. We knew Butch would do the same: wait, listen, and then attack, expecting to find Castellano with me and a few other men dedicated to his safety.

Distracted by Jackie's stubborn outburst at the office, I hadn't prepared for a prolonged stay. The hours passed, accompanied by hunger, and then thirst. Even though food and drink were available in the house, I didn't think it wise to expose our presence. I wondered how many more mistakes I would make, mistakes that might cost our lives. Martha had been right. The only way to survive was to view Jackie as expendable. That's how I treated women when on a mission during the war and that's what I needed to do now, for both our sakes. I was willing to die, not just this time, but for any of my clients once we had accepted their cases. That was the nature of the PI business. Now I'd have to accept the reality that Jackie had made the same commitment when we formed our partnership.

A few hours before dawn, we decided to head back home

and regroup with O'Reilly and my family. We needed to find a way to flush Butch out of hiding before he killed Carmine, if he hadn't already.

Reaching for the door handle of my car, I once again relived the sight of Butch tossing his cigar, igniting the gasoline that raced toward Antonio. The memory of Antonio's screams careened through my mind, and that's when I recalled what my subconscious had been trying to reveal since the night I watched over Castellano. I now had a pretty good idea where to find Butch and Carmine.

It was last year when Castellano handed me my first real case, to find out who'd killed his brother. My second meeting with Castellano took place at the end of an old, abandoned warehouse pier on Waters Street. We had met in secret. He didn't want anyone to know he suspected his brother hadn't committed suicide.

Butch had driven me to the meeting and delighted in telling me that the boss was angry. I had violated Castellano's expectations by working on another case at the same time I investigated his brother's death. Butch laughed when he warned me that no one would hear my cries for help if the boss turned nasty. He even went as far as telling me to run if Castellano got out of his car and walked toward the utility shack at the end of the pier. He said this as we entered the massive covered pier that was shrouded in darkness.

Thinking back, I remembered every detail of that night. The place was abandoned, filled with debris. Butch had to swerve several times to avoid holes in the crumbling cement floor as he drove toward Castellano's parked car. But my most vivid memory was the shack that loomed in the distance, backlit by the moonlight reflecting off the bay.

The city had condemned the pier, and it was now

scheduled for demolition. The shack, which had been used over the years by the shift foremen and night watchmen to store their gear and take bathroom breaks, was a perfect place to lay low, a perfect place to find an old, rusty bailing hook to bring along to a murder, and a perfect place to hide Carmine.

* * * * *

I turned off the car lights and stopped a hundred yards from the entrance to the pier. Taking our time, Jackie and I moved from one support pillar to the next, careful to maintain some cover. Every now and then the residents stirred: pigeons nesting in the rafters, rats scurrying overhead from beam to beam, an occasional owl—all mocking our presence in their decaying domain while watching to determine our intent.

Halfway to the shack, I stopped behind a concrete pillar and waved for Jackie to do the same. Once again it was time to take advantage of the most powerful weapon the army had trained me to use, a weapon that had saved my life countless times: the ability to control the rush of adrenaline that the body releases in dangerous situations and the patience to *feel* the environment in order to sense when something is out of place.

I slowed my breathing and heart rate and relaxed every muscle. The chill of the night dissipated. The concrete pillar and I melded into one and I listened. The wind gently whistled through cracks in the walls, discarded newspapers tumbled aimlessly, occasional drips of moisture fell from the rafters, and decayed pilings creaked. A thousand sounds formed a symphony that played a familiar rendition. Each setting and every building had its own song, a song that if left undisturbed by humans, repeated a chorus. We were ready to move again. I would know if an unfamiliar note drifted in: a careful step, a deep breath, even the sour smell of nervous perspiration.

We made our way over to a pillar near the back of the shack and noticed that several window panes were broken out. I crab walked over to the shack below the window and rested against the wall to slow my breathing again. Jackie waited in the shadows. I heard the sound of steel rubbing against leather. Jackie had pulled a chiv from her knife harness. She was ready.

In those few moments I felt a familiar sensation; Joey Batista was gone, and in his place was the man I had become in the war—a highly trained killer. I was a machine with one purpose.

I took a chance and called out for Carmine, waited a few minutes, and tried again, gun drawn.

Carmine responded in a whisper. "Who's there?"

"Batista. Is Butch around?"

"No. My family, are they okay?"

Not wanting to answer, I went around to the front, waited, and listened to the ongoing symphony before I pushed open the door to the shack. The stench caught me by surprise. I stepped back to catch my breath, a mistake that could have cost me my life if Butch had been hiding in the darkness. The inside of the hut was like a tar pit, devoid of light. Carmine said there was a switch on the right side of the door. I reached in, flicked it on, waited for my eyes to adjust, and entered low to the ground. Carmine sat in his own waste, strapped to a chair and table that were bolted to the floor. There were no closets or cubby holes where Butch could hide. Standing, facing the door, I looked down at the table and saw three wire cages holding large rats. Carmine was chained to the table by shackles clamped to his arms above his elbows.

I stared at what Butch had devised, unable to comprehend such evil. It looked like Carmine hadn't eaten since Butch took him from his home. When Carmine became desperate enough, he could reach a knife lying by the cages, grab any one of the rats, and kill it for food. I put down my gun and took hold of Carmine's arm to pull it free from the shackle. Carmine yelled for me to stop. That's when I noticed blood stains on the table.

"I tried that. The shackles have sharp spikes clamped into my arms."

Suddenly Butch appeared out of the darkness of the pier with Jackie's neck clutched in one hand. While she struggled against his grip, he wrestled the knife from her.

"I had a feeling you'd be the one to figure things out," Butch said to me, with the knife held to the side of Jackie's neck. "I went to get Castellano, but he was gone. Was that your doin'?"

"Put the knife away and I'll answer your questions."

"Answer or I'll put *her* away."

Jackie's only chance was for me to keep him occupied in the hope he'd drop his guard.

"What you planned for Castellano became obvious once I heard about your family. What I don't understand is why you didn't just shoot Castellano a long time ago? You must have had a million chances over the years."

"I wanted him to suffer like I did. We were looking forward to a new life, excited about the possibilities America offered. Castellano took it all away. I waited until he would know how it felt. How I felt."

"You're killing innocent people. They had nothing to do with your brother's accident."

"Accident!" Butch shouted. "That bastard killed my brother and parents. They were innocent. I was innocent. I lived in fear, eating rats and any scraps of food I could steal. What about your father and uncle? Are they innocent? Did they care what happened to me after my parents died? No, they didn't. Once Castellano is dead, they're next."

He ordered me to knock my gun off the table and toss the one still in my holster on the ground. Luckily he didn't realize I had a third tucked in my waistband around back.

"Release her first," I said.

He moved his hand away from Jackie's throat and gripped the collar of her blouse, then lowered the knife to his side. I tossed my gun at his feet.

Grinning, Butch yanked Jackie back and drove the knife into the small of her back. The force of the blow lifted her off the ground.

I knew from the sound of metal on metal that Butch's knife had hit the blade of one of the chivs in Jackie's knife harness, and I wasn't surprised when she pivoted in midair and landed an elbow to Butch's throat. Confused, Butch tossed her aside into the wall of the shack. I pulled my gun from behind my back and got off a clear shot.

The bullet hit Butch in the shoulder and slammed him against the wall, hitting the light switch. The room plunged into darkness. I knew Butch hadn't moved because Jackie's chiv, which he held with his damaged arm, fell to the floor. I had shifted to my left and decided not to fire again since I no longer knew Jackie's position.

Butch grunted and lunged forward, groping in the darkness with his good arm. One of his wild swings grazed my chest, sending me back out of his reach. Sensing he had me cornered, he charged, bouncing off several empty diesel drums and into the wall. When I smelled his foul breath, I squeezed the trigger several times, but my gun had jammed. I tossed it aside and pulled one of the knives from the vest Luigi had given me and lashed out, slicing across Butch's stomach. It felt like I had scraped my knife along a brick wall. He was so muscular that the knife hadn't penetrated very deep, but it sounded like it hurt like hell. His shrill scream caused the pier to come alive. Scores of pigeons took flight and rodents ran for cover. Enraged, Butch blindly charged ahead, smashing into the wall again and splintering several wooden studs. Fortunately, I dove to my right to get out of his path.

I felt for the gun I had thrown earlier at Butch's feet, jumped up, and turned on the light. Before I could get off a shot, Butch hit me with a crushing blow to the chest that sent me crashing to the floor.

When I came to my senses, Butch had his foot in the middle of my chest. His one arm dangled by his side, dripping blood from his shoulder wound. With his good arm, he gripped his sliced stomach muscles. He must have been in tremendous pain, but he grinned with the satisfaction of knowing he was about to crush the life out of me. He leaned back to gain leverage, releasing the pressure on my chest. This enabled me to reach behind my neck to grab another knife from the vest, but it was gone.

To my surprise, Butch let out a horrendous screech and fell sideways, smashing into the table that held Carmine captive, shattering it to splinters and freeing the rats from their cages. Butch was out of commission.

Jackie had crawled along the floor and severed his

Achilles tendon, above his right heel. Exhausted, she leaned up against a feces-encrusted toilet, staring at a bone that protruded from her leg. She looked pale and was drenched with perspiration. Jackie was going into shock. I had to act fast and get her medical attention. I went to free Carmine when I noticed Butch reaching inside his coat. He was so used to using his brute strength that he had forgotten he had a piece. I kicked him in the gut and grabbed his gun and patted him down for other weapons. Satisfied that Butch was no longer a danger to us I cut the leather straps holding Carmine to his chair and helped him get the circulation back into his legs. In spite of the pain from the shackles still around his arms, Carmine grabbed my gun and put it to Butch's head. I reached out in time to stop him.

"No, Carmine. He doesn't deserve a quick death."

The starving rats, smelling blood, inched closer to Butch. He pulled himself along the floor with his good arm until he was up against a wall and then fought off the rats with a piece of wood. That was the first time I'd seen fear in Butch's eyes. I had every intention of letting O'Reilly deal with what was left of Butch later, but then I noticed a small hole next to an old bailing hook lodged in a support beam of the shack. At that moment, images swirled inside my head of Kowalski dangling from a rusty bailing hook attached to a hoist and Antonio's limp body consumed by flames. Butch had shown no mercy, and neither would I.

I ripped a small section of rotting baseboard from the wall of the shack and kicked a hole in the wall by the ground. Then I picked up Jackie's chiv and sliced through Butch's left Achilles tendon so he couldn't stand. Ignoring his pleas, I barricaded the door, shutting in his screams, condemning Butch to hell where he belonged. The resident rats of the pier, hearing the squeals of their brethren, joined in on the feast.

I carried Jackie in my arms and headed for the entrance to the pier with Carmine hobbling beside me, clutching the slats of wood attached to his shackles.

*****

O'Reilly had noticed my car while he'd been checking on his men stationed around the neighborhood. He waited by the car suspecting I had found Butch. He knew it wasn't his place to get involved. If Butch walked out alive, then he'd take care of him.

I called out to O'Reilly. He placed Jackie in his car and sped off to the local hospital, while I helped Carmine to a shower station located at the entrance to the pier. O'Reilly had given Carmine a change of clothes that he kept in his car for emergencies and handed me the tools I needed to free Carmine from his shackles. Half an hour later, O'Reilly returned.

We thought it best to take Carmine to his wife, who was still with my parents, and then notify the police commissioner to release Castellano from jail.

Ma immediately took charge. She refused to give Carmine any heavy Italian food and insisted he eat a slice of bread and chicken broth for dinner. Too weak to steady his own arm, Angela spoon feed him. He asked several times for Antonio, which brought instant tears to Angela's eyes.

Seeing Angela's pain, an image of Butch trying to claw his way out of the shack with his good arm to get away from the hungry rats crossed my mind. The image didn't last long; Butch got what he deserved. I had no regrets.

After the meal, Angela and Carmine went into the parlor. We all heard Angela crying, and I'm sure they heard Ma's sobs as well. After a while, I went to join them and was surprised to see Carmine looking withdrawn, sitting away from Angela. She needed him, but he was deep in his own thoughts.

Chapter 52

Crises come and go in our daily lives, but the underlying fabric of the city continues undisturbed. Adults rush from place to place to make a living, youngsters seek new ways to entertain themselves, old timers sit on the same stoop spinning tales while watching life pass them by, and the ever-present leeches of society drain their neighborhoods of its morality to make an easy buck.

In a city the size of New York, it takes a catastrophic event to alter these dynamics and impact the character of an ethnic neighborhood. I had an uneasy feeling that such an event had taken place when Castellano had crumbled to the ground the night Butch tricked him into killing his only grandson. Castellano shielded our neighborhood from the harsh realities of the corruption interwoven throughout the city, and my fear was that his shield would also crumble over time.

Angela and Carmine buried their son and planned to stay with Castellano until they could find a new home; the old one held too many memories. The *Daily News* got their money's worth and scooped the other papers with sensational headlines and gory details of Butch's rampage.

Luigi focused on his speakeasy, and Pop keep busy with the shoe business. Ma spent most of her time in the kitchen or shopping for ingredients, while Rosalie focused on nursing school and helping Angela cope with her grief.

Jackie and Martha had prepared Frank Galvano and Sadie for the upcoming hearing concerning the injunction imposed on Ruth Capelli's estate and researched last-minute questions for Frank. I took the opportunity, while waiting for a new case, to sleep in late and jaw with some of the old timers and shop owners. Whenever I stopped by the office to ask Jackie and Martha about their investigation, they told me I'd get the details at the trial.

Our lives had returned to normal, along with the rest of the neighborhood, but as I feared, there was one notable exception. Castellano withdrew deeper into his own world, ignoring the neighborhood and the need to rebuild his organization. Carmine, recognizing the threat that Big Ben Napoli posed, promoted someone on his management team to oversee his international shipping company while he focused on running the docks.

Pop and Luigi became concerned when Castellano stopped going to his office behind the pizza shop. Castellano had been the one person who everyone felt comfortable asking for help when a crisis struck. We all knew that without Castellano, the neighborhood would begin to morph into something different.

One day, when the three of us were at Castellano's house, he asked me to take a walk around his compound.

"I know what you did," he said.

I stopped walking.

Realizing I was no longer by his side, he came back. "I've been over that night a million times. Butch tricked me into killing Antonio, didn't he?"

"You didn't have a choice."

"That's a lie, and you know it. There wasn't the smell of burning flesh."

"There's only one person to blame, and that's Butch. Believe me when I say he paid a steep price for what he did."

"That doesn't matter. What matters is that I'm through with this business."

"You're talking nonsense. What happened with Butch had nothing to do with the mob. There's no reason to step aside."

"Joey, look at me. I got the shakes. I don't have the stomach or the guts for this business anymore. I already told you, the other bosses can smell weakness, and when they do, they'll attack like a pack of animals."

I knew he was right and so did my pop and uncle. They had already expressed their concerns to me. "So what's the alternative? You think Carmine's ready?"

"I need someone who cares about the neighborhood and who can stand up to the other bosses."

"Carmine will do a good job," I said.

"Sure, he can run the business, but Carmine cares only about Carmine. I want *you* to take over."

We both stopped walking and faced each other. "I can't do that. I won't do it."

"Look, Joey. I've seen what you're capable of. Except for Big Ben, the other bosses won't risk goin' up against you. Ben's obsessed with the idea of taking over the entire waterfront. Always has been. The neighborhood needs you, just like they needed me years ago."

"This is different. Neither you nor my uncle wanted the responsibility. Carmine craves it."

"I know my son. His loyalty can be bought with money."

"We're not talking about money. We're talking about

power, influence, and absolute control over our slice of the city. Carmine expects to take over. He always has. Besides, I will not become one of Silvio's bosses and corrupt so many lives. I will not become one of them."

"You don't have a choice. I know you. You won't let everyone down."

"I have a choice. That's what I fought for; that's why so many died in the war."

"I'm telling you, Joey, if Carmine takes over, you won't recognize the neighborhood in a few years."

"I don't believe that and neither do you. But even if you're right, I can't take what rightfully belongs to Carmine. We would become mortal enemies and one or both of us would eventually die as a result of your decision. If you're dropping out, your only choice is to turn things over to Carmine."

We walked the rest of the way in silence until we got to the steps leading up to Castellano's house.

"Then promise me you'll help Carmine. He's a hot head and will get himself killed."

"Only if you do me a favor in return."

"What's that?"

"Spend time in your office. You're the one the neighborhood needs. Let Carmine run the docks, but you run the neighborhood. Carmine will eventually learn to do what's best."

"I hope you're right," Castellano said. "I hope you're right."

Chapter 53

The judge entered the courtroom, carefully adjusted his robes, and called the proceeding to order. As the gavel struck, Frank stood and asked permission to approach the bench. The judge looked startled when Frank went ahead and walked toward him before he'd given his response.

"Your Honor, new evidence has been uncovered indicating we may be dealing with more than a fraudulent will. My investigative team believes Ruth Capelli was murdered to prevent her from altering her recently modified last will and testament."

"Mr. Galvano, I could hold you in contempt of court for such behavior. Never approach this bench again without permission."

"Yes, Your Honor."

"Have you contacted the district attorney's office with your suspicions?"

"No, Your Honor."

"Are you a novice at this, Mr. Galvano?"

"No, Your Honor."

"Then you know if the DA asked for a continuation of the injunction for the reason you stated, it would be granted."

"I understand, Your Honor, but since the key evidence literally came together a few hours ago, there was inadequate time to schedule a meeting with the DA. This hearing also provides us with the rare opportunity to have all the people actively involved in Mrs. Capelli's life in one place to piece together the mystery behind her death."

The judge held his gavel in one hand and tapped his fingers repeatedly, staring down at Frank, until Doyle, Mrs. Capelli's legal representative, objected vehemently to Frank's maneuver and insisted he be allowed to approach the bench as well. Standing, the judge pounded his gavel.

"This session will recess for twenty minutes. Gentlemen, I'll see you in my chambers."

* * * * *

I took the opportunity to join Jackie and Martha, who were leaning over a banister jabbering with Sadie.

"Tell Frank to read this before he calls Mr. Doyle to the stand," Jackie said, handing Sadie a folder.

"Are you ladies gonna invite me into your little circle, or do I have to sit here all day to find out if you've been earning your keep?" I asked.

Jackie smiled and shrugged. "Your guess is as good as mine. It really depends on how Galvano uses the information Martha has gathered."

Martha moved over so I could sit between her and Jackie and told me to be patient.

The judge burst through his chamber door with a new sense of vigor, startling most in the courtroom. Frank followed and briskly walked to his table. In sharp contrast, Doyle waddled behind Frank with a scowl and stooped shoulders. He swore when he bumped his knee trying to get behind his table.

"I'll have none of that language in my courtroom, Mr. Doyle."

"Sorry, Your Honor."

Frank shook my hand, opened the folder Sadie handed him, and read it quickly.

"Bailiff, clear the docket for the rest of the afternoon. I believe, based on our conversation, Mr. Galvano has enough to entertain us for the day. Are you ready, Mr. Galvano, or do we have to wait for you to determine how you're going to proceed?"

"I call Mr. Doyle to the stand."

"I object!"

"On what grounds, Mr. Doyle?" the judge asked.

"Well, I . . . I'm a lawyer in this trial."

"This is not a trial, Mr. Doyle. This is a hearing. You do not get to object or cross-examine anyone unless I feel it's necessary. We agreed in my chambers to allow Mr. Galvano to present his evidence, and we shall do so. Take the stand."

Frank continued to read the file with his back to the witness stand. Once Doyle was sworn in, Frank dropped the folder on his table with some force and thoughtfully walked to the stand.

"Mr. Galvano," the judge said. "There is no jury to impress, so please get this over with as quickly as possible."

Frank nodded.

"Mr. Doyle, when did you first meet Ruth Capelli?"

"A few months ago."

"What were the circumstances?"

"She wanted to update her will."

"Did she seem agitated? Was there a sense of urgency?"

"Yes, she accused her nephew of stealing a priceless book and wanted to eliminate him from her estate."

"Did she make other changes?"

"Yes, she bequeathed a considerable amount of her assets to her domestic help and others."

"Did you encourage this change?"

"I didn't encourage nor discourage any action on her part."

"Since Mrs. Capelli is no longer with us, I guess we'll have to take your word on that. But you did become the executor of the will. Is that not correct?"

"Well, yes. Her nephew was the executor and that was no longer appropriate."

"If I compare both wills, you added a hefty fee and a percentage of all liquidated assets for your executor duties."

"No more than I usually charge."

"I agree. But under the old will, most of the assets were being transferred to her nephew and various charities in the form of deeds-of-trust, thus, eliminating the need for liquidation."

"Who can understand the rationale of an old lady?"

Frank walked back to his table mumbling, "Who indeed? Who indeed?" With his back to Doyle he picked up a ledger and asked, "How's business, Mr. Doyle?"

"I don't know what you mean."

"It's a simple question. Is your clientele increasing, decreasing, or remaining relatively flat?"

Doyle gripped the railing of the witness stand and said with a flushed face, "My business is just fine."

"Not according to your secretary's ledger of appointments. I would say you're having trouble keeping up with your expensive lifestyle," Frank said, handing the appointment calendar to the judge.

"How did you get that?" Doyle shouted.

"Maybe your lawyer will ask that question if you're ever accused of Mrs. Capelli's murder."

Doyle got up to leave the stand, "I resent that slanderous statement," he shouted.

"Mr. Doyle, you *will* remain seated," the judge said. "Mr. Galvano, that statement was out of line. Do you have any more questions for Mr. Doyle?"

"Just two, Your Honor."

"Then proceed."

"Mr. Doyle, how much is Ruth Capelli's estate worth?"

"I don't know."

"You don't know? How interesting, Mr. Doyle, since your fee would exceed two hundred thousand dollars if all her physical assets were liquidated. We had her estate appraised, and it just so happened we used the same firm you did," Frank said.

"Let me remind you, Mr. Doyle," the judge said, "that you are under oath."

"That's all for now," Frank said.

Doyle struggled to squeeze himself out of the witness stand when Frank turned and asked one more question.

"Sorry, Mr. Doyle, I almost forgot my last question. Who referred Mrs. Capelli to your office?"

"I don't recall."

"Thank you," Frank said. "Oh, by the way, that's a magnificent ring you're wearing."

Doyle popped out of the stand, put his hands in his pockets, and shuffled back to his seat. Frank called Ruth's Catholic priest to testify next.

"I gather from your robes that you're a Franciscan monk. Is that correct, Father Gallagher?"

"Yes."

"Did Ruth Capelli not understand that you had taken a vow of poverty, and any money she bequeathed to you would go to the church?"

"There is a lot Mrs. Capelli failed to comprehend about the Catholic Church."

"My understanding is that Mrs. Capelli was taking lessons from you on a frequent basis. Do you know why the interest in Catholicism when she was raised in the Jewish faith?"

"Once her husband passed away, she decided she should learn more about his religion. She said she had tried to convert him to Judaism but wasn't successful."

"Did you have any influence on her decision to rewrite her will?"

"We did discuss the topic. She was quite distraught about her nephew. I reviewed the joint will she had with her husband and suggested some changes."

"You didn't by any chance encourage her to leave considerable money to her domestic staff and others, or to liquidate her assets?"

Father Gallagher had a sudden coughing fit and pulled a handkerchief out of his long, brown, oversized monk sleeve. Once he recovered his composure, he responded to Frank's question.

"I hope you're not implying that I influenced Mrs. Capelli to include me in her will."

Frank had stopped moving, focused on Father Gallagher, and then turned to face Mr. Doyle. "No, of course not, Father. I would never accuse a holy man like yourself of such deception." Returning his attention back to the witness stand, he said, "But Father, you didn't answer my question."

"I did suggest she might leave a small sum to her domestic

help and those who had been of significance in her life. I never expected her to include me or be so generous."

"I believe you, but did you also suggest to Mrs. Capelli that she obtain the legal services of your *brother*?" Frank asked, pointing at Doyle.

A low murmur rose up in the courtroom. The judge pounded his gavel and called for the disturbance to cease. I whispered to the girls that I was impressed with their investigative skills.

"Mr. Galvano, explain your last statement. Are you implying that Mr. Doyle perjured himself when he said he didn't know who referred Ruth Capelli to him?" the judge asked.

"I'm afraid only Mr. Doyle can answer that question. It is, however, quite evident that Father Gallagher and Mr. Doyle are closely related since they have the same defective third finger and birthmark on their right wrists. I noticed that Mr. Doyle's index finger isn't the longest on his hand when I admired his diamond ring. I had also noticed the birthmark prior to that time. Naturally I didn't think anything of it until Father Gallagher coughed and exposed his hands outside his cassock."

Father Gallagher stood and addressed the judge. "I see nothing wrong in recommending my brother to parishioners in need of legal counsel. He's an honest man."

"I have no more questions for Father Gallagher," Frank said.

Father Gallagher walked back to his seat with his head bowed and arms folded in front of him, buried deep within his cassock.

The judge had leaned forward during the testimony and rubbed his beard as Gallagher left the stand. He then called a lunch recess.

* * * * *

The District Attorney entered the courtroom shortly before the hearing resumed, looked around, and sat down next to Jackie. She jabbed me in the side and we exchanged seats. She had no intention of sitting next to him.

"I didn't think Mrs. Forsythe was the type to hold a grudge forever. I just wanted to ask her how her leg was healing. After all, she did stop you from plugging me in the gut not that long ago," he said.

"That was the only time I've seen her use poor judgment."

"Oh, I'm sure you and I will butt heads again. When that day comes, maybe I'll let her convince me to return the favor, but I doubt it. I'd like nothing better than having a legitimate reason to put a bullet in your head."

I'd had enough of his chit chat. "What brings you here?"

"Your pal Galvano convinced the judge to call my office a short time ago to issue a *blank* subpoena for a murder charge. I always enjoy watching Galvano's maneuverings, so I came down myself. Besides, you never know when I'll be up against him again. I might learn something useful."

* * * * *

The judge called the proceeding to order to start the afternoon session. Martha took the witness stand.

"Miss Peone, please explain to the judge your role in this investigation," Frank said.

"I work for the detective agency you hired. I perform daily office duties and gather facts for the various investigations."

"In that capacity you searched Ruth Capelli's apartment for pertinent information. Is that correct?"

"Yes."

"Please tell the judge what you discovered."

"In my estimation, one of the most important pieces of information I uncovered was that Mrs. Capelli made an appointment with a different lawyer to change her will again the day after she held a party for the beneficiaries."

"Just to clarify your statement, Mrs. Capelli made an appointment with a lawyer other than Mr. Doyle. Is that correct?" Frank asked.

"Yes."

The judge interrupted. "How did you uncover this fact?"

Martha turned to the judge, threw back her shoulders, and said in a clear voice, "I noticed a scrap of paper stuck behind her phone with a number and the same date she was killed; naturally, I called. It was the office number for a local lawyer, a Mr. Vincent Rivisi. He confirmed she had called and made an appointment."

The judge nodded his approval. "Nice bit of work."

Martha turned back to Frank with a flushed face. I whispered in Jackie's ear, "Maybe the judge would be interested in Martha."

Jackie had a hard time suppressing a chuckle. "He'd have a heart attack in a week. She needs someone much younger and bigger, you know, more robust," Jackie said.

The DA interrupted our conversation. "Tell me, Joey, who's the murderer?"

"Not my case. You'll have to ask Jackie and she's not tellin'."

Frank continued his questioning. "Did you discover anything else of significance?"

"Yes. Copies of her prior will and deeds to her considerable real estate holdings."

"Can you confirm my statement that Ruth Capelli was a wealthy person?"

"Immensely, even her apartment furnishings are valuable. I had an antique dealer do an appraisal. Most items couldn't be valued. He said the entire apartment should be in a Victorian museum."

"Would that include her clothing?" Frank asked.

"Most definitely. I didn't find a stitch of modern clothing in her apartment."

"I understand you had the opportunity to examine the clothes she wore on the day she died."

"That's correct."

"Walking down the street dressed the way she was, do you think people took notice?"

"I'm sure she turned a few heads," Martha said.

Frank helped Martha off the witness stand. "Thank you, Miss Peone. I concur with the judge; you did an excellent job, and I believe your employer should give you a hefty raise," Frank said.

Sadie handed Frank a folder, which he promptly placed on the judge's bench. "You'll find that the original will we located in Mrs. Capelli's apartment is markedly different from the one Mr. Doyle crafted for her. The folder also contains a written affidavit from Mr. Vincent Rivisi, the lawyer Ruth Capelli was scheduled to meet on the morning of her so-called accident, along with a full appraisal of her estate."

The judge glanced through the papers and intently examined several pages. The judge looked up, but before he could say anything, Frank stated he would come back to the documents at a later time, and then he called his next witness, the chauffeur.

* * * * *

The chauffer approached the witness stand with a military demeanor, dressed in his black uniform. He took the oath with a clear, resounding baritone voice and sat at attention.

"It appears, Mr. Whitman, that you've found new employment since Mrs. Capelli's unfortunate accident."

"Yes sir."

"In fact, you have an uncanny knack for finding employment."

"Don't know what you mean, sir."

"I mean that in the last six years you've worked for four different employers."

"I haven't kept count, but I guess that's right."

"Do you often get fired?"

"Oh, no, sir. The old folks don't like to drive themselves in the city, and they just up and keel over from natural causes...most of the time."

"Did you know that all your employers were clients of Mr. Doyle?"

Doyle stood to object, scattering papers across the floor. He flopped back down under the judge's glare. The judge turned to the witness and asked him to answer the question, reminding him he was under oath.

"It seemed natural for me to ask my uncle if he could find me a job. He has all these wealthy clients who need help getting around town. I see nothing wrong in that."

Frank turned to the judge. "Your Honor, I believe I have established that the last will and testament of Mrs. Ruth

Capelli, an elderly woman estranged from her only relative, should be nullified due to the fact that she was deceived and unduly influenced by people she trusted. There was obvious collusion to influence her decisions in their own best interests. But before you rule on the document's legitimacy, I would like to have her nephew, Mathew Capelli, who is contesting the will, testify on his own behalf."

* * * * *

Mathew Capelli walked to the stand with a swagger.

"Mr. Capelli, why are you contesting your aunt's will?" Frank asked.

"My aunt called me the morning after she held a party for those included in her new will and—"

The judge interrupted his testimony. "This is the second time a party has been mentioned. Isn't giving a beneficiary party a rather strange thing to do?"

"Not for my aunt. She loved to entertain on a grand scale. In any event, she sounded outraged and said she had been deceived and was such a fool. She then apologized for accusing me of stealing a rare book from her husband's collection."

"Is that why you're not mentioned in her altered will that Mr. Doyle prepared?" Frank asked.

"That's correct."

"Did she say anything else?"

"She intended to contact a different lawyer and reinstate the original will she and her husband had agreed upon."

"Are you a beneficiary in the original?"

"Yes, I was to inherit my uncle's book collection and a significant portion of the remaining estate."

"Is the collection as valuable as the appraisers estimated?"

"Priceless."

"What happened next?" Frank asked.

"On the way to the new lawyer's office, she was struck by a car and died from her injuries."

Frank turned toward Sadie, and she handed him some papers.

"I have the police report. It states that the car sped away dragging your aunt for some distance before she rolled out from the undercarriage of the car."

"Yes, she died a gruesome death."

"According to the report, they never found the person responsible or the car. It was a Ford, much like yours," Frank stated.

"A very popular model, I can see how it would be impossible to locate the driver."

Frank abruptly switched subjects, catching everyone's attention. "What do you suppose caused your aunt to become so upset at the party?"

"She didn't say."

"Most likely she discovered a great many things that night. For instance, did you know that her rabbi collects old Bibles?"

Frank didn't give Capelli a chance to answer. "Yes, I know. It sounds strange at first, but I can see why a Hebrew scholar would be interested in knowing how translations of the Old Testament changed over time."

The judge admonished Frank for taking the court's time when he had already concluded the new will should be void. Frank didn't back down.

"Judge, I promised you a murderer, and that person is sitting in this courtroom."

All heads turned to Doyle, except Frank's. He continued to probe his client.

"Mr. Capelli, you might be interested to know that your aunt's rabbi has a close friend with a private book collection who recently purchased a Gutenberg Bible. In fact, he purchased the Bible from *you*."

"That's preposterous, I never—"

"There's no use denying that fact, Mr. Capelli. You've only told a half-truth. Your aunt did say she was going back to her old will, but with you still removed. One of the copies of the original will that Miss Peone found in your aunt's apartment has your name scratched out, along with your inheritance. She intended to bequeath her husband's collection of books to a museum and the rest of her estate to charity."

Capelli stood and shouted at Frank. "You have no proof that I killed my aunt! Why would I if I had nothing to gain?"

"That's a good question. Why would you kill your aunt if you're not mentioned in Mrs. Capelli's new will or in her intended revision of her original will? Maybe Vincent Rivisi can shed some light on that question."

The judge pounded his gavel and asked security to escort Capelli back to his seat.

* * * * *

"Mr. Rivisi, please state your profession," Frank said.

"I'm an attorney."

"Have you ever met Mathew Capelli prior to this hearing?"

"Yes, I have."

"In what capacity?"

"He asked me to look into the genealogy of Father Gallagher."

"Why would he make such a request?"

"He noticed the same birth defects you mentioned earlier and was concerned that his aunt had been influenced by Doyle and Father Gallagher to eliminate him from her will."

"Why didn't you mention this in your deposition?" Frank asked.

"I was never officially asked by any legal authority if Mr. Capelli was one of my clients. My client list and all conversations are confidential."

"Yes, of course. Please tell us now what you discovered about Father Gallagher's genealogy."

"Just what you had deduced, he's related to Mr. Doyle. In fact, they're fraternal twins."

"Once you presented this information to Mr. Capelli, did he give you any further instructions?"

"Yes. He asked that I inform Ruth Capelli of my findings by letter, and I was to pass this information on to you during this hearing if necessary."

Frank picked up a letter from his table and handed it to the judge. "Here is the letter Mr. Rivisi is referring to, which Miss Peone found among Mrs. Capelli's legal documents."

"So, this is the real source of your so-called deductive reasoning," the judge said.

"I just couldn't resist," Frank said, with a smile. "You'll notice that the birth defects are mentioned in the letter."

Frank returned his attention back to the witness stand. "Mr. Rivisi, I have to ask this question. Did you find any of this unusual?"

"Unusual, but not illegal. Mr. Capelli paid me handsomely for my services."

"Your Honor, I have no more questions of this witness and call Mathew Capelli back to the stand."

* * * * *

"Your Honor, I would like the court recorder to read back Mr. Capelli's last statement when he was on the witness stand," Frank said.

The court recorder stood and read aloud. *"You have no proof that I killed my aunt! Why would I if I had nothing to gain?"*

Frank pointed to Capelli. "You had everything to gain if your aunt died before changing her will again. Why? Because you knew her recent will would be overturned once the relationship between Father Gallagher and Mr. Doyle was revealed. Yes, Mrs. Capelli did call you and tell you she was changing her will again, but not back to the original. She felt betrayed by you and everyone around her. Unknowingly, she made a fatal mistake by mentioning to you she was walking to a new lawyer in the morning. You then deduced she had most likely contacted Vincent Rivisi, since his law office was within walking distance from her apartment and because she believed he had discovered the truth about her priest and Doyle."

Capelli laughed. "Everything you just said is speculation. You can't prove any of it."

Frank handed the judge two pictures. "You're right, but I can prove you killed your aunt," Frank said.

"We heard from Miss Martha Peone that your aunt was obsessed with the Victorian age and wore clothing common to that period. On her fatal day, she wore a plush velvet, Victorian Paletot coat trimmed in satin and lined with silk. A unique garment.

"The pictures the judge is holding prove you killed your aunt. The sleeve of her coat became caught in the undercarriage of the car that ran her down, which is why she was dragged such a distance. The coat ripped free, leaving behind a piece of the sleeve lodged in a Hassler shock absorber attached to the rear axle of your car. By the way, the Hassler is not standard equipment on a Ford. You had it installed after you purchased the car. Ironically, days before you killed your aunt."

"That's preposterous. You need to hire a better investigative team," Capelli shouted. "I have two cars and loaned that one to my aunt since her car was scheduled for repair. I loaned her the car with the new shock absorbers because it had a smoother ride. Anyone in her household with access to her car could have killed her."

"I can assure you, Mr. Capelli, that my investigative team is top-notch," Frank said. He then called his last witness, Ruth's companion and maid, Mrs. Althea D'Agostino.

* * * * *

"Mrs. D'Agostino, would you please tell the court about your relationship with Mrs. Ruth Capelli."

She turned to face the judge. "I was first employed by Mrs. Capelli twenty years ago when I was eighteen. She and her husband treated me like family, and Mrs. Capelli and I became good friends."

"Can you tell us about the night of the beneficiary party? Did anything unusual happen?" Frank asked.

"We were all excited to learn about the will and in a festive mood. That is, until Mrs. Capelli confronted Mr. Doyle, her lawyer."

"What exactly happened?"

"It's hard to say because they went into the library and

closed the door. Of course we were all curious so we did our best to listen. Mrs. Capelli was upset about her will. She came storming out of the room, turned toward Mr. Doyle, and said, "Consider yourself fired."

"Then what took place?"

"Mrs. Capelli went to her bedroom and slammed the door. The party was obviously over, so we all went about our business."

"Thank you, Mrs. D'Agostino. Now, tell us what happened the following day?" Frank asked.

"I brought her a late morning lunch in her study as she had requested. She stated that she had an appointment with a new lawyer and had decided to walk to his office since it was only a few blocks away."

"Was it unusual for her to walk alone around the city?" Frank asked.

"Oh, my, yes. I insisted on driving her, and she finally agreed."

"What happened next?"

"I took the car key off the hook by the backstairs, and we walked out of the apartment to where the chauffer parks the car."

"Why didn't the chauffer offer to drive her?"

"He got very upset when Mr. Doyle told him the night before that Mrs. Capelli intended to change her will. He took the day off."

"So, tell me why did Mrs. Capelli change her mind and walk to the appointment?" Frank asked.

"Oh, she didn't change her mind. The car was gone."

"And you had the only key to the car door that was in the apartment."

"That's right."

"Were you concerned that the car was stolen?"

"No, I assumed that Mr. Capelli, her nephew, took the car using a spare key in his possession. Mrs. Capelli's car was due back from the repair shop that afternoon."

Frank handed the judge another folder. "Your Honor, here are two sworn statements from local tenants in Mrs. Ruth Capelli's neighborhood that witnessed Mr. Capelli driving away with the car shortly before Mrs. D'Agostino and Mrs. Capelli exited the building with the intent of using the automobile."

"Is that all, Mr. Galvano?" the judge asked.

"Yes, Your Honor."

The judge called a recess and conferred with the DA. Upon returning to the bench, he ordered an investigation into the murder of Mrs. Ruth Capelli. He then ordered that Mathew Capelli be held for questioning. He also authenticated Ruth Capelli's hand-modified, original will that had been witnessed by the manager of her apartment building and the doorman on the morning of her death and, in so doing, nullified the will written by Mr. Doyle. He didn't stop there. The judge also suspended Mr. Doyle's law license for sixty days and issued an order to have the district attorney's office investigate the law practices of Doyle and Son.

Chapter 54

That evening we congregated at Maria's restaurant to celebrate Frank's victory and congratulate Jackie and Martha for their doggedness on the case.

"There was a time when we suspected every one of the beneficiaries. They all had one reason or another for knocking off the old lady," Jackie said.

"The deeper we dug, the more suspects popped up," Martha said. "The guy who married the companion is a professional swindler preying on lonely woman, the chauffeur kept working for widowed women who didn't last long, Doyle got most of his elderly clients from the Franciscan church, and the rabbi collected rare books."

Frank, who was drinking more than usual, was having trouble getting his thoughts together, but that didn't stop him from dropping a bombshell in the middle of the conversation.

"I can't prove it, but I think Rivisi…knew Capelli was guilty of murder and that…,excuse me, Capelli paid him handsomely to keep his mouth shut."

"Damn!" Martha said.

Everyone, except Frank, stopped drinking, and they had a good laugh.

"I know, I know. I have a knack for picking losers," Martha said. "I guess I should break my lunch date with him tomorrow."

Frank reached for another beer and missed his mouth, drawing attention away from Martha. He was so far gone already that he must have been drinking before we met at the restaurant.

"I don't blame you for getting smoked," I said. "We just lost a bundle of dough by proving your client killed his own aunt."

Frank put his mug down and looked at me strangely. "Oh, shit, I forgot to tell you guys. The judge, he...he... called me into his chambers...after the courtroom emptied and...he appointed me to be the executor of Ruth's estate, which means we...we...still get to split ten percent per our legal...ly binding hand...handshake." He grabbed his glass and raised it to Martha. "Not...not too bad for your first... case!"

"I can't take all the credit," Martha said. "It was Joey who wondered how Ruth got dragged so far."

O'Reilly had just stood to make a toast when Carmine came into the restaurant and waved me over to his table.

I noticed he had a gun under his napkin.

"What's goin on?" I asked.

"I need your help."

"Rosalie told me both Angela and your father aren't doing great. I haven't come by because there's not much I can do," I said.

"Angela is the least of my problems. It's my dad. His organization is falling apart, and he couldn't care less. He doesn't give a shit about anything. If we don't do something soon, the waterfront and neighborhood will be taken over. Some of Big Ben's boys are already strutting around as if they own the place."

"What do you expect me to do?" I asked.

"Back me up. My pop has given me the okay to take control, but I can't do it alone."

"Why me? You can hire guys for that job."

"Look, Joey. Whether you like it or not, the other bosses respect you and your family's ties to the Mafia. By rights, I'm next in line, but I need to show them I can handle the job, and that's where you come in."

"I promised your pop I'd do what I can, but only if you take care of the neighborhood."

"Fair enough. I knew I could count on you. I'll come by tomorrow and pick you up. We have a meeting with the syndicate at noon. Watch your back. The word's already out that you're standing with me."

"How did that happen?"

He holstered his gun and headed for the door. "Like I said, I knew you wouldn't let me down."

Chapter 55

Carmine arrived at the office on time, anxious to get to the syndicate meeting. I understood why. It's not a good idea to be late to your first meeting as a potential new boss. When the phone rang, Carmine swore.

"You guys need to get goin'," Jackie said. "I'll get the phone."

We were out the door and halfway down the stairs when Jackie yelled, "Joey, hold up. It's Lieutenant Sullivan from Staten Island. He said it's urgent."

Jackie stood at my side, leaning on her crutch, while I listened to the lieutenant.

"I'll be there at five," I said and hung up.

"What goin' on?" Jackie asked.

There wasn't an easy way to tell her the news, and she wouldn't want it sugarcoated anyway. "Debbie's missing and Gino's been shot. They don't think he'll make it."

Jackie leaned back against her desk for support.

Carmine yanked my arm. "Come on, Joey. We can't be late because of a street bum and a pro skirt."

I grabbed his arm, twisted it behind his back, and shoved him into Martha's office. "You damn well better give us a few minutes or you can face those goons yourself."

"Hey, take it easy, pal. I'm a little jumpy, that's all. I'll wait in the car."

Jackie came into Martha's office when she heard the door slam.

"Don't forget you might need Carmine on your side. Ronnie did this to Gino and Debbie, and he knows you're gonna come lookin' for Debbie. He'll be ready for you," Jackie said.

"I can handle Ronnie without Carmine's help. I'll meet you and Martha at the clinic as soon as this meeting's over. Sullivan can't get there until five to join us, so interview everyone at the clinic and be ready to give us a quick rundown when I arrive."

"Martha's on a lunch date with that young lawyer, Rivisi, and knowing her, she won't be back until tomorrow morning."

"I thought she was gonna break that date."

"She changed her mind. She figured everyone does something stupid once in a while, and didn't see why she should dump such a find just because Frank has a hunch."

"Do you feel good enough to go alone?"

"Sure, your pop can drive me to the ferry, and I'll take a cab on the island to the clinic."

"Stay off the leg as much as possible. Have any witnesses at the clinic come to you. I'm sure Dr. Schwartz will let you use his office."

"Don't worry. The leg is healing, and I'm getting pretty good with this crutch."

"There's one more thing. Contact O'Reilly to see if he can meet us there at five," I said, holding her tight. "Don't worry, they won't hurt Debbie, and Ronnie's days are numbered."

"What makes you so confident?"

"Ronnie came after Debbie so he could get back some

of his influential clients. They're not gonna pay for damaged goods."

"What about Ronnie?" Jackie asked.

"Let me worry about him."

* * * * *

Carmine and I got past the initial security team and gave up our rods and chivs. It wasn't until we entered the antechamber to the main meeting room that all hell broke out. We were told to strip down to our skivvies by two musclebound Neanderthals.

One of them shoved his palm against my chest. "You heard me," he said.

I noticed that the other guy had his eyes on Carmine, who was removing his jacket. Carmine needed to gain the bosses' respect and walking into the meeting in his underwear wasn't gonna do it. I had to move fast.

I pretended to follow orders, brushed aside the brute's palm, and reached for my lapel to remove my jacket. He relaxed and stepped back with a smirk. I surprised him with a swift kick to his groin, and as he bent forward, I grabbed his head with both hands and smashed his face with my knee. I quickly grabbed the gun from his holster and pointed it at the other guy who, by this time, had Carmine in a choke hold.

"Get his rod," I shouted to Carmine. When Carmine was ready, I shoved my assailant through the double doors. They flew open with a loud crash. The bloke smashed against the edge of the meeting table and fell backwards onto the floor, moaning. Carmine entered next with a gun to the head of the other goon.

Several of the bosses had ducked under the table. "What the hell's goin' on?" Vigliotti shouted.

"We'll not be treated like some two-bit hoodlums," Carmine shouted back. "I come here to broker a deal, and we're told to strip down to our skivvies? Is this how you conduct business?"

Vigliotti looked around the table. "Who gave such a ridiculous order?"

"I did," Big Ben said, pushing back his chair. "We all heard about the shit Batista pulled in Chicago, and after the threats he made last time he was here, he shouldn't be allowed anywhere near this meeting."

"Carmine, put the gun on the table and any other weapons you guys have," Vigliotti ordered.

Carmine frisked the guy he held the gun on, pushed him aside, and then slid the gun to Vigliotti. I did the same and removed my two army specialty knives hidden in the sleeves of my jacket.

"See, what the hell did I tell you?" Big Ben shouted.

"That's enough bullshit," Vigliotti said. "Let's get down to business. Carmine, what's your proposition?"

I stood by Carmine's side.

"First, let me thank you for locating my wife. She suffered great humiliation and emotional harm. If her enslavement in that dive lasted any longer, I'm sure she would have died, and in some ways, it might have been better if she had."

There was a lot of agitation around the table as Carmine spoke. Vigliotti shoved a copy of the *Daily News* toward us.

"Is this how your father keeps his word?" Vigliotti asked.

The front page had a graphic picture of the burnt skeletal remains of someone crucified upside down on the inside door of the Bayou speakeasy that had been gutted by flames.

There was no doubt in my mind that the image I stared at was the bartender who had paid Butch for Angela. I wouldn't have thought Carmine was capable of such brutality.

"Castellano never extended his offer of clemency beyond the family," I said. "As his consigliore, I speak on his behalf. Given how fast Angela was located and the death of Castellano's grandson, I never had the chance to make Castellano aware that I'd included other organizations in his offer not to take action against any boss who participated in her abduction or treatment, as long as they returned her safely."

Vigliotti shouted. "I thought I'd made it clear I didn't want to antagonize another ethnic organization."

"You did, but you also said doing nothing would be a sign of weakness, which is, in my opinion, more dangerous."

"So, that's your handiwork?" Vigliotti said, pointing to the paper.

"I don't need Batista to avenge a direct attack on my family," Carmine said.

Once again there was a rumble around the table that sounded like approval.

"Let's hear your proposition," Vigliotti said.

"You're aware of the atrocities inflicted on me and my wife and that my father had to shoot my son to stop his suffering from burning to death."

"We're all sorry for your loss," Vigliotti said.

"The circumstance of my son's death has affected my father to such an extent that he is no longer capable of running his affairs. He has turned his business over to me."

"That's for us to decide," Big Ben shouted.

Vigliotti had had enough of Big Ben's outbursts. "Sit down and keep your trap shut until it's time for you to speak." He turned to Carmine. "Get to the point. What is your proposal?"

"I'm here to commit to the same agreement you had with my father, with the addition of a guaranteed minimum contribution, starting a year from now—ten percent more than whatever Big Ben's organization delivers."

"That's a generous offer," Vigliotti said. "Your father has never exceeded Big Ben's income to the group. Exactly how do you plan on meeting that obligation?"

"That's my business. Do we have a deal?" Carmine asked.

Vigliotti looked around the room. "Does anyone object to Carmine's proposition?"

There was agreement, except from Big Ben. "You bet I do. This runt has never been an active part of his family's business. We can't afford to screw up such an important segment of our income."

"Do you have an alternative?" Vigliotti asked.

"You're damn right. I have lieutenants who know how to control the docks. This way the entire waterfront would be under one organization—mine."

"That is unacceptable to my father," Carmine said.

"Who the hell cares what he thinks? You said yourself he's done for. The only thing he ever did was run the docks when there's plenty of dough to be made in other businesses."

I spoke. "You want to know who cares? I care. The neighborhood cares. We will not allow a boss from across town to tell us what to do or interfere with our lives."

"I agree with Batista. The neighborhoods have always been run by local bosses," Vigliotti said. "Let's put it to a vote."

Everyone agreed, except for Big Ben.

"The motion passes," Vigliotti said. "Carmine, the rules are clear. Your father's territory is now yours, but Big Ben is free to challenge you. Any dispute is between you and him. Neither of you will get help from the other bosses. Just make sure innocents don't get caught in the middle."

Big Ben grinned.

"You have twenty-four hours to pull your men out of my territory," Carmine said.

"And if I don't?"

Carmine pushed the *Daily News* toward him and walked out while I picked up my knives.

"You best stay out of the way, Batista. This is between Castellano's family and mine," Big Ben said, tossing the *Daily News* in the air, sending the pages flying.

I pinned the cover page to the wall above Big Ben's head with my stiletto.

"There is a bond between Carmine and me, handed down from our fathers, and I intend to honor it."

"Brave words for a dead man."

"Remember this, Big Ben. I won't build an organization, nor will I fight in the streets alongside Carmine to advance his business interests, but I will cut off the head of the serpent who threatens me, my family, or my neighborhood. And I'm good at what I do!"

* * * * *

Once in the car, Carmine turned to face me.

"We're not two guys who grew up in the same gang anymore. I'm now the 'Boss,' and don't you ever forget it. You threaten me again like you did at your office, and one of us is gonna be dead."

"Damn, I'd hate for that to happen. I've already lost too many friends from the old gang," I said.

Carmine grinned and pulled into traffic. I looked at his profile and wondered how he was going to meet his financial commitment to Vigliotti.

Chapter 56

O'Reilly and I caught the same ferry to Staten Island and filled each other in on what was happening.

"Butch's body was found late last night by a hobo passing through town. He had ignored the demolition signs and was headed back to the shack for shelter from the rain when he stumbled over the remains."

I was surprised that Butch made it out of the shack alive. "How far did he get?" I asked.

"About twenty feet, it wasn't a pretty sight."

"Neither was Carmine's son lying in a pool of blood with his face frozen in pain and fear," I said.

O'Reilly looked away, no doubt remembering Antonio's face and the smell of smoldering flesh, still pungent when he arrived on the scene outside of Castellano's home.

O'Reilly came back to the present. "I took the call, so I was able to pay the bum what he wanted for the information and got him out of town on the next freight train."

"Why?"

"To save your ass from the DA, that's why."

"There wasn't anything to pin Butch's death on me."

"Do yourself a favor and don't underestimate the guy. The door was locked from the outside; there were bindings on the remains of a smashed table and chair, not to mention a bullet hole and a knife slit in Butch's shirt."

"Not enough to tie me to Butch."

"Everyone knows you fingered Butch as the guy who attacked Castellano's family. So, combine that with this," O'Reilly said, handing me the knife I'd lost during the fight.

O'Reilly had removed other pieces of evidence that might link me to the crime scene.

"The official word is that Butch ran into some of Castellano's men or friends of Bobby Stefano. The coroner thinks he was left for dead—he wasn't. His wounds weren't fatal, but they incapacitated him enough that the wharf rats did the rest."

"How did he get out of the shack?"

"It looked like he smashed the window and clawed his way up over the windowsill. I'm sure it took a hell of an effort. There was plenty of blood on the shards of glass still in the window frame."

O'Reilly picked up a discarded copy of the *Daily News* left behind on a bench next to where we sat.

"Is this your handiwork?" he asked, slapping the image of the charred remains of the bartender's crucified body nailed to the door of his speakeasy.

"Can't deny I intended to do something, but Carmine got there first."

"I hoped it wasn't you. Everyone has a *saligiare* moment in their lives, but committing two such deadly sins within a few weeks feels too sadistic."

O'Reilly looked at the picture again. "Carmine must have a side we haven't seen before."

"I wouldn't be too fast to judge. I saw what was done to his wife."

A young family sat down next to us, so we went outside on the main deck and stood by the railing, away from the tourists.

"Jackie didn't give me many details about what happened at the clinic when she called. Do you have any information?" O'Reilly asked.

"I went to a syndicate meeting with Carmine this morning, and when I returned to the office, Jackie had already left for the clinic. She should know more by the time we arrive."

"How did the meeting go?"

"Carmine's the new neighborhood boss, but Big Ben has challenged him. It's gonna get nasty."

O'Reilly flicked his cigarette overboard. "From what I hear, it already has. Toby Tobias, one of Castellano's former bodyguards, is now working for Carmine, and he beat a guy senseless this afternoon," O'Reilly said.

"I hope I did the right thing by backing Carmine today. He's not the kid I grew up with, not after what he did to the bartender at the Bayou and now hooking up with Tobias."

"Carmine needs to rebuild an organization fast, and Toby knows the business and the docks. More importantly, he can recruit the type of muscle Carmine's gonna need to fend off Big Ben," O'Reilly said.

"That's what I'm afraid of. They'll have more loyalty to Toby than to Carmine."

* * * * *

Jackie greeted us on the front porch of the clinic and had turned to enter when a passing car backfired. Both O'Reilly and I pulled our guns and shielded Jackie, thinking someone had taken a shot at us.

"I don't blame the two of you for being jumpy," Jackie said, taking us straight to Dr. Schwartz's office without introducing the staff, who sat in the parlor waiting for Lieutenant Sullivan to arrive.

Once in the office, Jackie hobbled in a circle, gripping her crutch. "Gino killed one of the bastards with a shotgun blast and was then shot in the chest."

I got up and stood in her path. She wiped away a few tears with her free hand and allowed me to walk her to a chair.

I pulled over a footstool and placed it under her injured leg. "I know it was difficult for you to interview everyone and hear what happened to Gino and Debbie, so it might be best if we ask you questions," I said.

O'Reilly started right in, "What time did this happen?"

"Around three last night."

"Was anyone else hurt?" I asked.

"Dr. Schwartz was with Debbie when a car smashed through the front gate. He opened the door to Debbie's cabin to see what was happening and got sapped on the head. Debbie screamed, and that's when Gino opened fire on two goons standing by the car."

O'Reilly looked over at me.

"I know what you're thinking, but it's not like that. Debbie wasn't his patient anymore," Jackie said.

O'Reilly continued his questioning.

"How many men were involved?"

"One of the girls looked out her window when she heard shots. She thinks there were four, including the one Gino killed."

"Where did Gino get the shotgun? I wouldn't think the doc would allow a gun anywhere near this place."

"No one knows," Jackie said.

"Pop told me he was missing one from his shop. Gino

must have taken it with him to the clinic after someone took a potshot at him. I think we now know it was Butch, since he was the one who killed Kowalski," I said.

Satisfied, O'Reilly peppered Jackie with more questions.

"How many cars?"

"Two black tops."

"What about the other two cabins? Did anyone who lives in them get a good look at these guys?"

"The gardener has the week off, and the nurse, who lives in the other cabin, was with a sick patient in the main house."

"How long did it take the cops to arrive?"

"About thirty minutes."

O'Reilly shook his head and swore.

"Plenty of time to make it over to Jersey by barge if things were prearranged," I said.

"How are we gonna get Debbie back?" Jackie asked me.

"You're in no shape to travel. I'll contact a couple of buddies of mine from the war for support and then leave for Detroit," I said.

"You never mentioned you could get help from anyone you knew in the war. We could have used them long before now," Jackie said.

"I don't know if they're available, but we were the only survivors of our outfit, and we went through detective training together before the army let us back to civilian life. I'm sure they have their own issues to deal with, but I have a feeling Ronnie is gonna be tough to take down."

There was a loud knock at the door, followed by a booming voice.

"Police, open up," Lieutenant Sullivan ordered.

O'Reilly let the lieutenant in, and they vigorously shook hands.

"Mike, I didn't expect to see you here. Do you have ties to the victims?" Sullivan asked.

"It's hard to explain," O'Reilly said.

"Don't bother. The doc already told me they're friends of Batista's."

He walked toward me and looked at Jackie's leg. "How is it, Batista, that anyone associated with you ends up dead or hurt?"

"Lieutenant, all you need to know is that none of this has anything to do with your jurisdiction. The men who came here last night are from Detroit, and they're not coming back," I said.

"What makes you so sure?"

"I'm gonna kill them."

"Look, Batista. I've got a young lady kidnapped and two guys in the morgue, and you expect me to do nothing. Just close the case? You gotta be out of your mind."

Jackie gasped.

"Sorry, I thought you knew. The guy named Gino didn't make it. His heart stopped on the operating table," Sullivan said.

I helped Jackie get up from her chair, and together we walked out, leaving O'Reilly to work things out with Sullivan.

* * * * *

A few minutes before the ferry docked at the Manhattan terminal, Jackie went to the ladies' room. While I sat alone, a middle-aged man with a limp sat down next to me. I paid no attention until he spoke.

"With the kind of enemies you're making, you need to be more careful," he said.

From the sound of his voice, I knew it was Cafiero, the retired Mafia hit man.

"I thought you blew town after the shootout at your apartment," I said.

"I did, once I knew Jackie was safe from those creeps who kidnapped her."

"So it *was* you who saved my life at the DA's safe house. My uncle said he didn't shoot the goon who was about to nail me by the outhouse."

"I tend to hit what I aim at."

"What brings you back?" I asked.

"You. I have a contract."

The fact that Cafiero was warning me wasn't much comfort, given his longevity in the business.

"You're supposed to be retired."

"I am, but thought it best to come out of retirement when I heard you were the target. You should feel good; there were no takers until the price got extremely high. Takin' out The Twins did wonders for your reputation."

"I guess friendship doesn't mean much to you."

"I took the job out of friendship. I didn't shoot when I had you in my sights at the clinic. The guy who hired me is very clever. He had another shooter in place waiting for you."

"So why didn't he shoot?" I asked.

"He never got the chance. I don't like competition."

"I didn't think the noise we heard on the clinic porch was from a passing car."

"You're forgetting what you learned in the army. Always trust your instincts."

My uncle said Ronnie was ruthless, but he left out the part about being clever. Ronnie knew I would go straight to the clinic when I heard Debbie was taken.

"Now what?" I asked Cafiero.

"I'll give you two weeks."

"To do what?"

"Kill Ronnie."

"I don't get it. You want me to kill the guy who hired you to kill me."

"If he's dead, I can't collect my money, so the contract is null and void."

"What happens if I'm unable to get to him in time?"

"I'll fulfill the contract."

"Why?"

"I have a reputation to protect," Cafiero said. He limped away.

Jackie came back and walked right past Cafiero. When she had known him, he had been disguised as an old man.

"Who was that?" she asked.

"No one, just a stranger."

Jackie moved closer and held my hand. "Be careful Joey. I have a real bad feeling about Ronnie."

We sat in silence until the ferry docked.

* * * * *

Carmine had caught up with me at my uncle's joint later that night. He wasn't pleased that I was heading for Detroit the next morning.

"What is this shit? We piss off Big Ben, and then you head out of town."

"I need to take care of some unfinished business with Ronnie. I'll be back in a few days."

"In a few days there might not be anything to come back to. Big Ben's goons have already set up shop in the union buildings. I don't have the manpower to stop them."

I thought Carmine was overreacting. I didn't think a few days would make any difference.

"Carmine, I'm leaving in the morning, and nothing you say will change my mind. I'm planning on locating a couple of war buddies of mine and convince them to head to Detroit with me, and when we're done with business there, I'll try to bring them back to help out."

Carmine reached for his gun, but then he shoved it back into its holster. "What is it with you and dames? They're a dime a dozen. You need to get your priorities straight," he shouted and stormed out of the speakeasy.

* * * * *

The next morning I dropped my gear outside the office and went in to say goodbye to Martha and Jackie. They were together in the inner office.

"I'm sorry I can't stay for Gino's funeral. I hope you understand," I said.

"Everyone does," Jackie said.

"You guys gonna be okay?"

"Sure, we were just talking about how to track down the guys who had killed Gino's wife and daughter. We had promised Gino that we'd find them, and we will," Martha said.

The girls reacted to several gun shots fired down the

street and ran to the window to see what was going on. That was a dumb move, no matter what was happening outside, especially with Big Ben's shadow looming over the neighborhood. I shoved them to the side and held them against the wall next to the window. Moments later two cars screeched to a stop in front of our building and opened fire. The windows in both of our offices shattered, and it sounded like bullets had also riddled Pop's shop windows below.

I ran downstairs to see if anyone was injured and bumped into my uncle in the hallway outside my parents' apartment.

"No one's hurt. Ma had prepared an early lunch for you, and we had just sat down to get started. Thankfully the sheets of steel I had installed to protect us from Stefano did the trick."

Pop stood by the entrance to the apartment holding a shotgun. I walked past him and wrapped Ma in my arms. She was shaking. That's when I decided Debbie would have to wait and to hell with Cafiero and his deadline. If I had to, I'd track *him* down. Big Ben had made the first move, and if I had my way, it would be his last.

One of our neighbors burst into the hallway.

"Castellano's been shot!"

About the Authors

Tom and Judy were both raised on Staten Island, New York. They met in high school and have been married for forty-three years.

Tom retired from Hewlett Packard Company after thirty years of service and Judy is a retired middle school teacher and registered nurse.

They are founding members of the Soaring Eagle Ecology Center located in Red Feather Lakes, Colorado. You can learn about the Ecology Center by visiting www.seecatrfl.org.

This is their second novel. They are currently working on *The Gumshoe Chronicles - 1922*, which will complete the trilogy.